APOCALYPSE
REBIRTH

BOOK ONE

BY

YORTH

APOCALYPSE REBIRTH

Book One
Copyright © 2025 Yorth

All rights reserved.

The characters and events portrayed in this book are fictitious. Any similarities to real persons, living or dead, are coincidental and not intended by the author.

No part of this book may be reproduced, stored in a retrieval system, or transmitted in any form or by any means, electronic, mechanical, photocopying, recording, or otherwise, without express written permission of the publisher.

Any use of this publication to teach, modify, improve, or train generative artificial intelligence (AI) technologies to generate text is expressly prohibited. The author and publisher reserve all rights to license any use of this work for generative AI training and development of machine learning language models.

ISBN (print): 979-8-88993-061-7
ISBN (e-book): 979-8-88993-060-0

Cover and Illustrations by Fernando Granea

Interior Design by Tangcu LLC

Published 2025 by MoonQuill
Arlington, VA

www.moonquill.com

TABLE OF CONTENTS

Table of Contents Continued

CHAPTER 1

Amidst the grandeur of his sprawling tent, where Lord Thorian had once strategized his battles and barked orders to his soldiers, now lay his broken and impaled body. A vicious spear had mercilessly pierced through his stomach, rendering him incapable of making even the most basic movements. The deadly weapon had destroyed his dantian, the vital energy center of his body, leaving him writhing in excruciating pain.

As he glared at the two culprits, Lord Thorian's eyes brimmed with fury and disgust. He was about to unleash his wrath upon them when an old man with a long, white beard entered through the scorched entrance of the tent, interrupting his thoughts.

"Even you, great-uncle?" Thorian's eyes filled with a sense of profound betrayal.

Unable to bear the weight of this terrible reality, he cast his gaze upwards. The roof was rich with the blue flags of their army, bearing the sigil of a sword and a lion that symbolized their family. However, most of them now fluttered in tatters, burned by his own fire.

"I'm sorry, my lord, but you have grown too ambitious." The old man's voice, deep and wise, reverberated through the tent. He walked towards his two accomplices through the ashes of the luxurious rugs that once adorned the floor. "Daring to bare your fangs at the royal family was truly a foolish thing to do."

Hearing the remorseful tone coloring his great-uncle's voice filled

Thorian with rage. His eyes stared swords and spears at the man he'd once considered his mentor.

"The capital was in our sight!" He coughed up blood, but his rage remained unquenched. "Our epithet—the great Steelblade name—would have been etched into the history books to be remembered for a thousand years!"

A man with a half-burned black beard and a stature that towered over the rest cast a pitying gaze at Thorian. "Your speeches are magnificent even on your deathbed, my lord."

The man was adorned in black-and-gold-plated armor. Perhaps it was that darkness that hid the ashes from Thorian's previous attacks. "It is a shame that very same tongue of yours spelled your eventual doom," he added solemnly.

"Let's end this farce."

The other man, with a clean-shaven face, raised his spear. His wounds were no less than those of the black-bearded man, with his left shoulder's skin burned and his flesh darkened. He was poised to deliver the final blow, but the old man intervened.

"Don't be hasty, General. Let us enjoy our final moments with our lord," he said gently, smiling at Thorian. "My lord, in your quest to achieve history and honor, you have forgotten your own men. You waged a brutal war against the capital with no sympathy for the soldiers who lost their friends, for the men who lost their families, for the wives who lost their husbands—"

"Aldrich!" Thorian growled. He turned his attention to the stoic faces of his betrayers, and to his own surprise, his rage gave way to uncontrollable laughter. "What did they promise you?" he asked with a low voice, eyeing them with suspicion. "Was it money? Land? Power? Or was it perhaps... the county?"

Aldrich's slight smirk told Thorian everything he needed to know.

"I see. So that's what it was."

The men stood silent as they looked at each other. Their eyes told the full story. After a few seconds, Aldrich finally opened his mouth. "Any last words, my lord?"

Thorian's eyes threatened to close as the bags beneath them grew dark and hollow. "Yes..." he said, his words slow and labored. "Please, come closer."

The black-bearded man let out a mocking laugh tinged with disbelief. "To think the day would come when I would see the lion of the lowlands grow so weak," he sneered.

The old man joined him in his mirth, his tone more gentle but no less amused. "Our lord is weary and tired. Let us listen to his will."

As Aldrich approached Thorian, triumph evident on his face, the two men followed closely behind. However, upon spying Thorian's lips twisting into a knowing grin, Aldrich's expression stiffened in shock.

Instinctively, he channeled mana into his eyes and scanned Thorian's body. There was a turbulent mass of orange-and-white mana concentrating on his mana heart, threatening to break it into a thousand shards.

"Run!" Aldrich's face contorted in horror while the two men stood dazed and confused. However, the terrible realization was for naught. The ball of fire expanded with Thorian as its center, and the three men were burned into nothingness before any thought could cross their minds.

The fire did not extinguish after the betrayers were reduced to ashes, instead expanding with fervor as it consumed the entire Steelblade army camp. Its flames blazed with such intensity and radiance that the people of the capital were convinced a third sun had risen.

As Thorian gradually regained consciousness, he became aware of muffled noises that pulled him out of the darkness of the void. His mind was a blank slate, devoid of any thoughts or memories. It was like waking up from a long night's sleep after dreaming an entire lifetime.

After a few seconds, his eyes adjusted to the new environment, and he could see the damp, rocky ceiling above him. Confusion sank over him for a moment before the memories of the past flooded back into his mind.

Wait, he thought in shock. *How am I alive?*

He could clearly remember the faces of the three men who betrayed him—his marshal, his grand general, and even his great-uncle. They and who-knows-who-else had conspired with the dogs of the royal family and betrayed him when the crown was within their reach. One final battle was all they'd needed to take control of the capital, and the remaining regions would have fallen right after.

Good thing I kept Sun Sacrifice a secret.

Thorian laughed to himself, remembering the look of pure horror on Aldrich's face. Sun Sacrifice, his self-destruction skill, had unleashed a power several times stronger than anything he had ever wielded before. By breaking his mana heart and releasing all the mana in his body, Thorian knew that none of his former allies could have survived the attack.

"But to think I would live too." Thorian cackled at the thought of his betrayers' plans all crumbling to ruins. "I, Thorian Steelblade, stand victorious!"

However, something felt wrong.

As Thorian looked at the rocky ceiling, he soon understood that he was in a dark cave. He stood and looked around to learn what was happening only to find himself surrounded by white-furred, wolf-like monsters.

"White kobloids?" Thorian frowned. "What am I doing amidst such weak and disgusting creatures?"

No matter how much he strained his brain, he could not come up with a reason for his stay in this cave. To make matters even more confusing, white kobloids were monsters that mostly appeared in the fens and the forests of Shelderwood, not the midlands where the capital was located.

Thorian clicked his tongue. "No matter. Let us get rid of these weaklings before we proceed any further." Acting on instinct, he reached for the mana heart in his chest and squeezed it, hoping to activate a spell.

However, nothing happened.

He did not understand what was going on, and neither did the small white kobloids. They looked at him with open confusion before carrying on with what they had been doing—mainly sleeping and playing around.

Is it because I destroyed my mana heart?

Such thoughts swirled in his mind before he looked down at his hand. To be more precise, he looked down to what he *thought* to be his hand but was now closer to a paw.

What?

Thorian inspected his body with ever-growing terror. There was fur everywhere—white fur. It was on his arms, his legs, his stomach, and his chest. With the thought solidifying itself in his mind and his heart beating louder than war drums, Thorian succumbed to the one thing he trusted more than even his own eyes.

Display panel, he commanded mentally.

Ding!

Race: White Kobloid
Lifespan: 40 years
Level: 1/15 (XP: 0/10)
Stats:
Strength: 8
Agility: 8
Constitution: 6
Mana: 3
Skills:
Minor Moon Boost (passive)

CHAPTER 2

Thorian's mind blanked as he looked at the proof that was laid bare before him. *I... What does this mean? How?!*

He stared at his own body in shock for a full minute. The white fur, his hairy and paw-like hands, his skeletal structure—all of it was unfamiliar to him. It was as if his soul had been ripped from his original body and shoved into this new one.

As rage bubbled inside his heart, Thorian took a deep breath and calmed his nerves. *At least I am alive... Somehow, even after Sun Sacrifice, I was given another chance.*

Thorian remembered the face of Aldrich as he screamed in horror, and a warm breeze cooled his raging heart. Even if he'd changed species, he was alive, and they were ash, burned by the flames of their greed.

The now-white kobloid cackled at the strange turn of fate. However, as he looked back at his own body, he couldn't help but click his tongue.

Did it have to be a white kobloid? Couldn't I have reincarnated in a stronger monster's body?

Thorian opened his system panel and focused on the skill displayed at the bottom.

Minor Moon Boost (passive)

Description: As a creature attuned to the moon, you gain power in its presence. Strength and Agility are boosted by 25% at night.

It is indeed as useless of a skill as I remembered. Thorian grimaced as he thought, *What use is there for such a thing when the night passes so swiftly?*

He furrowed what used to be his eyebrows as his mind turned over what to do next. Some of the other monsters littered about looked at him with curious interest, but he paid them no heed.

There's no use sitting here thinking. I need to see what's happening outside.

Thorian made his way to the entrance of the cave, each step carrying the confidence and bearing of a lord. Some of the kobloids sneered and growled at him for displaying such arrogance, but Thorian didn't feel the need to even acknowledge their presence.

It took a few seconds for his eyes to adjust to the new light when he walked outside. In front of him was a clearing with fairly tall grass and green shrubbery. The vibrant and healthy colors told Thorian that it was the middle of spring.

A smile parted his lips as he remembered the days before the apocalypse had happened. *Now that I think of it, it was spring when it happened. Almost ten years ago...*

He lifted his face to the sky to bask in the warmth of the sun and abruptly froze.

What in the world? Where is the second one?

Thorian gawked at the absurd vision laying above him. Ever since the apocalypse had begun with the introduction of the so-called "system," a second sun had stood alongside their old one. Ten years later, the dual stars had become a natural and welcome sight.

What's happening? Did I go back to before the apocalypse? No, I cannot be hasty in my assumptions. This could be a completely different world.

Thorian went back inside the cave, a frown marring his expression. His mind was a storm of warring thoughts and doubts. If this was a different world, then there wasn't much he could do. However, if he had indeed gone back in time, then a host of opportunities and risks had presented themselves to him.

I did hear rumors about monsters appearing even before the apocalypse began. If I did truly go back in time, then it should happen very soon.

Whether this was a different world or the past he once lived, Thorian needed to go out and explore. Staying in this dark cave without any knowledge of the outside world would drive him mad.

But I can't do it now. Thorian clenched his fangs. *If I meet other monsters, I will be at a great disadvantage when the moon is not shining.*

He cursed his fate for having reincarnated into a monster with such a glaring weakness but then took a deep breath. For now, the wisest choice would be to sit and wait for the sun to set.

After a few minutes of sitting amongst the noisy monsters playing around, Thorian tapped his feet in annoyance. *If only I could meditate and cultivate my Qi. This would be a perfect time for it.*

Then, the most outlandish idea took form in his mind.

Surely it won't work, but it doesn't hurt to try.

With hesitant movements, Thorian sat down in a lotus position. While the other white kobloids stared at him in confusion, he closed his eyes and took a deep breath. Slowly but with practiced ease, he performed the breathing technique he had been using for almost five years. Minutes passed and he could not feel any change.

As I thought, it doesn't seem to work.

Even as doubts crept into his heart, Thorian continued to practice his breathing technique. Since there wasn't much else for him to do, he didn't feel that it was time wasted.

After half an hour had gone and passed, he finally felt the ether in the air slowly breaking through his Qi paths.

What in the seven hells? I have never seen paths this filthy and clogged.

For a second, Thorian was about to stop his breathing cycle and curse aloud. In the ten years that he had spent practicing, training, and teaching, he had never seen a body with this much filth inside of it.

With any luck, I'll still reach the first realm in this session.

Even though this body was not the best suited for cultivation, happiness stole across his heart. One could only meditate for a single session each day; such were the rules enforced by the gods. Even the royals and imperials with their most luxurious cultivation halls could only meditate for six hours a day. A normal person without access to any facilities could only meditate for two. If this was another world that played by similar rules, then Thorian was glad that he hadn't wasted precious days and months before discovering that he could cultivate. However, if he had truly gone back in time, then this was a boon that could not be ascribed a price.

Minutes soon turned into hours as Thorian pushed the ether around him through his clogged and filthy Qi paths. His meditation felt like chiseling through stone with a blunt pickaxe, as he struggled to clear his blocked Qi channels using the natural energy of the world.

Just as his session was about to end, ether finally fully cracked through Thorian's Qi path and broke into his dantian. Once it reached its natural destination, it transformed from pure ether to a Qi that was truly his own.

Congratulations, you have unlocked the Cultivation System.
Display panel.
Ding!

Race: White Kobloid

Lifespan: 40 years

Level: 1/15 (XP: 0/10)

Cultivation Realm: Qi Gathering First Stage (7.9%)

Stats:

Strength: 10

Agility: 10

Constitution: 7

Mana: 3

Qi: 1

Skills:

Minor Moon Boost (passive)

As he looked at the system panel in front of him, Thorian grinned. *Good… A monster that can cultivate Qi? Now that is something unheard of.*

"Smelly poo!"

A deep, angry voice cast confusion over Thorian as he turned to look back. A monster that stood head and shoulders above the rest, a proper white kobold, pointed at him with an angry face. The other monsters were also disgruntled as they stole glances at him.

"Smelly poo! Go lake clean!"

Thorian looked around him. He was surrounded by a black goo-like substance, some of which even clung to his white fur.

"Smelly poo! Go lake!"

Thorian cocked a brow at the white kobold that was stalking towards him. The tone with which the monster was speaking to him made the hair on his neck stand as his body physically reacted to the challenge to his authority.

Is this thing trying to pick a fight with me?

Thorian instinctively pushed the small amount of Qi in his dantian to strengthen his body. However, just as the Qi exited his dantian through his channels, all of his muscles tensed and locked up.

No. This body isn't used to handling Qi yet.

As the realization hit him that he would not be able to move his body, the white kobold took Thorian's silence as an act of defiance. The last thing he saw was the monster's fist before it punched him in the face.

CHAPTER 3

Thorian slowly opened his eyes and craned his neck, feeling a throbbing pain pulsate through his face and down his whole body. As he looked around, he found that the cave was empty. A quick glance outside told him that the sun had already set.

So that is why. They have gone out to hunt.

Thorian knew that the white kobolds liked to hunt at night. Due to their skills, they tended towards nocturnal tendencies as a species that slept by day and hunted at night.

While he was still rousing himself from his forced slumber, a terrible smell assaulted his snout. He sniffed under his armpit, then turned his head with a grimace. "I do need to clean myself."

That black sticky goo was still around him. If this were any normal day, a maid would have cleaned it away already. Alas, this day was far from normal.

Thorian stood, intent on exiting the cave. However, just as he took a few steps, he found a dark silhouette in the corner.

"Who's there?"

No response. Thorian raised an eyebrow before clicking his tongue and walking towards the mysterious figure. As his eyes adjusted to the darkness, he could see a midnight-black kobloid sitting in the corner. The monster was just looking down at the ground, not saying a word.

"A night kobloid? Interesting..." Thorian muttered under his breath, before resuming his steps towards the mysterious creature. "Why are you staying here alone? Why did you not go with the rest of the pack?"

The night kobloid looked at Thorian with a cautious expression before looking back down at the ground. "Smelly poo, talk weird."

"You say *I* talk weird? That is quite presumptuous of you." His fist clenched. "And you dare call me Smelly Poo? That is laughable."

He frowned at the night kobloid before taking a deep breath and looking away. *What am I doing getting angry at a bunch of kobolds? Such behavior is beneath me.*

With a shake of his head, Thorian changed the topic. "So, why did you stay here? You should be with the rest of the pack hunting for food."

The night kobloid stayed silent, still looking at the ground. Seeing that the monster was not in the mood to talk, Thorian sighed and turned back towards the entrance of the cave.

"Me different. Me weak."

He stopped and looked at the night kobloid with a raised brow. "What? A night kobloid is weak? What sort of a joke is that?"

The black kobloid looked at Thorian with an open mouth before saying, "Smelly Poo, words many."

"Night kobloid, words too few, more like," Thorian immediately snarked back. Then he took a deep breath before shaking his head. "If you want to become strong, follow me."

Without another word, Thorian left the cave. Although the forest was dark, lit only by the moon, his eyes quickly adjusted.

I guess there are some benefits to being reborn as a monster. Proper night vision is something you only get at the second stage of cultivation.

Thorian walked amongst the trees and shrubberies before noticing some shuffling behind him. He glanced back only to see that the night kobloid had followed him.

He grinned. "You've made a wise choice."

"Me follow you, me strong?" the night kobloid asked with a hopeful gaze.

"If you follow my orders, you will reach a strength beyond your wildest dreams," Thorian confidently replied. "Now, let's go hunt."

The kobloid nodded, and the two continued their trek. However, before beginning the hunt in earnest, Thorian crouched down and smeared dirt and grass all over his body to hide his stench.

To think I will need to resort to such savagery. No, this is necessary if I want to hunt and level up. I am just making the most out of my unfortunate circumstances.

Having somewhat masked his odor, Thorian made sure to lay as low as possible and walk on all fours. That way, he could easily sneak up on any unsuspecting prey without it being able to see him from a distance away.

"Shh, stop." Thorian's ears perked up, and he raised his hand to stop the night kobloid. He peeked just slightly over a bush to find two small foxes playing around. Without saying a word, he signaled for the night kobloid to go in with his hand.

The two then rushed at the foxes with incredible speed. By the time their prey could notice them, Thorian's claws had already slashed at one of the foxes. He bit at its jugular, his fangs burying deep into the fox's flesh as sweet, sweet blood trickled down his throat.

I am not a beast!

Thorian threw the fox's corpse to the side before spitting out its blood, then looked to the side to find the night kobloid ravaging the other fox's innards with his mouth.

"Stop!" Thorian ordered and the night kobloid looked at him in confusion. "You need to stay hungry so that you can hunt even more," Thorian explained, his voice now low. "Only then can you become strong."

Those last words did the trick. The kobloid looked at the prey he had caught with sad eyes before standing up and nodding at Thorian.

"Good, now let's continue our hunt." Thorian smiled proudly. One sniff transformed that smile into a grimace, however. "We need to find a lake too."

As the two walked through the forest, Thorian opened his system panel to check his level.

Level: 1/15 (XP: 5/10)

So even normal beasts can give experience points. Good, we can make some progress tonight.

After a few minutes of walking around, the two found a doe eating some grass in a small clearing. Thorian knew it would be quite speedy, but kobloids were no slouches when it came to speed either. With a few hand signals, he laid out his plan to his night kobloid follower. As the latter slowly crawled his way around the clearing, Thorian refocused on the doe. It was still eating grass with a dumb expression on its face.

Good. Stay like that.

Thorian waited until the night kobloid was in position before pouncing full force at his prey. Catching the sound of bushes shuffling, the doe's ears perked, and it looked up immediately. By the time it saw Thorian, he had already closed half the distance.

With surreal speed, the doe galloped out of Thorian's charge. The night kobold swiftly pounced at his prey from the opposite side, only for the doe to jump over him. By the time Thorian could turn to look, it had already cleared the shrubbery and ran into the dark forest.

Thorian gritted his teeth before taking a deep breath. "What a speedy little thing." He looked down at his own body and smirked. "I guess I'm still not used to this weak body. We need to level up fast."

On the other hand, the night kobloid was downcast, with furrowed eyebrows and droopy ears. Seeing his follower in such a pitiful sight, Thorian clicked his tongue. "Don't feel down from such a thing. Failure is just part of the process. The next one will not escape us."

While the failure ate away at the night kobloid's enthusiasm, he still followed Thorian without a word of protest as they continued their search for new prey. Meanwhile, Thorian's focus did not waver and his head was clear. Letting past failures cloud his judgment was a mistake that he'd learned not to make ages ago.

After fifteen minutes of walking, Thorian's eyes picked up something to his right. There were trees, tall grass, shrubbery, and a fallen, ant-infested log. As he focused on the shrubbery next to the fallen log, he could see traces of something tawny brown. It was a sleeping doe.

Once again, Thorian signaled for his follower to walk around and cut off the doe's escape path. Slowly, without making a sound, the kobloid crept to the other side.

On the other hand, Thorian inched as slowly as possible towards his future prey. Once the kobloid reached his position, Thorian charged at the sleeping doe with all his strength. Just as he was about to reach it, his prey's ears perked up, and it jerked upright on high alert. It had fled before his eyes could even process what was happening.

Just as it galloped out of Thorian's reach, the night kobloid pounced at its legs. His fangs dug deep into its thigh, giving Thorian enough time to catch up. Rather than biting it as he did with the fox, he chose instead to slash its neck with his claws.

Level up!

Hearing the beautiful ding in his ears, Thorian knew that the doe was dead. A refreshing wave of energy coursed through his body, melting both pain and fatigue away. The numbing in his face cleared, his muscles were strengthened, and his tendons strummed with new vigor.

Thorian grinned at the feeling of his progress before looking at the night kobloid. "Did you level up too?"

"Yes." The kobloid nodded in enthusiasm. "Me strong."

"Don't rejoice yet," Thorian said, a hint of laughter in his voice. "You will grow much stronger tonight."

He turned his attention to his body. He may have felt great internally, but his physical exterior was not a pretty sight. On top of the black goo that was sticking to his fur and hide, he was now covered in blood.

"Do you know where a lake might be?"

"Yes," the kobloid answered. "Me know lake."

Thorian smiled at the good news. "Good, you'll need to show me the way."

With their destination now set, Thorian followed the night kobloid as he guided him towards the lake. On their way, they hunted and fought rabbits, foxes, and other small animals. By the time they reached the lake, they had both leveled up to level three.

Thorian immediately took a plunge into the lake. The refreshing feeling of water cleaning the filth from his fur was incomparable. It was as if he was reborn once again.

After cleaning himself for a bit, Thorian's mind finally cleared. Enduring the suffocating and disgusting smell stuck to him made it hard to think of anything else. Now that he was cleansed, he could finally check out his system panel.

Display panel.

Ding!

Race: White Kobloid

Lifespan: 40 years

Level: 3/15 (XP: 5/30)

Cultivation Realm: Qi Gathering First Stage (7.9%)

Stats:

Strength: 12 (15)

Agility: 13 (16)

Constitution: 8

Mana: 3

Qi: 1

Skills:

Minor Moon Boost (passive)

CHAPTER 4

Seeing the increase in his stats, Thorian couldn't help but grin. Even though he possessed nowhere near the strength of his past life, this feeling of rapid progression was one he had dearly missed. Now with his fur clean and his odor bearable, Thorian could finally focus on planning his next move.

I need to know where I am. This place does look like the forests of Shelderwood, but all forests look the same.

He needed to know, once and for all, whether he had gone back in time, or been transported to a different world altogether. To do that, he needed to expand his exploration.

He looked at the night kobloid bathing in the lake and asked, "Hey, what's your name?"

"Name?" The kobloid titled his head in a quizzical look.

Thorian clicked his tongue at his follower's dullness. "Yes, what's your name? I can't be just calling you 'You' the whole time."

The kobloid shook his head. "Me no name."

"That makes it hard." Thorian looked to the side in thought before his eyes brightened. "Oh, I've thought of a good one for you. Nox, your name shall be Nox from now on. It means 'night' in the old language."

"Nox..." The night kobloid puzzled over his given name before nodding with a smile. "Me like Nox. Me Nox."

Thorian chuckled. "Good, I'm glad you liked your name. Now, let's hunt for the whole night. We need to grow strong."

Nox nodded with a resolute expression. "Nox strong!"

Thus, the two walked back into the forest and started hunting once again. For two hours, they killed squirrels, rabbits, hares, foxes, deer, and other weak animals. However, as Thorian reached level 6, he noticed something.

Level: 6/15 (XP: 0/70)

Even after killing a few rabbits and squirrels, his experience points had not changed one bit.

Well, that was to be expected. Those small animals barely even counted when I was leveling up my class in the past.

Once the difference in levels was high enough, low-level monsters were just no longer useful to kill. Fortunately, Thorian was able to cruise through the early levels by hunting rabbits and hares, but now, he would need to focus on bigger and stronger monsters.

I hope those foxes and deer still provide some XP. Otherwise, I will need to start fighting true predators.

Thorian looked at Nox and gestured at him with his head. "Don't hunt rabbits and squirrels anymore. We need to focus on deer and foxes, you understand?"

Nox nodded. "Fox, deer. Nox understand."

The two continued their search for a few minutes before Thorian's eyes landed on a large, hollow log. He wordlessly signaled Nox to go to the other side, then walked towards the opening of the log with silent steps. As he looked down to see what was inside, a smile tugged at the corners of his mouth.

There were five foxes—two parents and three children.

Thorian felt no pity for the sleeping family. This was a kill-or-be-killed world, and he hated being the prey. The two kobloids needed less than a minute to massacre the fox family. Once woken, they tried to escape, but there was no escaping Thorian's strong jaws.

Level: 6/15 (XP: 19/70)

So, 3 XP for the small ones and five for the parents, huh? I guess that went down too.

When they'd started, small foxes had given Thorian five experience points, while the adults had given eight. While the decrease in gained experience was unfortunate, it was not the end of the world. At the very least, they could still hunt relatively weak animals and level up without much risk.

Before they could realize it, three hours had already gone by.

Level up!

After killing another sleeping deer and doe couple, the level-up screen appeared. His muscles grew, his frame became larger, and he gained around an inch in height. Even though the effects of the last few level-ups were not as potent as his first, their accumulation had profoundly changed him. He was now as tall as a normal human teenager.

Thorian smiled at his progress before turning to his follower.

"Did you level up too?"

"Yes." The night kobloid nodded. "Nox level 8."

"Good." Thorian then looked at the full moon illuminating the forest. His smile morphed into a full grin. "What do you say we go for some bigger prey now? These helpless lambs are becoming a bore to slay."

"Nox not understand." The night kobloid looked at Thorian with a confused look before his expression changed into excitement. "But Nox fight strong!"

Thorian laughed heartily at his follower's declaration. "You're truly simpleminded. But I do like that about you."

Let's check our status. I haven't seen it in a while. Display panel. Ding!

Race: White Kobloid

Lifespan: 40 years

Level: 8/15 (XP: 0/110)

Cultivation Realm: Qi Gathering First Stage (7.9%)

Stats:

Strength: 18 (22)

Agility: 19 (24)

Constitution: 8

Mana: 4

Qi: 1

Skills:

Minor Moon Boost (passive)

Seems like my mana hasn't increased much. Good... I don't need it right now. Strength and Agility are paramount when I don't have any skills that are worth anything.

They were walking through the forest when a sudden thought blazed across his mind. Thorian looked at Nox with a raised brow and asked, "Why haven't you used your skills yet?"

"Skills?" Nox looked at him in confusion.

"Yes, skills," Thorian confirmed. "Night kobolds are known for their shadow skills. When they reach the rank of a lord, they become truly horrifying to deal with."

Nox shook his head at the explanation. "Nox no skill shadow. Nox skill moon."

"Huh, interesting," Thorian remarked with a raised brow. "So you only have the moon passive. Maybe you will only gain the shadow skill once you evolve into a proper kobold."

Nox did not answer him verbally, but he did nod with great enthusiasm. His excited and happy face made Thorian chuckle.

Simple thing. I guess just the thought of evolving and becoming strong makes you happy... I do not dislike that.

While the two were talking with each other, Thorian's ears perked up as he heard shuffling in the distance. His attitude immediately changed, and his eyes focused on the darkness in front of them. After a few seconds, his pupils dilated, and he could see in the night as well as if it were a clear sunny day.

The two went down on all fours to camouflage their presence before they galloped through the bushes and shrubbery in the direction of the sound. It took them barely half a minute of running before they found the source of the noise.

"Awoo!"

A pack of five wolves was eating and yanking at the flesh of a hunted doe in the middle of a small clearing. A grin stole across Thorian's face as he watched the apex predators that served as the model for his own species. It was as if he were looking at his ancestors.

Well... I can't ignore them now, can I?

Thorian was more than confident he could win with his increased stats. However, he still wanted to know how these relics of the past compared to the monsters of the apocalypse.

With a curt head gesture, Thorian signaled for Nox to go in. The two bolted into action, the sluggish pace of their first hunt now left ridiculously far behind them. Before the wolves could even react, Thorian slashed the first one's chest and bit into its neck. With a herculean biting force, he yanked the wolf's corpse from the ground and threw it at the rest of the pack.

Nox used the opportunity to pounce at one of the disoriented wolves, savagely biting into its stomach. His fangs pierced through its underbelly like the flesh was made of soft fabric. The guts and innards of the wolf gushed through its open stomach, and the kobloid devoured them hungrily.

Thorian winced at Nox's savagery before focusing back on the last three wolves. Their ears were at attention and their fangs bared as they growled at the two kobloids.

In but a fraction of a second, two of the wolves rushed at Thorian from both sides, but to him, they were terribly slow. The first beast charged at him from the left, front paws high and maw gaping. In one smooth movement, Thorian sidestepped the attack and grabbed the beast by its back, locking his hands at his foe's stomach as it swiftly came to a stop.

The other wolf immediately charged at Thorian and bit at his calves, but its fangs could barely pierce through his flesh, let alone touch the bone.

"I have always wanted to do this." Thorian grinned as he lifted the wolf in his grip off the ground and over his head. With an explosive arching motion, he fell backwards, and the wolf's head crashed into the ground.

The beast whimpered in a stunned daze while the other wolf relentlessly bit at Thorian's leg. While his constitution was high enough that it couldn't break his bones, that didn't mean that it couldn't injure him. Blood dripped a trail along his leg from the knee down to his ankle. To add insult to injury, the last wolf also jumped into the fray and charged at him.

Noticing that the situation was taking a turn for the worse, Thorian yanked his right leg out of the beast's mouth before dodging to the side. Holes and wounds covered his calf—the white fur was stained with red blood.

Even with this injury, he was still able to generate enough force with his left leg to pounce at the third wolf and shove his claws into its neck. The beast that injured him before charged at him again, but Thorian was not going to fall for the same attack twice.

He grabbed the third wolf by the flesh of its neck while it gurgled and growled, then threw it at the charging beast, sending them both flying backwards. Without wasting another second, he pounced at the two using his uninjured leg and slashed through the second wolf's neck like a bolt striking from the blue. A fountain of blood sprayed out as the two beasts crashed to the ground

Thorian then shifted his attention to the last wolf. Although it was still in a daze from his suplex, the man-turned-kobloid did not want to give the beast any chance. He pounced, unwilling to let it regain its balance. Fang and claw tore into the beast's hide and flesh, severing the arteries and allowing blood to flow into his mouth.

Just as the sweet taste graced his tongue, Thorian stood and spat out the beast's blood with a grimace. He kept spitting until the taste completely left his mouth. By then, his prey had already stopped gurgling, its eyes hollow. Contrary to his feelings of disgust, Nox was feasting on his wolf's flesh like it was a harvest festival.

How utterly savage. I need to introduce some manners to this tribe if they're to become my subjects.

With the battle now over, the adrenaline rushing through his system ebbed and his past mistakes caught up to him. Wincing with pain, Thorian glanced at the mangled mass of his right leg. It was as if that one part of his body had changed subspecies.

Well, no matter. After a level-up or two, it should be as good as new.

With that thought in mind, Thorian checked his experience bar to see how far he was from leveling up.

Level: 8/15 (XP: 60/110)

Thorian raised his eyebrows and smiled at the number in front of him, then turned his gaze towards the corpses of the wolves around. He smirked.

So each one of them is worth 20 XP? Maybe we should be focusing on wolves rather than those poor foxes.

While lost in his thoughts, Thorian's ears suddenly perked up at a sound in the distance. He immediately looked at Nox and signaled for him to hide. The kobloid nodded at his signal, and the two ran to the bushes.

After a minute of waiting, they could finally see the source of the noise.

Humans.

CHAPTER 5

"Forget about seeing something like this again. I've never even heard of a beast like this one." A middle-aged man wearing leather armor grimaced as he looked at the creature he was holding by the leg. It had blue skin and the frame of an eight-year-old child, or at least, one that had survived his whole life on water and flour.

"You think we'll get some good cash for it?" Another, younger member of the group laughed as he eyed the creature. "I heard that the lord enjoys exotic animals. Maybe he'll like this one."

The older man matched the laugh with one of his own. "Maybe if we'd brought it back alive." He was better equipped than the rest, with shoulder plates and a chest piece covering his upper body. His small, well-trimmed beard showed that he was much better off than the rest of the soldiers. The fact that he stood at the front with confidence cemented that he was their leader.

"If we found one, we're going to find others," the young man declared, still smiling. He glanced back at the monster they were dragging by the ankle and said, "It probably got separated from its pack. We can search for them when the sun is out."

The captain of the squad of five smiled before looking forwards. As they approached a small clearing, though, he frowned. "Wait, careful."

He raised his hand to stop his squad before walking into the clearing. Five wolf corpses had been left there. Some of the beasts had been savagely ravaged, while others were killed in a more clinical and precise fashion.

"What in the world…?" The young man walked next to the captain and looked at the scene in front of them with an incredulous expression. "What could have killed these wolves? A bear?"

The captain shook his head. "Bears aren't usually in this part of the forest." He looked with concern at the bodies of the wolves before kneeling to check one of them. "Besides, bears are savages—they'll break all your bones and eat you by the chunk. Half of these wolves were killed with one strike."

"Then what? Was it some hunters?"

"Hunters don't have claws." The captain looked at the ravaged remains of the wolves. "And that wouldn't explain those two."

He looked with furrowed brows at the scene, deep in thought. Then his eyes, now adjusted to the darkness, spied a smidge of red. From it, he traced its trail to some shrubbery to his left.

Silently, the captain looked to the young man and signaled with his head to follow the trail. The two walked slowly through the grass and unsheathed their swords. Whatever was beyond the bushes, they did not want it to take them by surprise.

Their hearts palpitated. They clenched the grip of their swords hard and broke their slow crawl forwards to rush towards the bush. In a fraction of a second, they lunged toward shrubbery with their swords raised to swing.

There was nothing there.

The young man let out a sigh of relief. "That had me scared."

On the other hand, the captain did not say a word. He was looking down at the ground, trying to find any further traces of the blood. Yet somehow, the trail ended here.

He stood motionless for a few seconds, gaze intent and searching. Finally, he let out a deep breath.

"Let's go back. No use messing around here."

With the captain's order, the two returned to the rest of the squad and continued through the forest.

Thorian let out a deep sigh of relief as he watched the squad of soldiers finally turn back. The emblem of a bear and a shield embroidered on their clothes caught his eye even through the thick branches obscuring his vision.

Once the soldiers were out of view, Thorian and Nox jumped down from the tree into the bushes below. The former couldn't help but feel fortunate. If the two soldiers had looked up upon reaching the end of the blood trail, the two would have been found out.

I'm more glad for them than for me. Needlessly killing foot soldiers leaves a bad aftertaste.

"Creatures weak. Hide why?" Nox sent him a perplexed look.

"Those were humans," Thorian explained. "If we had killed them, it would have brought us quite a bit of trouble. A full squad disappearing will bring a lot of attention to the forest, and we wouldn't be able to hunt in peace."

The night kobloid's confusion was only accentuated by Thorian's explanation, but he simply shook his head. "Nox not understand. Nox trust..." He frowned at Thorian before finishing, "Smelly Poo."

Thorian arched a brow at the last two words.

Should I teach him a lesson?

Looking at Nox's simpleminded expression, Thorian couldn't help but sigh. "My name is not Smelly Poo. My name is Thorian, Th-or-i-an."

Nox's eyebrows pinched even further as he tried to repeat the name. "Thor?"

"It's Thorian, not Thor." Thorian clicked his tongue.

"Thor—*Thoreen*?" The syllables tangled themselves on Nox's tongue.

Seeing the poor kobloid struggle so much, Thorian shook his head and lamented. "I guess that's fine. I will need to educate this tribe later, as this cannot persist."

With their discussion over, Thorian thought back to the squad of soldiers. More precisely, he recalled the emblem that they all bore.

So this really is the forest of Shelderwood. We should be close to Locksley.

Thorian greeted the proof that he had been looking for with a grin. He was now certain. He had gone back to the past before the day of the apocalypse and somehow inhabited the body of a monster.

Locksley... Now that I think about it, was that Territory Altar not close to that city? It should be a few kilometers to its east if I remember correctly.

His thoughts turned to one of the best territories in the whole kingdom with three dungeons under its area of influence: Raven's Nest. It easily eclipsed Locksley as the most important city in the region. It had also become the Ravenwood family's base of operations.

As he recalled the chiseled face of the head of the Ravenwood family, his grin widened even further.

I'm sorry, William, but your fortune is going to be mine in this life.

"Thoreen face scary."

Nox's voice snapped Thorian out of his reverie. His expression mellowed as he turned to peer in the direction that the squad had taken.

"We need to follow them. Let's go."

While Thorian had a vague idea of the whereabouts of the Territory Altar, he was not the most familiar with this region. Most of his time had been spent in the lowlands in the south, where his city was located, so despite him having come to visit the Ravenwood family many times to partake in hunting with them as a diplomatic gesture, he did not truly know all of its ins and outs.

I need to reach Locksley to have a clearer idea. If we go from the east gate and follow the main road for five kilometers or so, I should find it. If memory serves me, the Altar wasn't that far off the road.

Using his wolf-like sense of smell, Thorian immediately picked up the scent of the five soldiers. They had not walked that far yet. With quick steps, the two ran through the dense trees after the squad. A few short minutes later, they could already see them again.

"Slow down," Thorian commanded, lifting his hand to stop Nox. "We need to follow them from very far away."

The two left two hundred meters between themselves and the human squad. With the darkness of the night and the noises of the forest, the soldiers had no hopes of detecting them.

The march was painfully slow as Thorian and Nox needed to follow the pace of the soldiers dragging the corpse of a monster. One glance at the blue-skinned creature was enough for Thorian to immediately identify the monster.

A blue goblin, huh? Quite the rare variety. I did hear from William that some of his men caught one before the apocalypse began. I thought he was just blowing smoke where there was no fire, but it seems that was not the case.

While Thorian was interested in the blue goblin's corpse, its existence did not change his plans in the slightest. His main priority right now was to find the Territory Altar. If he could claim it, the advantage that he would have over everyone would be monumental.

CHAPTER 6

After thirty minutes of following the squad of five, Thorian could finally see the sprawling stone walls that protected Locksley. He smiled at the nostalgic sight of a city without magical barriers or mana cannons.

This place would be razed in an hour if it was ten years in the future.

The two kobloids, one white, one black, stood at the edge of the forest and watched the soldiers from afar. The humans carrying the blue goblin continued their way down the main road and entered the city through the massive gate. Thorian looked up to the sky.

Which one was it again?

Even though the night cloaked the world in darkness, Thorian was greeted by a familiar expanse of twinkling lights above him. His great-uncle had taught him about the stars when he was young. Just the thought of that traitor hurt him, but he swallowed his pride and used the knowledge that his old mentor had passed down to him as he scanned the sky. A few seconds later, his eyes lit up.

So that's the south star.

Now that he'd found his point of reference, Thorian could easily find where the sun would rise. He grinned as he looked at the closing portcullis in front of them. It was the east gate.

"Let's move." Thorian smiled at Nox. "Tonight will go down in history."

Nox seemed confused, but he did not say anything. He just shook his head and followed the white kobloid.

As they no longer needed to walk at a crawling pace, the two crossed four kilometers in a few minutes' time. As they neared their destination, they paused.

Thorian looked at Nox and laid out his plan, "I'll search this side. You go to the other side of the road and search there. If you find a big stone with a demon's face on it, do not touch it. Come and find me immediately, do you understand?"

"Face demon?"

Thorian let out a sigh. "You will know it when you see it. Now, do you understand?"

The night kobloid nodded. "Nox understand."

"Good luck." Thorian patted him on the back. "I trust you."

With those words, Nox ran to the other side of the road and disappeared into the dark forest. Thorian turned around and started searching.

It should be buried somewhere around here, but not fully underground.

Thorian sped through the forest as he surveyed with his eyes. Whenever anything other than trees and shrubberies caught his eyes, he would stop and search it with great meticulousness.

The minutes trickled past as Thorian continued to search until his eyes landed on a rock protruding from behind some dense shrubbery. After making his way through the bushes, he circled the rock, his lips parting into a grin.

Found you.

Thorian covered his face with his hand to stifle a huff of glee. It took all of his self-control not to indulge in a maniacal burst of laughter. He then put his hand on top of the demon's face and said an incantation, one he hadn't had the opportunity to use in a very long time.

I, Thorian Steelblade, claim this territory by the divine right I have been given.

Thorian's vision shattered as screens popped into existence before him. It was as if he were looking at words through a shattered window.

System error…

The "system error" message repeated and repeated itself until finally, his vision was assaulted by a myriad of colors. Black, red, and gold all merged to accentuate a single large screen.

Create a dungeon… Become the dungeon boss!

While that one message took up most of his vision, Thorian could see that there was another message below it. Its screen was small and gray, making it easy to ignore when compared to the extravagance of the first one.

Create a village… Become the lord!

Thorian couldn't help but chuckle at the ridiculousness of the situation.

I see, so the system does not want me to create a village. Well then, I am very sorry, but…

Without wasting a second, Thorian chose the second message. At first, nothing happened, but his vision suddenly swirled with shadows and darkness.

System error.

System error.

Compatible host found.

System recalibration.

Congratulations, Thorian Steelblade. You have become a lord. Please choose a name for this village.

Thorian thought for a second before smiling. "Wolvendale. The village shall be named Wolvendale."

Let it be an homage to the future I have robbed from you, Raven's Nest.

A golden light emerged from the Territory Altar and merged with Thorian, digging deep into his flesh and bones and sinking deep into his blood. A sense of connection tied him with his territory, as if he could feel anything that was inside of it.

Four bursts of light shone from the four cardinal directions, each exactly forty meters away from the Altar.

The statues have emerged. This will prove useful.

As the apocalypse had not yet begun, Thorian was uncertain as to what extent the system was functional. He could only thank his good fortune that the class statues had appeared; he wouldn't need to wait for all the monsters to crawl out from the depths of the earth.

Thorian walked to the west where he found a two-meter statue of a woman wearing a robe and a hat while wielding a staff topped with a gem. He put his hand on the statue and a message appeared in front of him.

Would you like to choose the Magus class?

"Yes, I would."

A sky-blue light seeped from the statue and merged with Thorian. As with the golden light that had appeared from the Altar, this blue one also merged with his body at a fundamental level.

Choose one of these starting abilities.

Fireball: You conjure a fiery orb and hurl it at your enemies, leaving them charred and weakened.

Waterball: You summon a watery orb and launch it at your enemies, drenching them and knocking them off balance.

Rock Bullet: You create a barrage of rocks that fly towards your enemies, pummeling them and leaving them vulnerable.

Wind Gust: You summon a powerful gust of wind that can knock your enemies off balance, extinguish fires, and enhance your speed and agility.

"Fireball."

Thorian did not need even a second to think. In his past life, he had been a fire archmagus, one of only two in the whole kingdom. His flames had burned tens of thousands of his enemies to ashes and won him many wars. They'd even killed his marshal and great general, two of the greatest warriors of the realm.

Wait, wasn't there an amazing class that you could get?

Thorian's mind flashed with the image of a young man in a purple robe. As he remembered the terror that the young man was capable of, he tapped his foot in thought.

If I remember right, that brat Aiden got his class advancement by increasing the rank of all the starting spells.

Thorian laughed to himself as the thought took form in his brain. Aiden, a young magus who'd started three years later than everyone else, had joined the top ten magus council even without being an archmagus. The secret to his success stemmed from his first-class advancement, when he'd become an elemental magus. It was a class that was terribly hard to advance but afforded its users immense power. Even as a grandmagus, he was able to go toe to toe with archmagi that focused on only one element.

I won't be able to advance as early, but I will become that much stronger in the end.

Thorian weighed the pros and cons in his mind before shaking his head.

What is there to think about? It is one of, if not the *strongest class advancement possible. I'd be spitting in the face of my ancestors if I didn't take this opportunity.*

Thorian took a deep breath as he steeled his resolve. Now that he had become a magus, he would be able to accelerate his plans.

Display panel.

Ding!

Race: White Kobloid

Level: 8/15 (XP: 0/110)

Class: Magus

Level: 0/20 (XP: 0/10)

Lifespan: 40 years

Cultivation realm: Qi Gathering First Stage (7.9%)

Stats:

Strength: 18 (22)

Agility: 19 (24)

Constitution: 8

Mana: 4

Qi: 1

Skills:

Minor Moon Boost (passive)

Fireball (active)

CHAPTER 7

Now that he had become a magus, Thorian walked back to the Altar. He touched the head of the demon and tried to access his territory panel.

Display territory.

System error...

The Territory Altar has not been fully activated yet. Please wait until the start of the new world.

ETA: 21:37:16

Thorian raised an eyebrow at the system but huffed out a laugh all the same.

I shouldn't be too greedy. The fact that I got to become a magus even before the apocalypse started is an unbelievable advantage. Anyway, I should go bring Nox for now.

Thorian sniffed a couple of times before catching Nox's scent. With incredible speed, he then rushed towards his follower, and with no less than a minute gone, he had crossed the main road and found the night kobloid searching around diligently.

"Come with me. I have already found it."

Nox's eyes widened in pleasant surprise, and he followed Thorian with a happy expression. The two made their way to what was now the Wolvendale territory. Thorian was very familiar with the class system that the territories provided. As such, he confidently guided Nox to the Class Statue that he believed to be best suited for his follower. The two-meter-tall statue was that of a young man clad in a cloak and a hoodie that covered half of his face. He was wielding two daggers, along with multiple small weapons stashed all over his body and clothing.

"This is the Assassin statue," Thorian announced, then turned to look at Nox. "Place your hand on the statue, and when the message appears in front of you, just say 'Yes.' Do you understand me?"

"Nox understand," the night kobloid said, nodding enthusiastically. Although it was clear that he did not understand the significance of a class or the use of the statue, it seemed that he knew he would become stronger if he followed Thorian's words.

Simple but good. I'm liking this little fella more and more.

Nox put his hand on the Assassin Statue and a dark light merged with his body. The black aura was somehow even darker than the night kobloid's fur, giving him an ominous air about him.

A night kobold with assassin skills, huh? I wonder what kind of advancements will be available for him when the time comes.

The black aura slowly disappeared and fully merged with Nox, and the night kobloid turned and looked at Thorian with a confused expression.

"What skill did you choose?"

Nox wrinkled his forehead as he struggled to say the skill name. "Back—Backst... stab!"

Thorian nodded with a smile. "Good choice. It will work well with your shadow abilities once you evolve."

"Nox stab! Nox strong!" The night kobloid smiled from ear to ear. Thorian didn't know if it was cute or creepy.

"Well, let's continue our hunt." Thorian's expression turned serious. "We need to kill as many as we can before the apocalypse begins."

"Apocalypse?"

Thorian took in Nox's confused look before sighing and turning around. "You will know soon enough."

The two made their way in the direction of their original den for five minutes before spotting the opening of a burrow. As Thorian put his hand inside, he quickly understood that it was a large, complex structure.

Thorian grinned. "Good. This is the perfect opportunity to test my new skill."

Fireball.

A large amount of mana pulsated in his chest before making its way to his hand through thousands of channels. The mana traversing his body felt hot and violent, but it did not cause him pain, just a mild sense of discomfort.

Flames appeared above his palm and converged into a small ball. Thorian shoved his arm inside the burrow and launched his spell before instinctively yanking his arm back out. An explosion shook the ground below him, followed by flames rushing out of entrances all around the two kobloids.

Level up!

Level up!

Thorian frowned at the unexpected notifications before his eyes brightened up with understanding.

I forgot about the class. That should be what leveled up. Display panel.

Ding!

Race: White Kobloid

Level: 8/15 (XP: 0/110)

Class: Magus

Level: 3/20 (XP: 17/30)

Lifespan: 40 years

Cultivation Realm: Qi Gathering First Stage (7.9%)

Stats:

Strength: 18 (22)

Agility: 19 (24)

Constitution: 8

Mana: 4

Qi: 1

Free Points: 6

Skills:

Minor Moon Boost (passive)

Fireball (active)

Noticing the free points that he had accumulated, Thorian smiled. He was now finally able to control which stats rose with each level up.

My other stats increase naturally as I level up my race. I should put all my points into mana so that I can use my spells more.

Mana: 4 → 10

When Thorian cast Fireball, he'd sensed half of the mana in his core drain away, leaving him feeling somewhat drained. However, after increasing his mana stat, he felt refreshed once again. With his new mana pool, Thorian estimated that he could use his skill three more times before his mana ran dry.

"Thoreen strong!" Nox's mouth hung open and his eyebrows were raised high. He looked at Thorian as if he were a god.

"Let's find more burrows like these. They're very efficient." Thorian grinned before walking from the scene of his genocide as if nothing had happened.

The two continued terrorizing the forest, moving from one area to the next. Whatever animal they found, they killed. Rabbits, hares, foxes, wolves, deer, boars, and monkeys—none were spared. In this manner, another three hours quickly passed.

Level up!

This time, the notification was not about his class level but his race.

Level: 9/15 (XP: 0/130)

Finally! That took a while. The sharing of XP between my race and my class is going to make progressing in both truly grueling.

Amid hunting another wolf pack, Thorian had quickly noticed a peculiar phenomenon. The amount of experience that he gained from killing was split between his race and class level, most of which was going to his class level, which made progressing his race even slower than before.

"Did you level up too, Nox?" Thorian turned around to see his follower finishing off the last wolf with a bite through the neck.

The night kobloid yanked the dead beast to the side and walked towards him. Blood dripped down his face as he said with a grin, "Nox level 9!"

"Good progress. What about your class? What's your assassin level?"

Nox frowned for a second before answering, "Assassin, 7!"

"I see. I guess that only makes sense." Thorian looked down and checked his magus level.

Level: 8/20 (XP: 3/110)

After using all his free points, his mana grew by leaps and bounds.

Mana: 10 → 25

Even though his mana pool was now less than half full, Thorian could still use his Fireball spell three more times.

At this regeneration rate, my core should be full in two hours or so. That's if I don't use Fireball in the meantime, of course.

As rabbits and hares no longer contributed any experience to his class level, there was no reason for Thorian to use his spell. With his physical stats boosted by his passive, there were very few animals that could give him any trouble in the forest. Even a pack of wolves would fall in but a few moments to the two kobloids' assault.

The night sky was tinged a faint orange and red, mixed with the darkness of space. The beautiful twilight was a sign of the cracking dawn.

"Let's go back to the cave," Thorian ordered before his serious expression mellowed to a soft smile. "Let's show them your new self, Nox. Your strong self!"

Nox looked down with an open mouth for a second before looking at Thorian and bobbing his head up and down. "Nox strong!"

"I feel like I've heard those two words a thousand times now." Thorian shook his head. "Let's go."

As the two made their way to the cave, they made sure to hunt any big or strong animals that had the misfortune of being in their way. The scent of blood and damp earth filled the air as they traversed the dense forest, long shadows cast by the towering trees swaying gently above them. The distance that should have taken them a dozen minutes ended up costing them two hours, but it was well worth it. Both kobloids leveled up both their race and class again, their increased strength and abilities evident in their every move.

The sun had already risen high in the sky by the time they reached the entrance of the cave. Shafts of sunlight pierced through the canopy above, casting a warm glow on the dark, moss-covered rocks surrounding the entrance. The sound of crunching leaves and the occasional guttural growl marked the presence of the kobloids nearby. As expected, the pack that had gone hunting in the night had returned.

Inside the cave, most of the kobloids were feasting on fresh kills, tearing at the meat with their sharp teeth. Others were busy cleaning and sorting through the animal carcasses, preparing to store or preserve the leftovers. Meanwhile, a few weary kobloids were resting, their bodies sprawled across the cave floor after a long night of hunting.

Good thing I let my mana pool fill up to the brim before returning. I will be needing it.

"Attention, gentlemen. May I have your attention?" Thorian walked with confident steps towards the end of the cave. His boots echoed against the stone floor, a rhythm that seemed to captivate the monsters. After he passed by all the kobloids, he turned around and faced them, his voice echoing through the cavern. "From now on, this tribe will be under my rule. I will be your king!"

CHAPTER 8

Thorian's words resonated through the cave, drawing all of the monsters' attention. They stared at him in confusion and surprise, and then the white kobold let out a scoff.

"Smelly Poo! Smelly head!" The kobold's mocking scoff transformed into maniacal laughter. The rest of the kobloids followed his lead and a cacophony of laughter swallowed all sound in the cave.

Is that really the level of insults we are dealing with? Thorian raised an eyebrow but did not say a thing. He just stood with his chest held proud, looking directly at the kobold that stood half a meter above him.

"No Smelly Poo!" Nox shouted, stomping from the back in an angry huff towards the white kobold. "Thoreen strong!"

"That's not my name," Thorian muttered under his breath. However, he had a smile on his face as he looked at Nox confronting a stronger opponent.

"Thoreen?" The kobold's brows lifted, and a growl tumbled from his mouth. "Black weak! Smelly Poo weak!" He went to punch at Nox, but the latter quickly stepped back and dodged the attack.

The kobold clicked his tongue but did not say anything in response as Nox took a stance and readied himself for battle. At the same time, some of the other kobloids walked towards Nox and surrounded him.

"Stop!" the white kobold growled. "Me fight!"

Thorian blinked in surprise as the group dispersed to give Nox and the white kobold space. *I have underestimated you, creatures*, he acknowledged inwardly. *Your sense of honor is admirable.*

The two fighters stood at a standstill as they tried to read each other's movements before the kobold burst into action. In less than a second, he dashed towards Nox and swiped at him with his claws. The night kobloid sidestepped, but the attack was only the first of a flurry. Bites, swipes, hooks, and jabs formed a speedy combo delivered by the white kobold. However, with his small size, Nox was able to dodge most of the blows. Even the attacks that were too fast for him to side-step only grazed his fur and flesh.

Good thing I told him to put all his free points into Agility. His speed should be around the same as that white kobold.

Pride stole across Thorian's face as he watched Nox fight a being a full evolution ahead of him. While the white kobold had a much higher Strength and Constitution, he could not use that advantage if none of his strikes hit their target.

On the other hand, Nox was slowly chipping away at the white kobold with small counterattacks. Whenever the two-meter-tall monster would miss an attack, the night kobloid would sneak in a quick swipe to the stomach or a hook to the liver, and a few minutes later, his opponent was bloody and bruised.

"Black rat!" The white monster growled in rage. He opened up his palm, where a white light began to gather. Thorian immediately knew what it was.

Fireball.

The white light took proper shape in the monster's palm before he launched it like a lightning bolt at Nox. The night kobloid could only look in shock and confusion at the spell hurling towards him with unimaginable speed.

Boom!

A flash of red intercepted the white beam, and the two clashed brilliantly in front of Nox before dissipating into embers and ashes. It took half a second for him to understand what happened, then his eyes darted to Thorian.

"Stop! That is enough," Thorian ordered as he walked between Nox and the white kobold. He looked at the giant monster with calm, confident eyes. "If you want to fight someone, you can fight me."

The white kobold, his mouth hung slightly ajar and his cheeks hollow, gaped at Thorian with wide eyes. Noticing his own fear, the monster clenched his teeth and growled at the small white kobloid in front of him. "Smelly Poo! Weak!" Light sparked to attention once again atop the kobold's palm before he launched his white bolt at his enemy.

"Stupid." Thorian activated Fireball and launched it to counter the kobold's spell. Before the two skills could clash, he dashed to the side and closed his left eye. In a fraction of a second, the two spells collided against each other, letting out a burst of white and red. While Thorian had to squint against the harsh rays to see, it was nothing compared to the kobold who was forced to close his eyes so as not to be blinded.

Thorian rushed towards his visually impaired enemy and punched him right in the stomach with all his power. The wind was knocked out of the white kobold, and he took a few steps back, giving Thorian enough time to unleash another spell. Flames grew to life on the white kobloid's palm as he looked at his opponent with indifferent eyes. The moment the kobold regained his bearings, Thorian's spell was ready to cast. He launched it at the monster's chest.

A small explosion threw the white monster to the ground as flames burned his fur. He screamed and shrieked, rolling on the ground to put out the fire. However, he was already too late. The flames ate through patches of his fur right down to his skin, leaving the white kobold in excruciating pain.

Thorian issued a silent command. *Fireball.* Flames anew gathered atop Thorian's palm as he slowly strode towards the white kobold. The poor, pained monster shrieked at the sight and crawled away in fear.

"Do you admit defeat?" Thorian said in a low voice. "Do you accept me as your king?"

Fear and rage warred in the white kobold's eyes as his mouth bobbed open. However, it didn't take long for fear to overwhelm its opponent.

"Yes, Smelly Poo strong! Smelly Poo king!"

The scared white kobold's words served as a declaration for the rest of the cave, as they'd all been his followers. After a short pause, the cave was filled with chants.

"Smelly Poo king! Smelly Poo king!" Each utterance of those three words was like a strike of a hammer on Thorian's nerves.

He gritted his teeth and clenched his fists. "That is not my name!" The shout cut through the noise like the Red Sea's parting. Everyone looked at him with frightened eyes, afraid that they would be next on the menu to be roasted.

"Not Smelly Poo. Thoreen!" Nox walked forwards and explained with an enthusiastic expression, "Thoreen king!"

"Thoreen king!" Nox's words were like a lifeboat to the dozen or so kobloids who echoed the declaration in a chant.

That is not my name either... Thorian wanted to explain the misunderstanding, but in the end, he just sighed. His name was seemingly too hard for the kobloids and kobold to pronounce.

Minutes passed and the chants soon died down. After some

semblance of silence had finally returned to the cave, Thorian took center stage.

"As your king, my orders are absolute. If I say to do something, you will do it without question or complaint. You will also give your lives for me if need be, is that understood?"

Thorian scanned the cave with his eyes as the kobloids were nodding and responding with "Yes." Their facial expressions were undisturbed, free of any hint of unease.

Interesting... Either they are master-grade actors, or they are truly simpleminded.

"In exchange, I will make you strong." Thorian took a deep breath and spoke with power and certainty. "I will give you power that your brains could not even dare to dream."

Thorian glanced over at Nox as he said those last words. The night kobloid's expression was full of reverence and awe.

"Thoreen king!"

CHAPTER 9

"Silence." Thorian's voice cut through the shouts and howls. "Today, there will be no sleep while the sun is out. We will hunt."

It took a few seconds for all of the kobloids to understand his words, and they were not happy about them. The monsters glanced at each other in confusion and fear, lost as to what to do.

Thorian lowered his voice and spoke again, this time in a gentler tone. "I understand that you're afraid. But there is no need to be scared. You have seen it tonight, right? There aren't any strong monsters here. Almost everything can be killed."

Noticing that even his clear explanation did not inspire much response, Thorian lightly shook his head before opening his hand with a confident smile. A burst of flames raged as he conjured his spell. "Don't you want this power? Don't you want it now? I can give it to you!"

Thorian's Fireball dazzled the small kobloids as they looked with open eyes and mouths. They screamed and howled in excitement, with only a few intelligible cries of "Thoreen" and "King" shouted here and there.

This is surprisingly easy.

Charismatic speeches, something Thorian had practiced throughout his life, were something to which he had long grown accustomed. However, even with his level of experience, it would have taken him some degree of preparation to deliver a speech and achieve the same effect on a crowd of humans. For kobloids, though, it seemed there was no need to plant supporters in the crowd or even do any extensive research. Showing what they wanted to see was enough.

In that regard, perhaps the two are not that different.

"Nox." Thorian gestured to his most trusted follower. The night kobloid immediately made his way to Thorian's side with a serious expression. "Take everyone outside and wait. We will start our hunt soon."

Nox nodded before looking at the rest of the tribe. A slight smile parted his lips before he masked it with a neutral expression. "Outside, go!"

The group of fourteen or so white kobloids followed after the black one, leaving only Thorian and one other behind in the cave. The large kobold looked at Thorian with a mix of fear, rage, and bitterness, but Thorian did not say a word.

"Smelly Poo! Me no follow!"

"I can give you that right." Thorian walked towards the injured monster with confident steps. His demeanor conveyed a certain pride and arrogance as if he was the owner of the cave. "I can give you the right to leave."

Thorian got closer to the kobold and his words grew heavy. "You can leave the tribe, unharmed, and live the rest of your days in the wilderness. And when the true monsters come, you can live like a rat, hiding in whatever cave or corner you can find, afraid of the day when the truly strong ones will come and destroy you with a flick of their thumb."

Thorian stared deep into the injured kobold's eyes. He could see the uncertainty and fear there as he slowly spoke every word, making sure that the monster thoroughly understood him.

"Or you can follow me." Thorian's tone shifted to a gentle one as he smiled at the fearful creature. "Follow me and you'll grow stronger than any kobold ever has. You will command thousands. Armies will listen to your every word, and countries will fear you."

The kobold looked in shock at Thorian with his mouth agape.

After a few seconds, Thorian turned around and made his way to the cave entrance without looking back. He knew that his work was done.

Now, it's your choice and your choice alone.

Outside the cave, the kobloids were packed into the small clearing. The rabbits, squirrels, and small animals that stayed in the tall grass had all run away in fear into the dense forest.

"Nox, we will split the pack in two." Thorian grinned before continuing, "I will lead one group, and you will lead the other. You think you can handle it?"

Nox raised his eyebrows in surprise before lightly bowing. "Me handle group. Me leader!"

"Yes, you will now be a leader," Thorian said with a light chuckle, then looked up to the sky. The sun was already clearly visible, standing at forty degrees or so from the horizon. "We will be hunting until midday and then we will come back here. Do you understand what midday is?"

"Yes. Sunup!"

"Good, it's when the sun is up in the middle of the sky. And remember, hunt deep in the forest, and do not make a big fuss. Whatever you do, don't let humans see you."

Nox paused for a second before bobbing his head in acknowledgment. "Humans no see."

Seeing the slight hesitation, Thorian took a deep breath and looked at Nox with cold eyes. "If they find you, kill them immediately.

We cannot let them return home and tell the others about us. Not this soon."

After giving his directives, Thorian focused on the group of kobloids behind Nox. He pointed at seven of them at random.

"You all are now part of Nox's group, the night kobloid's. His words have the same weight as my words." His tone shifted to a low and aggressive one. "If I hear that you did not listen to his orders or disrespected him, I will personally take the head of the culprit, understood?"

Several gulps followed Thorian's statement before they responded with, "Understood."

"Good. The rest of you will follow me." Thorian grinned. "Let's turn this forest red."

Thorian was walking towards his group when he heard some shuffling behind him. The injured kobold was limping out of the cave with a conflicted expression plain to see above his burned upper body.

"Have you made your choice?" Thorian gestured at him with a frown.

The kobold let out a labored breath before nodding. "Me follow, me see."

"Oh, you will see." Thorian chuckled. "You will see everything."

Thorian bid farewell to Nox's group before leading his own to the left. Including himself, his group was composed of seven kobloids, and a large, though injured, kobold. Although the difference between his group and Nox's was striking, Thorian didn't think that Nox's group would have much trouble. Unless they somehow crossed paths with a bear or another monster species, few creatures of this forest could pose a threat to them.

As they walked through the dense trees, Thorian crouched to all fours with a click of his tongue. Even though he didn't like hunting in such an animalistic position, he couldn't deny its advantages. He raced through the bushes and around the trees while the rest of the group followed him. However, due to the massive difference in their speeds, Thorian was forced to slow down to the pace of their slowest member.

A few minutes passed before his ears suddenly perked up. With a hand signal, the whole group came to a stop. Without making a sound, Thorian peeked from the bushes to see a sounder of wild boars drinking from a stream. He couldn't help but grin at the unexpected prize.

He looked back at the rest of his group and signaled them to spread out. By taking up more space, there would be less of a chance for their prey to escape. Once everyone was in position, Thorian gave them the signal and rushed at the boars. Even though the poor animals reacted immediately, they could not handle what came next.

Fireball.

Thorian conjured up his spell and launched it at the boar that was furthest from him, making the others squeal in panic. He then pounced at the slow prey next to him, crushing its throat with a bite to the neck.

Meanwhile, even though the kobold was injured, he was still the fastest in the group. He jumped to the other side of the stream and cut off the boars' escape path. This gave the rest of the group enough time to catch up and hunt their prey.

Once the boar he'd first attacked stopped thrashing, Thorian jumped at the next closest and slashed its side with his claws. Blood and guts gushed out as the poor beast screamed and fell to the ground. With a merciful strike, Thorian sliced its neck open, leaving it to die.

The rest of the kobloids finished the job and killed all the boars before digging in fervently. Their eyes glistened hungrily as they ate their prey.

"Stop!" Thorian's order cut through the haze of victory. All the monsters looked at him in confusion. However, upon seeing his expression, their confusion soon turned to fear.

"We are here to hunt, to become stronger. Not to indulge in this gluttony." Thorian scanned each and every one of his group members with cold eyes. "Are you going to waste hours eating these weak beasts when you could be hunting more prey and growing stronger?"

He then walked out of the stream and without even turning back and looking at them, barked out his orders. "Stand up, let's move."

CHAPTER 10

The group of kobloids begrudgingly followed Thorian's orders, not that he left them any time to wallow in their frustration.

"All of you, tell me your levels."

The kobloids hesitantly answered the question. Other than the large kobold, they were all at level 4 or 5. Unsurprisingly, the kobold was level 1.

Not many monsters he can hunt that would give him XP. Maybe a bear? There was also that goblin that the soldiers caught. Those could increase his level a little bit.

"Good, your level is still low enough." Thorian cleared his throat. "Hunt anything that moves. If you can catch it, kill it. Do you understand me?"

"Understood," the kobloids said in unison, nodding.

With that, the hunt truly began. Wherever the small pack moved, a trail of blood followed. Squirrels, rabbits, raccoons, deer, boars, and foxes all perished to their fangs and claws. The level of mechanical, cold-blooded destruction on display was unnatural. It wasn't out of a need for survival or to eat; it was simply indiscriminate annihilation.

An hour later and all the kobloids were at level 6; the small animals no longer gave any experience points. As such, at Thorian's command, they swiftly changed targets to bigger and stronger prey.

After another two hours, Thorian looked up at the sun's position in the sky. They still had another hour or two left before their scheduled meeting.

Level up!

The poor wolf caged in Thorian's claws finally drew its last breath, pushing his class to level 10. Judging by his species' experience-point progression, he was close to leveling that up as well.

"Monster green!" One of the kobloids tasked with scouting the area came running from the bushes with a panicked face. "Close!"

Thorian frowned. "Green monsters? Are they goblins?"

Without wasting a single breath, Thorian and the rest of the group followed the kobloid scout. A brief walk through the bushes and shrubbery led them to a small cliff overlooking a clearing below. Thorian peeked from behind a tree only to see a pack of seven small green monsters led by a hobgoblin. They were finishing off a pair of wild hogs.

Thorian looked at the kobold next to him and grinned. "That's your prey."

The kobold also had a grin plastered over his face as he stared at the hobgoblin. Even though he was still injured from his fight with Thorian, his blood was boiling for a fight.

Thorian conjured a fireball and gestured to his group. "Once I throw it, go in."

Three, two, one.

Just as the hobgoblin was about to finish off the pig with a stab to the neck, a small fireball exploded in his face. The impact pushed him back, knocked his primitive spear out of his hands, and left him burning in flames. Before he could recover, another spell followed. This time, it was a burst of pure-white light that exploded with a massive shockwave, sending the poor creature flying in the air.

"Awoo!"

The bestial instincts of the kobloids took over as they charged at the confused and squealing goblins. Though the green creatures were armed with stone knives and daggers, they were no match for claws and fangs.

The kobold rushed through the small scuffles between the weaker monsters and pounced at the disoriented and wounded hobgoblin. Before the green monster could grasp his surroundings, the kobold shoved his claws through his neck.

Level up!

The notification told Thorian everything he needed to know. He switched his focus to the rest of the battlefield. While the kobloids had the upper hand, the goblins were still putting up a good fight. Their stone weapons might be primitive, but they were still sharp and effective.

Let's see if they can still give me experience. Display panel.

Level: 10/20 (XP: 47/150)

Seeing the massive experience increase in his class level, Thorian let out a chuckle. *Maybe I should be focusing more on these hobgoblins. They are truly generous.*

He conjured his Fireball spell once again and waited for an opening. Just as he saw a goblin and a kobloid back away from each other after a clash, he launched it.

Boom!

In less than a second, the poor little goblin was engulfed in an explosion before his flaming body was pushed out of the cloud of smoke and ash. A glance at his panel told Thorian everything he needed to know. The monster was dead.

Level: 10/20 (XP: 53/150)

So they give 5 XP? Really ten, since the other half goes to my race.

Thorian quickly compared this to the other animals he had hunted. Even the small goblins gave ample experience, similar to that of wolves. The realization drew him deeper into thought as the rest of the kobloids finished up the hunt.

According to his knowledge of the past, goblins usually lived in packs of fifty to a hundred. The bigger packs reached into the thousands and claimed whole forests as their land. Such a small group of goblins could only mean one thing: a bigger pack was close by.

A sudden shuffling in a bush to his right snapped Thorian out of his thoughts. He turned around, only to see an old man covering a small child's mouth as he looked at the clearing in fear.

For a second, Thorian's world froze in time. He knew what needed to be done, but it was as if his body were trying to shut itself down. As a myriad of emotions tangled within his heart, he closed his eyes and took a deep breath.

Almost in a flash, Thorian rushed towards the sitting pair of humans and towered over them. He looked at them with a cold, resolute stare. "Close your eyes," he said, his voice deep and low. Even though he understood that it was useless, he still wanted to give the pair a certain level of dignity and mercy.

The old man looked at Thorian with an open mouth, guttural sounds emitted from his throat as the words struggled to come out. "Please, god, have mercy." He tightened his hug over the little, sobbing child and pushed him to the ground in a last, desperate attempt to protect the boy with his body.

Thorian was about to execute the two when pieces of wood fell out of the old man's backpack. He looked dazedly at the cut branches and small trunks rolling on the ground when suddenly, an idea popped into his mind.

"Do you have an axe?!" Just as the words left Thorian's mouth, he realized their futility. He was a kobloid trying to talk to a human.

The old man looked up at Thorian with a face full of shock and terror. "Oh god," he muttered, the words struggling to escape him, "what in the heavens? A monster that talks? Is it the devil?"

Thorian's jaw hung open for a second before he understood the meaning behind the old man's words. "Can you... understand me?"

The man was still frozen in horror but managed to nod, shocking Thorian even further. All the knowledge he thought he knew as truth was now becoming a lie.

How does this even make sense? A kobloid could never talk with a human, only the evolved species can...

While Thorian was stunned in place, stuck in his turbulent thoughts, the old man looked down at his axe on the ground. With fidgeting hands, he inched closer to it.

"Don't." Thorian's voice startled the old man to the core. "Don't make my choice any easier."

Thorian grabbed the axe from the ground and threw it to the side in an absentminded fashion. His eyes were still blank, and his mind was as chaotic as when he first learned that he had been reborn as a monster.

"Don't move an inch from your place," he warned, looking at the old man and child with cold eyes. "You cannot run away from me, so do not even think about it."

With those words, Thorian walked to a nearby tree and sat down. He needed to think through his next actions thoroughly, lest he regret them for the rest of his life.

CHAPTER II

"What am I doing? I should just kill them and save myself the trouble," Thorian muttered to himself as he sat next to a tree. His course of action should have been clear: eliminate the two humans and avoid any future trouble they might bring. However, the fact that they understood him threw his mind into disarray. Had they been unable to understand a word he said, then communication would have been impossible. Without communication, there would be no possibility of coming to an agreement or an exchange. But now...

I wish I hadn't said a word. It would have made things much easier.

Thorian glanced to the side and noticed the old man's axe lying on a patch of grass next to him. His eyes locked onto the tool, mesmerized. Suddenly, his expression shifted, a grin spreading across his face as an idea struck him like lightning in a glass bottle.

With a determined stride, he stood, grabbed the axe, and approached the two humans. The old man was comforting the sobbing little boy with whispers and gentle embraces.

"You have a choice," Thorian said, his eyes filled with malice. "One of you will die, the other will live. You choose."

He tossed the axe to the old man, who caught it clumsily. The man's horrified eyes mirrored the young boy's as his arm shook, clutching the axe.

"Human?"

Thorian turned to see the kobold glaring at the old man and the young child. Just as the monster was about to take action, Thorian shouted, "Stop!"

The kobold looked at Thorian in confusion. "Human, kill?"

"No one is to touch them for now," Thorian said, taking a deep breath. "Not until I give the order."

The small pack of kobloids stared in confusion and interest at the pair, but they all stepped aside as the large kobold led them away with disgruntled growls.

With the kobold no longer posing an immediate threat, Thorian's attention shifted back to the two humans. His plan hinged on their next move.

"I'm sorry," the old man said, tears streaming down his face as he gently touched the little boy's cheek. "I'm so sorry, little Roo."

The boy, Roo, looked at the old man, his expression frozen and his mouth agape. "Grampa?"

But the old man didn't answer. He could only cry and sob, the axe trembling in his hand.

"Grampa, please!" Roo's face twisted in anguish as his emotions overwhelmed him. His once innocent eyes were now filled with terror, his pupils dilating rapidly as if seeking escape from the unfolding nightmare. His lower lip quivered uncontrollably, betraying his fear and vulnerability. Desperate to avoid the reality in front of him, Roo turned his head and closed his eyes.

Thorian, however, watched the old man intently.

Fighting his weakness and fragility, the old man's face contorted with a mix of emotions. Fear turned to sadness, then to anger and rage. With a scream, he raised the axe high before swinging it towards his own neck.

"Good," Thorian said, gripping the old man's forearm firmly, stopping the axe's descent. "You shall live... both of you."

The old man stared at Thorian, incredulous, and then a nervous huff of laughter escaped his throat before he was overcome by hiccups. As the reality of the situation settled in, he collapsed to his knees, sobbing.

Young Roo opened his eyes and, seeing his grandfather crying, also began to weep.

While the scene might have warmed the coldest of hearts, Thorian had neither the time nor the inclination to appreciate it.

"However, there is one condition."

Thorian's words were like a bucket of cold water, causing the old man to stifle his tears and look up at him, stiff with fear once more.

"I need you to go back to the city and bring me sixteen axes. I don't care if you buy them or steal them. I just want them in three hours."

Thorian placed his hand on young Roo's shoulder. Though the boy tried to jerk away, Thorian held him tightly in place, looking at the old man with cold eyes.

"The kid will stay here. If you don't return in time, I will kill him. If you don't bring all sixteen axes, I will kill him." He then smirked at the old man's terror-stricken face before conjuring a fireball in his free hand. "If you bring soldiers with you, I will kill him, kill you, and annihilate all the soldiers. Do not dare test my patience."

The old man stared at Thorian in shock before rapidly nodding his head. "Yes, I will bring them to you. Please don't hurt little Roo."

"You have my word," Thorian said, his expression neutral. "As long as you keep your own."

Thorian deactivated his spell, and the old man hurried away from the group of monsters. He stole a few glances back at his grandson before running with all his might.

After the man disappeared into the trees, Thorian looked down at the sobbing child. Roo had brown hair and brown eyes, an unremarkable appearance for this country. Tears streamed down his face, but Thorian couldn't blame him. No child in the world would have reacted differently.

"Roo," Thorian called, startling the tears from the boy's face. He immediately looked up, trying to control his shaking hands, though his lips still quivered. "Let me show you the kind of world you will grow up in, the kind of world you will need to face."

Thorian turned and walked towards his group of kobloids, chuckling as he gestured at the lead kobold. "How does it feel? Getting some experience after so long?"

Though the monster initially wore a sour expression, it quickly turned into a grin. "Good."

"I'm glad to hear that." Thorian nodded, surveying the rest of the kobloids. Their excitement was palpable, and they seemed confident in their growth.

"Everyone, what do you say we find more of those goblins?" Thorian exclaimed. "Fight them, kill them, and grow strong!"

"Grow strong!" The kobloids laughed and cheered, chanting, "Fight! Fight! Fight!"

"Good, you're truly worthy of being my men," Thorian said, smiling and nodding in acknowledgment before issuing his next command. "I want you all to search this whole area. Find those green monsters and come back. Do not fight them. Just observe their location and report back. Understood?"

The kobloids' excitement tempered slightly at Thorian's change in tone, but they replied, "Understood."

As his group dispersed in all directions, Thorian was left alone with the young boy. Roo was seated on the grass, his head buried deep within his arms as he rocked back and forth.

Thorian noticed the boy's strange actions but only shrugged. There was no need for further conversation, and it was better this way. Both of them would be left to their own thoughts.

As Thorian studied the child, he couldn't help but recall the families of foxes he had slaughtered, the pack of wolves he had killed. There had been young pups among them too.

This is just an exchange. Their survival or death is meaningless in the grand scheme.

Minutes passed quickly as Thorian questioned his own decisions again and again before a rustling grabbed his attention. One of the kobloids came back with a happy expression on his face.

"Monster green! Many!"

Those words, primitive as they were, sounded like a magical spell to Thorian as his lips parted in a grin.

CHAPTER 12

After the small pack of kobloids regrouped, Thorian turned toward the young child sobbing next to a tree.

"Roo." Thorian's voice made the little kid shiver as he looked up at him in terror. "Follow me."

The young boy immediately stood up without fuss. His knees and legs were shaking, and his face was streaked with dried tears and snot. Still, Thorian spared him no pity. He turned around and followed the scout along with the rest of his group.

As they made their way through the bushes and around the trees, the sounds of crunching and shuffling told Thorian all he needed to know. After a few minutes of hiking at a leisurely pace, they spotted a large horde of green monsters coming in and out of a dark cave. Each goblin was doing a specific task—some were sharpening their stone tools, others were bringing in animals they'd hunted, and others still were carrying captured humans.

Looking at the men and women stripped naked and tied with ropes, Thorian clicked his tongue. He knew what fate awaited them.

No more softheartedness. These people will only bring me trouble if I let them live.

Thorian looked at the horrified child next to him and couldn't help but grimace.

I guess in his eyes, I will always be a monster... Good. Only monsters survive.

Thorian shifted his attention to the rest of his group. This time, they couldn't just go in without a plan.

"We will bait them here," Thorian explained. "Two kobloids will go and get their attention and then run away towards the rest of us. We will then ambush the goblins that follow. If too many of them come for us, we run away. Do you understand?"

The group of kobloids looked confused but nodded all the same. "Go, run, fight?"

Thorian chuckled at this executive summary of his plan. "Yeah, that's right."

He then chose two of the kobloids and ordered, "You two will go in. Don't let the goblins get too close to you. Just get their attention and run towards us."

The pair of kobloids acknowledged his command and proceeded to circle the rocky formation before sprinting towards the large assembly of goblins. There were already about thirty goblins visible outside the cave—the number of those lurking within remained a mystery.

"Be prepared." Thorian looked at the kid with a serious expression. "We might have to run at any moment."

The kobold grunted at the special attention Thorian was giving the human child before focusing on the two kobloids in charge of baiting. They screamed and howled at the goblins to get their attention.

The green monsters sharpening their weapons and bringing in the dead animals stopped what they were doing and focused on the two white-furred kobloids. Dozens of goblins and three hobgoblins charged with mad zeal at the two, laughing and squealing at the apparent gift from heaven.

Thorian and the kobold prepared their spells as their two comrades and the dozens of enemies ran towards them, including three hobgoblins, who sped past their green kin and rushed towards the two kobloids. All three had short spears in their hands, ready to thrust through the poor monsters' white fur.

Just as they were about to reach their targets, a fireball burst the first hobgoblin into flames while a moon bolt launched the second one backwards with a blinding white light.

"Now! Fight!"

With Thorian's war cry, the group of kobloids charged into the melee. The large kobold rushed towards the burned hobgoblin while Thorian focused on the unharmed one.

While the hobgoblin's spear had good range, a fireball had even more. Thorian launched his spell at the monster's face, smothering it in flames. The hobgoblin shrieked in pain and dropped his spear, only for the screams to get stuck in his throat as Thorian followed with a punch to the liver. The green beast's body collapsed to the ground, its muscles convulsing from the combined force of the searing magical flames and the devastating physical blow. Thorian shoved his claws through its throat, crushing its windpipe and severing its arteries.

Just as he finished off his enemy, two more goblins rushed towards him in the chaos of the battlefield. Thorian jumped back to get some distance before the white kobold pounced at one of the goblins from the side. One bite was all he needed to sever its head from the rest of its body.

While the kobold was handling the two goblins, Thorian took a glance around the battlefield. The first hobgoblin he had set ablaze had been killed by the kobold, leaving only one more evolved threat. As for the small goblins, even though they outnumbered the kobloids, the latter were still handling them well enough. Each kobloid was able to fight off two goblins.

Seeing the last hobgoblin stagger to its feet, Thorian used his last bit of mana to conjure a final fireball. Before the disoriented monster could regain its bearings, an explosion engulfed it in flames and burned off its skin.

The kobold, having already dispatched the second goblin, seized the chance to strike. As the flames continued to flicker, he tore into the hobgoblin's abdomen with his sharp claws, causing guts and blood to spill from the gash.

Level up!

Level up!

The two notifications brought a smile to Thorian's face. A refreshing feeling washed away his fatigue, and he felt even more energized than before.

Thorian and the white kobold pounced from one goblin to the next with incredible speed. Without any more hobgoblins, the tide of the battle quickly shifted in the kobloids' favor. Even without using his Fireball, Thorian was much stronger than the low-level goblins, and he had an additional lifetime's worth of combat experience.

In just a few minutes, the green grass turned red with the goblins' blood. Bodies littered the battlefield and heads rolled on the ground. With all the goblins dead, Thorian took a moment to look at the little kid. He was retching with hollow eyes and shaking hands, looking like he might lose consciousness at any moment.

"Squii! Shrii!"

Loud squeals and shrieks coming from the cave captured Thorian's attention immediately. As he looked at the entrance, his expression froze.

"Run! Now!"

An army of countless goblins charged out of the cave, led by more than half a dozen hobgoblins. Even if Thorian had ninety lives, he wouldn't survive a fight against them in his current state.

Thorian rushed at the vomiting little kid and grabbed him by the waist, while the rest of the kobloids followed suit. As they exited the clearing and entered a dense patch of the forest, Thorian immediately laid out his order.

"Split up, right now! We shall meet at the cave!"

The kobloids split up in three directions at Thorian's order, leaving him running straight ahead with the now-unconscious kid under his left arm. After a few seconds, he looked back to see three of the hobgoblins running after him. Their speed was marginally faster than his own, allowing them to slowly but surely catch up to him.

Display panel.

Agility: 22 → 31

Thorian invested his remaining skill points into agility, significantly enhancing his speed. His muscles transformed and expanded as a sensation of weightlessness permeated his entire body. It felt as though he had been carrying a heavy burden all his life, and only now was finally able to release it.

Even with the young boy in his arms, Thorian's speed now outpaced that of the hobgoblins. With his improved agility, he was able to jump on top of broken tree trunks and climb up cliffs without losing much speed. After a few such maneuvers, Thorian could no longer see the hobgoblins behind him.

However, he did not slow down or stop. He continued running at top speed, taking a long detour towards the cave. Minutes quickly passed, and the sun reached its apex, signaling their scheduled time for the meet-up. As Thorian neared their so-called home, he couldn't help but think of the rest of his group.

Most of the hobgoblins followed me. The others shouldn't have too much trouble.

As Thorian crossed the dense forest and reached the clearing where their cave was, he was greeted by Nox's group, along with three of his own kobloids.

Nox looked delighted at Thorian's return before his expression shifted to confusion as he looked at the young boy in his arms. "Human... kid?"

CHAPTER 13

Nox's reaction was something Thorian had already predicted, but he had acted with a specific purpose in mind.

"I have made a deal with this child's protector. No one is to touch him, understood?"

Nox and the rest of the kobloids nodded, but they couldn't shake off the strangeness of the situation as they stared at Thorian in surprise and confusion.

"The deal I have made is very beneficial for us. Don't worry."

With those words, Thorian made his way inside the cave, knowing that there was no use in explaining himself further. The cavern was dimly lit by the light filtering in from outside, leaving the shadows in its corners untouched. Thorian sat down in one of those shadows, placed the sleeping child on the ground next to him, and began meditating in a lotus position.

This is the best time to cultivate Qi. I will need to wait for my mana to fill up either way.

Thorian practiced his breathing technique. For the first ten minutes, the energy in the air had difficulty entering through his Qi paths. Despite having undergone a cleansing the previous day, his channels were still more clogged and filthy than those of a typical human practitioner.

The minutes passed slowly, and Thorian was able to use the surrounding energy to clear his channels. It was only after an hour had passed that a small droplet of Qi reached his dantian.

With the Qi having reached its destination, Thorian could do what he hadn't been able to do the day before: circulate it through his meridians.

I should start with the Vermilion Bird. My fire powers will be unmatched if I can strengthen that meridian path.

Thorian pushed the two drops of Qi he'd gathered towards the entrance of the Vermilion Bird meridian. However, no matter how he tried to force them to enter, the path was clogged beyond repair.

How frustrating. I can't dig through this filth even with two drops of Qi?

Thorian cleared his mind and continued his breathing pattern to calm his emotions. Since circulating the Qi internally was out of the question for now, he could just focus on gathering more of it.

Once again, Thorian pushed the surrounding energy through his external paths. With them already slightly more clear than before, the process was much smoother and faster. In the hour he had left to cultivate, he was able to gather another two droplets of Qi.

As Thorian opened his eyes, the first thing he checked was the child beside him. The boy was still sleeping soundly.

Display panel.

Ding!

Race: White Kobloid

Level: 11/15 (XP: 27/180)

Class: Magus

Level: 11/20 (XP: 13/180)

Lifespan: 40 years

Cultivation Realm: Qi Gathering First Stage (31.6%)

Stats:

Strength: 21

Agility: 31

Constitution: 10

Mana: 25

Qi: 4

Free Points: 0

Skills:

Minor Moon Boost (passive)

Fireball (active)

Not too bad. Hopefully with this growth, I can start with Qi circulation tomorrow.

With two hours of meditation under his belt, Thorian felt refreshed. His mana was replenished, and he no longer felt fatigued. He stood and turned, only to see Nox and the kobold looking at him with scrunched noses and furrowed brows.

Wait... Oh no, not again. A couple of sniffs under his armpits were all he needed to understand the severity of the situation. His body and the ground below him were covered with the same black goo that had stuck to him the day before.

"I will be going to the lake," Thorian announced, pointing at the child on the ground. "You two keep an eye on him. Don't let anyone hurt him. He is still needed for my exchange later." With that order established, he made his way out of the cave while the kobloids looked at him with furrowed brows. The reason for their wrinkled noses and narrowed eyes was quite clear.

Thorian rushed through the forest with ghostly steps, his speed comparable to that of the kobold. In less than fifteen minutes, he reached the lake where he had baptized Nox.

Thorian couldn't enjoy his bathing session for long, as the meeting time with the old man was drawing near. After a few minutes of scrubbing the goo out of his fur, he walked out of the lake and hurried back to the cave. Thankfully, the child was still soundly asleep, with no one disturbing him.

Good... If they could not even handle such a simple task, they would truly be undeserving of my protection.

Thorian carefully picked up the child and looked at Nox and the kobold, who were resting along with the other kobloids. Their eyes were threatening to close as they dozed off.

"Nox, kobold, wake up." Thorian's voice sent shivers through their bodies, making them jerk upright as they shook their heads. "I need you two to help me bring in those sixteen axes. I can't handle them all by myself."

"Axes?" Nox asked in half-awake confusion.

"Yeah, we need them to build the village," Thorian replied but did not explain further. The two didn't inquire either and just followed him out of the cave.

The path to the meeting point was clear in Thorian's mind, and he had no trouble guiding the two. After twelve minutes of walking, Nox and the kobold were wide awake, and they reached their destination.

As they crossed the bushes, they saw a figure at the edge of a small cliff. The old man jumped to his feet and looked at them in fear before his expression shifted into hope when he saw the child in Thorian's arms.

Thorian attuned his ears to the environment before asking the old man, "Did you bring the sixteen axes?"

"Y-Yes." The old man hurriedly leaned down and picked up a large piece of cloth stuffed with axes. The makeshift bag was made of layers of clothes and fabric, all of which were of different colors. "Please, take them. There are sixteen axes, just like you asked." He laboriously handed the heavy makeshift sack to Thorian, who opened it right away. There were indeed sixteen axes inside.

Thorian sighed deeply before grinning. "Good, you have done your part of the deal."

There were a couple of seconds of awkward silence before the old man tilted his head and nervously asked, "So, you will let us both live?"

"Of course, that was our deal," Thorian responded with a smile before his expression turned serious. "However, if you go back to the city right now, you will cause me a lot of problems. You see, I can't have humans knowing about my existence this early."

"But what about our deal?!" the old man reacted with a scream before primal fear took over his actions, and he cowered back.

"Our deal was that I would let both of you live," Thorian stated as a matter of fact. "And I fully intend to honor that deal. I just ask you to wait a few hours until the sun sets before you go back. That should be more than enough."

The old man looked at Thorian with a doubtful expression. "Will you really let us go when the sun sets?"

"Yes, I will," Thorian stated simply. "I will even escort you right to the gates of the city. No harm will come to you under my watch, I swear upon my name."

Hearing those words calmed the old man as he slowly lowered his guard. "Okay... then we will stay for a few hours. Is little Roo all right? Is he hurt anywhere?"

"Look for yourself." Thorian handed the child to the old man, the young boy slipping in and out of consciousness as his protector held him in his arms and checked every inch of his skin.

"Thank God. Thank God you're all right."

CHAPTER 14

As Thorian secured the cloth holding the axes with a knot, he snuck a look at the humans in front of him. Though he smiled as he held the young child, it was obvious that the old man was weak and weary. His arms shook, barely able to support the weight of the boy, and his legs were bruised and cut. The fabric holding the axes also had several tears, presumably from the edges of the weapons.

Thorian heightened his senses to their limits, his ears perking up as he sniffed the air. However, he could neither hear nor smell anything but the natural sounds and scents of the wilderness.

I should still take the long way, just in case.

Thorian handed the makeshift bag to the kobold and said, "Hold this for me. Be careful not to drop it, or you will get hurt."

The kobold grumbled but took hold of the axes as instructed. Nox, on the other hand, looked at Thorian with confusion.

"Sound not understand. Humans not understand." Nox tapped Thorian, who returned a puzzled look. "Thoreen human understand?"

Thorian's mind went blank at Nox's statement before he regained his composure.

Of course, this should be the natural reaction. Low-level kobolds shouldn't be able to understand human speech.

"Yes, I understand the words of the humans," Thorian responded confidently. "I am sure you will too when the time comes."

Once you become a kobold "champion," you definitely will.

Thorian then turned to the two humans and declared, "We will be returning to our cave. That will be your residence for the next few hours."

With their destination set, Thorian guided the group through the longest path possible to the cave, confusing his two followers. However, Thorian wanted to provide as many opportunities for potential ambushers to reveal themselves before reaching a sensitive area like their home cave.

It took an hour to reach their destination, and by the end of it, the old man could barely walk, even with Thorian's support. Though his frame was sturdy due to his menial job, this level of exertion would tire anyone, regardless of age.

By the time they reached the cave, it was already deep into the afternoon. Though he didn't have anything precise like a clock, Thorian estimated that they had three to four hours before dusk. "Consider this place your home for the next few hours." He guided the old man and sleeping child inside. "I apologize for the slight mess."

When the old man entered, he immediately scrunched his nose and brow. Despite his fatigue, the lingering smell took him aback.

I would clean this place, but I have neither the tools nor the time to do so. I suppose it matters not, as today will be our last here.

"Gentlemen," Thorian announced to the kobloids sleeping and resting. "I'm afraid the time for rest will be short today."

The pack of monsters groggily woke up, much to the old man's terror. His eyes widened as he saw the monsters from folktales filling the cave.

Thorian turned to the night kobloid and asked, "Can I trouble you with a task?"

Nox frowned before guessing, "Humans me protect?"

"Yeah, I want you to keep an eye on them."

The night kobloid thought for a few seconds before nodding. "Me humans protect."

"Good." Thorian then turned to the kobold who was eyeing the human pair. "You can set the axes down. We're going to distribute them now."

The kobold dropped the makeshift sack with a grunt, the sixteen axes clanging on the hard ground. Thorian, on the other hand, looked back at the kobloids who were slowly standing up and stretching. "Everyone, come here." The pack of monsters walked towards Thorian with grunts and growls, nearly waking up the little child. "All of you, take one axe each."

The kobloids looked at the unfamiliar tools, unsure of what to do. One of them approached and grabbed the axe by the edge of its blade.

"Stop!" Thorian interrupted the display of ignorance and stupidity before him. "What in all the seven hells are you doing?"

Do I need to explain everything?

Thorian sighed and properly grabbed the axe from its handle, then swung it a couple of times in the air to demonstrate its use. "This is how to hold and handle it."

With Thorian's demonstration, the kobloids were at least able to hold the axes properly by their handles. Using them, however, was another matter entirely.

One of the kobloids grasped the axe handle with a smile, attempting to swing it as Thorian had demonstrated. However, after just one swing, the axe flew from his hand and hurtled towards Thorian's face. For a second, Thorian saw his short life flash before his eyes as he ducked, narrowly dodging the projectile.

Thorian could only blink at the incredible turn of events.

Is this a rebellion? Thorian glared coldly at the perpetrator before noticing the kobloid's frozen expression. *No, he is just stupid.*

"Okay, some training is in order here," Thorian concluded. "None of you swing these axes, just hold onto them. Is that understood?"

Thorian made sure to say the last three words as clearly and slowly as possible. Only when all the kobloids nodded did he breathe a sigh of relief.

After each kobloid grabbed an axe, there were three left. They were for Thorian, Nox, and the large kobold. However, since Nox was staying in the cave for the time being, Thorian handed an axe to the large kobold and kept the last two for himself.

No need to keep a weapon lying about. It will only invite trouble.

With preparations in place, Thorian led the small army of kobloids towards the Territory Altar. On their way, he noticed the large kobold looking at his axe and grumbling to himself.

I should clear the air now before whatever is brewing in his mind boils over.

"What's on your mind?" Thorian gestured at the kobold with his head. "Is something troubling you?"

The kobold looked at Thorian before growling, "Axe useless! Claw strong!"

"Oh, so that's what it was." Thorian chuckled at the simplicity of the comment. He then pointed at a nearby tree, its trunk large and sturdy. "You see that tree? Do you think you can cut it with your claws?"

The kobold's eyes widened for a second as he looked at the tree before puffing out his chest and saying, "Claw strong! Tree weak!" He took a combat stance before charging at the tree with all his might, using all the kinetic energy and momentum he had to deliver a powerful strike with his claws.

"Awoo!"

Thorian covered his forehead with his palm and shook his head as the kobold screamed in pain. Observing his pitiful appearance, Thorian couldn't help but wonder, *Is he a kid?* The pack of kobloids circled the kobold as he rolled on the ground in pain. Some looked concerned, while others snickered under their breath.

Still, looking at the tree proved that the kobold's strike wasn't without effect. There was a deep gash in the trunk where he'd made contact, but it was far from enough to cut the sturdy trunk down and certainly wouldn't have resulted in a clean cut.

After a minute or so, the pain subsided, and the kobold stood up with a neutral expression. Everyone would've believed he was fine if not for the fact that he was hiding his hand behind his back and his legs were slightly shaking.

"Okay. Now that you've seen what happens if you do that, behold the power of using an axe." Thorian did not comment on the kobold's obvious state and just walked leisurely towards the tree.

He grabbed the axe's handle with both hands and took a stance in front of the tree. With one fluid motion, he struck the same area the kobold's claws had damaged earlier.

The kobold let out a painful chuckle. "Axe weak. Claw stronger," he insisted, eyeing the tree that hadn't been felled in a single blow.

Thorian rolled his eyes at the comment but didn't address it. He simply struck again, and the cut went a little deeper this time. One strike followed the next with a stable rhythm, and before long, the large tree fell to the ground.

The sound of the tree crashing onto the rocks and dirt provided the perfect backdrop for the kobold's shocked expression. Both his eyes and mouth opened wide at the sight before him.

"This is the power of an axe," Thorian explained, his eyes scanning all the kobloids. "Even though one strike might not be strong, you can do many. With each strike you cut a little bit deeper, until even the largest and strongest trees fall."

CHAPTER 15

With his demonstration over, Thorian issued another order. "Let's clear the branches of this tree. It will be a good exercise for all of you to learn how to use an axe." Thorian pointed at a random kobloid and said, "You, come here."

The kobloid looked confused for a second before walking towards Thorian with his axe in hand. Thorian took a stance and said, "Look closely at my hand. This is how we cut the branches." He cleared the leaves from a large branch before striking it continuously with his axe. After a couple of hits, the large branch fell with a thud. "Do the same thing I did but take your time and make sure your grip is firm."

The little kobloid nodded before following his steps. He also cleared the leaves from the branch, but his left arm was precariously aligned with the axe's trajectory, which immediately set off Thorian's internal alarms.

"Not like that." Thorian stopped the kobloid before disaster could strike, repositioning his hand so it was no longer in the natural trajectory of the weapon. "Careful with your hand. An axe can cut through your wrist with a single strike."

The kobloid nodded, oblivious to the danger he was just in, before striking the branch. The cut wasn't the best—it hit at a diagonal angle, and the edge wasn't properly aligned—but it still did the job. After seven or eight strikes, the branch was cut.

"You did well," Thorian praised the young, furred monster before looking at the rest of his pack. He pointed at another random kobloid and said, "You come next."

The second kobloid wasn't as hesitant as the first one and stepped forwards confidently. He followed Thorian's directions, but as with the first kobloid, his hand placement was terrible. After correcting the mistake, the second monster was also able to cut a branch with relative ease.

Thorian calmly taught every one of his followers the basics of handling an axe and cutting branches. Even the large kobold surrendered and learned after seeing everyone participating in the activity.

After fifteen minutes of work, the large branches were all cut, leaving a large naked trunk on the ground.

"We will be carrying this trunk with us," Thorian announced with a grin. "You're all strong and tough, so I don't expect any complaining."

The kobloids laughed and howled, high on their achievement. Thorian's slight compliment also helped boost their morale and make them eager to work.

The pack of fifteen monsters raised the large tree trunk and put it on their shoulders. They then followed Thorian's lead to the Territory Altar.

"Demon."

The kobold looked in shock at the altar and so did all the other kobloids. Their bodies were shivering, and they looked like they wanted to run away from this place at any moment.

"Calm yourselves, gentlemen." Thorian put down the trunk and walked towards the scary altar, touching the demon's face. "There is nothing to be afraid of. It is just a rock."

The kobold still looked apprehensive, but he slowly inched towards the altar. With shaking hands, he lightly touched the rock. Seeing that nothing happened, he touched all parts of the demon's face with more confidence until the fear fully dissipated. The kobloids also slowly took up their courage and walked towards the demon's face on the Territory Altar. Once they were sure it was safe, they started playing around and jumping on top of it.

How fickle are these creatures? One moment they're experiencing primal fear, the next they're playing like children.

Now that they had reached their destination, Thorian's true plan could finally commence. He cleared his throat to get the attention of everyone. "We will now need to cut down all the trees. Don't ask for the reason, as you will understand soon. I just want everyone to take their axes and cut as many trees as they can. Whoever finishes with the most trees cut will become the tree-cutting champion."

Thorian's words created an uproar as the kobloids chanted, "Champion! Champion!" Even the kobold seemed excited and made his way to a tree with a grin on his face.

Truly simple-minded.

Seeing their open excitement over a non-existent title, Thorian could only shake his head at the simplicity of his new species. However, it was that same simplicity that allowed him to unlock their potential with such ease. Thorian did not mind it.

Wait... Maybe they're getting too excited.

The kobloids were striking the trees with their axes with no regard for their own or others' safety. If they continued at this rate, catastrophe was sure to strike.

"Stop!" Thorian shouted with a commanding voice. Thankfully, whether it was due to respect or fear, the kobloids followed his order and stopped to look at him. "Be careful of where the tree will fall after you cut it. Do not crush your comrades due to your stupidity. Do not rely on others to know what to do. Keep an eye out if a tree is falling towards you and be safe."

The kobloids nodded at Thorian's words before nervously fidgeting in place, awaiting his next words.

"Continue." With Thorian's blessing, the kobloids resumed their work, but with less savage fervor.

Minutes slowly passed, and Thorian's worries did come to fruition, though to a lesser extent than expected. The kobloids who finished cutting through a tree trunk represented less of a danger to others and more of a danger to themselves. They almost always cut in such a way that the tree would fall on top of themselves and would need to hurriedly scurry out of the way lest they become shredded pancakes.

Fortunately, Thorian did not have to intervene many times, as the kobloids were fast enough to ensure their safety. It was only those cutting the tallest trees that Thorian had to keep an eye on. If he felt that they were about to cause irrevocable harm, he would stop them mid-work and finish the cutting process in their stead. For now, the safety of his subjects was paramount.

The hours flew past as the monsters cleared out the patch of the forest that the four statues surrounded. By the time the sun was about to set, all the small trees around them were already cut, along with a significant portion of the medium-sized ones. Only the truly gigantic trees had not touched, as Thorian did not have confidence that they would be able to fell them without sending one of his subjects to meet Amay and the seven hell princes.

With the work now almost done, Thorian walked towards the kobold who was busy cutting through a medium-sized tree. His movements were now much more fluid and honed with practice. His edge was properly aligned in most of his strikes, and his rhythm relatively consistent.

For someone who didn't want to use an axe, he learned the craft in a short time.

After the tree fell and the rumbling stopped, Thorian finally spoke. "I will give you the responsibility of keeping an eye on everyone while I go back to the cave. When I am absent, you speak in my tongue. Your orders are to be followed."

The kobold grinned at Thorian's words. They sounded better than an angelic choir to his ears.

"For now, just keep clearing more trees. We will need as many as we can get."

The kobold looked at Thorian in confusion. "Tree cut, why?"

"They will be useful very soon," Thorian responded simply. "Even if I try to explain it to you right now, you won't understand it until you see it. So just wait until you can see it."

Although his words were not particularly convincing, the kobold still nodded. "Tree cut, me strong?"

Thorian chuckled at the question. *I forgot. I should have gone with such an explanation in the first place.* He then nodded and responded, "Yes, the more trees that are cut, the stronger we will all get."

The kobold grinned yet again and gripped the handle of his axe tighter. Working without much sleep for so many hours should have left him relatively weary, yet the thought of becoming strong pushed him to start cutting the next tree.

Seeing the kobold get back to his work, Thorian walked towards the Territory Altar and checked the time.

Display territory.

System error...

The Territory Altar has not been fully activated yet. Please wait until the start of the new world.

ETA: 06:22:38

Six and a half hours? That should be enough time to get the necessary amount of wood. We also need to hunt in these last peaceful hours before the Apocalypse truly begins.

CHAPTER 16

As Thorian returned to the cave, he found Nox sitting at the entrance and the two humans at the back. The little boy had woken up and was hiding behind the old man, stealing occasional glances at the night kobloid. Nox, on the other hand, seemed unfazed, simply ignoring the two.

"Thoreen, done?" The night kobloid's expression brightened as he saw Thorian approach. He seemed terribly bored, doodling in the dirt with his claws.

"You did an amazing job," Thorian complimented his trusted follower. "And yes, we can start hunting in a bit."

Nox stood up with a grin. "Hunt, me strong!"

The simplicity of the kobloid's thoughts and words never failed to make Thorian chuckle. He walked past Nox and focused on the grandfather and grandson. While the old man was relatively at ease, the young boy was understandably shivering in fear.

"Are you going to let us go now?" The old man cautiously asked with doubtful eyes.

Seeing the man's attitude, Thorian quickly dispelled his doubts. "I have promised to escort you to the city safe and sound after the sun sets, and I do not go back on my words."

He then turned around and said, "Let's go, I don't like wasting time."

The old man's doubtful expression morphed into surprise before he turned to the young boy. The child was still scared, his lips quivering and eyes red from tears.

"Come here, little Roo." The old man scooped the boy into his arms. "It's better this way, right?"

Roo nodded and curled into a fetal position in the man's embrace. Now ready, the old man followed Thorian, who had been patiently waiting.

"Hunt now?" Nox asked, seeing Thorian was free.

"No. First, we will protect these two on our way to the city." Thorian gestured to the pair behind him. "We will hunt after."

Nox nodded with a disappointed expression but remained silent.

The walk towards the city was uneventful. When a pack of wolves or a stray bobcat dared to ambush them, Thorian's Fireball quickly turned the aggressor into valuable experience points.

While Nox had fun relieving his boredom, the two humans could only watch in horror as he tore apart wolf flesh as if it were old parchment. The little boy could barely hold himself together during the first few encounters before quickly fainting once again.

After an hour of slow walking, they finally reached the west gate of Locksley. Fortunately there wasn't much commotion, and the guards were only doing their usual patrols.

With the gates in front of them, Thorian turned back to see the old man nearly collapsing to his knees. Tears streamed down his face as he gazed up at the tall watchtowers guarding the city.

"You are now free to go. And don't go babbling about what you saw," Thorian warned, and the old man frantically nodded.

As the man slowly walked past Thorian, the latter had a sudden thought. He clicked his tongue before saying, "Oh, and here's some advice."

The old man looked back with a confused expression. He was obviously eager to reach the safety of the city walls, but Thorian knew that those same walls would soon become the bars of their birdcage.

"Before midnight, go to the city plaza in the center. You'll thank me."

The old man's confusion only grew at Thorian's cryptic words. "Why is that?"

"Just do as I say," Thorian sighed and turned away. He had already fulfilled his end of the deal and more. What the two humans would do from now on was no longer his concern.

Nox followed quietly after Thorian, and the two delved deep into the forest, out of the prying eyes of any would-be onlookers. Only after they had covered a significant distance did Thorian turn eastward, heading to the Wolvendale Territory where his Territory Altar was located.

I should have them unlock a class right now. That way, we can raid those damned goblins.

Thinking back to the pack of hobgoblins present in that cave, Thorian knew that he and his kobloids would be unable to defeat them for now. While hobgoblins were weaker than kobolds in individual combat, there were just too many of them. Taking into account the size of their horde, Thorian was certain that his subjects would stand no chance if they fought at this moment.

But a kobold with a class, can I handle that?

Recalling the large kobold, even though he was obedient for now, it all rested on the precondition that Thorian was stronger than him. If the thought that he had grown stronger than Thorian ever germinated inside the kobold's mind, there would be dire consequences.

Thorian glanced back at Nox and asked, "What's your level right now?"

"Eleven," the night kobloid responded with a toothy grin. "Assassin ten!"

That's good enough, Thorian thought before furrowing his brow in confusion. *Wait, his speed doesn't seem to match his level.*

"How many free points do you have left?" Thorian inquired with narrowed eyes.

The night kobloid furrowed his brows, his eyes darting. Then, his pupils widened, and his mouth drooped with newfound realization. "Nox stupid. Free points fifteen!"

Thorian smirked at his follower's words before saying, "That cleared up my confusion. Put twelve of the points in Agility and three in Strength. That ratio should be good enough for now."

Nox looked at the invisible stat panel with serious eyes before his lips parted in a deep, satisfied smile. He examined his body with a sense of wonder, as if he had just transformed.

Thorian laughed. "It feels much better, right?"

Nox's eyes sparkled as he exclaimed, "Nox light! Nox fast!"

Thorian continued to laugh as he thought, *With Nox, I shouldn't have any trouble with the kobold, especially before he can level up his class.*

The two continued on their way towards the Wolvendale territory. The usefulness of the points Nox spent on his Agility were immediately put on display, as Thorian had to run with all his might just to keep up with the night kobloid's relaxed pace.

His agility should be around fifty. I don't think the kobold even has one stat higher than thirty-five.

Feeling more assured than ever, Thorian formulated a plan in his head. Being cautious was important, but Thorian knew that never taking a risk was the biggest risk of all.

In less than ten minutes, Thorian and Nox crossed the length of the forest and reached the main road. After a few carriages passed and the path cleared, the two made their way to the territory where they found the kobloids still madly cutting down one tree after another. The kobold was also busy striking a medium-sized tree with his axe, sweat dripping down his forehead.

After the tree fell and the kobold let out a deep breath, Thorian walked towards him and said, "Good work, everyone seems to be doing well." He then scanned the kobloids with his eyes before focusing back on the kobold and continuing, "Let's stop the tree-cutting operation here. I hope everyone kept track of the trees they cut."

"Me cut trees many," the kobold pounded his chest and grinned.

"I'm sure you did." Thorian chuckled before focusing on the other kobloids. "Stop! Everyone, bring all your trees in front of the altar!"

The kobloids ceased their work and looked at Thorian, who continued his announcement, "Whoever has cut the most trees shall be named the tree-cutting champion, a warrior with strong determination, focus, and power."

Thorian's words thrilled the kobloids, who slowly carried the trees they had cut closer to the altar. They'd removed the branches and only left the trunks, as carrying a full tree was a truly impossible task for their current strength. One minute turned to two, then fifteen while the monsters carried out this laborious task.

Since the trees were too heavy for most of them to carry alone, they took turns helping each other. After around half an hour, they were finally done. Each of the thirteen kobloids stood wearily next to their stack of tree trunks, both tired and satisfied after their work.

Other than the kobold, who had twelve trunks stacked on top of each other, the rest's count averaged around five and six. One of the kobloids stood above the rest with his stout figure and strong muscles. He had cut eight trees and carried them all by himself.

Now that the preparations were finished, Thorian took center stage. "Kobold, as the one with the most trees cut, I declare you tree-cutting champion."

The kobold loudly howled to the sky and screamed, "Champion!"

I guess that is the only word he cares about.

The rest of the kobloids also chanted and praised the kobold for his strength. After the claps, howls, and cheers finally died down, Thorian pointed at the stout kobloid.

"As for you, while you are not the tree-cutting champion, you have still shown incredible abilities as a kobloid. You are a warrior who is determined, focused, and has a strong will. I declare you the unyielding warrior."

The kobloid looked with surprise at Thorian before also cheering, "Warrior!"

The rest of the kobloids also screamed and whistled in admiration for their stout brethren. Even the kobold nodded and clapped.

Once the small festivities ended, Thorian laid out his most important announcement, waiting until everyone was silent before speaking with a low but powerful voice. "Now, let us talk about your true rewards. You shall all receive a class—a power and a blessing from the gods that will give you strength beyond your comprehension!"

CHAPTER 17

"Class?" The kobold looked confused at Thorian, but the cheering of the other kobolds was contagious, and a grin quickly formed on his face.

"It will be easier to show you than to explain." Thorian turned and looked at the Magus Statue in the distance. With most of the trees already cut, he could see it even through the night.

"Follow me."

Thorian led the excited pack to the statue while Nox walked next to him. Once he arrived at his destination, he turned around and said, "This statue will give you magical abilities like my Fireball."

Thorian opened his palm and activated his spell. The fireball floating in his hand had its intended effect and mesmerized the simple kobloids. "You can get Fireball like me, Waterball, Wind Gust, or Rock Bullet. They are all good spells, and we will need all of them. Who wants to become a magus?"

At Thorian's question, almost all the kobloids screamed and shouted, "Me!" with enthusiasm clear on their faces.

Thorian sighed. "Not all of you should become magi. The other classes are equally as impressive and important."

Knowing that they would waste even more time if he let them choose as they pleased, Thorian randomly pointed at four kobloids. "You four will become magi. From right to left, you'll get the Fireball spell, Waterball, Wind Gust, and Rock Bullet. Is that understood?"

The four kobloids did not even wait for Thorian to finish speaking before howling in happiness. Their tails whipped left and right with enthusiasm, and their eyes gleefully sparked.

"Put your hand on the statue," Thorian said with a shake of his head.

The kobloids jumped for joy and ran towards the statue as if it were a race. Once they touched the statue, they raised their eyebrows in surprise as a blue light encompassed them. They looked blankly in front of them, presumably reading through the invisible screen panels that gave them the choice for their starting skills.

After a few seconds, their eyes finally focused, and they looked around in excitement. One of the kobloids opened his palm as Thorian had done so many times, and a fireball appeared. However, unlike Thorian, the kobloid could not control the spell and launched it to the side, setting a small tree on fire.

Thorian clicked his tongue and turned towards the second kobloid who was taken aback by the situation. "Hey, you. You have Waterball, right?"

The small kobloid looked shocked and confused for a second before hesitantly nodding.

"Go to that tree and use Waterball before the fire spreads. And you." He looked back at the perpetrator, whose expression was frozen in fear. "Don't just randomly throw your skills around. You could have killed someone."

The small kobloid hastily nodded. "Sorry."

Thorian took a deep breath before focusing back on the kobloid whom he'd ordered to quench the fire. The poor little monster made his way towards the fire with hesitant steps before raising his palm and pointing it at the burning tree. The fire was rapidly spreading through the roots and the grass on the ground.

A ball of water appeared in front of the kobloid's palm and rapidly grew to a considerable size. Once the spell reached its maximum capacity, the kobloid launched the waterball and recoiled, sending the spell zooming towards its target. The water skill destroyed the tree with its impact, but the fire was almost immediately extinguished. A large amount of steam covered the area, blocking everyone's view, but the orange hue of the flames was nowhere to be seen.

After a few seconds, the steam dissipated. What remained was a charred and destroyed tree and a few embers amidst the ash on the ground. Thorian made his way forward, examining the scene of the crime.

If I let this pass, they may become unhinged and unruly. A good talk is in order.

After stomping out the last few embers with his foot, Thorian turned around and said, "Let that be a lesson. Do not get high on your power and maintain vigilance. If that fireball had hit someone's face, I would have taken personal revenge in their stead."

Thorian then focused on the perpetrator who was shamefully looking down and laid out his decree. "As punishment for causing such trouble, you shall spend the next hours guarding this place and cutting trees. By the time we finish our hunt, I want those big trees to be cut and cleaned of all branches. Is that understood?"

The kobloid nodded and meekly said, "Understood?"

Thorian clicked his tongue at the weak response. "I can't hear you, speak up!"

The kobloid hesitated for a second before shouting, "Understood!"

Even though the little monster did not dare maintain eye contact with Thorian, the latter did not bother him much longer. He just said, "Your duties start now. Pick up your axe and get to cutting."

Not willing to waste any more time, Thorian focused back on the rest of the kobloids. Some were looking at the fire magus with pity, while others just snickered and grinned.

"Let us continue. There are still three other classes left."

Thorian took the lead while the rest of the kobloids formed a beeline behind him. Only Nox and the kobold walked with relaxed strides beside him.

The second statue was one of a man clad in armor, brandishing a menacing battle-axe. His fierce expression and poised stance exuded a warrior's spirit.

"This is the warrior class statue," Thorian explained. "For those of you who want to fight up close and personal, this is a perfect class. A true warrior can delve into an army of enemies and slaughter them all with his weapon and indomitable will."

Half of the kobloids that did not have a class looked at the statue with bright eyes, wishing to be chosen. Even the kobold looked with interest after Thorian finished his explanation.

"Warrior strong. Me like."

"Whoever wants the warrior class can become one," Thorian simply stated. "I do not have any specific inclinations towards any skill, so you can choose whichever you want."

Thorian's words were like that of an angel opening heaven's gates to the kobloids. They all walked excitedly towards the statue, with the kobold taking the lead.

Green-hued light illuminated the dark forest as four kobloids and the one kobold shone brightly. After a few seconds, their eyes regained focus, signaling to Thorian that they had finished choosing their skills.

"No wasting time. Let's move to the rest."

As such, the group made their way to the Assassin Statue. This time, only three kobloids chose the class and were filled with the shadow aura. After they chose their skills, Thorian led them to the final class statue.

Venturing south of the Territory Altar, they discovered a two-meter-tall statue of a woman draped in ceremonial robes. Her delicate hands were raised in a gesture of blessing, while her serene expression conveyed an aura of divine wisdom.

Looking back at the group, Thorian thought, *Only two are left? I guess that's good enough. We just need those two skills.*

"You and you. One of you will choose Healing, the other will choose Radiance. I don't care who chooses what, just choose fast."

The two kobloids were taken by surprise before one of them pointed at his chest and said, "Me Healing."

Thorian nodded. "Good, that makes things easy. Now go and claim your class."

The two hesitantly walked forwards before placing their hands on the statue. A dim golden light covered them as they chose their skills. Once they were done, Thorian could finally breathe out a sigh of relief.

Good, with this much power, we should be able to deal with the hobgoblins fairly easily.

After the two new priest kobloids joined the rest of the pack, Thorian laid out his next plan.

"I am sure that all of you must be feeling great with your new powers." The kobloids grinned, and some of them whistled and howled before Thorian continued. "But do not get too cocky. The opponents we will be facing are not easy. We will go to the goblin cave and exterminate all of them."

The kobold's eyes glinted at the proposal, while Nox looked confused. However, neither of their thoughts nor feelings mattered in front of the excited howls of the kobloids.

Thorian turned towards Nox and smiled. "You will understand soon enough. Killing the hobgoblins is going to help us tremendously."

As usual, Thorian did not waste any more time. With his plan now clear, he guided the pack of monsters through the forest. Even though they needed to run at the speed of their slowest member, the pace they had set was still much faster than any human could hope to achieve.

On their way to the goblin cave, they found all kinds of animals, predators and other things. Seeing all of them as free bags of experience, the kobloids razed the forest and left a trail of blood behind them. Any animal large enough to be seen was large enough to be killed.

After half an hour of hunting and running, they finally reached the rock outcropping close to the goblin cave. Their class levels averaged around 3, with the kobold already at level 4 and inching close to 5.

Peering at the cave from behind the large rocks, Thorian couldn't see any of the green monsters outside.

Perhaps they are asleep. Good for us.

Without saying a word, he signaled for the pack of kobloids to follow behind him. Tonight, carnage was on the menu.

CHAPTER 18

With Thorian in the lead, the group of kobloids inched towards the entrance of the cave. Thorian looked at Nox and signaled for him to go in first. The night kobloid followed the instructions and entered the cave. His black fur was perfect for the job, as only his eyes could be seen in the darkness.

After a few minutes, Nox walked back out and gestured for everyone to enter. Thorian followed Nox inside, and the rest of the kobloids did so as well. Their footsteps were light and careful, ensuring they wouldn't wake any goblins before their surprise attack.

As they ventured deeper into the cave, they found more and more small green monsters lying on the ground. Suddenly, Thorian raised his hand, and the kobloids behind him all stopped. In front of him was a sleeping hobgoblin.

A fireball materialized above Thorian's raised hand, signaling the start of the battle. He launched it at the hobgoblin's face, putting the weary monster to eternal rest.

"Squii! Shrii!" The goblins shrieked and cried as they woke from the sound of the blast. However, the squeals were easily overwhelmed by the kobloids' powerful war cries.

The burning face of the hobgoblin cast the cave in dim light, revealing the three kobloid magi as they conjured their spells. A rock bullet flew with incredible speed towards one of the goblins, piercing a hole through its head. The water magus hurled his spell at a group of green monsters, and the ball of water exploded, leaving the goblins injured and stunned.

Just as the last magus prepared his spell, Thorian sprang into action. He conjured a fireball and timed his throw with the wind gust. The fireball followed the wind spell, growing into raging flames that seared the goblins' skin off.

It's similar to a small fire wave. It's fortunate I am still proficient with these low-level spell combinations.

The other kobloids were not standing still either. The warriors charged into battle, their axes at the ready, and activated their skills. Two of the kobloids rushed with incredible speed at their enemies, slashing them through the waist with their weapons. The other two were slower, but their axes shone with blue light, empowering their next attack. Skulls were cracked open, and guts dripped onto the ground.

Nox and the three assassins blended with the shadows, killing any stray or confused goblins. Nox's Backstab was especially effective, his axe plunging through enemies' backs and protruding from their bellies.

"Shrii!" Thorian's attention shifted to the aggressive shrieking, only to find six hobgoblins charging towards them from the depths of the cave.

Seizing the opportunity, the kobold rushed into battle with a maniacal grin on his face. With a bloody axe in hand, he leapt at the hobgoblins who didn't even have time to grab their spears. His axe shone with blue light, and a hobgoblin's head rolled on the floor with one swing.

I know you're excited, but I won't let you get all the XP on your own.

Thorian conjured a fireball and launched it at the hobgoblins surrounding the kobold. One explosion knocked down a monster, and the white kobold wasted no time, plunging his weapon straight through the injured monster's chest before spinning and hacking at the next.

Level up!

Level up!

Thorian ignored the notifications and conjured another spell as soon as his mana calmed down. He unleashed fireballs at the four hobgoblins until they were nothing but charred, mangled corpses.

Sensing that he'd depleted half his mana reserves, Thorian switched his axe from his left hand to his main one. Scanning the area around him, he spotted a group of goblins fighting his kobloid warriors to a stalemate. With his superior speed, Thorian charged in and cracked a goblin's skull open.

With Thorian amongst them, the kobloids' fervor grew to unimaginable heights, and they hacked and slashed without regard for their own safety. The battle was not a painting of blood or a dance of death; it was a pure, unadulterated massacre. Green heads rolled on the ground before the kobloids stomped on them, crushing their skulls. The goblins that fell were immediately trampled to death by the frenzied white monsters.

Truly savage.

However, Thorian did not reprimand his subordinates. This level of savagery was what they would need to survive in this world.

After killing the last goblin in his group with an axe slash, notifications appeared in front of Thorian once again.

Level up!

Level up!

Good. Just a bit more and I will evolve.

Thorian turned around to scan the battlefield, only to be surprised when he spotted the kobold and Nox fighting against one opponent. It was a hobgoblin, with a spear in its hand and a ferocious look on its face. Muscles ripped through its ragged clothes, and its frame was much bigger than that of its dead kin.

Thorian conjured a fireball while thinking, *A high-level hobgoblin? It should have some spear skills.*

Like clockwork, the hobgoblin's spear flashed with a red light as it lunged with incredible speed at the kobold. The latter could barely block the attack by imbuing his axe with blue light, and even then he was pushed back slightly.

Boom!

Just as the hobgoblin stopped after its attack, a fireball exploded in its face. Nox reflexively jumped in and slashed through its hamstring, forcing it to fall. Just as the hobgoblin's knees touched the ground, the kobold's shining blue axe slashed through its neck.

Its burning head rolled across the ground. When the flames naturally died, only the dead, hollow eyes of its charred face were left to stare into the void. Its hatred and resentment were burned into its pupils, deeper than the flames had pierced through its skin.

Thorian's focus shifted to the rest of the battlefield. They were winning on all fronts, with the magi providing long-range support and damage, while the two priests healed and buffed the fighting kobloids. While he could stay in place and throw fireballs, his leveling efficiency would be severely hampered. As such, Thorian gripped his axe handle tight and charged into the fray.

Wherever there was a battle, he would rush towards it and kill as many goblins as possible.

Soon there was no more squealing in the cave, only the howls and screams of the kobloids. Delighted by their success, Thorian looked at the last two notifications he had received.

Level up!

Level up!

That should make level 14 in both my species and class. Display panel.

Ding!

Race: White Kobloid

Level: 14/15 (XP: 4/300)

Class: Magus

Level: 14/20 (XP: 4/300)

Lifespan: 40 years

Cultivation Realm: Qi Gathering First Stage (31.6%)

Stats:

Strength: 25

Agility: 35

Constitution: 11

Mana: 25

Qi: 4

Free Points: 9

Skills:

Minor Moon Boost (passive)

Fireball (active)

Thorian grinned as he looked at his stats. The nine free points were especially pleasing to see.

I should leave them for emergencies. There's no telling what stat will serve me best when the time comes.

Snapping out of his daze, Thorian looked around to see the kobloids still cheering and shouting. Even Nox and the kobold were laughing with each other as if their past grievances never existed.

Huh... Well, they deserve to have their moment after such a bloody battle.

After the ruckus eventually died down, Thorian took the lead and walked out of the cave. "Come. The time will soon come."

Both Nox and the kobold looked at him with confused eyes. "Time?" the latter asked, furrowing his brows.

"You will see soon enough," Thorian simply replied. "Let us return to our territory. We need to hunt as much as we can along the way while we still have the chance."

Hearing the word "hunt" was all the kobold needed to completely forget Thorian's previous talk. The pack of kobloids happily followed as they laughed and giggled amongst themselves.

While walking back to the territory, Thorian turned towards Nox and asked, "What level did you reach?"

"Thirteen." The night kobloid grinned. "Me strong! Me fast!"

"What about you?" Thorian shifted his focus to the kobold.

The white monster grinned and said, "Warrior nine."

Seeing that the kobold did not speak of his species' level, Thorian could guess that it had not leveled up.

So it's the same as what happened to us before. The experience points all go towards the class level until both levels are close to each other.

With this new piece of information in mind, Thorian asked the rest of the kobloids about their progress. Their average species level reached nine while their class levels hovered between seven and eight.

CHAPTER 19

The journey back to Wolvendale territory was uneventful. Now that all the kobloids had reached a high level in both their species and class, most animals they could hunt simply didn't offer any experience. As for the predators, they were not easy to find in large enough numbers to satisfy a full pack of fifteen monsters.

Once they reached the territory, Thorian saw the fire magus kobloid still striking trees with his axe. In the few hours they had left him alone, he'd managed to cut down four large trees and remove their branches. Even now, he was tirelessly swinging his axe at the fifth giant tree.

With one final crack of a swing, the tree fell with a deafening thud.

"Enough." Thorian walked up to the young kobloid. "You have finished your punishment. You can now rest."

The fire magus looked at Thorian with relieved eyes and bowed slightly. "Thank you."

Thorian nodded and turned back towards the rest of the pack. "All of you, take the next few hours to rest. We will need all the energy you can muster for later in the night."

The kobloids cheered at Thorian's order, but the kobold looked at him with furrowed eyes. "Hunt no more?"

"You will get to hunt as much as you want after." Thorian said with a smile. "For now, just rest."

The kobold shrugged his shoulders and found a patch of grass to sleep on. Nox and the rest of the kobloids also settled down to rest.

Thorian made his way to the Territory Altar to check the time until the apocalypse would begin.

ETA: 03:25:43

About three and a half hours, huh? That should be enough time to rest. My meditation earlier helped a lot with my fatigue already.

With the matter settled, Thorian lay down next to the altar. He wasn't so picky that he would ask for a bed in such a situation. A patch of grass was more than enough.

Hours quickly passed before a slight shuffle awoke Thorian from his slumber. He instinctively looked to the right in search of a threat, only to find Nox snoring and rolling around on the ground.

Thorian huffed out a laugh at his overreaction before looking around. While most of the pack was sleeping, some of the kobloids were playing with their skills. The warriors illuminated their axe blades with their abilities, while the magi threw their spells around. The fire magus, however, was sound asleep, his mouth open and tongue drooling after hours of exhausting work.

Good... Rest as much as you can now, because you won't be able to catch your breath for the rest of the night.

With that thought in mind, Thorian touched the altar, only to find that there were only two minutes left until the apocalypse. A mixture of dread and anticipation brewed inside his heart. He had seen it all before—the monsters that would appear by the thousands, the heroes that would rise against them, and the lords who would protect their citizens and lead them to new heights.

Glancing back in the direction of the city, he couldn't help but wonder how many would die. Five thousand? Ten thousand? Maybe even more.

As the head of the Steelblade family, the duty to protect his citizens was ingrained in his bones. However, those living beyond Locksley's walls were not his own. The only people that mattered now were the fourteen kobloids and the kobold who had sworn their fealty to him.

I am no longer a human. I am simply the king of the white kobloids.

"Wake up!" Thorian's voice was low but powerful. The kobloids that were scattered around sleeping slowly opened their eyes while yawning and stretching. Some of the kobloids were heavy sleepers and did not wake up from Thorian's shout. Nox was one of them. Seeing his most trusted follower snoring less than a minute away from the start of the apocalypse, Thorian shook the night kobloid's shoulders until he jolted awake. He then turned around and ordered the kobloids that were already up on their feet. "Wake the rest of them up right now. We only have a few seconds until the apocalypse starts."

While the kobloids shook and tapped those next to them, Thorian walked back to the altar to check the time once again.

Display territory.

ETA: 00:00:03

Thorian's mind blanked before he looked up at the sky. Dark clouds were quickly forming, hiding behind the bright full moon. Lightning struck amidst the clouds, illuminating the darkness below.

Wait... The time is over.

Seeing that the apocalypse was only starting to ramp up and hadn't fully begun, Thorian once again thought the words, *Display territory.*

Wolvendale Village
Realm: Village Stage 1
Resources:
Gathered Experience: 0

Wood: 0

Owned Buildings

Warrior Class Statue: The Warrior Statue embodies the strength, resilience, and martial skill of a formidable combatant. Warriors excel in physical combat, wielding a variety of weapons and armor to protect their village and charge fearlessly into battle.

Magus Class Statue: The Magus Statue represents the essence of arcane knowledge and mastery over the elements. By channeling their magical energies, magi can wield destructive spells to vanquish their foes and lay waste to the land before them.

Assassin Class Statue: The Assassin Statue epitomizes the art of stealth, precision, and cunning. Assassins excel in striking from the shadows, dealing lethal damage to their targets before slipping away unnoticed.

Priest Class Statue: The Priest Statue symbolizes the divine connection between the mortal realm and the gods. As conduits of divine power, priests can heal and support their allies or smite their enemies with holy wrath.

Available Buildings

Wooden Wall (Stage 1): The Wooden Wall is a sturdy barrier designed to protect the village from external threats and encroachments. Crafted from strong timber, this defensive structure forms a circular perimeter with a radius of two hundred meters from the Village Altar. The wall is equipped with watchtowers and gates to enable monitoring and control of access to the village.

Cost: 1000 Wood Units

Village Hall (Stage 1): The Village Hall serves as the central hub of administration, communication, and community for the village. Within its walls, the lord and villagers can gather to discuss important matters, plan for the future, and assign tasks vital to the village's growth and success. As the heart of the village, the Village Hall provides access to quests, both daily and non-daily, that help drive progress and development.

Cost: 750 Wood Units

Wooden House (Stage 1): The Wooden House is a simple yet cozy dwelling designed to provide shelter and comfort for the village's inhabitants. Constructed from durable timber, the house features a sloped roof to protect against the elements, a small porch, and an interior that can be customized to meet the needs of its residents. Each house can accommodate a small family, offering them a safe and warm place to call home.

Cost: 300 Wood Units

Attributes

Ether Line Nexus: A powerful convergence of ether lines lies beneath Wolvendale Village, creating a nexus of magical energy. This nexus enhances the potency of magic used within the village and accelerates the recovery of mana for magi. It also promotes the growth of magical flora and fauna within the Sherwood Forests, offering unique opportunities for research and discovery.

Upgrade Conditions:

100 registered citizens

1000 gathered experience

Upgrade the four statues into guilds

Like I thought, the Ether Line Nexus was this territory's unique attribute.

While Thorian's eyes scanned the territory screen, the storm brewing above him grew louder by the second, scaring some of the kobloids. Thunderclaps came in droves while lightning bathed the dark skies in blue and white light.

While the monsters looked up in terror at the start of the apocalypse, Thorian laid his palm on the Territory Altar and issued a command: *Absorb wood.*

The massive cut trees positioned all around the altar shone with a dark blue light before disintegrating into specks of neon light. To the shock of all the kobloids, these specks formed a whirlwind before being absorbed by the demon's face. The stone face shone with the light for a few seconds before finally dimming.

Territory resources.

Resources:

Gathered Experience: 0

Wood: 1800

Thorian let out a sigh of relief. He had enough wood for what he needed.

Build Wooden Wall and Village Hall.

With that command issued in his mind, the earth rumbled. Timber wood grew out of the earth behind the Territory Altar faster than bamboo ever could, and after a few seconds, a full building appeared. Looking even further beyond, past the statues and the trees behind them, a circular wall was erected with watchtowers standing even above the tall trees.

However, Thorian was not interested in the wooden walls right now. What he needed lay inside the building in front of him.

"Don't be dazzled, and come inside." Thorian took the lead and walked towards the Village Hall. It was a two-story wooden building with an unassuming door and barely any paint on its frame.

After entering through the squeaking door, Thorian and the rest of the group found themselves in a spacious, yet modestly decorated room. In the center of the room, an elven woman stood behind a plain wooden desk. However, her elegant demeanor was immediately broken as she laid her eyes on Thorian and the rest of the kobloids.

"Monsters? How?!

CHAPTER 20

"**W**ell, that was quite rude," Thorian retorted while walking towards the surprised elf. "I must have you know that we are distinguished and civilized gentlemen."

He turned back to the rest of the kobloids, who were looking around the room in awe. The kobold's focus, on the other hand, was dead centered on the elven woman, with narrowed eyes and furrowed brows.

"She is not an enemy, kobold." Thorian smiled before looking back at the still-shocked woman. "In fact, she should of great help to us."

The slender elven woman wrinkled her brow at Thorian before her eyes suddenly widened. "A-Are you the lord of this village?"

"Yes, I am." He bowed slightly. "Thorian, lord of Wolvendale Village."

"A kobloid is a village lord..." The elf's pupils dilated, and her mouth hung slightly open. Noticing the rudeness of her reaction, she shook her head and matched his bow with one of her own. "I am terribly sorry, Lord Thorian. It is the first time I have ever seen a monster claim a territory."

Just as the elf finished her sentence, a thunderous rumbling shook the room along with an earthquake that threw them all off-balance. The tables and chairs fell, and so did the kobloids and the elf. Fortunately, the building was not damaged by the seismic event, and no one was truly hurt.

"Monsters of a thousand worlds!" a deep and ancient voice shouted in Thorian's ears, making him instinctively plug his ear holes. "Roam the earth. Devour, evolve, and conquer!"

Wait, the words are a bit different... Is that what the monsters heard on the day of the apocalypse?

Just as Thorian formed the thought, a screen appeared in front of his eyes.

Monster Quest Unlocked!

Kill (0/50 humans)

Reward: Level +1

Kill (0/100 humans)

Reward: Previous rewards and an E-tier skill

Kill (0/250 humans)

Reward: Previous rewards and Level +2

Kill (0/500 humans)

Reward: Previous rewards and a rare variant in the next evolution

Time Left: 47:59:56

Reading through the screen in front of him, Thorian's mind blanked for a second. He looked back at the kobloids behind him only to find them also staring blankly at a point in front of them. "Do you see the monster quest?" he couldn't help but ask.

"Human kill, reward many," Nox nodded and responded.

The kobold cackled and with a maniacal laugh teasing the edge of his voice, he said, "Me kill human many! Me strong become!"

The rest of the kobloids joined him in screaming and cheering. Seeing the reaction of his subjects, Thorian looked down at the wooden floor with a turbulent mind. *So the gods are telling me to reject any lingering sense of humanity I have left... I see. I will play your game, then.*

Thorian clenched his teeth and stood up with renewed resolve. He shifted his attention back to the elf who was disturbed by the ruckus happening around her.

"This place gives quests, correct?"

The elf looked up at Thorian at his question and nodded. "As the lord of the village, you can receive the available quests right now." She then looked at the rest of the kobloids and smiled wryly. "As for your subjects, they will need to register as citizens first."

Thorian nodded at the elf's explanation. "I see. Show me the quests first." He, of course, already knew where to find the quests, but he did not want to put his future knowledge on full display for all to see. He still needed to ask questions that were expected from him.

"Of course, my lord." The elf bowed lithely before pointing to the side. "You can simply take whichever ones you want from the bulletin board and give them to me to register with the system."

Thorian nodded and walked towards the bulletin board while the kobloids looked on in confusion, not knowing what to do. With a quick perusal of the board, Thorian could see the normal daily quests for monster subjugation and material gathering, each of which gave a certain amount of experience points and arcane coins. However, Thorian was not interested in the daily quests. He wanted the rare and unique ones that only appeared in specific periods or when certain events happened.

Found you.

Thorian took a quest from the bulletin board and looked at it more closely.

Pact with the Wolven Guardians

Description: The wolves that roam the Sherwood Forests are known to be intelligent and fiercely protective. Legend speaks of a unique bond that can be formed between the village and these Wolven Guardians, granting both parties mutual protection and co-operation. The quest calls upon you to venture into the heart of the forests, find the wolf pack's alpha, and establish a bond of trust and respect between the village and the wolves.

Quest Objectives:

Enter the Sherwood Forests and locate the wolf pack's territory.

Approach the wolf pack cautiously, demonstrating peaceful intentions and respect for their territory.

Earn the trust of the alpha wolf and establish a pact of mutual protection and cooperation between the village and the Wolven Guardians.

Rewards:

Wolven Guardians' Loyalty: The wolves pledge their loyalty to the village, serving as additional protectors and patrolling the outskirts to alert the villagers of any potential threats.

Wolven Communication: Villagers gain the ability to communicate with the wolves on a basic level, allowing for cooperation in hunting, scouting, and defense.

Wolf Totem: A totem representing the pact with the Wolven Guardians is erected in the village, granting a passive bonus to the village's defense and fostering a sense of unity between the village and its newfound allies.

Thorian couldn't help but chuckle seeing the rewards of the quest. *No experience or coin, but the rewards are beyond worth the trouble.*

He grabbed the Wolven Guardian quest along with the daily ones and presented them to the elf at her desk. After a quick look, she took out a golden stamp from under her desk along with a container of beeswax and stamped the quests. With each stamp, the paper on which the quest was written disappeared and reappeared once again on the bulletin board. Naturally, only the Wolven Guardian quest did not reappear after being stamped.

After stamping the last quest, the elf sent him a smile. "The specified quests have been registered, Lord Thorian. You can view them by thinking the command 'show journal.'"

Thorian nodded before voicing the command in his mind. A colorful screen quickly appeared before him, displaying the quests he had accepted.

Journal:

Subjugate 10 monsters (daily)

Cast a spell 20 times (daily)

Cultivate your Qi for two hours (daily)

Gather 100 Wood Units (daily)

Clear one dungeon (daily)

Pact with the Wolven Guardians

With his accepted quests now stored in his journal, Thorian looked back at the elf and asked with interest, "What's your name, miss elf?"

The elven woman raised an eyebrow before answering, "My name is Melina, my lord. It is my pleasure to serve you."

"The pleasure is all mine," Thorian responded before looking back at the kobloids who were waiting for him to finish with impatience. "Can you please help my subjects become official citizens?"

"Of course. Please have your subjects form a line and I will begin the procedure right away."

"You heard her, everyone," Thorian said, raising his voice to catch the kobloid's attention. "Form a line in front of Melina to become official citizens of Wolvendale Village. This is our first step towards total conquest."

The kobold grinned at the word "conquest" and was the first to walk forward. Nox followed right after him, and the kobloids soon formed a line in front of Melina's desk. Witnessing such a large number of monsters following orders and organizing themselves left the elf's eyes wide and mouth agape.

"You can start the procedure."

With Thorian's reminder pulling her out of her daze, Melina shook her head and took a stack of parchments from under her desk. She then twisted the wooden handle of the stamp before separating it from the piece of metal underneath. The wooden handle had a small needle poking out from its base.

"Prick your thumb with this needle and then press it on this empty part of the paper here," Melina explained while looking cautiously at the large kobold towering over her.

The kobold nodded and did as told. After a few seconds, the paper disintegrated into golden specks of light that surrounded the kobold and melted into his fur and skin.

"Huh? What happened? What are these things?"

Thorian looked at the kobold with an arched brow, not daring to trust his own ears.

Did I just mishear him speak?

CHAPTER 21

Looking around, it became clear that Thorian was not the only one shocked. Melina and all the kobloids stared at the kobold in shock and confusion.

"Kobold word many. Kobold talk Thoreen!" Nox, who was standing behind the kobold, appeared visibly stunned.

The kobold only looked at the night kobloid with a baffled expression. "Nox? Stop messing around and talk normally."

"That is how he has always talked," Thorian interjected while scratching the fur on his chin.

The kobold was even more surprised as he turned towards Thorian. "Thoreen? Since when can you speak normally?"

"I have not changed the way that I speak. It is you who has changed." Thorian turned toward the equally shocked Melina and asked, "Do you have any idea what is happening here?"

"No. I'm sorry, my lord," Melina shook her head. "I have never heard about a village with monsters as citizens, so I have no information as to what may have happened."

"What is happening now? Why did everyone change the way they speak all of a sudden?" The kobold growled and looked around the room with confusion and a bit of fear.

"It is not we who have changed our way of speaking, kobold." Thorian clarified, "It is you. You changed the way you speak when you became a citizen."

The kobold's mouth hung open as he blinked with dazed eyes. "That makes no sense. Why do I hear everyone differently, then?"

"That, we will need to find out." Thorian nodded, gesturing for Nox to proceed.

The night kobloid walked forwards and pricked his thumb with the stamp needle before pressing his blood on a new piece of parchment. As with the previous one, the paper scattered into specks of light that Nox's black body absorbed.

"Can I speak like you two now?" Nox turned around with an excited and expectant look on his face, much to the horror of the kobold and the delight of Thorian.

The latter grinned and replied, "Yes, you can. This is truly fascinating."

"Oh? Thoreen speaks normally!" Nox's eyes widened at Thorian's speech, and the latter could only chuckle and shake his head.

"Thorian, not Thoreen. Now that you can speak properly, you would do well to not make that mistake again."

"Thorian, huh? But I liked Thoreen better..."

Thorian rolled his eyes and ignored Nox, choosing instead to focus on the kobold. The white monster looked like he was experiencing an existential crisis.

Meanwhile, the kobloids followed Nox and continued with the procedure. As the line gradually shrank, Thorian's focus shifted from them to the bulletin board at his side. There were still many quests that were not daily, but most required a level of strength miles above his current level. His assessment of the board eventually brought him to a quest with a two-day time limit.

Interesting. I'd never heard of a quest like this. Thorian snatched the quest from the board and read it.

Revenge on the Monsters

Description: The apocalypse has started, and monsters are roaming the world. Bloodthirsty, heartless, and cruel monsters slay and devour anyone who would dare cross their path. Raise your weapon and take revenge for your fallen kin. This quest can be partially completed. The more milestones you cross, the better your reward.

Quest Objectives:

Kill as many monsters as you can.

Milestones:

Slay (0/50 monsters)

Reward: Level +1

Slay (0/100 monsters)

Reward: Previous rewards and a class skill of your choosing

Slay (0/250 monsters)

Reward: Previous rewards and Level +2

Slay (0/500 monsters)

Reward: Previous rewards and a Purple Cloud weapon specific to your chosen class

The contents of the quest drew an involuntary laugh from Thorian, scaring Melina and the kobloids behind him.

"Thorian, are you all right?" Nox tapped him on the shoulder and looked at him with concerned eyes, while Thorian had trouble containing his own laughter.

After a few seconds, he finally took a deep breath and turned around. "I'm sorry, it just seems that the heavens like to play the cruelest games."

He looked back at the quest in his hand and smirked. *So you're giving me a choice, and a clear one at that. Either renounce any lingering feelings, or act like some kind of hero of humanity.*

Without waiting another second, Thorian handed the quest to Melina and said, "Add it to my journal."

The elven woman obliged and flipped the stamp back around. She marked the new quest using the beeswax next to her and the parchment disappeared. Thorian confirmed that the quest was added to the end of his journal.

With his job finished inside the Village Hall, Thorian turned around and said, "Follow me outside once everyone has become an official citizen. Our hunt shall begin swiftly."

Remembering one last detail, he looked at Melina. "Show them how to get their daily quests. They will need to do it on their own from tomorrow onward."

"Of course, my lord," Melina obliged with a nod. "That will be my pleasure."

When he walked out the door, the storm was still raging with dark clouds blocking the moon and torrents of rain pouring onto the ground. Thorian trudged through the mud and rain and headed for the walls beyond the tall trees. Looking around, he heaved out a sigh of relief.

Seems like none of the apocalypse monsters appeared inside the village. Our luck is good.

However, the closer he was to the walls, the more a frown pulled at his brow. He could hear screaming, shrieking, and increasingly loud strikes and thuds.

Thorian rushed through the dense trees and climbed up the stairs of the watchtower. From his vantage point, he could see dozens of monsters trying to break the wooden walls with all their might.

The bulk of the monster horde was made of goblins and hobgoblins. However, there was also a pack of five giant cat-like monsters, each with a large boulder stuck at the end of their tail. With every swipe of their tails, the boulders would strike the wooden wall with immense speed, cracking it slightly.

Oh, chaskas? Those cute little things.

Thorian smiled as he watched the monsters try their best to invade his territory. If such a scene had occurred only a week before, he wouldn't have been able to stop himself from bursting into laughter. The thought that such weak creatures would try to pick a fight with him was ironic in and of itself.

Let's see if the Ether Lines Nexus lives up to its reputation.

Thorian conjured a fireball within his palm and launched it at one of the chaskas chipping away at his village's protection. The spell pierced through the rain and illuminated the night sky before striking one of the cat monsters straight in the head.

He didn't give his enemies any chance to breathe and conjured another spell as soon as the creature fell. Like a god of fire, Thorian launched one fireball after the next towards the wave of monsters beneath him. Because they were so densely packed, he didn't even need to aim with pinpoint accuracy to hit one or two of them at a time. The torrential rain made it so that he didn't need to waste a second worrying about starting a forest fire either. By the time his spells claimed the lives of their victims, the rain had already quenched the flames and stopped them from spreading.

Quickly scanning the battlefield, Thorian immediately noticed the most imminent threat. A hobgoblin was stretching his bowstring, its aim clear upon Thorian's face. The would-be target could only smirk at the attempt.

Without even needing to time his attack or keep track of the arrow, Thorian conjured another fireball and launched his spell along the path the arrow would take to reach him. Just as he expected, the fireball flickered midway as it burned the arrow before continuing on its path towards the hobgoblin's face.

Level up!

Level up!
Level requirement achieved for evolution!
Choices available:
White kobold
Flame kobold
Without hesitation, Thorian chose the second option

CHAPTER 22

Starting evolution...

Apeculiar energy swirled around Thorian's body, enveloping his skin and muscles. An intense surge of vitality welled within him, causing his bones and muscles to expand painlessly. His once snow-white fur began to shimmer with a golden radiance. As the light gradually subsided, his fur underwent a stunning transformation, emerging a brilliant shade of crimson red.

Display panel.

Ding!

Race: Flame Kobold

Level: 1/30 (XP: 0/500)

Class: Magus

Level: 15/20 (XP: 0/330)

Lifespan: 40 years

Cultivation Realm: Qi Gathering First Stage (31.6%)

Stats:

Strength: 35

Agility: 40

Constitution: 17

Mana: 35

Qi: 4

Free Points: 12

Skills:

Minor Fire Affinity (passive)
Flame Resistance (passive)
Fireball (active)
Combustion Touch (active)

As Thorian scanned his skills, he couldn't help but click his tongue. *So I lost the Moonlight Boost... A shame, but I've got better skills now.*

Eager to explore his newfound abilities, Thorian quickly realized the monsters below wouldn't afford him that luxury. The final chaska was scaling a tree, poised to leap into the village, while hobgoblins relentlessly assaulted the wooden walls with their spears.

Fortuitously, Thorian's evolution had restored his mana pool to its maximum capacity. Drawing upon his power, as he had done countless times before, he conjured his trademark spell. However, the fireball that materialized atop his palm was strikingly larger than any he had previously summoned.

Is this the effect of Fire Affinity?

He unleashed his spell at the airborne chaska, engulfing the beast in a torrent of flames. The feline creature plummeted to the ground, writhing in agony as the fire consumed its fur, skin, and flesh.

Without hesitation, Thorian rapidly summoned a barrage of spells, raining them down upon the monsters below in a cascade of hellfire. In no time, the hobgoblins lay incapacitated or lifeless, while the remaining goblins fled in terror back to the safety of the forest.

As Thorian exhaled a deep, steady breath, the very fabric of space itself began to shudder and fracture with a thunderous cacophony. A swirling vortex of darkness and light coalesced before the village walls, casting an eerie, pulsating glow on the surrounding area. The air crackled with palpable energy, and a sense of foreboding settled over the village, heralding the arrival of an unknown force.

"A portal appeared this close? This will be problematic," he muttered.

Without wasting a moment, Thorian sprinted down the stairs, his speed not in the least bit hindered by the rain or the muddy terrain. Within seconds, he dashed through a dense cluster of trees and arrived at the Village Hall, just as his group of kobloids emerged one by one.

"Everyone, gather here! Immediately!" Thorian commanded, his booming voice startling the kobloids. The pack hastened to their king, a mix of intrigue and excitement on their faces. Yet, none were aware of the impending danger that lurked nearby. "A horde of monsters is rushing towards us from the northeast side. We need to slay them before they breach the wall," he explained quickly.

His words ignited the kobloids' spirit. As the group rushed towards the spot Thorian had just come from, the white kobold looked at him with interest.

"How many are there? I want to hunt them all." Only after expressing his desire for battle did he notice the change in Thorian's fur. "And why are you red? Is that blood?"

"It's my evolution," Thorian said. "I am now a flame kobold."

The kobloid's eyes widened in shock, while Nox smiled with unbridled joy.

"Really? That is so cool!" the night kobloid exclaimed. "I heard so many stories about flame kobolds. They're very strong!"

Thorian chuckled at Nox's reaction. "You can tell me all about those stories later. We need to focus on the monsters outside right now. They are going to be a hassle."

Just as he finished speaking, loud thuds that threatened to crack the walls shifted his attention. Without saying a word, he rushed towards the watchtower alongside Nox and the kobloid.

"Are those... goblins?" Nox asked.

The monsters were indeed green like goblins, so Nox's confusion was warranted. However, they were much bulkier, with two small tusks protruding from their mouths. They were also riding giant armored boars and wielding mighty battle axes in their hands.

"No, they are orcs," Thorian explained in a low voice. His attention then shifted to the high orc commanding his army from the back. He was riding a blood boar that was much larger than the other armored mounts, with mightier tusks and a meaner look on its face.

Meanwhile, the kobloids reached the bottom of the watchtower and stood in a daze, not knowing what to do.

"Only the magi go up the stairs. The rest stay down," Thorian commanded before looking at the kobold. "You go and take the warriors to fight them on the ground. We will provide long-range support from above."

The kobold grinned. "I was waiting for you to say that. I will tear those overgrown pigs to shreds!"

"Do not enter the frey immediately," Thorian warned, shooting him a stern look. "Give us a few minutes to thin out their army first."

"You got it, King. I will wait ten minutes before charging in."

After the four magi reached the top of the watchtower, the kobold walked upstairs and gathered the warrior and the priests. Nox followed after him, along with the assassins.

Meanwhile, the orcs were still charging at the wall beneath them with their armored boars. Each time they struck it, the wall would cave in a little or crack.

Does the low-level wall have trouble even against these lousy attacks? I need to upgrade it as soon as I can.

He looked at the wind magus and ordered, "Prepare your Wind Gust. I will launch my Fireball right after you use your spell." He then turned around to face the fire magus. "Try to time your attack with mine and launch your Fireball in the same direction."

The two kobloids nodded and aimed their open palms in the direction of the orc army below them. The green pig-like monsters almost numbered in the hundreds, with most of them standing unmounted and guarding their king in the back. The cavaliers that were riding the warboars were around twenty-strong, separated into squads of five that took turns ramming the wooden wall.

Noticing the trajectory of the wind magus' arm, Thorian grinned. *I like your guts, wind boy.*

The moment the Wind Gust was unleashed, Thorian launched his Fireball spell, and so did the fire magus behind him. The three spells flew in tandem above the mounted orcs and foot soldiers before reaching the high orc commander.

Boom!

The moment the Wind Gust struck the orc commander, the two fireballs exploded into a flaming pillar that rose higher than the trees. The explosion engulfed the high orc and a dozen of his subordinates in skin-melting flames.

"Another one!"

Following Thorian's order, the wind and fire magi prepared their spells once again and launched their strategic combo. Another explosion struck the high orc with the flames of hell, heating its armor until it glowed red.

Faced with two back-to-back explosions, the rain could not quench the flames, allowing them to spread across the battlefield and devour the fleeing orcs that stood in their path.

"Fire everything!"

This time, the earth and water magi also joined in launching their spells at the scattered enemies. Naturally, the water magus focused his spells on the mounted orcs that were closer to them, knocking them off their boars and drenching them in water and mud. Meanwhile, the rest of the green monsters ran away from the raging fire.

Level up!

Without needing to look at his panel, Thorian already knew that it was his class that leveled up. His focus remained firm on the battlefield, keeping track of every moving piece on his chessboard.

While some of the orcs ran deeper into the forest, most of them were forced to charge towards the wall. The unquenching flames cut off their paths of retreat, and their only hope was to either break through the wall or climb it. Unfortunately, that task was not going to be easy.

"Charge!" The white kobold raised his woodcutting axe and charged at the orcs alongside the warrior kobloids. The two priests stayed far back to provide support to the warriors without putting themselves in danger.

While the warriors charged into the melee, Nox and the assassins snuck their way to the backline using the shadows of the dense trees as cover. Whenever they saw an opening, the assassins would pounce and tilt the tides in the warriors' favor.

Meanwhile, Thorian and the magi focused their support on the orcs that were closest to the warriors. With their long-range support, even though the kobloids were disadvantaged in numbers, they could not be overwhelmed.

With each strike from the white kobold's axe, an orc's head would be sent flying or a limb would be severed. The stout warrior kobloid also showed remarkable prowess and kept up with the kobold. His axe shone a brilliant blue while dyed in the purple of orc blood.

"Roar!"

The high orc, whom everyone had deemed dead, rose from within the flames with a charred body. Its blood boar had already been melted, burned, and turned to ashes, and so was half of the commander's body. However, it persevered with an iron will, showing all of its subordinates that it was still alive and ready to fight.

"Fireball."

Thorian's simple incantation launched another spell at the orc commander's face, pushing it straight back into the tongues of hell.

Level up!

CHAPTER 23

Silence enveloped the battlefield as all eyes focused on the plummeting black silhouette of the high orc, engulfed in bright orange flames. The orcs stared in horror as the faint glimmer of hope that had begun to swell within their hearts was brutally extinguished.

"*Raaagh!* Break the wall!" One of the mounted orcs took the lead, charging at the wooden barrier with the rest of the orcs following in his wake. Their eyes turned red, and a sinister gray aura enveloped their armored bodies, lending them a menacing appearance. The mounted units hurled their warboars against the wall with reckless abandon, while the infantry brandished their axes and pursued them.

"Blast them! Do not let them break the walls!" Thorian commanded while launching a fireball of his own. However, no matter how many spells they threw at the mad orcs, it did nothing to stop their charge. Whenever one of the orcs would die, another would immediately take his place and hack away at the wooden wall.

Is this the orcs' Berserk skill? Truly fearless... But their backs are open to the warriors.

Casting a swift glance at the kobold and his subordinates, Thorian realized that this war of attrition was not to their advantage. Although the kobold was dispatching orcs with ease, their sheer numbers were overwhelming.

"Attack!" The mounted orc who had initially led his kin on this perilous endeavor readied himself for one final charge. The gray aura surrounding him intensified, encompassing the warboar he was riding. Both orc and boar swelled in size, the boar's determined expression matching its rider's resolve.

Thorian noticed the danger and laid out his order immediately. "Kill him!"

He, along with the rest of the magi, conjured their spells and aimed them at the charging mad orc. "Strike!" Elemental spells, representing all four forces of nature, hurtled towards their target with breakneck speed. However, before they could make contact with the formidable enemy, a group of self-sacrificing orcs leapt into the path of the magical onslaught. They were torn apart and reduced to ash, valiantly shielding their ultimate hope from destruction.

Thorian's eyes widened in disbelief at the scene before a sudden tremor and a powerful shockwave threw him off balance. The orcs had successfully infiltrated their defenses.

"Stay here and provide cover fire!" Thorian commanded as he quickly regained his footing and positioned himself on the ledge, poised to leap into action. "I will prevent them from advancing any further."

Much to the kobloids' astonishment, Thorian fearlessly jumped from the watchtower, plunging into the surging mass of green orcs. The thundering horde of beasts, mounted on their warboars, shook the ground like a relentless stampede of a thousand buffalo.

Let's see what this new skill does.

With a daring grin, Thorian embraced the imminent challenge and lunged at the oncoming monsters with remarkable swiftness. Blinded by their bloodlust, the frenzied orcs only saw red and continued their charge with increased intensity, intent on crushing Thorian beneath their boars' hooves.

Thorian delivered a forceful strike to one warboar's snout using the palm of his hand, just before initiating his spell. *Combustion Touch*. A surge of mana, far more potent than that of a mere fireball, flowed through his body and converged in his outstretched palm.

Boom!

The orc before Thorian was swiftly consumed by flames, which then fanned out in a fiery cone to incinerate the surrounding adversaries. The explosive shockwave hurled three mounted orcs backward, their bodies scorched and blackened by the relentless inferno.

Interesting, thought Thorian. His grin broadened in response to the awe-inspiring demonstration of raw power. *It reminds me of the final part of the Flaming Phoenix Dance.*

Sensing that his reserves of mana were running low, Thorian opened his panel and allocated all of his free points.

Mana: 36 → 51

Feeling his body brimming with mana, Thorian refocused on the battlefield. The rest of the mounted orcs along with the foot soldiers were charging through the broken wall like ants out of an anthill.

"Let us dance."

Thorian assumed a battle-ready stance and lunged at the approaching green foes with the steely resolve of a seasoned warrior. Each palm strike he delivered to an orc produced a fiery cone that eliminated another two or three of their brethren. Empowered by his Flame Resistance skill, Thorian remained unscathed by the blazing bodies, feeling neither pain nor burns. He gracefully navigated through walls of fire, overwhelming the orcs with his unmatched speed and strength. On this battlefield, he was a deity, cleansing the tainted souls of the orcs with his purifying flames.

As the devastation unfolded, the frenzy in the orcs' eyes gradually subsided, supplanted by the dreadful realization of their impending doom. The valiant kobold warriors assailed their enemies from behind, the watchtower magi unleashed the fury of all four elements upon them, and the stealthy assassins eliminated any who attempted to flee.

Most disheartening of all was Thorian's sheer superiority. His formidable fire skills proved overwhelming, and his ability to maneuver within the flames rendered him virtually invincible. Ultimately, they were left with only one option if they wished to survive.

"Mercy!" The orc who had breached the wooden barrier was the first to yield, pressing his forehead firmly into the muddy earth. His warboar lay lifeless, seared by Thorian's incendiary magic. Even he bore the scars of battle, with burn marks and singed skin marring his body.

Witnessing their makeshift leader reduced to such a submissive state, the orcs were taken aback.

"Zogthar, have you lost your mind? They killed the commander!" One of the orcs bellowed at the prostrate figure, only for Zogthar to shoot him a lethal glare. The dissenting orc promptly recoiled in terror and turned to Thorian with trepidation.

Thorian furrowed his brow at this unexpected turn of events, and noticing that the orcs had ceased their assault, he too halted his destructive rampage.

However, the warrior kobloids failed to grasp the situation and viewed this as an opportunity to eliminate more enemies and gain experience. Observing his troops ruthlessly cutting down the barely resisting orcs, Thorian decided to issue new orders.

"Stop!" Thorian's voice thundered across the chaotic battlefield, bringing the kobloids to an immediate halt. He then directed his attention to the orc named Zogthar. "Have you assumed the role of their leader?"

"I am Zogthar the Fierce, leader of the Mounted Legion and second-in-command of the Blacktusk Warband," Zogthar declared, placing his fist on his chest in a military salute before bowing even lower. "Please, show us mercy."

Hesitantly, the remaining orcs followed suit, emulating their vice-commander and kneeling before Thorian. Not one of them dared to meet his gaze.

"Please, have mercy on us!"

Thorian stroked the fur on his chin thoughtfully before motioning for the kobold and Nox to join him.

"What do both of you think? Should we accept their surrender?"

"We should kill them," the kobold declared with a sinister grin. "I'm just one kill away from leveling up."

Thorian chuckled at the response before turning his attention to Nox, who was deep in thought. "I believe it would be better if they joined us. We would become stronger!"

Thorian nodded, carefully considering both options. On one hand, killing the orcs would be the safest choice and provide immediate rewards in terms of experience. However, they were also critically short on personnel. Their "army" of kobloids barely constituted two and a half squads, far from a complete company.

"Thank you both for your input," Thorian said, his gaze shifting past Nox and the kobold to the kneeling orcs awaiting their fate. "As you mentioned, Nox, our numbers are limited, and we need more fighters. We won't kill them, but they can't simply join our ranks immediately either. That would create chaos. First, they must repair the damage they've caused."

Thorian then addressed the dissatisfied kobold. "Do you enjoy chopping trees?"

The kobold tilted his head and furrowed his brow. "No, not really. I'd rather hunt and grow strong."

"I thought as much." Thorian smiled. "But we need more wood to improve and repair our village. We'll have the orcs handle the tree-cutting while we focus on hunting."

"Thorian, you're smart." The kobold's eyes widened, and his lips broke into a broad grin. "I like that idea a lot!"

Thorian chuckled. "I'm glad you approve."

He then strode alongside Nox and the kobold towards the orcs. What had begun as a small incident involving a portal materializing before their walls had ultimately resulted in an unexpected boon for their village.

CHAPTER 24

The relentless rain doused the crackling fire as the kobloids gathered in front of the kneeling orcs.

"First things first. Remove your armor and hand over your weapons." Thorian's command caused a stir among the orcs, but Zogthar took the lead and dropped his battle axe on the ground. Removing his armor piece by piece, his scarred and wounded body revealed itself. By the end, he was left with only a loincloth to cover his genitals.

Observing their new leader's compliance, the other orcs followed suit, rising to their feet and removing the pieces of their armor one by one. The sight of twenty muscular orcs, with their imposing physiques and battle-hardened bodies, standing exposed to the pouring rain was truly a spectacle to behold. Rivulets of water cascaded down their broad shoulders and chiseled torsos, accentuating the scars and marks that told the stories of countless battles.

Thorian turned to the kobloids behind him and commanded, "Gather their armor and store it in the Village Hall."

"Understood."

"Yes, sir!"

The kobloids approached the orcs, collecting the discarded armor as the orcs stood unflinchingly in the downpour. Their eyes remained locked with Thorian's, who stared back at them with a composed expression.

As the kobloids carried the armor away to the hall, Thorian advanced without breaking eye contact with Zogthar.

"From this moment on, until I say otherwise, your sole task will be to cut down these trees," Thorian declared, gesturing to the dense forest surrounding them. The orcs followed the path of his hand, taking in the extent of the task. "You will neither eat nor sleep until I release you from this duty."

"You want us, the proud orcs of Butarand, to be your menial workers?!" An orc who had been kneeling at the back stood up, glaring fiercely at Thorian. "You'll pay for this transgression!"

Thorian could only sigh inwardly at the absurdity of the situation as the enraged, naked orc charged. *Oh well. Roasted pig is always delicious.*

Just as Thorian prepared to unleash a Combustion Touch, a powerful fist landed squarely on the charging orc's jaw, sending him flying to the side.

"Barmaloth!" Zogthar's eyes glowed red, radiating a murderous aura. "You dare defy the orders of your leader? You deserve death!"

Zogthar strode over to the stunned Barmaloth, striking him with a powerful knuckle blow, then another and another, until he was pummeling the hapless orc with a flurry of hammer fists, bruising bones with each impact. Barmaloth's grunts soon transformed into pleas for mercy as Zogthar's relentless assault threatened to reduce him to a pulp.

Nox winced at the brutal display unfolding before him and glanced towards Thorian. However, Thorian remained impassive, choosing not to intervene. As the minutes passed, Barmaloth's cries for help eventually ceased.

He had died.

While everyone's attention was fixated on Zogthar's fatal assault on Barmaloth, Thorian noticed movement off to the side and quickly shifted his focus. A small goblin was entering the village through a gap in the damaged wall.

Tsk, that's why I didn't want the wall to break.

Thorian conjured a fireball and dispatched the goblin, sending it to join Barmaloth on the journey along the River Styx.

"Kobold, Nox, watch over the orcs. I'll handle things outside."

With that command, Thorian leapt through the makeshift opening in the wall, only to discover a sizable group waiting for him outside.

Twenty goblins and five hobgoblins.

Taking stock of the mana within his body, Thorian realized he had only a third of his pool remaining. Nevertheless, he was confident it would be more than sufficient.

As the hobgoblins charged towards him with their spears, Thorian swiftly conjured a fireball and hurled it in their direction. As the spell made contact, he lunged at the five hobgoblins, searing their defenseless bodies with the intense flames of his Combustion Touch.

Level up!

Thorian dismissed the notification and swiftly closed in on the remaining dazed hobgoblin. After delivering two rapid punches to its gut, the green humanoid crumpled to its knees. Thorian then struck its neck with a powerful thunderclap.

The goblins, who had been following the lead of the hobgoblins, were bewildered by the speed at which Thorian dispatched their leaders. Just as they were about to flee in fear, a white blur rushed past Thorian from the side.

"You won't escape! You're my level-up!"

The kobold charged at the group of goblins, a wide grin adorning his face. He darted from one side to the next, slaying two or three goblins with each swing of his axe. Whenever he spotted one of the green creatures attempting to make a run for it, he hurled his lunar bolt, stopping the fleeing goblin dead in its tracks.

I thought I told him to keep an eye on the orcs.

Thorian shook his head and chuckled at the kobold's antics before deciding to return to the village. If the kobold was up to the task, there was no need for Thorian to expend any more mana on mere grunts.

Display panel.

Ding!

Race: Flame Kobold

Level: 3/30 (XP: 7/600)

Class: Magus

Level: 17/20 (XP: 123/410)

Lifespan: 40 years

Cultivation Realm: Qi Gathering First Stage (31.6%)

Stats:

Strength: 37

Agility: 42

Constitution: 19

Mana: 52

Qi: 4

Free Points: 3

Skills:

Minor Fire Affinity (passive)

Flame Resistance (passive)

Fireball (active)

Combustion Touch (active)

Huh, so I leveled up twice? I guess I missed a notification when fighting the orcs.

Thorian felt a sense of satisfaction from his progress. Although his current capabilities paled in comparison to those from his past life, he had reached a level where he could at least hold his own in the early days of the apocalypse.

Snapping back to reality, Thorian glanced around to find Nox and the orcs all staring at him intently. Zogthar, having killed Barmaloth, had returned to his position and was waiting.

"What are you standing around for?" Thorian furrowed his eyebrows. "I have given my order. Cut the trees."

As usual, Zogthar was the first to take the lead. He lifted his battle axe from the muddy ground and approached one of the trees to begin cutting. The rest of the orcs followed suit after exchanging a few grunts. However, none of them voiced any complaints, likely fearing a fate similar to Barmaloth's.

As the orcs busied themselves with cutting trees, the kobloids returned to Thorian after completing their task. Just as before, Thorian instructed the magi to ascend the watchtower for a better vantage point. This time, he also included the two priests, as their abilities had a sufficiently long range to be cast from that height.

Meanwhile, the warriors joined the kobold who was manically massacring monsters as if they were sheep in a slaughterhouse. The original pack of goblins had already been killed, Thorian noticed, spying their lifeless bodies strewn across the ground.

Are those rabbarians?

The kobold and the warrior kobloids were now engaged in combat with large, humanoid rabbits. Their eyes were red, and their ears flopped around, but their fists were incredibly fast, enveloped in a red aura.

CHAPTER 25

The warriors' blue light and the rabbarians' red aura clashed fervently as both sides fought for their lives. Thorian approached Nox and said, "We need to patrol around the wall. Other monsters might breach us from another spot."

Nox furrowed his eyebrows and suggested, "Should we go with the assassin team?"

Thorian glanced at the three assassins who were awaiting his command before nodding. "The more, the better."

One of the three assassins chuckled and said to the other two, "I'm almost done with the monster-slaying quest. Only have one left."

"Lucky," another kobloid said with a click of his tongue. "I didn't get the chance to kill many. I still need five before I'm done with that quest."

The topic drew Thorian's attention, and he opened his journal.

Journal:

Subjugate 10 monsters (daily) **(completed)**

Cast a spell 20 times (daily) **(completed)**

Cultivate your Qi for two hours (daily)

Gather 100 Wood Units (daily)

Clear one dungeon (daily)

Pact with the Wolven Guardians

Revenge on the Monsters **(partially complete)**

Noticing that two of the quests had already been completed, Thorian turned his attention to the remaining quest.

Milestones:

Slay (50/50 monsters)

Reward: Level +1

Slay (88/100 monsters)

Reward: Previous rewards and a class skill of your choosing

Slay (0/250 monsters)

Reward: Previous rewards and Level +2

Slay (0/500 monsters)

Reward: Previous rewards and a purple cloud weapon specific for your chosen class.

Huh. I guess even the kills I shared with wind boy and the other fire magus were counted. Good, that makes the process much easier.

Thorian closed his journal and concentrated on the patrol. He kept his ears open for any sound or noise that might indicate something was amiss. After a few minutes, Thorian's ears perked up as he heard loud, rhythmic thuds in the distance. He glanced at Nox, who was also focusing on the same spot, and said, "Someone is trying to break the wall."

Without wasting any more breath on words, the group hurried towards the source of the noise, weaving through trees and leaping over bushes. Unfortunately, once they reached the section of the wall where the thuds were coming from, there was no watchtower to provide them with an advantageous position.

"Let's scale the wall," Thorian ordered before sprinting towards the wooden wall with all his might. With one powerful leap, he reached most of the wall's height and grabbed the ledge. In a fluid motion, Thorian hoisted himself on top of the wall to gain a full view of the perpetrators.

Giant rabbits with twisted goat horns confronted him. The white monsters numbered in the dozens, each of them glaring at the wooden wall with rage-filled eyes and salivating, growling mouths.

Checking his mana, Thorian was pleasantly surprised. *I still have a quarter left. That should be enough.*

Nox and the other three assassins swiftly followed Thorian, assuming a ready position to pounce on the giant rabbits. Aware that Nox's abilities were now stronger than a typical level 1 kobold due to the Minor Moon Boost, Thorian wordlessly permitted him to join the fray alongside the other assassins.

The group of white kobloids leapt down from the wall while Thorian launched a fireball at one of the giant rabbits. However, the white ball of fluff somehow bounced to the side, evading Thorian's spell entirely.

I forgot how annoying these thumpalopes are.

Realizing that merely standing at a distance and hurling fireballs would not suffice, Thorian followed Nox and the assassins, jumping off the wall's ledge.

Nox and the assassins darted across the battlefield with their exceptional agility. However, the giant rabbit thumpalopes were nearly as fast, giving the kobloids no chance to strike without risking being surrounded.

Thorian charged into the fray, facing the pack as they bounced around, attempting to catch him off guard. Three of the thumpalopes sprang towards him from the left with incredible speed, determined to impale him with their horns.

Boom!

Before they could even reach him, Thorian struck them with a Combustion Touch, immersing all three in infernal flames.

"Rampathump!"

With one final cry, the three thumpalopes were incinerated. The remaining rabbits shifted their focus from the kobloids and zeroed in on Thorian with wrathful eyes.

"Ramparampathump!"

Dozens of the giant rabbits lunged at Thorian from all directions, leaving no room for escape. Left with no choice, Thorian crouched and placed his left palm on the ground.

Combustion Touch.

With a massive explosion, Thorian was propelled into the sky, evading the imminent threat and causing the thumpalopes to collide with one another. The fortunate ones merely butted horns and were left dazed, while some of the rabbits impaled each other with their razor-sharp horns.

However, Thorian did not escape unscathed. Although his Flame Resistance protected him from most of the burn damage, the shockwave itself was enough to force his elbow into an unnatural angle.

Tsk, it is very badly dislocated

After landing on the ground. Thorian rushed back in without any hesitation. The pain from his injury could be dwelled on later. Right now, he needed to kill. With a strike from his right palm, Thorian activated Combustion Touch once again, killing five of the rabbits in one hit.

Naturally, the remaining uninjured thumpalopes couldn't sit idly by. They clearly understood that Thorian was their greatest threat and focused on him. However, as they left their backs exposed, Nox and the assassins swiftly moved in and severed their spines with their axes.

Four of the remaining rabbits closed in on Thorian, only to be met by a Combustion Touch. The flames instantly killed the first three thumpalopes, leaving the last one severely burned.

"This one is for me. Thank you!" Nox nonchalantly beheaded the rabbit with a single swing of his axe, while Thorian gulped in labored breaths.

"I'm out of mana," Thorian gasped before pointing at the injured thumpalopes. "Finish them."

"You don't need to tell me twice, boss." One of the assassins pounced on the opportunity with a grin, as the others followed right after him. Nox and the assassins didn't need much time to dispatch the injured and stunned monsters. In less than a minute, they completed the task.

Level up!

Thorian's eyes widened at the notification, and his lips formed a slight smile. Although he had seen this same screen countless times before, he couldn't be happier that it appeared at this moment.

Thorian's dislocated elbow gradually realigned itself, as if guided by an invisible force. However, unlike with a normal procedure, there was barely any pain or discomfort. There was only a sense of relief as his left arm became usable once again.

With the hunt over, Thorian scaled up the wall alongside the other kobloids. He was fatigued and his mana already depleted. Trying to fight in this state would be simply unproductive.

"I will take some time for my mana to recharge," Thorian stated after walking a few steps from the wall. "Continue patrolling the wall. If there are enemies you can't handle, report back to me in the Village Hall."

Nox, who had already noticed Thorian's state, nodded and smiled. "Don't worry about us, we won't have any problems. I'm just a few kills away from evolving."

Thorian opened his eyes wide in surprise before chuckling. *That makes sense, his level has always been close to mine.*

Thinking about the abilities of a night kobold and their synergy with the assassin skills, a weight was lifted off Thorian's shoulders.

The rest of the kobloids also smiled, and one of them said, "Rest well, King. By the time you come back, all of us will be strong!"

CHAPTER 26

Upon returning to the Village Hall, Thorian found Melina sighing as she sipped her tea. As he entered, the young elven woman immediately tensed and placed her cup back on its saucer.

"Be at ease, Melina," Thorian said, smiling as he approached her. "I'm just here to claim the rewards for a couple of quests I've finished."

"Right away, my lord," Melina replied, giving a light bow before retrieving three parchments from beneath her desk. "You have two quests completed and one partially finished. Would you like to claim them all, or just the daily ones?"

"Just the daily ones."

Melina retrieved her stamp and beeswax once more. After impressing the seal on the two parchments, a notification materialized before Thorian.

Level up!

Personal resources.

Arcane Coins: 200

After reviewing the rewards from the two quests, Thorian's gaze shifted towards the bulletin board. To his disappointment, he was unable to locate the "Revenge on the Monster" quest.

Nonetheless, Thorian noticed a new quest that hadn't been there previously. Raising an eyebrow at the unexpected opportunity, he made his way over to the board and removed the quest.

Hope it's a good one.

Purification of Eärendil's Sanctuary

Quest Chain

Description: Venture into Sherwood Forest and locate the entrance to the Lost Elven Sanctuary of Eärendil.

Quest Objectives:

Reach the entrance to the Lost Elven Sanctuary.

Solve the riddle given by the Whispering Trees to gain access to the sanctuary.

Rewards:

200 Arcane Coins

500 Experience Points

Eärendil? Isn't that the dungeon with the corrupted tree monsters?

A wide grin split Thorian's lips at the words "Quest Chain." By completing the chain, he would receive incredible, unique rewards that would set him apart from his competitors.

Eärendil isn't the type of dungeon I can clear right now, but the quest is simply about finding it and solving that riddle.

Though Thorian hadn't spent all his time around Locksley in his past life, he had heard rumors of a perplexing riddle that had cost the lives of five squads.

I don't remember what the riddle was, but Hearth was the answer.

With his plan in place, Thorian glanced back at Melina, only to find her staring wide-eyed at the quest parchment in his hand. Noticing his gaze, she quickly shook her head and resumed her usual demeanor, as if nothing had happened.

Lost Elven Sanctuary, huh? Maybe she knows something.

Thorian handed the quest to Melina, who took out her stamp while avoiding eye contact. As he observed the elven woman busily sealing the quest with beeswax, he broached the subject.

"Do you know of a place called Eärendil?"

Melina hesitated just before stamping the quest, then continued her task. As the parchment slowly disintegrated, she looked up at Thorian and smiled. "I'm sorry, I'm not familiar with it. There are many elves across the thousand worlds, so it might be a city in a world I have no information about."

Thorian furrowed his brow for a moment before shrugging. "That's indeed possible. If your memory is ever jogged and you recall something about this 'Eärendil,' please let me know."

"Of course, my lord. I am at your service," Melina replied, bowing slightly.

Thorian nodded, letting out a small breath before glancing back at the bulletin board. To his surprise, the quest he had just accepted reappeared on the board.

"Can that quest be claimed by multiple people?" Thorian asked Melina with interest.

She nodded. "Yes, my lord. This first part of the chain quest can be claimed by anyone who wishes to do so."

"That is wonderful news," Thorian remarked with a smile. "I'll share it with my subjects very soon."

With that, Thorian left the Village Hall and headed for the dense patch of forest where the orcs were tirelessly cutting down trees. The mastery of their weapons and the sharpness of their battle axes made them far more proficient woodcutters than the kobloids. Zogthar, in particular, was quite impressive, having already felled two medium-sized trees while the others had managed only one.

"Stop!" Thorian commanded as he strode among the orcs. "Take the trees you've cut and follow me."

The orcs grunted and nodded. Thorian anticipated that Zogthar would struggle with the two trees he had cut, but the orc simply enveloped his entire body in a gray aura and hoisted the two trees, one under each arm.

His strength is truly a sight to behold. His base stats should be even higher than mine.

Just imagining the formidable team of warriors the orcs would become once they received their classes had Thorian's lips quivering with excitement. The orcs' high Strength and Constitution made them an ideal fit for the warrior class.

But not now. They need to be assimilated into the pack first.

After several minutes of laborious transport, the orcs, led by Thorian, arrived at the Territory Altar. Their eyes widened, and they dropped the trees they were carrying as soon as they caught sight of the demon's face.

"Return to your duties," Thorian ordered. "You shall place your work in front of this altar every two hours until you are relieved of your duties. Do you understand?"

Zogthar was first to regain his composure and answered with a respectful, "Yes, understood." The other orcs followed suit before heading back to the forest.

With the orcs gone, Thorian placed his palm on the demon's face and mentally commanded, *Absorb wood.*

As before, the cut trees disintegrated into specks of light before being absorbed by the altar. A glance at the territory resources had Thorian grinning. There was enough wood.

Repair wall.

Though he couldn't see the result of his command, Thorian felt a slight tremor beneath his feet. Once the tremor ceased, he knew the repair process had been completed.

That should give me enough time. Once Nox evolves, the kobloids shouldn't have trouble with most monsters.

After spending five hundred wood units on repairing the wall, Thorian made his way towards the Village Hall. He then sat cross-legged right in front of the door and started his meditation, easing into his breathing technique. Immediately, Thorian sensed a significant change. The amount of ether he could grasp from the air was much higher than usual.

So this is the effect of the Ether Lines Nexus? No wonder that miserly William didn't want me to meditate here when I visited.

As Thorian guided the dense ether through his Qi channels, he found it much easier to penetrate his relatively clogged pathways. Minutes swiftly passed as Thorian cleared his channels using the dense ether enveloping him. In just under fifteen minutes, the first droplet of Qi materialized in his dantian.

Excellent! With this pace, I should be able to break through the Vermilion Bird's gate.

WIth a goal now clear in mind, Thorian continued his breathing technique. The second droplet reached his dantian even faster, taking only ten minutes. The third one took eight minutes, as did the rest that followed. After practicing his breathing technique for an hour and a half, Thorian had amassed a total of ten Qi droplets.

This should be enough.

With fourteen Qi droplets now circulating in his dantian, Thorian directed them towards the entrance of the Vermilion Bird meridian.

It's still stuck?

Undeterred, Thorian pushed the Qi droplets again and again, gradually chipping away at the obstructed entrance. The process was challenging, akin to trying to dig through hard ground with layers of roots underneath using a small shovel. Nevertheless, Thorian persisted. For the remaining thirty minutes, he continued to push his Qi, slowly clearing the entrance.

Finally, with only a minute remaining in his meditation time, one of the Qi droplets broke through the entrance and entered the meridian. The other thirteen Qi droplets followed suit and flowed through the grimy path. Although the path itself was dirty, it wasn't obstructed and allowed for relatively smooth passage. The end of the path, however, was another matter.

When Thorian's Qi reached the end of the meridian path and the entrance to the first node, it became stuck once again. The node's entrance was as clogged as the meridian's gate, if not more so.

CHAPTER 27

Unable to cross through the barrier of the first node, Thorian exhaled deeply and opened his eyes. His meditation session had come to an end.

Rank up!

Oh, my cultivation stage ranked up? Display panel.

Ding!

Race: Flame Kobold

Level: 4/30 (XP: 30/650)

Class: Magus

Level: 18/20 (XP: 230/450)

Lifespan: 40 years

Cultivation Realm: Qi Gathering Second Stage (5.3%)

Stats:

Strength: 41

Agility: 46

Constitution: 23

Mana: 53

Qi: 14

Free Points: 6

Skills:

Minor Fire Affinity (passive)

Flame Resistance (passive)

Fireball (active)

Combustion Touch (active)

I'm close to hitting a wall in my class, Thorian noted, eyeing his class level. *I cannot advance until I master all four basic spells.*

Thorian concentrated on his fireball spell to reveal more information.

Fireball: You conjure a fiery orb and hurl it at your enemies, leaving them charred and weakened.

Proficiency: 87.35%

Thorian nodded in approval at the proficiency featured at the end of the skill description. *Good, I'm almost done with Fireball. I just need to concentrate on the other three skills.*

The train of thought sent his gaze toward the patch of forest where the orcs were cutting trees. *The first building I'll upgrade is the magus statue. I need the guild to be built as soon as possible.*

As he rose from his cross-legged position, Thorian was assaulted by a disgusting stench. The black goo had spread all over the place, its viscosity and volume even greater than usual.

Is that the filth from my Vermilion Bird meridian? What a god-forsaken body.

Thorian approached the Territory Altar, surprised by the number of tree stumps surrounding it. What had taken the kobloids a good part of the afternoon and night to accomplish was achieved by the orcs in just a few hours.

I should be able to upgrade the magus statue with this much.

Wearing a broad smile, Thorian placed his hand on the demon's face and commanded it to absorb the trees. Once they had entirely disintegrated, he checked his resources.

Resources:

Gathered Experience: 1230

Wood: 1150

Upgrade magus statue, he commanded.

Magus Statue

Description: The Magus Statue embodies the essence of arcane knowledge and mastery over the elements. By channeling their magical energies, magi can wield destructive spells to vanquish their foes and devastate the land before them.

Upgrade:

Gathered Experience: 750

Wood: 1000

Do you wish to upgrade the Magus Statue into the Magus Guild?

"Yes."

A noise from the west indicated that the upgrade process had begun. From a distance, Thorian could see a wooden building taking shape where the statue of the magus once stood. Eager to explore the village's newest addition, Thorian hastened towards it with quick strides.

Upon entering the newly built Magus Guild, Thorian was immediately struck by the modest yet captivating atmosphere of the interior. The wooden structure, though simple, exuded an aura of mysticism and potential. The guild's low level was reflected in its relatively small size and limited furnishings, but it was evident that it had been designed with growth and expansion in mind.

On the left side of the guild, there was a room dedicated to testing the potential of aspiring magi. The room contained an assortment of magical artifacts and testing devices, designed to measure the innate magical aptitude of those who wished to join the ranks of the Magus Guild.

Good, we can finally recruit proper magi and not just haphazardly choose candidates.

While the room on the left was important, Thorian's interest lay in the room on the right. There, he spotted the guildmaster's desk, cluttered with scrolls, half-dried parchments, and massive arcane tomes. However, most intriguingly, the guildmaster was nowhere to be seen.

"Yagh, I can't reach," a small squeaky voice came from the other side of the room. Confusion tugged at Thorian's brow as he walked towards the desk. When he checked behind it, he discovered a small creature with lavender skin and a head that was disproportionately large compared to its tiny body. Its hair was white, and although unkempt, it looked silky smooth.

Seeing the poor creature struggling to jump off the chair and reach the desk, Thorian couldn't help but feel sympathetic.

"Do you need some help?"

The creature turned towards Thorian, frowning, but as it looked at him, its expression changed from confusion to pure surprise.

"You are the lord?" the creature asked with wide eyes. "I have never seen a monster become a village lord. That is marvelous!"

As the creature opened its arms wide, Thorian lifted it onto the desk and said, "Well, I happen to be quite special."

"And you're a magus too?!" The creature's eyes glistened. "Not only are you special, but you are also wise. Magi are the wisest and strongest, capable of turning the tides of a battlefield with a single spell."

Thorian furrowed his brow as he examined the lavender fluffy creature. While he had never seen one that looked like this before, he had heard of a species with a similar description.

"Are you a buzzlekin?"

"Y"Yes, I am." The creature proudly placed its hand on its chest. "I am Thimblewick Fizzlegrin, seeker of the highest truth and the master of this here village's Magus Guild."

Thorian arched a brow at Thimblewick's sudden declaration. He had encountered guildmasters of many different species in his past life, but a buzzlekin was a first.

Now that I think about it, Melina wasn't the Village Hall reception-ist of this territory when I visited it in the past. The magus guildmaster was also that elder nymph, Safia.

While Thorian was lost in his thoughts, Thimblewick cleared his throat. "Ahem, ahem. Do you require anything? Maybe a skill?"

The buzzlekin wore an expectant look on his expressive face as he lightly rubbed his hands together like a stereotypical merchant. Observing the guildmaster's demeanor, Thorian wasn't sure whether to laugh or to frown.

"I need the Waterball skill first to get rid of this stench," Thorian answered.

"A civilized monster, now isn't that rare?" Thimblewick nodded approvingly as he rummaged through the scrolls in his desk. Upon finding the scroll he was searching for, Thimblewick handed it to Thorian with a childish smile. "This is the Waterball scroll. Since you are the lord and the first to purchase a skill, I'll offer it to you for only two hundred arcane coins."

Thorian nodded, accepting the buzzlekin's proposal.

It's been so long I'm not exactly sure, but I believe that they normally cost five hundred coins.

As Thorian accepted the skill scroll, Thimblewick chuckled child-ishly before muttering to himself, "My first-ever deal. I'm so happy..."

Thorian shook his head at the peculiar scene before saying, "I'll leave you for now. The other magi should come soon to buy their skills too."

"Good doing business with you. Until next time!"

With Thimblewick waving at him with a smile, Thorian left the Magus Guild and tore open the skill scroll. The yellow parchment shimmered with a sky-blue light before disintegrating into specks that Thorian's body absorbed.

Waterball skill has been learned.

Waterball: You summon a watery orb and launch it at your enemies, drenching them and knocking them off balance.

Proficiency: 0%

I need to use my basic skills whenever possible. The longer I spend without fully maxing them out, the longer I'll be stuck without a class advancement.

With his mana now full, Thorian headed straight in the direction of the orcs. He needed to return and hunt the monsters beyond the wall to continue progressing.

INTERLUDE 1

Half an hour before the apocalypse...

"Grampa, are we really going to the plaza in the middle of the night?" The young boy, little Roo, had a much-improved complexion compared to when he was with the pack of kobloids. However, he was still shivering and maintained a closed-off demeanor.

The old man offered a gentle smile and said, "We're just taking a stroll. Some fresh air never hurt anybody, right?"

Though Roo remained unconvinced, he nodded and followed his grandfather without any further complaints. In the middle of the night, the usually bustling streets were practically empty. The shop stands were closed, and only a few horse carriages and boisterous drinking buddies populated the streets.

The old man, of course, knew the city like the back of his hand. He understood precisely which roads to take and which streets to avoid. The underbelly of Locksley was a dark place, and he certainly didn't want to escape one dangerous situation only to be ensnared by slave merchants—or worse.

As he walked through the streets with his fidgety grandson at his side, the old man's thoughts drifted back to the talking, white-furred creature.

A monster who speaks like a noble offering advice? I would be mad if I didn't at least check the plaza to see what happens.

The old man's years of experience had never prepared him for an encounter with a creature that was something straight out of folklore. However, he understood how fickle lady fortune could be. Opportunities often came only once, so he knew the importance of recognizing them for what they were and seizing upon them when they arose.

Upon reaching the plaza, the old man and little Roo scanned the area, noticing a single small group occupying the entire square. The group consisted of six individuals, with three of them sitting by the fountain, engaged in conversation and laughter, while the other three stood with puffed-up chests and stoic expressions on their faces.

"Those people look scary," the young boy muttered under his breath.

The old man couldn't help but agree. Careful not to make much noise or attract any unwanted attention, he took little Roo's hand and led him to the other side of the plaza, well out of the group's sight.

As they walked towards the edge of the town square, the old man couldn't resist stealing glances at the group, particularly the three individuals sitting by the fountain with relaxed expressions. The one who immediately caught his eye was a large man with broad shoulders and bulging muscles. Even while seated, he towered over the other two with his imposing frame.

Wait, isn't that the Beast?

The old man suddenly stopped, which surprised little Roo as he looked up at him in confusion. However, the old man's facial expression quickly conveyed everything the young boy needed to know.

He was horrified.

For a decade, the old man had heard rumors of a man with the physique of a beast, capable of wrestling a bull and tearing a child in half with his bare hands. A ruthless killing machine that served the criminal underworld, committing heinous crimes and spreading fear and terror to anyone who dared to cross his masters.

There's no way, right?

A dismissive chuckle escaped the old man at his overactive imagination. The man before him was smiling and laughing, a far cry from the cruel and emotionless beast he had heard whispers of in the taverns. *Those drunken fools sure do like to spin tales. A man that can tear a child in half with his hands? Give me a break.*

"Eh, grampa?" The little boy nudged at the old man's pants, bringing him back to reality. Noticing the lost and confused expression on Roo's face, the old man smiled and continued walking towards the edge of the plaza. There, they sat down together on a bench, waiting for the appointed time to arrive.

As the minutes passed, the old man's gaze drifted back to the group by the fountain. This time, he chose not to focus on the muscular one but on the other two.

To the left was a man with a slender build. He was wearing a light brown long-sleeved linen shirt with a laced-up neckline, a truly unremarkable outfit. However, it was clean, which told the old man that he was either wealthy enough to afford new clothes or diligent enough to properly repair and regularly clean old ones.

Without much thought, the old man's focus shifted to the center, where a lithe woman sat between the two men. Her wavy, raven-black hair was tied into a ponytail. As for her attire, she wore a form-fitting, dark-green fabric. Such clothes were not easy to come by and required skillful tailoring, which only deepened the old man's curiosity.

As time continued to pass, the old man grew silent. Although he attempted to distract himself by engaging in conversation with little Roo, his mind couldn't help but entertain wayward thoughts and imagined scenarios.

Any moment now...

While the old man was lost in thought, gazing at the ground, little Roo nudged him from the side.

"Grampa... Those people are coming."

The old man snapped out of his reverie and looked up, only to find the group of six slowly approaching them.

"Wait here, everyone. You're going to scare them." The lady in green halted the rest of her group and continued walking alone towards the old man and the young boy.

"Hey there, what might your names be?" The lady asked with a friendly smile.

She had green eyes, the old man noticed, ones that seemed to pierce through the very depths of his soul. And her light makeup perfectly complemented her heart-shaped face.

"Whoa... Pretty lady."

Both the old man and the black-haired woman looked at little Roo in surprise. Seeing the innocent expression on the boy's face, the lady chuckled softly. "Thank you, you're a well-mannered little fellow. What's your name?"

"My name is Roo!" the boy answered excitedly. His earlier tension seemed to have vanished as he talked with the slender woman.

"Nice to meet you, young man. My name is Nalia." She then smiled and looked at the old man. "And what's your name?"

"I am Robert," the old man replied curtly. Although the lady before him was friendly and the atmosphere seemed relaxed, he couldn't shake the feeling that something was amiss.

As his gaze shifted from Nalia to the men behind her, he noticed their intense expressions. The three stoic men, who had not said a word, appeared especially fearsome as they scrutinized him and his grandson with cold eyes.

"Were you planning on staying the night here, Mister Robert?" Nalia's question brought his focus back to her. She wore a questioning and puzzled expression, accompanied by a mix of compassion and sincerity.

"No, of course not." Robert nervously chuckled at the unexpected question. "We're just here for a breath of fresh air."

"A breath of fresh air, I see." Nalia smiled and nodded. She then looked up at the sky with a melancholic expression on her face. "It is indeed a beautiful night to stroll around. The skies are clear, and the moon is captivating."

Nalia gazed at the sky for a few more seconds before looking back down and smiling at the old man. "I won't make things more awkward for you, Mr. Robert. I hope you have a great night."

She then walked back towards the rest of her group before making their way back to the fountain. Robert's eyes couldn't help but remain fixated on them. Even though he didn't know who they truly were, he understood instinctively that they were people he should definitely avoid.

INTERLUDE 2

The dark clouds overhead thickened, shrouding the night sky. The once-radiant white moon disappeared, leaving only intermittent lightning strikes to pierce the darkness below, with booming thunderclaps echoing behind. Each one sent a deep, rumbling vibration through Robert's core.

Roo clung to the old man's arm in terror, letting out a yelp with each thunderous roar. "It's a storm," Robert said, urgency in his voice. "We should move before it rains."

Just as the old man rose from the bench, the earth trembled, throwing him off balance. He stumbled, gripping Roo tightly to shield him from harm. Though he regained his footing, a flicker of fear latched onto him as he said, "That felt like an earthquake. We need to find shelter, now."

Just as Robert prepared to scoop up Roo and make their escape, a surreal scene unfolded before him. Multiple rocky protrusions burst from the plaza floor, birthed from the very earth. The ground fractured as these objects emerged from beneath the surface with unnatural speed, resembling a gushing stream of water from a spring.

"I thought you had gone crazy," a muscular man said with a cackle, capturing Robert's attention. The man's eyes were filled with madness as he gazed at the rocky structures surrounding them. "The end of the world is truly here."

Hearing those words from the strong man's mouth, Robert's mind went blank for a moment.

The end of the world?

As if determined to fulfill the prophecy, the storm intensified. Torrential rain drenched Robert and Roo, while the plaza continued to tremble from the emergence of the rocky structures.

When the tremors finally ceased and the structures stopped growing, Roo mustered the courage to cling to Robert, crying out, "Grampa, I'm scared!"

Robert shivered, uncertain whether it was the cold rain trickling down his back or the chaos surrounding them that chilled him. He hugged the young boy tightly with one arm and reassured him, "Don't worry, Roo. Grandpa is here. There's nothing to be scared of."

The old man's attention turned to the group of six. The three stoic men had lost their composure, staring in horror at the structures that had erupted from the depths of the earth around them. The muscular man continued to laugh maniacally while the slender one glanced around with a mixture of surprise and fear.

Only Nalia appeared unfazed. Her posture was relaxed, and a slight smile graced her lips, as if the unfolding events were merely a mild source of amusement.

That white creature told me to come here. Is it because of these things?

The old man chose not to dwell on the six enigmatic individuals, instead concentrating on the structures that had appeared throughout the plaza. They were immense, towering over any house and rivaling the watchtowers that lined the city walls.

As Robert's focus sharpened, he realized their true nature. *Are these... statues?*

The craftsmanship of the four giant stone figures surpassed anything he had ever seen. The existence of one such impeccably carved, colossal statue would have been miraculous enough, but the presence of four could only be the work of a deity.

Robert's gaze settled on the statue nearest to him. It portrayed a man clad in armor, with a voluminous yet neatly trimmed beard and a fierce expression on his face. He wielded a menacing battle-axe, poised to strike any approaching enemy.

Despite being a statue, Robert felt as if it were alive. Its spirit seemed palpable, and the intricate details of the carving gave the impression that a giant warrior had been turned to stone mid-battle.

Entranced by the statue's beauty, Robert led Roo closer to it. The young boy followed his grandfather without hesitation, his own eyes filled with curiosity and wonder.

As Robert reached out and placed his hand on the exquisite stone, a mysterious message materialized before him.

Would you like to choose the Warrior class?

What...? Am I seeing things?

Robert blinked and shook his head, but no matter what he did or where he looked, the message remained centered in his vision. He couldn't escape it.

"Grampa? What are you doing?"

Robert tried to look at the young boy beside him, but the message obstructed Roo's face. He couldn't even see his grandson's expression with the floating text in the way.

"Yes. Yes, I do," Robert replied aloud, frustration seeping into his voice. He could feel Roo's hand trembling in his grip, a telltale sign that the old man's behavior was becoming increasingly bizarre.

Choose one of these starting abilities.

Power Strike: You imbue your weapon with magical power and strike the enemy with an attack that deals additional damage.

Charge: Allows the warrior to quickly close the distance to their target, potentially stunning or knocking them down with a small shockwave.

Taunting Shout: Provokes enemies to focus their attacks on the warrior, protecting more vulnerable party members.

Weapons Proficiency (passive): Allows the warrior to use various types of melee weapons effectively, such as swords, axes, and maces.

Shield Proficiency (passive): Grants the ability to use shields for added defense, helping to block or deflect incoming attacks.

Robert was baffled by the colorful screen that appeared before him, but the more he examined it, the more he felt something was amiss.

How... How can I read this? How do I understand this language?

"Grampa? Can we go back home?" Roo tugged at Robert's sleeve, his voice quivering as tears threatened to fall.

The plea spurred Robert to take charge of the situation. "Yeah, Roo. Just give me one second."

No longer questioning the strange occurrences, Robert quickly scanned the abilities presented before him. After a few moments, he made his choice.

"I choose Power Strike," he muttered under his breath, hoping the gods could hear him and that Roo couldn't. The last thing he needed was to seem even more unhinged.

Congratulations, you have become a warrior. You can check your information by simply saying or thinking "Display panel."

The message vanished after a few seconds, revealing Roo's worried expression as he gazed at his grandfather.

Robert sighed, about to tell his grandson they would head home when a sudden thought struck him.

Roo should get this class thing too.

He didn't fully understand his reasoning, but he instinctively felt that this was an opportunity he couldn't let Roo miss. The muscular man's words echoed in his ears: *"The end of the world is truly here."* Considering the monsters he had encountered in the forest while cutting wood, and the fact that the intelligent creature had directed him to this place, Robert was nearly convinced that these classes would be crucial. Gaining such abilities could be a significant advantage for both of them.

"Roo, can you touch the statue?" Robert asked with a warm smile.

The little boy hesitated at first before nodding. As he placed his hand on the colossal sculpture, he suddenly yanked it back with a yelp.

"Grampa, I'm seeing words! What are these things?"

"Calm down, little Roo," Robert said soothingly, placing a hand on the boy's shoulder. "Just follow what the words say."

Roo swallowed hard and admitted, "This is scary." Despite his fear, he obeyed his grandpa's instructions without further complaint. Robert could feel Roo's trembling subside as the child focused. After standing in the pouring rain for half a minute, Roo looked back at the old man and announced, "I did what the words said. It says I am now a warrior."

Robert nodded gravely before turning his attention back to the group of six. Inexplicably, a large stone building had materialized on the other side of the plaza. It boasted a grand entrance, and the exterior was adorned with decorative statues, which, upon closer inspection, were miniature versions of the sculptures encircling the square.

Five of the six individuals were seated outside, seemingly waiting, when Nalia suddenly emerged from the building's entrance, a devious smile spread across her face.

Oh, hell no.

Seeing the woman's expression, Robert immediately grabbed Roo by the wrist and walked out of the plaza as quickly as he could. His many years of life experience had taught him that staying near people who practically radiated the word "underworld" was far from wise.

CHAPTER 28

Although dark clouds lingered above the village of Wolvendale, the downpour had mostly ceased. Thorian sniffed at his damp fur and realized that he couldn't meet his men reeking as he did. Placing a hand on his head, he called upon his magic to remedy the situation.

Waterball.

The spell struck Thorian with great force, but he managed to power through. As the jet of water washed over him, it deeply cleansed the skin and fur on his head and shoulders. Although it helped, the stench still reeked from the other parts of his body. Determined to rid himself of the odor, Thorian extended his arm as far away as possible from his torso and aimed a waterball at his own chest.

The force of the spell sent him tumbling a couple of steps backward, but Thorian quickly regained his balance. Resolute, he continued using his magical ability to cleanse every spot on his body. Reaching his back proved to be a challenge, but he was able to twist his arm and launch a spell, nearly dislocating his shoulder in the process. Despite the discomfort, Thorian's efforts paid off, leaving him feeling refreshed and free of the unpleasant odor.

Finally, the smell is gone. Each cultivation session feels like eating a marrow cleansing pill, but with just the smell and none of the benefits.

Now that he was presentable, Thorian set his sights on the forest. He made haste, traversing the muddy terrain with purpose as he moved towards the orcs. Upon entering the forest, the sound of powerful axes striking tree trunks echoed from every direction. Each orc was singularly focused on their task, their well-developed muscles tirelessly working to chop down trees with impressive speed.

If they could use Power Strike, their speed would be even higher.

Excited by the possibilities, Thorian eagerly anticipated the day when the orcs would obtain their warrior classes. They were destined to become the most formidable tree-cutters in the entire kingdom. Alas, for now, he would have to be patient and wait for that day to come.

Seeing that the orcs were performing their tasks dutifully, Thorian continued his journey without uttering a word. In no time, he reached the wall, where he observed magi hurling spell after spell from their watchtower at an enemy beyond.

With a single, powerful leap, Thorian landed on the wall's ledge, gaining a full view of the battlefield. The kobloids were engaged in combat with a pack of chaskas, while the kobold faced off against their enemy's evolved form—the formidable tailmasher. This giant beast stood at six feet tall, almost towering over the kobold even while on all fours. Its muscular body was cloaked in thick, dark fur adorned with faint, glowing stripes.

While regular chaskas had a single boulder at the end of their tails, a tailmasher's tail was split into three sections, each resembling a smaller and more agile boulder connected by sinewy, flexible tissue. The sight of this terrifying opponent only heightened the intensity of the battle.

The tailmasher clenched its three tail sections into one massive boulder before swiftly whipping it at the kobold. Despite barely managing to block the attack using Power Strike to parry, the kobold was sent tumbling backwards several steps, its arms bruised from the impact.

As the beast lowered its head, poised to pounce once more, it was met with a barrage of magical spells. Like a volley of arrows, the combined forces of all four elements struck the tailmasher's face, momentarily halting its advance. The display of raw power and cooperation from the defenders was truly a sight to behold.

Good combo.

Silently commending the four magi, Thorian charged towards the evolved chaska with an open palm. As he struck the beast, a fiery cone-shaped blast erupted from its back.

The tailmasher roared in pain, but this only provided an opportunity for the kobold. "Catch this!" the kobold cried out, as a blue light enveloped its axe. Gripping the weapon with both hands, he struck the beast, effortlessly slicing through the tailmasher's skin and flesh. This impressive display was made possible by his exceptional skill and the increased stats gained from leveling up his class. Indeed, the kobold's strength was in a league of its own.

Wasting no time, Thorian launched a fireball at the tailmasher and charged in once more with an open palm. As the initial spell exploded, he followed up with a Combustion Touch, propelling the flaming beast into the air.

"Good throw!" the kobold laughed, sprinting after the airborne tailmasher. With a single leap, the kobold reached the creature and delivered an overhead slash, cleaving its chest open.

The beast plummeted to the ground, and the magi in the watchtower unleashed their skills once more, bombarding it with a powerful four-element barrage. Thorian also joined the fray, hurling an additional fireball of his own to ensure the tailmasher's defeat.

As the dust settled, the kobold shouted triumphantly, a wide smile across its face. "It's dead! I just leveled up."

Thorian's expression remained unchanged, his focus shifting to the rest of the battlefield where the kobloids continued to battle the chaskas. The four warriors were giving it their all to hold their ground against the relentless onslaught, but the powerful boulder strikes from the overgrown cats proved too formidable for them to handle.

With hurried steps, Thorian charged towards the chaskas, closely followed by the kobold, who clicked his tongue in anticipation. With his allies in such close proximity to the enemies, Thorian couldn't risk using his Combustion Touch skill. Instead, he relied on his brute strength and agility, pummeling the chaskas with relentless punches before slashing them open with his claws.

The kobold proved to be even more effective, employing his Power Strike skill and superior combat abilities to quickly overwhelm the chaskas, felling them with his axe.

The arrival of Thorian and the kobold quickly turned the tide of battle. The beleaguered warrior kobloids, who had been steadily losing ground, found renewed strength and began pushing back their foes. In a matter of minutes, the pack of chaskas lay defeated, thanks to the combined efforts of Thorian and his allies.

With the monsters defeated, Thorian surveyed the battlefield before assessing the condition of the wall. It was battered, having sustained damage from sharp blades and blunt objects alike. Thorian wouldn't be surprised if it were breached again in the near future.

"Let's head back inside," Thorian instructed. "I need a report on what transpired during these past two hours."

"A report?" the kobold asked, face scrunched in puzzlement. "What's that?"

Once more confronted with the ignorance of his new allies, Thorian took a deep breath and replied, "Let's return to the village first, and then we can discuss it."

As the group of white-furred creatures and Thorian climbed the wall and re-entered the village, Thorian clarified, "A report is an update on important information. Tell me who leveled up, how many times, if anyone was injured, or if there's anything significant that I should be aware of."

"All of us leveled up, boss," one of the kobloid warriors supplied with a chuckle. "I've already leveled up three times in both my species and class. I'm getting so close to an evolution!"

"Same here," another kobloid chimed in. Thorian recognized him as the one who'd placed second in the wood-cutting competition. "We're all getting stronger. Just a few more levels and we'll become a true army."

"Like they said." The kobold grinned. "Everyone leveled up, even me. My warrior level is 15, and my species is now level 3."

Thorian nodded in approval. "That's excellent progress on all fronts." Then, turning his attention to the magi descending the watchtower stairs, he asked, "What about you? What's your level?"

"We're now level 13 in both," the wind magus replied with a chuckle. "Choosing this class was the best decision. We level up so quickly."

The fire magus bobbed his head in agreement. "We just have to hit the monster from far and we get all the experience. It's so good."

"You guys have it too easy," one of the warriors commented. "If I were a magus like you, I would've already evolved."

"Is that jealousy I'm hearing?" the wind magus retorted as the other magi laughed.

While the kobloids chatted and bantered with one another, a thought that Thorian had pushed to the back of his mind since his reincarnation resurfaced.

"All of you need names."

CHAPTER 29

"Names? Why do we need names?" The kobold raised an eyebrow at Thorian's unexpected proposition. The other kobloids also stared at Thorian, their eyebrows furrowed, clearly not understanding the purpose of his suggestion.

Thorian let out a sigh before explaining, "Imagine one of your comrades is injured while battling a monster. How would you inform me about it?"

"I would tell you that he was injured..." the kobold replied, the incredulity in his voice unmistakable.

Thorian clicked his tongue. "And how would I know who 'he' is? It could be anyone."

His subordinate's expression froze, and after a few seconds, he looked away in embarrassment. The kobloids also began murmuring amongst themselves, their confusion shifting to intrigue.

The stocky warrior raised his hand and said, "But we will know who got injured when we bring everyone together."

"That only works when we're this small," Thorian immediately countered. "When we become a hundred, a thousand, or even more, do we need to gather all of us together just to know who we're talking about?"

At that, the kobold cleared his throat and said, "I understand. These names seem very important. Will you be the one giving them to us?"

"Yes, I will name you first." Thorian scratched his chin in thought before an idea came to him. "You are a strong moon kobold. From now on, your name shall be Forlune, which means 'strong moon' in the ancient language."

Hearing the meaning of his name, the kobold grinned. "Forlune, I like that name. A strong name for a strong warrior!"

The kobloids cheered and roared as the kobold received his name, causing Forlune to blush slightly.

"Congratulations, Forlune." One of the warriors slapped the kobold's back with a hearty laugh. "You got a good name."

As the kobloids cheerfully joked around with one another, Thorian's eyes shifted towards the magi.

They are the easiest to name, I will just use their elements.

"You, fire magus," Thorian pointed at one of the magi. "Your name shall be Ignis."

The fire magus was initially confused, but his expression quickly morphed into joy. "That is a great name. Thank you, King!"

Thorian then named the rest of the magi Ventus, Aqua, and Saxum, respectively. Each name represented the element of the skill they possessed.

Turning his attention back to the kobloid warriors who were expectantly waiting for their names, Thorian let out a sigh.

This is truly spreading my creative spirit thin.

Thorian pointed at the warrior who had placed second after Forlune in the woodcutting competition. "Your name shall be Caedar."

Caedar smiled and nodded gratefully at the name he had been given. Thorian then looked at the rest of the warriors, bestowing them with names as follows: Bellafor, Crimen, and Inly.

After finishing his naming spree, Thorian took a deep breath. *This is even harder than slaughtering a full army of orcs.*

The stocky warrior, Caedar, took a deep breath. "King, thank you for gifting us these names," he expressed with sincere gratitude.

"Thank you, King," the rest of the kobloids echoed.

Seeing all the kobloids bowing down to Thorian, Forlune was flustered before he too joined them and bowed down.

"Raise your heads," Thorian ordered with a relaxed voice. "I need to take a look around the village and see what Nox has been doing. He can't possibly protect all sides with just the small team that he has."

As Thorian voiced his thoughts, Forlune looked up at him and asked the question that had been gnawing at him for some time. "King, when are we going to kill the humans? We need to complete that quest. It's too good to pass up."

Forlune's words immediately grabbed the attention of the kobloids. They were also intrigued by the quest and eager to complete it.

Thorian shook his head. "We can't do it now. It's too dangerous."

Forlune furrowed his eyebrows in confusion at Thorian's response. "Why is it dangerous? If the humans are like the ones we captured earlier, we could kill thousands of them without any problem."

"The humans are not the problem," Thorian explained. "If we leave, the village will be unprotected. No one would be around to keep an eye on the orcs, and even if they don't misbehave, other monsters could break in and destroy everything we've worked for."

Thorian's eyes drifted in the direction of the Village Hall before he continued his explanation. "I don't care about the wall. If it's destroyed, we can easily repair it. However, if they break in, destroy the Village Hall, and kill Melina, we will be in deep trouble."

Forlune tilted his head in confusion. "Why? If the village is destroyed, can't we just repair it or build another one? With the orcs helping us, we can gather enough wood very quickly."

"It's about Melina," Thorian let out a deep sigh. "If she dies, we will need to wait for a full month for her replacement to arrive. That's a full month of not being able to do the Village Hall's quests because there will be nobody to approve them."

Forlune's mouth hung slightly ajar at Thorian's explanation. After a few seconds of processing the information, he couldn't help but ask, "How do you know all of this?"

"I have my secrets," Thorian curtly responded, leaving no room for further questioning. As Forlune looked away to avoid eye contact, Thorian softened his voice and assured, "That said, it doesn't mean we will just ignore that Monster Quest. We just need some preparation first."

The kobloids, who had been feeling down, brightened up at Thorian's last words. Inly, one of the warriors, excitedly said, "Is it that we need to evolve first? After our evolution, we will become strong enough to protect the village easily."

"Oh, that's true!" With rejuvenated spirits, the kobloids nodded and voiced their agreement with Inly.

"Evolution will be helpful indeed, but it's not enough. Truthfully, we are just not a big enough pack. We can't even properly guard all four gates," Thorian explained.

Forlune thought for a second before suggesting, "Do we need to bring in more monsters? Like the orcs?"

Thorian nodded. "Monsters like the orcs would be fine. However, if we can bring in other packs of kobloids and kobolds, that would be ideal."

"There was that pack of brown kobloids earlier," Ventus remarked.

"Yeah, but they ran away immediately after they saw our skills," Ignis laughed, joined by the other kobloids.

So there are brown kobloids are nearby. That is good to hear.

"Regardless, this discussion is fruitless," Thorian concluded. "What you need to focus on right now is simply your evolution. Once all of you become strong enough, we will be able to bring in as many monsters as we deem fit. To our glory!"

"To our glory!" the kobloids repeated with cheerful voices.

After the cheers died down, Thorian focused on Forlune. "I will be taking a look around the village. If those brown kobloids come back, make sure to bring them in. Use whatever means necessary."

Forlune grinned and nodded. "As you wish, King."

Having completed his work in this part of the village, Thorian jumped up onto the ledge of the wall and began walking around the periphery of the village.

Monster corpses littered the ground beyond the walls. At first, the corpses were mostly charred with fireballs and hacked by the warriors' axes, but as Thorian continued, the wounds became much less obvious. Some had their throats slit, while others had their backs hacked by axes. This was the work of the assassins.

However, the wall was far from spotless. Cracks, chips, and dents adorned it in a constant stream, revealing the efforts of the monsters trying to break in from all sides.

After a few minutes of surveying, he noticed movement far in the distance. Goblins were using ropes to scale the wooden wall.

CHAPTER 30

"Tch, what is Nox doing?" Thorian wondered as he conjured a waterball and launched it towards the three climbing goblins. The green creatures screamed as they fell onto their backs.

Combustion Touch.

In less than a second, Thorian leapt towards the falling goblins and struck the first one with his flaming fist. The water from the fireball evaporated, creating a small mist, while the green body of the creature turned charred and black.

Fortunately, Thorian's Flame Resistance protected him from the scorching mist, making it feel only slightly hot. He glanced around to see the other two goblins running in opposite directions.

You think you can escape?

Eager to test the proficiency of his new skill, Thorian launched a waterball at one of the fleeing creatures before chasing after the other with lethal intent. He slashed the goblin's back with his claws, eliciting one final scream as it fell to the ground. Thorian crushed its skull with a single stomp, ending its life.

Like an unfeeling machine, Thorian turned around to look at the other fleeing creature, only to find it lying on the ground. Its clothes were torn to shreds, and its skin was wounded from the waterball's impact.

Thorian rushed towards the weakened creature and stabbed through its chest with his claws, crushing its heart in his grip. Whether that was a testament to his strength or the frailty of the goblin could not be determined.

Having eliminated all the goblins that had been attempting to infiltrate the village, Thorian looked back at the walls. To his surprise, he spotted another one of the green creatures standing on the ledge. The goblin's knees shook as it took in the grisly scene Thorian had created before hastily descending the rope into the village.

Unfortunately for the creature, Thorian was not in the mood to let it escape and engage in a cat-and-mouse game. With swift strides, he rushed towards the wall and scaled it in a single leap. Looking down, he could see the goblin had just barely descended the wall and was about to rush into the dense patch of trees.

You're too slow.

Thorian conjured a waterball and launched it at the fleeing green monster. The impact from the spell sent the creature soaring through the air, screaming for its life. Without wasting another second, Thorian conjured a fireball and engulfed the unfortunate monster in its flames.

Was he the only one inside? No, I need to make sure.

Thorian took a deep breath and focused on his sense of smell. The scent of flames and the corpses littered around the village was overwhelming, but as he concentrated, Thorian could make out subtle differences. After a few seconds, his keen nose was able to sift through the stronger odors and detect the scent of the escaping goblins within the village.

There are three of them... No, four.

From the goblins' scent, Thorian could tell they were running as a single pack—it would be easy to track them down. Sneering at their obvious mistake, Thorian rushed through the trees and tall grass at his top speed. In less than a minute, the odor of the goblins became more distinct.

Thorian emerged from the patch of trees to find a group of four goblins running through the open space in the center of the village. Upon noticing that Thorian had caught up with them, all but one of the creatures turned and brandished their stone daggers. The last goblin simply stared at the flame kobold in horror, slowly inching backwards while the rest of its kin prepared to launch their final attack.

"Weak little things." Thorian waited until the green creatures rushed towards him before conjuring a fireball and launching it at the incoming goblins. The spell instantly took out the first attacker, sending its charred body flying between its two comrades. The duo glanced back at their fallen kin as Thorian rushed forward, grabbed them by their heads, and smashed them together.

Combustion Touch.

The goblins' facial orifices burst with flames under the influence of Thorian's spell, and they were quickly engulfed in the ensuing explosion. Their bodies didn't even have time to thrash, as their nervous systems were seared by the intense heat.

With only one goblin remaining, Thorian charged at the last survivor, determined to finish the job. However, just as he reached the goblin, the creature immediately dropped to its knees and began shrieking.

"Squii! Shrii!"

Seeing the quivering goblin kneeling and begging for mercy, Thorian conjured a fireball and was about to launch it when a thought crossed his mind.

Wait... It might be useful.

After a few seconds of contemplation, Thorian launched his fireball next to the goblin, causing it to yelp in fear. Its horrified eyes met Thorian's for a moment before it pressed its head to the ground, not daring to maintain eye contact.

"Why should I keep you alive?" Thorian asked, immediately regretting his decision to speak.

"Shrii, squii! Squii Squii!" The goblin looked up and passionately explained all the reasons it deemed sufficient to keep it alive. Unfortunately, Thorian couldn't understand any of them.

Watching the creature try its hardest to convince him, Thorian grinned in amusement.

It's quite the lively goblin... I could have it chop wood alongside the orcs.

As the goblin remained focused on Thorian's expression, trying to decipher its fate, Thorian glanced at the Village Hall behind it.

The kobloids gained proper language once they became citizens. I wonder if it will as well.

With a plan in mind, Thorian looked back at the goblin and said, "Follow me."

Those two words were like an angel's choir to the green creature, as it smiled in happiness and relief. As Thorian strode towards the Village Hall, it excitedly followed behind him.

"Hello, Melina," Thorian entered the Hall and greeted the elven lady. "I have an unusual guest for you today."

Melina furrowed her eyebrows in confusion and inquired, "Who would that be, my lord?" Her question was soon answered as the goblin entered through the door, an ugly grin plastered across its face. Melina's confusion only deepened as she looked at Thorian and asked, "Did you bring this goblin to become a citizen, my lord?"

Thorian simply nodded in response.

The elf opened her mouth to say something, but as the emotions warred in her eyes, she couldn't find the words and simply closed it once more.

"Go to Melina," Thorian ordered the goblin. "And follow her instructions properly."

"Shrii! Shrii!" The goblin nodded with over-the-top enthusiasm. It then walked with careful strides towards the elf before stopping at her desk.

Melina, still shocked by the events unfolding around her, absent-mindedly retrieved the stamp and parchments from beneath her desk and began the procedure.

As with the kobloids, the goblin punctured its thumb with the needle in the stamp and pressed its bloodied finger at the bottom of the parchment. The piece of paper disintegrated into specks of light before being absorbed by the goblin's body.

"Huh? What was that? Magic?"

Hearing the goblin's squeaky voice, Thorian grinned.

That proves it. Any monster that becomes a citizen gains the ability to speak.

The possibilities this discovery unlocked raged within Thorian's mind. With this ability, creating a monster kingdom would not be a dream.

"Good, now that you have learned how to speak, you will go and cut the trees alongside the orcs."

Thorian immediately turned around and walked out of the Village Hall, expecting no complaint or retort against his order. As expected, the goblin nodded and followed him without hesitation.

As the two were walking towards the dense patch of trees where the orcs were chopping wood, the goblin cautiously asked for Thorian's attention.

"Master, forgive me, but may I ask you one thing?"

Thorian furrowed his eyebrows at the goblin's suspiciously servile attitude. "Speak."

"Thank you, master," the goblin said, rubbing its hands together and smiling. "I believe I can be of more use to you than a woodchopper. I came from a large tribe. I can show you where our cave is."

Thorian stopped dead in his tracks at the goblin's words before looking back at it with narrowed eyes. The little green creature had a smile plastered on its face as it gazed at Thorian.

This little thing, Thorian thought, raising an eyebrow in surprise. *Is it really willing to sacrifice its tribe to gain favor with me?*

CHAPTER 31

As Thorian stared at the cunning little goblin, the image of his great-uncle Aldrich superimposed itself onto the green creature. The longer he gazed at it, the more vividly he recalled the treacherous smirk on his betrayer's face in those final moments.

"Shrii! I'm sorry!"

The goblin's high-pitched plea of desperation shattered the illusion, revealing to Thorian the diminutive, retreating green creature as it quivered with fear.

Thorian glanced away and down, only to realize that he had clenched his fist so tightly that his claws had punctured his own palm. He could feel the tension in his face, a menacing fury so intense that the terrified creature couldn't help but beg for its life.

Don't lose your temper, he counseled himself. *He can be useful.*

Thorian took a deep breath and relaxed before looking back at the goblin with a neutral expression. "What's your name?"

The goblin stuttered for a few seconds, regaining his composure, before he answered, "My given name is Skabrixpride, but everyone calls me Brix."

Thorian curtly nodded. "Brix, you will now go and chop trees with the orcs. Is that understood?"

"Yes. Yes, of course!" Brix nodded enthusiastically, relieved that the situation had de-escalated.

With that brief exchange over, Thorian turned and continued

walking through the central part of the village. However, just as they entered a patch of trees, Thorian's stomach let out a rumbling growl.

Surprised by his body's natural reaction, Thorian glanced down at his stomach. *Ah, yes. I haven't eaten anything in the past two days.* He grimaced as he recalled the taste of blood on his tongue. His bestial instincts urged him to hunt and consume a prey's raw flesh, but Thorian refused to let them overpower him.

What kind of sick joke is this? The head of the Steelblade family eating like a savage animal?

While his pride dictated his course of action, reality offered Thorian few alternatives. It was either continuous starvation or swallowing his pride.

However, as he looked back at the wary Brix following him, an idea sparked in Thorian's mind.

Goblins eat cooked meat, don't they.

"Brix," Thorian gestured at the goblin with his head. "Do you have any experience cooking meat?"

"Cooking meat?" Brix's forehead wrinkled in confusion before he nodded hastily. "Yes, of course I can cook. I can prepare the best meals around!"

"Good," Thorian acknowledged with a slight smile. "There aren't any utensils around, so I'll need you to be creative. The thumpalopes' meat should still be safe to cook. It's only been a few hours since I killed them."

"Thumpalopes, master?" Brix asked hesitantly.

"They're large rabbits with twisted goat horns.Have you never seen them before?"

"No, I've never seen them." Brix followed Thorian as he veered away from the direction of the orcs and headed to the right. "But they sound delicious."

The goblin attempted a laugh to break the ice, but Thorian merely glanced at him with a neutral expression. The awkward laughter abruptly ceased as the green creature stiffened, maintaining a safe distance as he trailed behind Thorian.

"You'll skin them, clean them, prepare them, and cook them," Thorian instructed. "My men have been eating their prey raw, but they need to experience the true delicacy of a cooked meal. Make it good."

"Of course, master." Brix nodded ever-so-enthusiastically. "Once they taste my cooking, they'll never want to go back to eating raw meat again."

Thorian remained silent. After about a minute of traversing along the tree line, the pair finally reached the village wall.

This should be the spot.

Thorian turned to Brix and said, "Take my hand."

The goblin hesitated at first but ultimately accepted Thorian's offer. The flame kobold gripped him firmly before leaping atop the wall ledge in a single bound.

As they landed, Brix yelped and exclaimed, "Master is truly strong."

However, Thorian paid him no heed. He knew that Brix was only trying to flatter him because of the precarious situation he'd found himself in.

Instead, Thorian focused on the scene before him, where the dozens of thumpalopes should have been lying dead. What greeted him instead made him pause.

Something was wrong.

Instead of dozens of the giant rabbits, Thorian could only see five of the large creatures scattered on the ground. *Did some thieving scavengers come and take them?*

Thorian grimaced in annoyance before leaping off the wall on his own. One by one, he gathered the dead thumpalopes and tossed them inside the village. However, as he reached the last one, an idea crossed his mind, and a grin spread across his face.

I should leave this one as bait. Let's see who these thieving rats are.

With his plan in mind, Thorian jumped back up the wall and brought Brix down with him. As they reached the ground, Thorian issued his command, "I want you to cook all of these rabbits in the center of the village. I don't care how you do it or where you get your tools from, but if you burn them or make something inedible, you won't have a good time. Understood?"

Brix reflexively flinched, but quickly hid his expression and nodded nervously. "I understand, master. Don't worry, I will cook them properly."

"Good. Now go."

With that final command, Brix grabbed one of the giant rabbits by the leg and, with all his strength, slowly dragged him towards the village center. The thumpalopes weren't quite as tall as goblins, but they were thicker and fluffier. The small creature struggled, attempting to pull a beast whose body was significantly heavier than his own.

While Brix hauled the thumpalope to the center of the village, Thorian leapt back up onto the village wall, casting one last, smirking glance at the flailing Brix.

If he tries to escape, then so be it. He will just be food to the monsters roaming the forest.

With that settled, Thorian shifted his focus to his next objective: meeting up with Nox. He sprang into action, running atop the wall as he kept an eye on both the inside and outside of the village for any unnatural disturbances. The last thing he wanted was for monsters to sneak inside the walls and launch an attack on his men from behind.

After a few minutes of tireless sprinting, the sounds of battle caught Thorian's attention. He instantly increased his speed, and before long, he reached the battlefield.

A pack of twenty rabbarians was engaged in combat with a similarly sized group of brown kobloids, led by a couple of kobolds. However, the latter were at a distinct disadvantage. Only the evolved kobolds could strengthen their hide with their skills to counter the rabbarians' red-aura punches, while the kobloids merely served as punching bags.

However, the disadvantage was short-lived, as a silhouette lunged from the shadows. A tall kobold with midnight-black fur and streaked with silver that shimmered under the moonlight moved with dizzying speed. In but a moment, his body was enveloped in shadows, which then spread and struck a couple of rabbarians. The shadowy aura coated the white, humanoid rabbits from head to toe, where the dark kobold then struck them with his axe, cleaving them in half with a single slash.

Is that Nox? Thorian thought, his face etched with disbelief. *But that's not the appearance of a night kobold. Those streaks... Is he a shadowstalker?*

Just as Thorian finished the thought, three more kobolds emerged from the shadows. Their fur was a pristine silvery-white, and their lithe figures showcased their astounding agility. They too had streaks covering their bodies, only theirs were dark.

The moment the trio touched the ground, their feet shone with brilliant light before they darted across the battlefield. They were like unrelenting arrows claiming the lives of the rabbarians with each strike. Their opponents simply could not fight back, as the silver kobolds' speed left no room for counterattacks.

CHAPTER 32

Thorian watched with bated breath as the tide of the battle turned in their favor. Nox and his three assassins made quick work of the remaining rabbarians, their precise strikes and agile movements stamping out any resistance before it could sprout. The brown kobloids, inspired by their allies' display, pushed their advantage and began to overwhelm the rabbit humanoids. Sensing their impending defeat, the last of the rabbarians fled the battlefield with their tails between their legs.

As the dust settled, Nox called out, "Priests, come and heal our friends!"

The wooden gate opened and the two priest kobloids walked out. They made their way towards the brown kobloids that were bruised and injured from the rabbarians' powerful strikes.

While the priests were tending to the wounded, Nox approached the two brown kobolds, a grin spreading across his face. "You took quite the beating there. You all right?" he teased.

One brown kobold chuckled, flexing his muscles. "Nothing, nothing. Beating more."

The other kobold also used his brown aura technique to showcase his tough body. "Rabbit weak. No injuries." The three kobolds laughed heartily at their jokes.

Thorian, still standing atop the wall, stared down at the scene below in astonishment. A wave of elation washed over him as he realized the significance of Nox's accomplishment. The shadowstalker had managed to forge friendly relationships with the brown kobloids and kobolds. This would be a great boon for their tribe.

You surprise me, Nox. I didn't take you for the diplomatic type.

As Thorian's thoughts raced, the brown kobloids began to notice the figure standing on the wall, illuminated by the moonlight. They murmured in a mix of awe and fear, "Flame kobold..."

The whispers soon reached Nox, the assassins, and the brown kobolds, who all turned their gazes towards Thorian. The air filled with reverence and curiosity.

Nox's eyes lit up with excitement as he recognized Thorian. He beckoned to the three assassins, and together they approached their leader. "Thorian, we won!" he exclaimed in his innocent, youthful tone.

Thorian smiled, pride swelling in his chest. "You all did an excellent job." He then glanced at his evolved comrades, who now matched his height. Their lithe figures perfectly complemented their agile nature. "You have come a long way too. The other kobloids are still far from evolving."

"That's all thanks to Boss Nox!" one of the silver-white kobold assassins exclaimed.

"Boss Nox is really the best," added another with a chuckle.

Thorian tilted his head in confusion before focusing on Nox, who was scratching the back of his head in embarrassment.

"I didn't do much. You guys all worked hard," Nox said modestly.

Hearing Nox's meek voice, the first silvery-white kobold who had spoken earlier immediately jumped on top of him and playfully scratched his furry head. "Don't be so humble, Boss Nox!"

While the two were messing around, the last assassin who hadn't spoken yet looked at Thorian and explained, "Boss Nox gave us all the kills after he evolved. That's how we leveled up so fast."

"His skill really helped too," the second assassin added. "When he places his shadows on the monsters, our axes can cut through them with ease."

A damage amplifier skill? Thorian's brow furrowed as he tried to remember the shadowstalker skills. *Oh, Shadow's Embrace. I forgot about that skill.*

Thorian couldn't help but grin at the possibilities that had just been unlocked. Having access to a damage amplifier skill was something he never expected to happen so soon.

"I've said it before, and I'll say it again: you all have done an amazing job. Your growth has been remarkable," Thorian praised the assassin unit, his eyes lingering on Nox, whose expression betrayed his delight.

Thorian then shifted his gaze towards the brown kobolds, and he couldn't help but frown slightly in confusion. "But how did you meet these new friends?"

"It's a funny story, boss." The assassin who had been scratching Nox's head hopped off his back and laughed. "We found them trying to steal those rabbits we had killed earlier. But just as we were about to have a word with them, a bunch of goblins came out from the woods and ambushed them."

Well, that at least solves the thumpalopes mystery.

The silver-white kobold looked at Nox with a teasing grin before continuing, saying, "Boss Nox wanted us to help them because they're kobolds like us, so we did. And before we knew it, we were already making jokes and became friends."

Nox grumbled at the assassin's teasing tone before adding, "They didn't seem like bad guys. They just wanted food. And they helped us a lot after we teamed up."

"That they did," the third assassin, who was usually quiet, nodded in agreement with Nox's statement before letting out a sigh. "Guarding the wall was much easier with more people."

Thorian stayed silent as Nox and the silvery kobolds then explained their strategy with the brown kobolds, waiting to see if he could pick up any interesting nuances.

From what Nox relayed, it seemed that the bulk of their small army was situated in front of the southern gate, where they currently were, diametrically opposite to Forlune, who was near the northern gate. Nox and the assassins left the task of guarding this part of the wall mostly to the brown kobolds while they scouted the southeast and southwest sides. It was only when dealing with truly strong opponents, like the rabbarians, that all of them would concentrate their efforts in one spot.

That explains why things have been going relatively smoothly. I expected at least one big hole in the wall after spending two hours cultivating.

Nox and the assassins being so dependable filled Thorian with pride and relief. Having competent people beside him who wouldn't require his input for every decision was a luxury he hadn't expected this early. And witnessing these once-kobloids, whom he had initially dismissed as weak creatures, transform into reliable subordinates was a pleasant surprise.

Nevertheless, while he appreciated Nox's actions, Thorian still couldn't fully trust the brown kobolds. He studied them out of the corner of his eye as a plan formulated in his mind.

I should make them citizens, but they shouldn't get a class yet. Let's wait and see where their hearts truly lie.

Noticing Thorian's gaze on the brown kobolds, Nox shifted his attention to his two newfound friends and called for them to join. "Brown kobolds, come here."

As the two approached after being healed by the priest, Nox introduced them. "This is Thorian, our king. Like I told you before, he's the one who made us strong."

One of the brown kobolds nodded at Nox's admiring explanation before staring at Thorian with wide eyes. "You... flame kobold?" he asked, his voice filled with awe and disbelief.

Thorian furrowed his eyebrows at the unexpected question before nodding. "Yes, I am."

The other brown kobold chimed in, excitement laced in his words. "Flame kobold strong. Me saw one. Powerful!"

Although the kobold's fragmented sentences were difficult to decipher, Thorian had grown accustomed to them after spending a full night with Nox before he'd become a citizen. However, it was the meaning behind their words that truly puzzled him.

"You saw a flame kobold before? Where?"

"Back home," the brown kobold responded with a reminiscing look. "Flame kobold many killed. Forest all fire."

Back home, huh? Thorian scratched his chin in thought. *So like those people that appear with the buildings, these monsters have come from another world?*

Although Thorian was curious to learn more, now wasn't the time for such a discussion. He had more pressing matters to attend to.

"Did you like your stay here?" Thorian probed, cautiously observing the brown kobolds' facial expressions.

"Me like!" The first brown kobold laughed heartily. "Me hunt, me eat! Nox no take food. Nox friend!"

The other kobold also lightly chuckled but didn't say anything.

Seeing the two's genuine attitude, Thorian slightly relaxed. While the possibility that they were only faking their expressions was always present, kobolds were not known for their cunning nature. They were usually painfully honest creatures.

"If you like it here, then why don't you become true citizens?" Thorian proposed. "It will give you many benefits."

"Great idea!" Nox excitedly remarked. "They can speak better then. It will make it so much easier to talk."

"Citizens?" The brown kobold furrowed his eyebrows before looking at Nox for advice. "Good?"

"Yeah, it's very good," the shadowstalker nodded with excitement. "It will help us a lot."

"Nox says good. Good!" The other brown kobold heartily laughed. "Citizen become."

CHAPTER 33

Thorian led the two brown kobolds back to the village hall, where they would be officially initiated as citizens. Their trusty and ever-elegant elven receptionist, Melina, greeted them with a warm smile.

"Ah, my lord. More citizens to join our ranks?" she inquired, her voice soft and melodic, betraying an air of familiarity with the various creatures that had approached her desk that day.

Thorian noticed the subtle change in her demeanor but chose not to remark upon it. Instead, he glanced back at the two brown kobolds, who were curiously surveying their surroundings. "Yes, these two fine gentlemen have expressed a desire to join our community."

"Citizen, here?" One of the brown kobolds asked, venturing further into the hall, his eyes wide with wonder.

"Yes, please come here." Melina gently beckoned the two brown creatures to her desk, where she had already prepared the stamp needle and citizenship parchments. After pricking their thumbs with the needle and pressing the parchments with their blood, the two kobolds became official citizens. As the golden dust settled, their eyes cleared, and they gazed at Melina and Thorian.

"Did we become citizens now?" one of them inquired.

"Yeah, was that it?" the other chimed in.

Thorian chuckled lightly at the exchange. "Yes, you are now proper citizens of Wolvendale Village. Congratulations."

"Oh, I can understand you clearly now," the brown kobold remarked, raising his eyebrows in surprise, his companion mirroring his reaction.

"Well, the feeling is mutual," Thorian replied before turning towards the door. "Let's return to the gates. We'll need the rest of your group to come here as well."

The two kobolds nodded and followed Thorian outside the hall. As they meandered through the quaint village, one of the kobolds couldn't resist asking, "Is there more to this citizenship?"

"There are additional benefits, but those will come later," Thorian explained, not breaking stride. "For now, simply being able to communicate effectively is more than enough. Isn't it better now that you can fully understand me?"

"That is indeed true," the kobold acknowledged. "You seem wise, flame kobold, much like the elders back in our cave."

"My name is Thorian. You may address me by my name," the flame kobold said, casting a brief glance at the two before continuing. "And what cave are you referring to?"

"It's our little home in this world," the brown kobold revealed with a sigh. "Our entire tribe lives there, under the rule of our chief."

Thorian nodded, allowing a brief silence to settle between them as they walked. He could sense the somber mood in the air.

"Were there issues within your tribe?" he finally inquired, prompting a lengthy sigh from the brown kobold.

"Of course there were. The chief took half our food." He clicked his tongue and shook his head, clearly disheartened by the memory.

Observing his friend's agitation, the other kobold chimed in. "That fat tyrant, his body could feed the entire tribe."

As the two conversed and exchanged jests, Thorian asked a more pointed question. "Is your chief strong?"

The response was a mere gulp. The two kobolds fell silent, but their reticence spoke volumes to Thorian. He looked ahead, realizing they were nearing the southern gate, where the two priests stood on standby beside the watchtowers.

This is a heaven-sent opportunity, Thorian mused, scratching his furred chin in contemplation. *If their chief is such a despot that his own men would rather remain with strangers than return to him, the entire tribe will soon crumble.*

A sly grin tugged at the corner of Thorian's mouth.

And when that happens, I'll be there to capitalize.

The clamor of battle reached Thorian's ears even before he opened the gate. Outside, the brown kobolds were locked in combat with a horde of goblins, commanded by spear-wielding hobgoblins. Nox and the three assassins dealt with the more-formidable green adversaries, while the brown kobolds managed to overwhelm the smaller, weaker goblins.

As the battle drew to a close, Thorian and the two brown kobolds approached Nox and the assassins.

"Ah, Thorian!" Nox, the shadowstalker, exclaimed in his innocent voice, noticing his king. His eyes flicked to the brown kobolds. "And you two! Did you become citizens?"

"Yes, we did." The two brown kobolds chuckled as they strode towards Nox. Thorian could see how much more at ease they were in the company of the guileless shadowstalker. "It's so much easier to understand you now. My head hurt whenever we talked before!"

"Same here, my friend. It was so difficult to comprehend you two," Nox laughed along before turning to Thorian. "So, what's our next move?"

Thorian surveyed the battlefield. As usual, the priests moved among the brown kobolds, tending to the wounded. Meanwhile, the three silvery-white assassins sat on the ground, catching their breath.

With a strategy forming in his mind, Thorian turned to Nox and explained, "I need you to instruct the three assassins to escort the brown kobloids to the village hall, where they can become citizens. The four of us, along with the two priests, will remain here to guard the wall."

"Ah, we're going to fight together?" Nox's face lit up at Thorian's words. "Yes! It's been so long!"

Thorian chuckled at his follower's endearing reaction. "What do you mean, 'It's been so long'? It has been just a little over two hours."

"Yeah, but I wasn't evolved back then. Now I can show you my true skills!" Nox replied excitedly, while the two brown kobolds chuckled at the exchange. The shadowstalker then turned towards the three assassins and declared, "I'll go tell them to get moving. Their break has been long enough."

As Nox strode towards the group of assassins, Thorian took a moment to clear his thoughts and devise a plan for the future.

First and foremost, I need to focus on my personal growth. It doesn't matter if I have to slay monsters or humans. I simply must become stronger. The secondary priority is leveling up the village. We don't have enough registered citizens yet, but we can still upgrade the statues to proper guilds.

Absorbed in his contemplations, Thorian glanced around to see the pack of kobolds following the three assassins into the village. *The final part of the plan is assimilation. We need to reach one hundred registered citizens to upgrade the village.*

As their comrades passed through the gate, the two brown kobolds sidled up to Thorian and inquired, "Is there something we need to do now that we're citizens? Share our food?"

"Everything you hunt is yours," Thorian said with a chuckle. "Believe me, you'll have so much food you won't know what to do with it all."

As Thorian and the two kobolds bantered playfully, the brown kobolds filed into the village and the gates closed. Nox, who had been attentively monitoring the operation, returned to the trio.

Thorian glanced at the approaching black kobold and remarked, "Good timing. We were just about to discuss our defense strategy."

"Oh? That sounds interesting. Strategy..."

Unfazed by Nox's child-like enthusiasm, Thorian voiced his concerns. "Our current approach to defense is, at best, clumsy. Concentrating most of our military force at the two poles while leaving our east and west sides virtually unprotected is unwise."

"Should we split the two groups in half, then?" one of the brown kobolds suggested. "That way, we can station one team in the west and the other in the east."

"That's one possibility," Thorian acknowledged. "But the north side has its own challenges to contend with, and dividing their forces might invite more trouble than we're prepared to handle."

There are still the orcs on that side. I cannot be naive and weaken the north.

"I believe the two of you should manage the west and the east," Thorian proposed, catching the brown kobolds off guard. "You'll divide your pack in half, and each oversee one side."

The pair exchanged glances before addressing Thorian. "Since the kobloids have leveled up significantly, we shouldn't have trouble against weaker creatures like goblins. But if a large horde of them appears or if any particularly strong monsters come by, I'm not sure we'll be able to handle them on our own."

"You don't need to worry about that," Thorian assured them with a smile. "The way you've been handling the defense hasn't been very strategic. Typically, an army should stand behind the wall, not in front of it. You should only venture out if you're confident you can manage the threats beyond."

"But then how will we see what's happening outside?" The brown kobold inquired, puzzled by Thorian's line of thinking.

"You can use those," Thorian said, indicating the two watchtowers flanking the gate. "By climbing the watchtowers, you can get a clear view of what's happening outside without exposing yourselves to unnecessary danger."

"Oh! You are indeed wise and knowledgeable," the brown kobold marveled at the watchtowers before praising Thorian. "I don't think even the elders would have known such a thing."

"This is nothing for Thorian. He knows everything," Nox responded, pride swelling in his voice as if Thorian's accomplishments were his own.

Thorian dismissed the excessive compliments with a shake of his head. Then, his ears caught a sound from the forest. His eyes immediately shifted towards the shadowy woods in the distance, where a tall silhouette emerged from beyond the trees.

It had a lithe, inhuman figure, with a diminutive core and torso that contrasted with its length and size. Its limbs extended into scythe-like claws, and its face featured twitching mandibles, eager to tear into the flesh of its victims.

Is that a thri-kreen?

CHAPTER 34

Nox's gaze followed Thorian's, his eyes narrowing as he spotted the danger lurking in the shadows. "What's that thing?"

As he took a step forwards to investigate, Thorian's arm shot out, halting him.

"Stop. That thing is dangerous."

Thorian's eyes remained locked on the thri-kreen emerging from the dark forest. Bathed in moonlight, the creature's immense, mantis-like body came into focus. Its green exoskeleton was adorned with brown markings, but what caught Thorian's attention was the absence of any purple streaks.

Good, it's not a psion, he thought with a sigh of relief. *We can handle a warrior-type without too much trouble.*

The thri-kreen clattered its mandibles, emitting a menacing hiss as it readied itself for battle. Its powerful thighs tensed, reminiscent of a tightly coiled Roman slingshot.

Noticing that the creature was poised to attack, a brown kobold bravely stepped forward, intent on blocking the oncoming assault. Thorian had no time to react before the thri-kreen sprang into action.

Swish!

With agility rivaling even Nox's, the colossal mantis charged at the brown kobold. In response, the defender raised his guard and fortified his forearms with his Rocky Armor skill.

The thri-kreen leapt into the air, its silhouette framed by the luminous moon. Its razor-sharp claws gleamed silver as it descended upon the kobold. Bracing for impact, the defender ensured his rocky arms covered his vital organs. Alas, the creature's claws proved too sharp.

Shring!

The thri-kreen's gleaming claws tore through the kobold's rocky armor with a resounding crash, sinking into the flesh beneath. Just as it seemed the kobold would lose his arms, a shadowy figure darted in from the side, delivering a powerful kick that sent the creature reeling.

Thorian, having prepared his Waterball spell, seized the opening provided by Nox. He unleashed his attack on the thri-kreen before it could regain its footing. A tremendous splash followed as the gargantuan mantis was hurled backward, creating an opening for another strike. Nox pounced on the opportunity, slamming his axe into the falling behemoth and shattering one of its colossal claws.

As Nox noticed Thorian advancing beside him, he activated his Shadow skill and enveloped the wounded thri-kreen in a cloak of darkness. Thorian closed in, his hand ablaze with fiery red energy.

Combustion Touch.

Thorian's inferno enveloped the thri-kreen in a hellish blaze. After a final, feeble struggle, the colossal mantis succumbed to the flames.

As Nox's shadows receded, the thri-kreen's charred remains collapsed into a heap. All that lingered were Thorian's searing flames and the remnants of steam from the earlier waterball.

"Brother, are you okay?"

Thorian looked over to see the brown kobold attending to his injured sibling. Blood stained the wounded kobold's brown fur a deep crimson, and Thorian caught a glimpse of white bone through the torn flesh.

"I'm okay," the injured kobold gasped through the pain. "That bastard cut through my armor like it was nothing."

"Priests, come out and help!" Thorian called beyond the gate before he and Nox approached the injured kobold.

Visibly concerned, Nox hurried to his wounded friend and asked, "Are you okay? Is it just a flesh wound?"

"Thank you, Nox." The brown kobold managed a pained smile. "If you hadn't helped me, I'd have lost both my arms."

"Still..." Nox gazed down at his friend with sadness as a kobloid priest hurried to the scene.

"Healing." The white kobloid invoked his spell, and golden light emanated from his hand, tenderly enveloping the brown kobold's wound. Gradually, flesh mended, concealing the exposed bone, while veins reconnected, and the skin fully healed.

"Huh." The brown kobold flexed his forearm, rotating it left and right to ensure its proper function. "Much better." He looked at the kobloid priest with gratitude. "Thank you, you saved me."

"That skill is truly a miracle," the other brown kobold remarked with an impressed whistle. He glanced at his healed brother and teased, "You would have become a cripple without it."

"I would still have had my other arm. I'd have no problem beating you up with just one."

The concerned brother shook his head and clicked his tongue at the playful retort. "I can't believe you're still in the mood to talk smack after almost losing your arm."

As the brown kobolds bantered and laughed with Nox, the once-injured kobold's expression turned thoughtful. "But how did that bastard break through my rocky armor? Are its claws just that sharp?"

"That's its skill," Thorian explained. "That giant mantis is called a thri-kreen warrior. One of its abilities is armor-breaking, which is why it could slash through your skill with ease."

The two brown kobolds stared at Thorian, their mouths agape, before casting their gazes downwards. "That is a concerning thought. To think that there are skills that can bypass our armor so easily."

"That depends on the strength of your armor," Thorian countered. "If it were much stronger, the thri-kreen wouldn't have been able to break through."

The brown kobold looked up at Thorian with an arched brow before bursting into hearty laughter. "So you're saying we just need to become stronger, and we won't have to worry about it. I like that."

"That is the one rule of this world." Thorian shrugged before changing subjects. "Anyway, now that you're healed, we need to move.

"We will patrol along the village wall," he said, turning to Nox. "You'll cover the east side, and I'll take the west. You two brown kobolds will keep watch from the watchtower at this gate. If you spot monsters approaching, engage them if you think you can defeat them, but stay inside if you can't. It doesn't matter if the wall is breached. Your lives are more important."

The two kobolds took a moment to process the orders before nodding, while Nox gazed at Thorian with a hint of sadness. "So we're not going to fight together?"

Caught off guard by the unexpected response, Thorian's mouth hung open for a few seconds before he chuckled. "It's just until the assassins and the brown kobloid army return. After that, we'll fight together."

Nox reluctantly nodded and then turned his attention to the two brown kobolds. "See you in a bit, you two."

"Don't die," one replied.

With a light chuckle, Nox and Thorian sprang up onto the wall. They then sprinted along the ledge, each heading in opposite directions.

While patrolling the village, Thorian encountered goblins, chaskas, thumpalopes, and rabbarians. Fortunately, he didn't come across any group too large or powerful for him to handle. Employing his Fireball and Waterball spells, he bombarded his foes with ranged attacks before closing in and finishing the job with his Combustion Touch.

It took forty minutes for the group that had ventured to the village hall to return to the southern gate. During that time, Thorian successfully leveled up both his magus class and his flame kobold race.

Display panel.

Ding!

Race: Flame Kobold

Level: 4/30 (XP: 30/650)

Class: Magus

Level: 18/20 (XP: 230/450)

Lifespan: 40 years

Cultivation Realm: Qi Gathering Second Stage (5.3%)

Stats:

Strength: 43

Agility: 47

Constitution: 24

Mana: 54

Qi: 14

Free Points: 9

Skills:

Minor Fire Affinity (passive)

Flame Resistance (passive)

Fireball (active)

Combustion Touch (active)

Waterball (active)

So I have nine free points left? I should leave them be for now. They can prove useful in a pinch.

Upon checking his system panel, Thorian quickly refocused on the scene unfolding before him. The small brown kobloid army was making its way towards the southern gates, guided by the three assassins. Now that they possessed enhanced language abilities, the kobloids were more talkative than ever, engaging in ceaseless whispering, laughter, and conversation.

As Thorian observed the brown kobloid group, he spotted an intriguing interloper—a small, green humanoid who fidgeted nervously, glancing left and right.

Brix?

Thorian raised an eyebrow and smiled at the unexpected presence. However, he remained silent and simply watched from a distance.

As the group of brown kobloids neared the gates, the green creature caught sight of Thorian standing atop the wall, and its face lit up with recognition.

"Master, I was looking for you!" Brix called out.

Thorian furrowed his brow. "I thought I had already given you your orders. Did you already cook the thumpalopes?"

"About that…" Brix scratched the back of his head. "It's been raining a lot, and the rocks and branches are all wet. It's very hard to start a fire."

The frown between Thorian's eyebrows deepened even further at the goblin's excuse. "So? Are you not going to follow my orders, then?"

"No, of course I will!" Brix exclaimed, then continued in a quieter, more timid voice. "I was just wondering if you could help me a little. If you could use your spell to start a fire, it would help me a lot!"

Thorian thought for a bit before concluding, *It is not an unreasonable demand.*

"Sure, I can help you," he agreed, much to Brix's delight. He then glanced at the watchtower where the brown kobold stood. "Split the group as we discussed earlier and stay here. You can move to the east and west gates after I return."

"Sure. You got it, Thorian," the kobold replied.

With the matter settled, Thorian jumped down to join Brix and said, "Lead the way."

The little, green creature happily scampered through the forest, with Thorian following closely behind. After passing through a dense patch of trees and reaching the center of the village, Thorian was greeted by an unusual contraption.

Two large and sturdy branches supported an orc chest plate above them, like a makeshift pot. Beneath the chest plate were several branches, arranged to resemble a fire pit.

"Are you going to use the chest plate to cook the thumpalopes?" Thorian asked, turning towards Brix.

The goblin, proud of his resourcefulness, smiled and said, "Yeah, I found them in the village hall and thought it would work well as a pot!"

Thorian sighed heavily at the goblin's shortsightedness before pointing out the significant flaw in his plan. "What about the sweat? Are you going to cook thumpalopes with orc sweat flavor on top?"

Realizing his mistake, Brix yelped and stepped back, fearing Thorian's retaliation. However, Thorian could only shake his head at the goblin's simplistic thought process.

No matter how shrewd, a goblin is still a goblin.

Silently, Thorian removed the chestplate from the two branches and placed it on the ground. He then conjured his Waterball spell and launched it at the inside of the makeshift pot.

With a loud splash, the force of the resulting waterball caused the chestplate to sink into the ground beneath it. But Thorian wasn't finished. He conjured a fireball and launched it inside the chestplate.

Following a small explosion, the water transformed into vapor and steam, which enveloped the area. Unfazed, Thorian walked through the hot steam, retrieved the orc chestplate, and sniffed it.

Still has the smell of sweat.

Thorian launched his spells one after the other until the smell was purged from the makeshift pot. The chestplate was deformed in some spots due to the temperature shock, but Thorian wasn't concerned about that. The smell was a far greater issue.

With the task completed, Thorian glanced back at the goblin, whose eyes sparkled with amazement. "Can you handle the flames without burning the whole place down?"

The dazed goblin took a few seconds before nodding. "Yes! Yes, I can."

"I hope so," Thorian said with a click of his tongue, then turned back to the pitiful-looking fire pit Brix had created. He conjured a fireball and launched it a couple of meters to the side of the firepit.

"Use that fire to light up your pit," he instructed, glancing back.

Eagerly, Brix sprang into action, removing branches from his firepit and lighting them using Thorian's fire before using the smaller branches to ignite the entire pit. Once done, he placed the chestplate on top of the larger branches and fetched the thumpalope pieces he had cut up and placed on a leaf bed nearby.

At least he skinned them well. I guess he is not too useless after all.

Seeing that things were progressing smoothly, Thorian used his Waterball spell to extinguish the fire he had started earlier before heading back towards the southern gate. Dusk was approaching, and the day was about to begin. It was sure to be a long day, without a moment to catch their breath.

CHAPTER 35

Thorian settled onto the wall's ledge, surveying his surroundings. Just moments ago, the area had been teeming with kobloids, but now, they had dispersed to the east and west gates under the guidance of the two brown kobolds.

Now that I think about it, I should give them names too. It gets tiring calling the both of them "brown kobold."

The three silvery-white assassins were also nowhere in sight. They had gone to patrol the perimeter of the wall under Thorian's orders, lending support to all four sections. Recalling their unique appearance, Thorian's expression grew thoughtful.

I wonder what evolution they received. Their form doesn't look like that of a normal white kobold, especially with those black streaks decorating their fur.

As Thorian lost himself in thought, the sky above transformed into a mesmerizing tapestry of hues. Dusk descended upon the landscape, bathing everything in warm shades of orange and pink. The sun's final rays danced along the horizon, gracefully outlining the clouds before disappearing beneath the skyline.

This stunning vista stood in stark contrast to the reek of death that hung heavy in the forest. The putrid scent of decaying corpses and congealed blood, mingling with the saturated soil, served as a haunting reminder of the apocalypse. It was an evolutionary hellscape, where only the most ruthless emerged triumphant, and emperors reigned over realms of devastation.

"Thorian, we have some guests," Nox called out from the watchtower, pointing to their right. Following his gesture, Thorian spotted a small group of goblins charging towards the wall, ropes clutched in their hands.

Without hesitation, Thorian summoned a Fireball spell and unleashed it upon the hapless creatures. Nox swiftly followed Thorian's assault, closing in on the goblins with an almost supernatural speed. Caught off guard, the goblins could only flail helplessly as the shadowstalker's axe cleaved through them with ruthless efficiency.

What a strange weapon for an assassin, Thorian couldn't help but chuckle at the sight. *Hopefully we'll get some good gear once we challenge the dungeons.*

As Thorian contemplated the dungeons, a subtle grin crept onto his face. The Wolvendale territory, or Raven's Nest as it was known in his previous life, was highly coveted not just because of the Ether Lines Nexus attribute, but also due to the dungeons that surrounded it. These dungeons were a veritable treasure trove for anyone who ruled over the territory.

Still, we need to solve the issues here first. The orcs should bring enough wood to upgrade all the statues in a few more hours, but it's the hundred-citizen requirement that's truly putting a wrench in our wheels. We need to upgrade the village so that we can gain access to better walls.

Thorian clicked his tongue and lowered his gaze, lost in contemplation. Though numerous opportunities awaited beyond the village, he knew he couldn't leave, at least not yet.

Once our main force evolves to kobolds, our defenses should be strong enough that my presence wouldn't be absolutely required. I can then go explore the dungeons or start on all the quests I have already gathered.

Time passed as Thorian and Nox guarded the southern gate together. With their combined might, none of the forest monsters managed to breach the walls. The pair decimated chaskas and their evolved form, tailmashers, as well as goblin and rabbarian hordes. Two more thri-kreens emerged from the dense forest, but with their previous experience, Nox and Thorian had no trouble dispatching them.

After three hours, Thorian had leveled up twice in his magus class and three times in his flame kobold race. Just as he was about to check his system panel, he heard footsteps approaching.

Glancing to the right, Thorian saw one of the assassins running towards him and Nox, a pleased expression on his face.

"The magi! The magi have evolved!" the assassin announced breathlessly as he raced towards the pair.

"Finally?" Nox raised an eyebrow as the kobold reached them. "Took them long enough. Have they been slacking?"

The assassin couldn't help but chuckle at the response. "Boss, we only advanced so quickly because of your help. They couldn't hunt as effectively in the north. But enough about that." He shook his head, his expression brightening as he turned to Thorian. "One of them evolved into a flame kobold, just like you, boss!"

"Oh wow, another flame kobold!" Nox exclaimed, while Thorian's eyebrow lifted in pleasant surprise.

So it's like I thought. The skills you use are what determines your evolution path.

Thorian's smile widened at the incredible news. Having another flame kobold on their side would help them immensely, especially in freeing up the assassins who wouldn't need to spend most of their time on the east and west sides assisting the brown kobloids.

"What about the other magi? What did they evolve into?" Thorian inquired curiously. While having a flame kobold was great news, he was already familiar with that race's abilities and powers. He was most curious about the other evolutions.

"They evolved into their specific elements," the assassin replied curtly. "Water, wind, and earth."

"Oh, how do they look? Are they cool?!" Nox, excited by the new evolutions, couldn't help but exclaim his emotions.

"The water one is blue, the wind one is yellow, and the earth one is dark brown. As for their abilities, I haven't seen them yet, boss."

Nox turned towards Thorian and stared at him with expectant eyes. Thorian obviously understood that Nox wanted to go and see the newly evolved kobolds with his own eyes.

"We can't yet," Thorian said, shaking his head as he focused back on the assassin. "What about the rest of the kobloids? Did they evolve yet?"

"Not yet. But they're close! I think in, uh, half an hour or so, they should evolve too."

Thorian grinned at the good news before looking back at Nox, "Then we can meet up with them in half an hour."

"Yay!" Nox jumped up in joy. "I wonder what kind of skills they'll have. I'm sure they will be really cool!"

Both Thorian and the assassin rolled their eyes at Nox's theatrics. The matching reaction from the assassin made Thorian chuckle softly, but he reigned in his amusement to issue his orders. "Go see what the orcs have been up to and report on their progress. Once the other kobloids evolve, return with four capable, evolved kobolds to stand guard here while we investigate the northern gate. Understood?"

"You got it, boss!" The assassin offered Thorian a two-fingered salute before executing a backflip off the wall and into the village.

What a showoff. Thorian shook his head as the assassin vanished into the dense foliage. He then turned back to Nox, who was still clenching his fist in anticipation of the new evolutions.

In a way, Nox's enthusiasm touched Thorian. The fact that he was so thrilled by the evolution of his brethren revealed Nox's true nature. Despite having been virtually ostracized just days earlier, he was now wholeheartedly supporting his group.

I suppose he's still a child at heart.

Taking a deep breath, Thorian redirected his attention from the black kobold to his own progress.

Display panel.

Ding!

Race: Flame Kobold

Level: 7/30 (XP: 15/840)

Class: Magus

Level: 20/20 (XP: MAX)

Lifespan: 40 years

Cultivation Realm: Qi Gathering Second Stage (5.3%)

Stats:

Strength: 47

Agility: 52

Constitution: 27

Mana: 57

Qi: 14

Free Points: 15

Skills:

Minor Fire Affinity (passive)

Flame Resistance (passive)

Fireball (active)

Combustion Touch (active)

Waterball (active)

Now that Thorian had reached the limit of his class, he needed to attain maximum proficiency in all four skills before he could pursue class advancement. With this realization, he turned his attention to examining the proficiency of each skill.

Fireball: You conjure a fiery orb and hurl it at your enemies, leaving them charred and weakened.

Proficiency: 100%

Waterball: You summon a watery orb and launch it at your enemies, drenching them and knocking them off balance.

Proficiency: 23.5%

Still quite a long way to go, and I haven't even started with the two last skills yet.

Reflecting on the final two starting skills, Wind Gust and Rock Bullet, Thorian scratched his chin as he considered their cost. Each skill carried a price tag of five hundred arcane coins. Although he could purchase one of them using the rewards from his quests, he would still come up short for the other.

I suppose I need to go to the dungeons, then.

CHAPTER 36

As Thorian and Nox approached the northern gates, the shadowstalker clenched his fists, barely containing his excitement. "Inly looked so cool after his evolution!" he exclaimed, glancing at Thorian. "Those red tattoos on his face—savage!"

Nox's infectious enthusiasm brought a smile to Thorian's face. Reflecting on the image of the transformed warrior, he couldn't help but draw a comparison to the berserker class.

That might be a good class advancement for them.

Contemplating the potential that lay before them, Thorian's own excitement grew. Assembling a full squad of kobloid berserkers at this early stage of the apocalypse could pave the way for future glory.

Returning to the present, Thorian and Nox arrived at the northern section of the village. Like a relentless swarm of termites, the orcs methodically stripped away the forest that stood before the gates, clearing an unobstructed view towards the village hall.

"Wow, they're fast!" Nox marveled. "We spent the whole afternoon cutting trees, but they've already cut so much more than us."

Thorian nodded, his smile reflecting their impressive progress. With this much, they should have enough wood to upgrade the last three statues into guilds. The only requirement left would be to have a hundred registered citizens.

He scratched his chin, contemplating the brown kobloids. *I want them all to evolve into proper kobolds before we approach their tribe. That would make the negotiations significantly easier.*

As the two neared the gates, they discovered the group of newly evolved kobolds gathered within the village, exchanging jokes and laughter. The warriors retained their distinct white color, but their faces and bodies were now embellished with tribalistic red tattoos.

Forlune sat among them, but he no longer exuded the same aura of strength and power he once had. The kobolds were now as large and powerful as him, if not more so, rendering his appearance rather ordinary in comparison.

Though the moon kobold laughed and conversed with the others, his energy seemed subdued. His gaze would occasionally drift into the distance, and his posture lacked the commanding presence it once held.

"Is he okay?" Nox observed the moon kobold's unusual demeanor and whispered to Thorian. The latter merely shook his head and continued walking towards the group.

"Forlune," Thorian called out, capturing the kobold's attention. "Everyone, I see you have all evolved."

"Fighting those monsters is so much easier now, King," Bellafor proudly declared, flexing his enhanced muscles.

"I never thought our evolution would be this good," Crimen added, turning to Thorian and offering a respectful bow. "It's all thanks to you, My King."

Thorian surveyed the group of warriors, his eyebrows knitting together in concern. Including Forlune, there were only three of them.

"Where is Caedar?" No matter where he looked, Thorian couldn't locate the final warrior—the one who had placed second in the woodcutting competition and displayed the most potential among the kobloids.

At Thorian's question, the two warriors exchanged glances, leaving Forlune to provide an explanation. "He was badly injured."

The moon kobold rose to his feet, directing his gaze towards the rightmost watchtower. "The healer priest is taking care of him right now."

"Is he okay?" Nox inquired, concern evident in his voice as Thorian and Forlune strode towards the watchtower. Sensing the change in atmosphere, the shadowstalker trailed quietly behind them.

Upon reaching the base of the watchtower, Thorian discovered the kobloid priest tending to Caedar, who was lying on the ground. The priest chanted a spell, focused on his patient.

Noticing Thorian's approach, the priest offered an explanation. "The bleeding has stopped, but his arm is gone."

Thorian's eyes fell upon Caedar, who emitted pained, labored breaths. His arm had been cleanly severed at the elbow, and the wound was now sealed thanks to the priest's healing skill.

"I'm sorry, King." Caedar managed a pained smile as he looked at Thorian. "I have become a cripple."

Thorian closed his eyes and took a deep breath. *Well, I cannot say that was unexpected.* He then glanced at Forlune, who wore an expression of both shame and sadness. *But they were still your responsibility.*

"What happened?" Thorian asked Forlune, seeking answers. "How did things come to this?"

"It was that giant mantis," Forlune sighed and explained. "Half an hour ago, just after the magi evolved, the giant mantis appeared and caught us off guard. It was incredibly swift. By the time Ventus could react, it had already taken Caedar's arm."

Thorian nodded at Forlune's explanation, deciding not to probe any further. *If it was a thri-kreen, then it was understandable. Without a proper grasp of its strengths and weaknesses, it might be one of the most challenging monsters to fight in the forest at the moment, at least among the normal ones.*

Thorian glanced back down at Caedar, pondering the situation as he scratched his chin. Nox, on the other hand, could only fidget in silence while Thorian was lost in thought.

If it's just one arm, then it shouldn't be too much of a problem. Good thing it happened recently, too.

With a strategy in mind, Thorian turned to the group and declared, "From now on, do not kill any of the monsters that come knocking at our doors. Strip them of their limbs and allow Caedar to deliver the final blow."

All eyes were fixed on Thorian as he outlined his plan, a mixture of confusion and curiosity filling their expressions as they tried to understand his reasoning.

"King... why?" Caedar inquired weakly.

"You'll find out soon enough," Thorian replied, casting a reassuring smile at the injured warrior. "Just rest for now."

Forlune, initially taken aback by Thorian's plan, quickly adapted and regained his composure. He addressed the two bewildered warriors, saying, "You heard our king's orders. Let's move."

"Understood, boss." Crimen acknowledged, nodding at Forlune as he and the other warrior trailed behind the moon kobold. The trio effortlessly scaled the wall in just a few steps, while Thorian observed from the side, pleased.

He is shaping up in his role quite nicely.

Impressed by Forlune's demeanor, Thorian turned to Nox and suggested, "Shall we head upstairs?"

Nox, who had remained silent throughout, eagerly nodded in agreement. "Yeah, let's go!"

Thorian chuckled softly at his companion's enthusiasm before they both ascended the watchtower stairs. Reaching the top, they found Ventus and Aqua surveying the battlefield below.

"You're looking sharp, Ventus," Thorian praised the light yellow kobold—a coloration he had rarely seen among their kind.

He then turned his attention to the blue kobold, adding, "You too, Aqua."

"Thank you for the compliment, my lord," Aqua replied with a graceful bow, his words imbued with an uncommon elegance rarely encountered among kobolds and kobloids.

"You too, King!" Ventus boomed with a hearty laugh. "We're looking good, but you two are looking even better!"

Feeling bashful from the compliment, Nox scratched his head and laughed. "Thank you!"

Meanwhile, Thorian simply smiled and joined the two magi as they gazed out from the watchtower. Below, the group of warriors stood by the wall, poised for any ill-fated creature that might dare approach.

"I'm curious. What kind of skill did you acquire from your evolution?" Thorian asked the pair.

Ventus' expression swelled with pride at Thorian's question. "I think it's better if I show you, King!"

The yellow kobold extended his arm, pointing his palm towards the forest. Taking a deep breath, he bellowed, "Gale Slash!"

A crescent wave of wind surged from the watchtower, slicing cleanly through several sizable trees.

"Wow! It's so powerful!" Nox cheered. Ventus basked in the praise, scratching his nose.

"Did you have to shout the name, though?" Aqua sighed, casting a disappointed glance at the wind magus.

"No, but it does sound cool that way!" Ventus replied, bubbling with excitement.

As the trio bantered, Thorian nodded in appreciation of Ventus' skill, deep in thought as he scratched his chin.

"Gale Slash is a very useful skill," Thorian remarked, much to the wind magus' delight.

"I know, right? It cut through that big mantis immediately! But it does use up quite a bit of mana, though."

Thorian nodded at Ventus' explanation, then continued sharing his thoughts. "That is a good use for the skill, indeed. But I think I have a better one."

Ventus raised an eyebrow, curiosity piqued. "And what is that, King?"

"Cutting trees."

CHAPTER 37

A few seconds of silence passed as Thorian and Ventus exchanged glances. Thorian's gaze held a mix of interest and gravity, while Ventus looked incredulous.

The wind magus chuckled nervously. "That was quite the joke, King. You have a great sense of humor."

Thorian's furrowed brow at Ventus' response made the latter gulp in anticipation. "I don't joke about such matters, Ventus," the flame kobold stated in a low, controlled voice, emphasizing the finality of his words. He then glanced back at the fallen trees in the distance, a smile gracing his lips. "Gale Slash is the ideal skill for the job. It sliced through four large trees more cleanly than an axe ever could."

"But it consumes a lot of mana," Ventus retorted. As his voice rose slightly, Thorian fixed him with a stern gaze, prompting the wind magus to flinch. Ventus continued, his tone now more subdued. "Wouldn't it be better to use it to slay monsters and defend the walls?"

Thorian scratched his chin for a few moments. "It is true that we are still sorely lacking in power, particularly at the eastern and western gates."

Ventus' face brightened at Thorian's reply. "Exactly! I need to be on the frontlines to provide as much support as possible. We can't afford to assign a powerful magus like myself to tree-cutting duty."

Thorian absentmindedly nodded before adding, "Nevertheless, we still need more wood to upgrade the statues into guilds."

"Guilds?" Ventus asked, tilting his head in confusion. The word also piqued the curiosity of Aqua and Nox, who leaned in closer.

Thorian conjured a waterball atop his palm, captivating the three evolved kobolds.

"Did you acquire a new skill, King? How?" Ventus asked excitedly.

"That's the primary function of guilds," Thorian explained. "They allow you to purchase new skills using your arcane coins."

"Arcane coins?" Ventus furrowed his brow before shaking his head, a wide smile spreading across his face. "Wait, so we can buy skills at these guilds? And we just need more wood to create them?"

"That's the gist of it," Thorian shrugged as Ventus appeared lost in thought.

"Why don't you do it?" Aqua nudged the yellow kobloid. "I wouldn't mind learning a new skill."

"I want a new skill too!" Nox chimed in enthusiastically. "I'll become stronger! That would be amazing!"

Ventus frowned and grumbled under the peer pressure from the two kobolds before throwing his hands in the air in defeat. "Agh! Fine! I get it! I'll cut those trees! I'll cut all the trees!"

Seeing Ventus agree to his new duties, Thorian smiled and instructed, "Speak with Zogthar first and inform him of your plans. The orcs will need to adjust their pace to accommodate you."

"Don't worry, King. I'll talk to them," Ventus assured as he placed one foot on the watchtower's ledge, ready to leap. "I'll cut all those trees within the village before the sun sets!"

With that declaration, Ventus jumped from the watchtower into the village, leaving the three kobolds behind. As they continued their conversation, Thorian heard shrieks and screams from beyond the wall. Glancing downward, he saw the warriors led by Forlune effortlessly dispatching a small group of goblins.

Seeing no major threat, Thorian redirected his attention to Aqua. "What about you? What skill did you acquire?"

Aqua grinned in response to Thorian's question. "I actually acquired two skills." He then raised his arm and pointed at Thorian, creating a water membrane that fully enveloped the king.

Thorian surveyed his body, noticing the water that encased him from head to toe. Nevertheless, it didn't feel constricting or suffocating in any way.

"Water Shield?" Thorian asked, looking back at Aqua. "That's an excellent skill."

"Oh, what's that?" Nox inquired, puzzled as he moved closer to Thorian.

"Why don't you touch it and see?" Thorian suggested.

Accepting the invitation, Nox approached and attempted to poke through the blue membrane. To the shadowstalker's surprise, his claws failed to pierce the Water Shield.

"It's quite sturdy, isn't it?" Thorian observed, then looked back at Aqua, whose expression was tinged with pride. "What's your other skill?"

Seeing both Thorian and Nox watching him with interest, Aqua smiled and looked beyond the watchtower. "It's called Triple Jet Stream," he explained as he pointed his finger past the walls and conjured his water spell. A fist-sized waterball hovered in front of his finger for a fraction of a second before splitting into three shards, which launched into the ground. The three jet streams struck the earth in different locations, leaving burrowing holes in their wake. "Much more powerful than a simple waterball, right?"

"Whoa! That's powerful! You could kill three monsters with one strike!" Nox exclaimed, his eyes shining with admiration.

"It is indeed superior to a waterball," Thorian praised the water magus while observing the warriors battling various monsters beyond the wall. Whenever they dispatched a foe, one of the kobolds would carry the severely injured prey back inside for Caedar to finish off.

Things are going well on this front. I should go back to the altar and check how much wood we already have.

"I need to attend to some matters," Thorian announced before turning to Nox. "Stay around here and keep an eye on things, at least until Caedar evolves."

Nox frowned but nodded in agreement. "Okay, I'll do that."

With that, Thorian descended the stairs to find Caedar still lying on the ground, with the priest attending to him. Surrounding the pair were the mutilated corpses of various monsters—goblins, chaskas, and thumpalopes. The condition of the bodies bore witness to the warriors' efforts before presenting their prey to Caedar.

"You, priest, I need you to go out there after Caedar evolves," Thorian instructed, pointing at the bewildered kobloid.

"Me?" he asked, puzzled.

Thorian nodded and explained, "Yes, you need to heal your brothers while they're fighting so that you gain more experience and level up. At this rate, you're going to be left behind."

The priest's mouth hung open before he lowered his gaze in shame.

Thorian sighed and looked up. Fortunately, Aqua was also watching him from the watchtower.

"Aqua, keep an eye on your brother. Help him evolve quickly."

The blue kobold nodded at Thorian's command. "Don't worry, King. He'll be a kobold by the time you return."

Thorian chuckled at Aqua's confident statement before turning and continuing towards the altar. As he walked through the clearing among the trees, he could see several of them falling with a loud thud in the distance.

Ventus is already getting to work. That's good to see.

As Thorian strode towards his destination, his stomach rumbled faintly. Feeling a moment of embarrassment, an image of a certain small green figure flashed in his mind.

Brix should be done cooking the meat by now.

Thorian smiled as he thought back to the little, green goblin. Thumpalope meat was renowned as a great delicacy, even among the upper class, so he had high expectations for the meal Brix was preparing.

He might be a goblin, but thumpalopes are very easy to cook. It would be a travesty if he messed it up.

With a smile on his face, Thorian passed by the village hall and continued to the altar behind it. As he approached, shock left his jaw slack and sent his eyebrows shooting up.

That's a lot of trees.

The altar was surrounded by cut trees stacked on top of each other, higher than Thorian was tall.

How much is that? Four times—no, five times the amount I saw last time? Their pace has definitely increased.

Surprised and delighted by this turn of events, Thorian rushed towards the mountain of trees and leapt over it. With one swift motion, he crossed the ocean of wood and landed in front of the altar.

As he had done multiple times already, Thorian placed his palm atop the demon's face and commanded it to absorb the trees.

Territory resources.

Resources:

Gathered Experience: 9242

Wood: 5965

Seeing the screen floating in front of his eyes, Thorian's grin stretched from ear to ear.

Good, this is so much more than I expected. The only thing left to do is to get more citizens.

With that thought in mind, Thorian laid out his command. *Upgrade assassin statue.*

Assassin Statue

The Assassin Statue epitomizes the art of stealth, precision, and cunning. Assassins excel in striking from the shadows, dealing lethal damage to their targets before slipping away unnoticed.

Upgrade:

Gathered Experience: 750

Wood: 1000

Do you wish to upgrade the Assassin Statue into the Assassin Guild?

"Yes, I do."

Hearing the rumbling in the distance, Thorian continued his task. After upgrading the Assassin Statue to a guild, he did the same with the priest and warrior statues.

Satisfied by the progress, Thorian walked towards the village hall before locating Brix's cooking spot. The strong fire engulfing the makeshift cooking pot was hard to miss in the open field.

"You sure took your time, Brix," Thorian approached the green goblin, who was startled by the kobold's voice. "It has been hours since you started cooking."

"I am very sorry, my lord! I messed up and burned a couple," Brix scratched the back of his head in embarrassment. "But that was just the first few! I got better, and I made you one that's really good!"

The goblin pointed to the side, where a large roasted thumpalope thigh rested on a bed of leaves. The fatty aroma it emitted, thankfully, overpowered the smell of ash and char from the previous failed attempts.

"That does look appetizing," Thorian smiled as he walked over to the roasted thigh. Strangely enough, his hunger only intensified as he took in the aromas with his sharp sense of smell.

However, just as he was about to take a bite, he glanced back at the green goblin and handed him the prized food.

"Here, why don't you take a bite?"

CHAPTER 38

The goblin hesitated for a moment before accepting Thorian's invitation. As he grasped the piece of meat from the thigh bone, he looked up at Thorian and asked, "Can I ask why, master?"

"It's tradition in our tribe," Thorian explained nonchalantly. "Whoever hunts the prey gets to eat first. Now, this wasn't a hunt, but I believe the same principle should apply."

Hearing Thorian's explanation, Brix nodded and took a bite from the tender piece of meat. Just as he was about to return it to Thorian, the latter stopped him.

"Take a bite from the other side too. I want you to thoroughly taste the results of your hard work."

Brix nodded and said, "Thank you, master." He then followed Thorian's instruction to a tee, taking a bite from the other side of the meat.

Seeing the goblin obeying his orders, Thorian nodded with a smile. Without a word, Brix handed the thigh piece to Thorian who immediately took a large bite out of it.

It's not bad.

Although it lacked salt and spices, the roasted thigh had enough fattiness and juiciness to provide a satisfying flavor and aroma. The tenderness of the cooked meat made eating it all the more enjoyable. Most importantly, it was civilized. The mere thought of becoming a savage and having to eat raw meat repulsed Thorian so much that he would have rather starved himself to death.

Without uttering a word, Thorian finished his meal with delighted bites. After cleaning the bone, he glanced back at Brix, who looked at him nervously.

"That was perfectly cooked. Good job." Thorian nodded in approval, while Brix let out a deep sigh of relief.

"I'm glad you enjoyed it, master." The goblin smiled before looking back at the remaining uncooked meat. "Should I roast the rest too?"

Thorian followed Brix's line of sight. While he would have liked the other kobolds to experience the delicacy of a cooked meal, Thorian still had reservations about the goblin.

"No, don't cook them yet," Thorian shook his head. "Go around the village and try to make yourself useful."

"Okay, master." Brix bowed slightly. "I will do as you tell me."

As Thorian looked at the goblin's meek appearance, a sudden thought flashed in his mind. *Should I allow him to use my name for his safety... Wait, he was marching with the brown kobloids last time I saw him. How did he do that?*

Thorian frowned and asked the goblin, "Last time, you were walking alongside the kobolds. How did you do that without getting hurt?"

Brix's eyes widened as he scratched the back of his head. "Ah, about that? Honestly, those kobold assassins almost killed me. They were so fast! But when I mentioned your name, they thankfully stopped and listened."

"You're a sharp little thing, aren't you?" Thorian's slight smile betrayed his hidden emotions. He then scratched his chin with a pensive gaze, recalling Brix's earlier proposition. "As for your tribe, we'll discuss that matter later. I hope they're as smart as you are."

Brix's expression brightened at Thorian's suggestion. "The tribe chief is a shaman, master. He's really wise and smart. I'm sure he'll listen to you properly!"

"A goblin shaman..." Thorian looked down in thought before shrugging. "Well, that's a matter for later. Don't just slack off. Make yourself useful, you understand me?"

"Yes, master," Brix enthusiastically nodded his head. "I will do my best."

With that, Thorian turned around and walked towards his new destination of the eastern gate. With quick strides, he crossed the patch of trees and reached the wooden wall, where he found three of the kobloids sitting next to the gate, battered and wounded. Beyond the wall, the war cries and the sounds of battle raged on. Thorian jumped atop the wall and saw the group of kobloids fighting against three chaskas.

While the brown kobold had little problem blocking the overgrown cats' attacks with his armor skill, the other kobloids were not as fortunate. The agile chaskas darted from one side of the battlefield to the other, smashing the hapless brown creatures with the large boulders attached to the ends of their tails. Kobloids were sent flying through the air from the strikes, their ribs and bones likely broken.

However, the chaskas could not do as they pleased either. Whenever they struck one kobloid, another two or three would take their place and surround the chaska. With their sharp claws and fangs, they would tear apart the large cat's flesh.

It was a good thing they didn't face a tailmasher. That would have been a real issue.

As Thorian scanned the battlefield, he saw that two of the kobloids were heavily injured from their encounter with the chaskas. Adding them to the three that were sitting inside the village brought the tally of injured to five.

That leaves ten capable of fighting in this group—eleven if you count the kobold.

As the battle came to a close, Thorian jumped down from the wall, attracting the attention of the kobloids. Soon, the brown kobold noticed the commotion and turned around as well.

"Oh, Thorian, you have come."

Thorian walked towards the brown kobold while the kobloids around them murmured "flame kobold" and "King." None of the kobloids, however, dared to speak up or ask for Thorian's attention.

"I see that many of yours have taken a beating," Thorian commented, looking around.

The brown kobold bit his lower lip and looked down. "It's my fault. I thought there were only two chaskas, but a third one appeared after we started the fight."

Looking around, Thorian motioned with his head towards the gate. "We should go inside. It is not safe here."

The brown kobold nodded before issuing his order to the rest of his group. "Everyone, inside. Handle the two injured with care."

The group of kobloids immediately sprang into action. Four of them tended to the injured while the rest entered the village.

As they passed through the gate, Thorian looked at the brown kobold and said, "Your numbers are running low. It will be much harder to defend the walls like this."

The brown kobold bit his thumb and replied, "I'm sorry. I was too incompetent."

"No." Thorian shook his head. "You were just too weak."

The brown kobold looked down without saying a word, leaving an awkward silence between the two. However, Thorian did not immediately break it. He needed that silence for the kobold to more deeply understand the situation.

After twenty seconds or so, Thorian looked up to the wall and asked, "When do the assassins usually come here?"

Surprised by the change of subject, the brown kobold took a few seconds to answer. "Every half an hour or so? They should be here any minute now."

"Good, that's good," Thorian nodded before looking back at the kobold. "Like I said, you are weak. But you do not need to be."

The kobold raised an eyebrow at Thorian's statement before nodding in understanding. "You're right. I need to hunt more so that I level up and become strong."

"That's one way, but it is not the method I was referring to." Thorian looked intently at the kobold, who was engrossed in his words. "Have you ever wondered why all the kobolds you've seen here are so much stronger than usual?"

"Is it because of you?" The brown kobold tilted his head in confusion. "Nox said that they became stronger thanks to you."

"In one sense of the word, that is true." Thorian chuckled. "But the true reason is that I gifted them a class."

"A class?" The brown kobold inquired, his face a mix of curiosity and confusion. "What is that?"

"For now, just think of it as a way to level up twice, and get double your normal stats. It will also provide you with a variety of skills, which will make you that much stronger."

"That's—That's amazing!" the brown kobold couldn't help but exclaim. However, his loud voice drew the attention of the kobloids in the area, which displeased Thorian.

Noticing Thorian's facial expression, the brown kobold made an apologetic face before speaking in a lower voice, "I'm sorry."

"Just be calm," Thorian responded before his gaze shifted to the wall. Spotting three figures rushing atop it, he slightly smiled. "And I think they have finally arrived."

CHAPTER 39

Upon spying the three assassins scaling the wall, a smile played upon Thorian's lips. His original intent had been to assist the brown kobold in unlocking his class, but he recognized the imprudence in leaving the kobloids to their own devices.

"Oh, is that the boss?" One of the assassins, sensing Thorian's presence, dropped from the wall and strode towards him. "Had we known you were here, we wouldn't have bothered. You alone are more than capable of safeguarding everyone."

"Your presence is appreciated, nonetheless," Thorian responded, shaking his head. His gaze then shifted to the brown kobold. "We have a matter to attend to in the village center."

The assassin's brows knit together in momentary confusion, soon replaced by understanding. "Ah, are you about to acquire a class?" He shot a smile at the brown kobold, nodding in acknowledgment. "Excellent, you'll be significantly stronger!"

The brown kobold laughed nervously, managing a "Thank you" in response.

Thorian's attention returned to the assassin, the topic of conversation shifting. "You've been on patrol for some time. What's the state of the western gate?"

"It's much the same as here," the assassin said, sighing. "We have four injured, but they should manage well enough against the standard goblins and a couple of chaskas."

Thorian scratched his chin in response. *Could we use the same idea as with Caedar? No, broken bones will need two or three level-ups to heal. We must get more priests with the Healing skill.*

Thorian cast his gaze over the brown kobloids who had congregated into distinct clusters and cliques. Each group occupied its own corner, immersed in conversation and punctuated by bouts of laughter. *I can't have them all leave their spot at the same time. It will leave us undefended for too long.*

Decision made, Thorian clucked his tongue and returned his attention to the assassin. "I will entrust this position to you. We shouldn't be gone long."

The declaration was met with a robust laugh. "Take all the time you need, boss. No one's getting past these walls on our watch."

"That's reassuring to hear," Thorian said, chuckling lightly. He then glanced back at the brown kobold and gestured with his head towards the village center. "Shall we proceed?"

As they ambled towards the village hall, Thorian began to elaborate, "There are four classes to choose from: warrior, assassin, magus, and priest. Each one has its own unique strengths and weaknesses."

The brown kobold absorbed the information with a thoughtful expression, then turned to Thorian and asked, "Which class did Nox choose?"

"Assassin. They specialize in agility and lethal strikes, and while they may not excel at handling multiple enemies simultaneously, they can deliver decisive blows to a single target."

At Thorian's explanation, the brown kobold's demeanor transformed, his features alight with excitement. "Can I also become an assassin?"

Thorian took a moment before responding, "Ultimately, the choice is yours. However, one advantage of being in a guild is that we can assess your aptitude. After the test, you'll know which class best suits your abilities."

Scratching his chin, the brown kobold nodded in understanding. "That's logical. I should choose the class where my talent lies. That way, I can become stronger in the future."

Well, you don't strike me as the assassin type, but I have been surprised before. I guess we will see when we will get there.

As they journeyed towards the Assassin Guild, the brown kobold shot a curious glance at Thorian. "Can you change your class after you've chosen it?"

"You can," Thorian confirmed, a chuckle escaping his lips. "But it's usually not desirable. Changing classes means losing all your levels and forfeiting the progress made in your class skills. Unless you're aiming for a specific type of class, it's not a decision taken lightly."

"A specific type of class?" The brown kobold cocked his head in confusion. "I thought there were only four classes."

Thorian's smile was gentle as he said, "You needn't concern yourself with that for now. Special classes aren't something you can attain simply because you wish to. They require exceptional luck."

Upon reaching the Assassin Guild, Thorian immediately noted the austere silence that pervaded the space. The guild was unpretentious and functional, its emphasis on practicality over flamboyance, typical of a low-level guild. The walls, constructed of dark, polished wood that swallowed the light, lending the space an air of clandestine seclusion.

To the left of the entrance, the training room stood out, purpose-built for assessing the skills of potential recruits. The area was bare and spacious, furnished with an array of training dummies, weapon racks, and an intricate sequence of obstacle courses meant to test agility, stealth, and precision.

As in the Magus Guild, the guildmaster's desk was situated to the right. The sleek, undecorated surface held only a few meticulously organized parchments and a single, gleaming dagger serving as a paperweight. Instead of a regular figure, however, Thorian could only discern a void-like silhouette seated on a chair before the desk.

"What's that?" The brown kobold murmured from beside him, his gaze also locked onto the shadowy entity.

Oh, a shadowkin?

The guildmaster bore a slender, agile figure. His skin was a deep obsidian black, mirroring the color of the midnight sky, yet it radiated an ethereal shimmer when struck by the right angle of light. Another extraordinary feature gleamed brightly: his eyes. They were almost luminescent, with a silver hue that stood in stark contrast against his dark skin. Reflective and profound, they spoke to Thorian an ocean of unspoken tales. His hair, as black as his skin and cascading down to his shoulders, was styled back to keep clear of his face.

Most strikingly, the shadowkin guildmaster was enshrouded in a robe of shadows. These shadows undulated and flowed around him as if they possessed a life of their own.

"Kobolds... intriguing." The guildmaster lifted his gaze from the parchments on his desk, focusing his attention on Thorian. "Are you the lord of this domain?"

"I am." Thorian stepped forwards to address the shadowkin. "I'm Thorian. It's a pleasure to meet you, guildmaster."

"Impressive," the shadowkin replied, a slight smile revealing a captivating blue light hidden behind his lips. "A monster ruling over a territory is indeed a rare sight."

Thorian acknowledged the sentiment with a tilt of head, gesturing over to the brown kobold. "We are here to ascertain this individual's potential. Could you please administer the test?"

"A brown kobold, I see." The shadowkin's gaze shifted to Thorian's companion. "The standard test won't suffice. It's designed for humans who have yet to receive their classes and unlock the system. A monster who has already undergone its first evolution would pass it with ease."

"Does that mean I can become an assassin?" The brown kobold asked eagerly, buoyed by the guildmaster's words.

His question was met with a shrug. "The physical examination is just one aspect. Your personality and mental prowess are equally crucial."

"So, do I possess the right personality for it?"

"That's what we need to determine," the shadowkin replied with a smile, striding past the duo. "Let's head outside. We don't want to risk breaking anything if we spar indoors."

While the brown kobold appeared confused, Thorian couldn't suppress a grin.

It's been a while since I saw a shadowkin fighting. Their skills and spells are the most frustrating thing to deal with.

As the shadowkin strode outside, the brown kobold turned to Thorian, his brows furrowed in a silent inquiry.

Observing the kobold's questioning expression, Thorian simply shrugged. "Go ahead. It should be a beneficial experience."

Thus, the trio exited the guild, with the brown kobold and the guildmaster adopting fighting stances. The kobold positioned himself widely, primed to spring at the shadowkin and rend him with claws and fangs.

In contrast, the guildmaster stood in a relaxed pose, hands clasped behind his back. They were roughly the same height, but the shadowkin's gravitas gave the impression that he towered over the brown kobold.

"Come, give it your best shot." He beckoned, his gesture seemingly taunting the kobold.

Provoked by the shadowkin's words, the brown kobold gritted his teeth before charging at the guildmaster. With a fierce war cry, he lifted his arm high and aimed a clawed slash at the shadowkin's form.

The guildmaster sidestepped the kobold's predictable attack with ease. Yet the latter wasn't finished. The moment the shadowkin evaded his slash, he followed up with an uppercut, which the shadowkin also deftly avoided.

The kobold launched a barrage of attacks, all of which the guildmaster nimbly dodged. Each strike appeared as though it might hit, but the shadowkin always managed to elude them by the merest fraction.

"Let's stop here." After deftly sidestepping one final attack, the guildmaster seized the brown kobold by the shoulder. His grip was so firm that the unfortunate kobold was unable to move a single muscle.

Once the brown kobold relaxed and crumpled to the ground, the shadowkin loosened his hold and stepped back.

Thorian, witnessing his subordinate's defeat, was not surprised in the least. If the result had been any different, it would have been a miracle.

"You're not suited to be an assassin." The guildmaster delivered his verdict. "Your attacks are too direct, and you lack the necessary cunning for a proficient assassin."

"Let's fight again!" The brown kobold growled, leveling a glare at the shadowkin. "I was so close to hitting you. Just give me one more chance."

"You weren't close to hitting him," Thorian sighed. "And even if you had, it wouldn't have made a difference."

Without diverting his gaze from the brown kobold, Thorian suddenly sprung forwards with astonishing speed, aiming a spinning high kick at the guildmaster's neck. However, his foot simply passed through the shadowkin's body as if it were a mirage.

Maintaining his silent communion with the shadowkin, Thorian turned back to the brown kobold to conclude his point: "Because hitting him achieves nothing."

CHAPTER 40

The brown kobold could only watch in sheer horror as Thorian's foot swung through the guildmaster's form as if he were crafted from nothing more substantial than mist. The shadowkin, however, seemed unperturbed, a hint of a grin playing on his lips as he returned Thorian's gaze.

"Lord Thorian, your capacity for surprise is unending," the guildmaster remarked, his voice laced with amusement. "Your wisdom and knowledge exceed your years... Quite remarkable."

"I just happen to be special," Thorian replied curtly, refusing to divulge any more than that.

The shadowkin glanced down, a low chuckle resonating in his chest before his gaze returned to the petrified kobold. "Don't let this dishearten you. It merely suggests you're more suited to a different class. Warrior, I believe, should fit you perfectly."

The brown kobold cast his gaze downwards, shame flushing his cheeks as he gritted his teeth. With a heavy sigh, he lifted his eyes back to the shadowkin, asking, "What does a warrior do?"

"Your role is defined by your specialization," the guildmaster replied in a low, measured tone. "You can serve as the shield of your team, drawing the enemy's attention and soaking up the damage. Or, you could become a relentless berserker, fueled by an insatiable bloodlust and a passion for close combat."

The kobold's gaze dropped again, his brow furrowed in thought. As he mused over the options, Thorian turned his attention back to the shadowkin.

"Thank you for your time, guildmaster," he said, stepping towards the kobold to conclude the conversation. But just as he took that step, he paused, glancing back over his shoulder. "I realize I neglected to ask your name."

The shadowkin's silver eyes gleamed brightly as if peering into a distant horizon. "I lack a formal name, but some refer to me as Whisperwind."

"An honor to make your acquaintance, Whisperwind," Thorian responded, his head dipping in a respectful nod. "May our relationship be enduring and prosperous."

"The honor is mine," Whisperwind returned, his lips curling into a small, knowing smile. "Overseeing a lord as special as you promises to be most fascinating."

With no further words exchanged, Thorian moved towards the brown kobold, who was now gradually pulling himself upright. Seeing the kobold's downcast, crestfallen expression, Thorian softened his gaze. "Don't fret," he reassured, "The guildmasters are currently insurmountable beings to us. There is no dishonor in your defeat."

The brown kobold glanced up at Thorian and nodded, albeit reluctantly.

As they resumed their journey, the kobold trailed behind Thorian. When they'd walked some ways, he couldn't help but voice a question that had been gnawing at him. "If they're so powerful, why can't they help us fight the monsters outside? We'd level up incredibly fast with their help!"

Thorian chuckled at the kobold's proposition. "It would indeed be advantageous if that were possible. But the guildmasters are significantly limited outside of their guild areas. They lose all their powers and become extraordinarily weak if they venture beyond a certain radius."

The kobold stared at Thorian in disbelief, his jaw slack. With great disappointment, he sighed. "That's a shame. It would have been so amazing for us if we could receive their help."

"Do not let greed cloud your judgment," Thorian replied, a smile playing on his lips. "At this moment, you're about to transform into a being unlike any other in the world. Take pride in that."

As the brown kobold absorbed Thorian's unwavering confidence, his eyes widened in surprise, and he followed him with newfound respect. The pair continued their journey until they reached another guild.

Upon entering the newly minted Warrior Guild, Thorian was immediately enveloped by an aura of grit and resolve. The guild was unassuming yet formidable, reflecting its recent evolution from a mere statue to a thriving hub of martial prowess. The walls, carved from sturdy wood, bore the scars of axes and swords, silent testimonies to the vigorous training conducted within.

To the left, a capacious training room was designed to push the physical limits and martial aptitude of budding warriors. The room was outfitted with weighty training dummies, an assortment of melee weapons, and a sand pit reserved for wrestling and close combat drills.

At the guild's rear, Thorian noticed a modest study where the guildmaster would craft battle strategies and inscribe skill scrolls for sale. Shelves brimming with military treatises and maps encircled a humble wooden table. Scattered across its surface were pieces of parchment, each inked with meticulous diagrams and battle tactics.

The guildmaster's desk, a thick slab of oak, was situated to the right of the entrance as usual. However, Thorian's gaze was immediately drawn to the hulking figure perched on a large chair, busily inscribing words onto parchment. The desk, which would have seemed sizable under normal circumstances, appeared diminutive compared to the guildmaster.

A mountain goliath? The variety of races of these guildmasters is truly interesting. Most of my previous ones were simple humans.

His skin had a rough, stone-like texture and a grayish hue, adorned with unique patterns that mountain goliaths regarded as marks of honor and age. His face was weather-beaten, crisscrossed with deep lines carved by both time and laughter, a testament to a life abundantly lived. He was bald, with a thick beard woven with beads and small trinkets accrued from numerous battles.

The mountain goliath glanced up from his desk and noticed the new arrivals. A broad smile lit up his face, and he rose so abruptly that his chair toppled over. Standing at well over eight feet tall, his head nearly grazed the ceiling. Had he stretched, his hands would have punctured the guild's roof.

"Are you the lord of this territory?" The goliath regarded Thorian before his features creased into a frown. "It's a pity that you're already a magus. You would have made a formidable warrior, leading your troops into the thick of battle!"

Thorian received the compliment with a smile. "Alas, I'm more inclined towards strategy." He then gestured towards the brown kobold at his side. "But my companion here harbors an interest in the warrior's path. Perhaps you could evaluate him?"

"A brown kobold, eh?" The goliath stroked his beard contemplatively, his face soon breaking into a wide grin. "I like it. Brown kobolds are a hardy folk with big hearts. I once counted one among my friends."

Caught in a moment of nostalgia, the goliath's gaze drifted upwards before snapping back to the present. He refocused on the brown kobold. "Regardless, I'll need to assess you to determine if you have what it takes to become a mighty warrior." His eyes slid to the training grounds on the left, a thoughtful click resonating from his tongue. "A standard test won't be enough. How about a friendly spar?"

Upon hearing the guildmaster's proposition, the brown kobold visibly shrank back. Words failed him as his gaze darted nervously between the towering mountain goliath and Thorian.

Recognizing his subordinate's plea for intervention, Thorian stepped in. "I fear a spar might be rather unfair given the significant size disparity. Wouldn't you agree, guildmaster?"

The goliath responded to Thorian's comment with a broad grin. "My name is Rumblestone, Lord…?"

"Thorian."

"Yes, Thorian. That's a fine name." Rumblestone nodded approvingly. "And if size is the concern, we can easily remedy that."

Assuming a firm stance, Rumblestone tensed his muscles. A low growl resonated from his chest as a black aura enveloped him, and he began to shrink rapidly. In mere seconds, the aura subsided, revealing a significantly leaner form.

Rumblestone now matched the brown kobold's height. Despite his trimmer silhouette, his muscles were still markedly larger than the kobold's, his biceps seeming to strain against the confines of his clothing. Although he bore the signs of age, his strength remained undeniably formidable.

Rumblestone cast a glance at the training room before returning his gaze to the brown kobold. "Let's go outside. That training room isn't designed to accommodate our level of strength. It'd crumble within a few minutes of our sparring."

The brown kobold, still taken aback by the guildmaster's transformation, found Rumblestone's new form somewhat reassuring. At least now he didn't have to crane his neck to make eye contact. Together, they exited the guild, with Thorian trailing closely behind. Much like with Whisperwind earlier, the two assumed their positions, ready for a friendly bout.

"Come! Show me what you've got!"

Spurred by Rumblestone's challenge, the brown kobold lunged at the grinning elder, aiming a right hook at him. The goliath effortlessly deflected the strike, but the kobold was quick to follow up with an uppercut.

Grinning, the guildmaster nimbly sidestepped before launching a counterattack. His fist, as solid and formidable as a slab of meat, sped towards his opponent in a swift, downwards punch.

Seeing the blow hurtling towards him, the brown kobold raised his hand to shield himself, encasing it in a protective armor of rock. The force of the guildmaster's punch forced him to stagger back a step, but his armored guard successfully absorbed the impact.

"Quick reflexes!" The old goliath roared with laughter. "Your snout would've been flattened if you hadn't blocked that."

However, the brown kobold was in no position to share the humor. His gaze remained riveted on the elder as he launched himself at him once more.

While the kobold unleashed a torrent of punches, the guildmaster either blocked or evaded each attack. However, just as he was about to parry another of the kobold's strikes, the latter encased his fist in the same rocky armor.

Bypassing the elder's defense, the kobold's punch connected squarely with his face, causing him to bleed from his lips. Without granting him a moment's respite, the kobold unleashed a barrage of attacks—kicks, punches, swipes, and even bites. It was a brutal brawl, where instincts reigned supreme.

"You're a clever little rascal, aren't you?" Even amidst the flurry of the kobold's onslaught, the elder couldn't contain his laughter. As the kobold readied a powerful haymaker punch, Rumblestone swiftly closed in and tackled him to the ground.

With the kobold held firmly in his grip, Rumblestone tightened his hold, his grip audibly cracking the kobold's back as the latter futilely clawed and punched at his captor.

Watching the skirmish devolve into chaos, Thorian decided to intervene. "Why don't we call it a draw? I believe this suffices as a test."

"Oh, it seems I got a bit carried away." Rumblestone rose to his feet, laughing heartily while the brown kobold gasped for breath. The guildmaster's bear-like embrace had left him winded and on the verge of having his bones crushed.

"You've passed." Rumblestone beamed at the brown kobold. "You possess a fearless spirit and fierce instincts. With the right training and guidance, you'll grow into a formidable warrior."

Caught off guard by Rumblestone's declaration, the brown kobold looked from him to Thorian, a proud smile stretching across his face. Despite his labored breathing, he couldn't suppress his ear-to-ear grin.

CHAPTER 41

Upon seeing the brown kobold's expression, Thorian's face broke into a warm smile. "You've performed remarkably well. Congratulations," he praised.

At that moment, Rumblestone sauntered over to the young kobold, extending a massive hand. The kobold clasped it gratefully and rose to his feet. Rumblestone's hearty laugh echoed around them as he shook his head in amusement and confessed, "You truly surprised me. I didn't anticipate you'd use your armor skill in such an aggressive manner."

"It was purely instinctual, brought about by the heat of battle," the brown kobold admitted with a modest chuckle.

Rumblestone gave his shoulder an appreciative pat, admiring his fighting spirit. "You have keen instincts," he declared, before posing a pivotal question. "But what path will you choose, warrior? Do you desire to immerse yourself in the heart of battle, or would you prefer to control the chaos from afar as a strategic leader?"

The brown kobold's brows knit together in confusion. "I'm not entirely sure what you mean, but I suppose I'd prefer to be a leader? I already lead my band of kobloids. I'd like things to stay that way."

Rumblestone let out a robust, hearty laugh at that. "Good, that's an excellent answer. Given your choice, I'd recommend 'Taunting Shout' as your starting skill. It would synergize perfectly with your rock-hard armor."

As the guildmaster laid out his proposition, the brown kobold cast a questioning look towards Thorian, seeking his approval. Thorian couldn't hide his smile upon noticing the kobold's pleading eyes. "It's an enticing suggestion, indeed. Acquiring these two skills so early on would make you one of the most formidable frontline soldiers in the region."

Bolstered by Thorian's approval, the brown kobold gave a firm nod. "All right, I choose this 'Taunting Shout' skill."

"Good choice," Rumblestone approved, his gaze wandering away from them and fixing onto a distant point. Thorian understood that the guildmaster was likely viewing a screen much like the ones he had access to.

"Oh, I see it now," the brown kobold exclaimed, his brows shooting up as he gazed at an unseen point in the air. Observing the pair respond to invisible prompts prompted Thorian to chuckle at the absurd spectacle.

It's funny how such a thing is now considered normal. After ten years, it's almost hard to even notice the ridiculousness.

Once the brown kobold had secured his starting skill, Rumblestone appraised him curiously. "Why not purchase an additional skill? Since it's your first, you'll get a two hundred arcane coin discount. It would cost only three hundred."

A look of confusion spread across the kobold's face. "Arcane coins?" he echoed inquisitively.

Thorian cut in swiftly with an explanation. "He has yet to receive any quests," he clarified. "We were pressed for time, and not all have been properly inducted as citizens."

Rumblestone offered a wry smile before nodding in understanding. "That is quite a pity." He then turned to the brown kobold, his grin broadening. "Nevertheless, once you've completed your quests and earned some coin, come find me. I'll be able to sell you a new skill. We can even spar again to discover the one that suits your fighting style best."

The brown kobold chuckled nervously and gave a dismissive shake of his head. "That won't be necessary. You could just show me the skills, and I'll choose the one I like."

The goliath feigned a disappointed pout. "Oh, that's too bad. I was eager for another sparring match."

Meanwhile, Thorian was lost in thought, scratching his chin. Finally, he made a decision. He addressed the brown kobold, saying, "Once we return to the eastern gate, take your men and tour the village. Head to the hall and ask Melina to show you how to get quests. You can also visit the guilds, so that the kobloids can choose their classes."

"Come to mine first," Rumblestone interjected, addressing the brown kobold. "I want first dibs on promising new talents before that shady character gets his hands on them. He'll spoil their pure and courageous spirit."

The brown kobold chuckled in response and reassured, "I can at least promise you that much."

With their plans set, Thorian and the kobold bid farewell to the guildmaster before making their way towards the eastern gate. Along the way, Thorian explained the concept of quests and the benefits of their rewards. He also introduced the notion of arcane coins, emphasizing their role as the universal currency within the territories.

Upon reaching the gate, the sounds of battle echoed from beyond the walls. Thankfully, only the kobloids Thorian had seen injured before were resting within the village, indicating no fresh casualties.

As the gate swung open, Thorian could see that the skirmish was nearing its conclusion. Led by the trio of assassins, the kobloids were dispatching the remnants of the goblin pack that had dared to threaten the village with their spears and daggers.

Turning to the brown kobold at his side, Thorian queried, "What's the average level of the kobloids?"

He scratched his head, considering Thorian's question. "I'm not sure. They used to hover around level 10. A few reached level 11, and I think one managed to hit 12."

"That's a commendable rate of progress," Thorian noted approvingly. "Their class levels should ascend swiftly and bolster their strength a considerable amount. Your group should find it easier to handle smaller chaska packs, but you'll still need to exercise caution around a tailmasher. As for thri-kreens, your best strategy at your current level is simply to flee."

"Thank you for the advice, I'll definitely remember it," the brown kobold responded with a solemn nod. Thorian reciprocated with a firm nod of his own.

"Boss! You're back?" One of the assassins spotted Thorian's return and promptly bolted towards him.

Seeing the assassin's beaming smile, Thorian couldn't help but be reminded of Nox's guileless demeanor. *I guess they're taking on some of his personality. Not bad.*

"Yes, I have given our friend here a tour of the village. He even managed to pick up a class along the way."

The assassin turned his curious eyes to the brown kobold. "Oh? What class? Did you opt for the assassin class like us? It's the best one!"

"No, I've chosen to be a warrior," the brown kobold replied, his chest puffed up with pride.

Upon hearing this, the assassin clicked his tongue in disapproval. "Tch, that's boring."

"And who are you calling boring?" the brown kobold shot back, his eyebrows knitting together. "I'll have you know, the warrior class is perfect for a leader like me. A youngster like you wouldn't comprehend such subtleties."

Observing the friendly banter teetering on the edge of an argument, Thorian cleared his throat twice, bringing their bickering to a halt.

"Ahem. The plan now is for the kobold to lead his group on a tour of the village and help them all select their classes." Thorian turned his attention to the assassin and spelled out his instructions. "Since I'll be assuming responsibility for guarding this gate, you can return to your patrolling duties. The eastern side will be secure under my watch."

"Understood, boss," the assassin responded, flashing a two-fingered salute. "I'll go notify the others to shift positions."

"I'll do the same," the brown kobold chimed in. "I'll gather the kobloids and brief them on our next steps."

With a clear plan in mind, the two kobolds sprung into action. The trio of assassins promptly resumed their patrol as Thorian had instructed, while the brown kobold congregated the kobloids to inform them about classes, quests, and various aspects of territory know-how. After a brief explanation, the group proceeded into the village, escorting the injured members along so they could receive immediate healing once some of the kobloids ascended to priest classes.

With Thorian left alone, he couldn't help but think back to the two brown kobolds.

I should at least name those two, and also the rest of the original tribe. As for the rest of the brown kobloids, I should have someone else do the honors. Maybe Melina?

However, Thorian quickly relegated those thoughts to the back of his mind. There would be time to attend to that task later. His immediate responsibility was protecting the wall and neutralizing any monster that ventured too close.

Upon checking his mana pool, Thorian was surprised to find it almost completely replenished. He could readily feel the effects of the Ether Line attribute—merely taking short rests was sufficient to recharge his mana fully.

While the brown kobloids were off on their tour, Thorian single-handedly fought off all the monsters that dared approach his territory's border. While this responsibility might have seemed daunting to others, for him, it was a significant advantage. He didn't need to share his kills with anyone, thereby claiming all the experience points for himself.

As per his routine, Thorian hunted goblins, chaskas, rabbarians, thumpalopes, and a few thri-kreen. Intriguingly, it wasn't the giant mantises that presented the biggest challenge, but instead the goblins. Similar to what happened with the orcs, a spacetime distortion occurred in front of the eastern gate, giving rise to nearly two hundred goblins. With a considerable number of hobgoblins amongst them, it was a formidable task to repel them all.

Initially, Thorian leveraged his height and range advantage, employing a blend of fireballs and waterballs to reduce the number of hobgoblins. Having eradicated the evolved species, he then dove into the fray and accumulated experience points. By utilizing his Combustion Touch skill and his overwhelming stats, he managed to cut through the swarm of green monstrosities with ease, dispatching several with each strike. The tricky part wasn't the killing, but rather preventing them from climbing the wall after scattering. Some managed to infiltrate the village, but Thorian's keen sense of smell enabled him to track them down and eliminate them.

After the two-hour interval, Thorian thought it best to check his status screen.

Display panel.

Ding!

Race: Flame Kobold

Level: 10/30 (XP: 238/1050)

Class: Magus

Level: 20/20 (XP: MAX)

Lifespan: 40 years

Cultivation Realm: Qi Gathering Second Stage (5.3%)

Stats:

Strength: 52

Agility: 56

Constitution: 31

Mana: 60

Qi: 14

Free Points: 15

Skills:

Minor Fire Affinity (passive)

Flame Resistance (passive)

Fireball (active)

Combustion Touch (active)

Waterball (active)

CHAPTER 42

Thorian's gaze sharpened as it rested on the last skill displayed on his stat panel. Upon concentrating on it, the screen metamorphosed, providing detailed information on the selected skill.

Waterball: You summon a watery orb and launch it at your enemies, drenching them and knocking them off balance.

Proficiency: 38.9%

It is a decent increase in proficiency, but at this pace, it is going to take a few more days before I can finally advance my class.

The requirements to progress his class to an elemental magus weighed heavy on his mind, twisting his face into a grimace. He had been engaged in relentless combat for the past three days, and he was still not halfway there.

I also need to get more arcane coins to buy the last two skills.

Thorian's mind wandered to his pending quests. It had been several hours since his last status check on the monster-hunting quest. Given that he had obliterated entire tribes of monsters during that period, he deemed it high time to consult his quest journal.

Journal:

~~Cultivate your Qi for two hours~~

~~Gather 100 Wood Units~~

Clear one dungeon (daily)

Pact with the Wolven Guardians

Purification of Eärendil's Sanctuary

Revenge on the Monsters (in progress)

Noticing that two of the quests had already been completed, Thorian turned his attention to the remaining quest.

Milestones:

Slay (50/50 monsters)

Reward: Level +1

Slay (88/100 monsters)

Reward: Previous rewards and a class skill of your choosing

Slay (250/250 monsters)

Reward: Previous rewards and Level +2

Slay (479/500 monsters)

Reward: Previous rewards and a Purple Cloud weapon specific to your chosen class.

The tremendous progress he'd made with his quests had a wide grin splitting his face. Yet, just as he began to revel in the anticipation of claiming all the rewards from the "Revenge on the Monsters" quest, he drew in a deep, steadying breath.

I need to stay calm and refrain from claiming the rewards right away. The value of instant level-ups increases with each level, so it would be wise to wait.

Yet, as sound as this line of reasoning was, Thorian couldn't ignore the pull towards a different strategy. Gaining strength as rapidly as possible carried its own benefits, primarily the ability to take control of the situation and minimize potential mishaps. In the end, he realized he'd need to strike a balance between the two approaches.

I will wait until I reach the maximum proficiency in Waterball. After that, I will claim the rewards and get my next skill.

His choices were narrowed down to Wind Gust and Rock Bullet. The wind spell would sync beautifully with his Fireball, but he was aware of his inability to cast the two spells swiftly enough to capitalize on this synergy. On the contrary, Rock Bullet clearly demonstrated offensive superiority. Unless the adversary deployed a defensive skill such as Rock Armor, it would penetrate the defenses of most regular monsters. This one-shot, one-kill type of ability would likely prove more valuable and easier to cultivate compared to the supportive Wind Gust skill.

But that's after I finish training my Waterball skill. I need to focus on the present now.

From his position atop the wall, Thorian discerned the rhythmic sounds of marching brown kobloids emanating from the tree line. A band of sixteen furred creatures approached the eastern gate, their faces alight with excited smiles. Even those previously injured now moved with ease, their bodies showing no sign of any wounds.

"Has everyone received their classes?" Thorian inquired, leaping from the wall to land before the brown kobloids. A mixture of respect and fear filled their eyes as they turned towards him, and the reverent murmurs from before started up again.

I guess they heard legends about flame kobolds in their world. Their reaction is understandable.

"Yes, they've all received their classes," affirmed the brown kobold, casting a glance over his comrades. "Eight have chosen the path of the warrior, two are magi, and five have become priests."

"Five priests—that's excellent news," Thorian acknowledged, his nod of approval given eagerly. He then shifted his gaze back to the brown kobold, querying, "How many have selected the healing skill?"

"Three of them have. The remaining two picked Radiance. I figured that having that skill could significantly help us on the battlefield. The increase in Strength and Constitution it offers can be very useful."

"Your foresight is commendable," Thorian replied, his smile glowing with pride. "While the healing skill is indeed beneficial outside of combat, Radiance can provide the edge needed to survive or even triumph over enemies who might have previously claimed your life."

His gaze swept over the fifteen kobloids assembled before him. A few stole glances in his direction while others stared unabashedly. Whether such attention was out of curiosity about his species or reverence for his status, Thorian couldn't be certain.

They don't have any assassins, but this is a good enough composition to guard the wall. I would have liked a bit more magi for long-range fire, but I guess brown kobloids don't have the best affinity for that class.

Noticing Thorian lost in thought, the brown kobold prodded him back to the present. "Should we assume our positions now and resume our duties?"

"Yes, but before that, there is an important task that needs tending to," Thorian answered. "I need to bestow upon you a name."

"A name?" The kobold's brow furrowed in puzzlement before his face lit up. "Ah, like Nox has? Yes, please grant me a name."

Acknowledging his request with a nod, Thorian rubbed his chin thoughtfully. "Your name shall be Lapis, a term that translates to 'stone' in the old language."

Surprise flickered across Lapis' face before giving way to a smile of gratitude. "Thank you, Thorian. You've been so generous to us, yet you don't for anything in return."

"Don't mistake my intentions. It's far from a one-sided transaction," Thorian corrected, shaking his head. "You will repay me by safeguarding everyone in this village—those currently here, and those yet to arrive."

Lapis placed his hand over his heart and bowed slightly. "I would lay down my life for this cause."

"There will be no need for that," Thorian reassured him, his chuckle accompanied by a comforting pat on the shoulder. "Just concentrate on nurturing your troop's growth. I want them all to evolve into kobolds as swiftly as possible."

"You can count on me, Thorian," Lapis replied, his grin broad. "You'll be commanding the strongest army in this forest in no time."

Thorian smiled at Lapis' audacious promise but didn't comment. He simply bid him and the brown kobloids goodbye and made his way towards the western gate.

There, he found a scenario strikingly similar to the one he'd encountered at the eastern gate a few hours earlier. With the injured count at six, the trio of assassins couldn't perform their patrolling duties, instead staying behind to offer aid. As he did with Lapis, Thorian accompanied the other brown kobold around the class guilds to identify the one that suited him best. Interestingly, despite being a brown kobold, he exhibited a high affinity for magic and thus chose the path of a magus. Opting for efficiency in medium to large-scale battles, he chose the Wind Gust spell over Rock Bullet.

Once the brown kobold settled on his class and spell, Thorian did not immediately exchange places with his group, unlike before.

I need Nox to hunt with me so that I can focus on just raising my Waterball proficiency.

As he approached the northern gate, Thorian could easily discern the results of the orcs' and Ventus' efforts. The section of forest encircling the village center had been almost halved. Even from a distance, the impact of the Gale Slash sent a billow of dust and dirt clean into the air with each cast of the spell, slicing through three or four trees in the process. Thorian's thoughts drifted as he gazed at the fallen trees from afar.

I need to go and talk with Zogthar and the orcs. If they are to offi-cially join our village, I cannot only give them the stick. They also need a carrot. Still, my priority remains with the western kobloids. If they're to acquire their classes, I need to go relieve them of their guard duties.

Thus, Thorian chose to first make his way towards the northern gate, where he was greeted by the sounds of battle cries emanating from beyond the wall. The resonating impact of spells and the clash of steel, interspersed with the grim stench of death, created a vivid tableau of a typical apocalyptic battlefield.

Ascending the watchtower stairs, he discovered Aqua, relentlessly casting spells at the enemy on the other side of the wall. His Triple Water Jet skill was being deployed with rapidity, each successful strike culminating in a small but potent explosion.

Other than Gale Slash, that should be the strongest long-range attack we currently have. Though I haven't seen Saxum's skills yet.

Thorian was rather confused by Aqua's intense look of focus. He found it hard to imagine many adversaries that could command such attention from the water kobold, especially with the support of the other evolved monsters.

A swift appraisal of the scene outside swiftly laid Thorian's skepticism to rest. The opponents his men were contending with were un-doubtedly formidable enough to warrant such diligence.

The berserker kobloids were engaged in combat with a horde of chaskas, while Nox and Forlune squared off against a pack of tail-mashers, with Aqua providing long-range support. The tailmashers were commanded by a creature that towered above the rest, its furry body marked with streaks of purple and blue. Its claws crackled with sparks of lightning, while the three rocks at the end of its tails rever-berated like thunderclaps each time they struck the ground.

CHAPTER 43

Beholding the formidable creature at the head of the three tail-mashers, Thorian's brows knitted together. *A thunder-masher? Can they manage to face it alone?* He cast a sweeping gaze across the battlefield.

By comparison in number, the kobloid forces seemed dwarfed. Their three evolved warriors were locked in ferocious combat against the swarm of chaskas. Each of their mighty axe strokes claimed the life of an oversized feline, yet the relentless tide of adversaries did not wane.

Meanwhile, the priest lingered at the rear of the tumult, his stature now elevated, his fur transformed from a dirty white to a silvery hue reminiscent of the assassins. Only the vibrant blue markings and lunar tattoos distinguished him clearly from his deadly counter-parts.

With a fervor imbued in his eyes, the priest chanted a lengthy incantation until a silver radiance enfolded the warriors. Their movements instantly quickened, each blow they delivered carrying enhanced might.

A support skill? And one that affects a large area at that? These evolutions are truly wondrous. It's roughly equivalent to the power of a first advancement shaman or a similar tiered class.

While the tide of battle was decidedly in favor of the kobolds on one flank, Nox and Forlune found themselves in a precarious situation. Despite Aqua's protective Water Shield enveloping them both and his Triple Jet Stream assaulting the tailmashers, they were still struggling against the thundermasher. Each swing of its lightning-imbued claws left Forlune paralyzed and scorched, rendering him vulnerable to a merciless lashing from the beast's tail. The thundermasher had the ability to amalgamate the trio of boulders on its tail into a colossal one, using it to strike the moon kobold with fearsome force.

Yet the blessing of victory was not entirely lost. The priest had another ace up his sleeve. With a concise chant, a beam of moonlight descended upon the beleaguered Forlune, mending his wounds.

Long-range healing as well? Thorian's face bore a complex mix of surprise and delight. *We need more priests to evolve.*

Concurrently, Nox grappled with the three tailmashers. His shadow skill enveloped the beasts in a sinister aura, amplifying the effectiveness of Aqua's abilities. However, the liberated thundermasher soon intervened, making the odds even more perilous for Nox.

Should I intervene?

Thorian's foot grazed the edge of the watchtower, poised to leap into the fray at a moment's notice. Nox was now contending with four adversaries simultaneously, and while three were battered, the fourth proved unyielding. The thundermasher moved with astonishing speed, keeping pace with Nox even as the latter employed his shadow skills. Kobold's dark aura collided with the thundermasher's blue lightning, but the overwhelming luminescence was gradually eroding the shadows.

Just as Thorian braced himself to join the battle, a resonant roar arrested his movements. His muscles tautened instantly, attention abruptly pulled towards the source of the roar: the three warriors.

Their combined might reverberated in an awe-inspiring howl, striking terror into the hearts of their feline adversaries. Even the thundermasher halted its assault, casting a glance intermingled with rage and fear at the origin of the roar. This gave Nox a brief reprieve, allowing him to retreat and put some distance between himself and his foes.

Aqua wasted no time capitalizing on this chance. He directed his Triple Jet Stream solely at the thundermasher's face, causing the beast to howl in agony. The watery assault shattered its nose and jaw and gouged one of its eyes, blood dripping down its mangled visage.

Rejuvenated by the lunar beam, Forlune rose to his feet and barreled towards one of the tailmashers. Witnessing the moon kobold's courageous charge, Thorian couldn't help but smile as he summoned a sphere of water.

Just as Forlune's axe cleaved into the belly of his target, Thorian launched his spell at another tailmasher, which was darting towards the moon kobold from the side. Just as the beast prepared to strike Forlune, the waterball collided with its chest, sending it sprawling to the ground.

This is a good time to begin practicing this spell.

Armed with a clear strategy, Thorian hurled waterball after waterball at the tailmashers, skillfully denying them any suitable angle of attack on his comrades. Meanwhile, the three warriors were cutting a swath through the petrified chaskas, their bodies swiftly joining the growing pile of defeated foes.

Bodies blanketed the earth before the wall, the majority of them heaped directly against it. In a matter of hours, there would hardly be a patch of ground untouched by the fallen.

The chaskas contributed incessantly to the gruesome pile, succumbing to the warriors' axes by the dozen with each passing minute.

Unyielding, the kobolds carved their path towards the other end of the battlefield where Nox and Forlune were engaged in their arduous combat.

As the minutes slipped by, Aqua and Thorian continued to provide sustained long-range assistance to Nox and Forlune, who employed a strategic hit-and-run tactic. It wasn't long before the three warriors eradicated the remaining chaskas, leaving only the thundermasher and a severely injured tailmasher in their wake.

Faced with the combined onslaught of the evolved kobolds, the final two adversaries stood little chance. They were soon brought to their knees and subsequently defeated.

"I leveled up," Aqua declared, a note of satisfaction underscored by his emerging smile. "I've now attained the highest level for my class."

"Congratulations," Thorian commended. "You're now eligible to advance your class. You have the choice to transition to a water magus straight away and gain increased power, or you can choose to hold off."

The water kobold, initially nodding along with Thorian's words, cocked his head at the last comment. "Wait? What am I waiting for, exactly?"

"Potentially a superior class," Thorian explained, grinning. "The more basic skills you master, the better the class you can progress into. For instance, if you acquire proficiency in Wind Gust alongside Waterball, you'll be eligible for the ice magus class, which wields wind, water, and ice magic."

"That's... That's amazing!" Aqua's eyes sparkled with enthusiasm. "I want to become an ice magus. I'll be significantly more powerful that way."

But as Aqua's initial excitement faded, a note of confusion surfaced. "But how can I learn the Wind Gust skill? You've said something about a guild earlier. Can I get the skill there?"

"No, you'll need arcane coins to purchase it," Thorian corrected, shaking his head. "The quests you received from Melina reward arcane coins. You must have completed a few of them by now, right?"

Aqua's eyes glazed over as he browsed his invisible screens. After consulting his Journal, he turned his gaze back to Thorian and replied, "I've completed three quests. All that's left to do is to gather one hundred units of wood and clear a... dungeon. What is a dungeon?"

"For the wood, you can take the trees the orcs have chopped down and left beside the altar. I'll have everyone collect some later," Thorian suggested. "As for the dungeon, we will clear one very soon. We just need all the brown kobloids to evolve so we can fortify our defenses here before we set out."

Aqua initially furrowed his brows before casually shrugging. "I see. That seems like a sensible plan."

"King!"

While the two magi conversed in the watchtower, a voice from below interrupted them. Looking down, Thorian spotted Caedar bowing to him.

"Thank you, King. Thank you for giving me this opportunity. Thank you for allowing me to evolve."

Hearing the heartfelt emotion behind Caedar's words, Thorian matched the gravity of the moment. "Your gratitude is appreciated, but unneeded. Much of the effort to evolve was of your own doing."

He then let his gaze drift across the battlefield, strewn with the bodies of their adversaries, "And in this battle, you have more than repaid the favor. You've displayed your bravery and honor." Thorian then turned his attention to the other warriors. "All of you have. You are extraordinary and commendable warriors."

"You're overdoing it with the praise, King!" Crimen hollered, his laughter reverberating across the battlefield.

"We merely did what was expected of us," Bellafor chimed in, a chuckle punctuating his words.

Thorian's gaze landed on the priest standing solo near the wall. "Priest, I am proud of you too. Even though your class doesn't equip you with many tools for combat, you still ventured out and hunted enough to evolve. Your courage will not gone unnoticed."

With a gracious bow and a smile, the priest responded, "Thank you for the praise, My King."

Meanwhile, Nox was helping Forlune to his feet. Despite the priest's healing, the moon kobold was still fatigued and slightly injured. When he heard Thorian's praise for the warriors, he could only look down, his face a tapestry of mixed emotions.

"You too, Forlune."

At the sound of his name, the moon kobold glanced up in surprise. Thorian, catching the look of astonishment on his subordinate's face, could only offer him a sympathetic gaze.

"Even in the face of grave danger, you refused to retreat and directly confronted the most formidable adversary. You are a true leader."

Forlune's eyes widened, then he shook his head, "It's nothing. I simply did what was required."

Hearing the moon kobold's response, Thorian smiled gently. He then turned his attention to the shadowstalker. "Last but certainly not least. Nox, you performed excellently. I needn't say this, but you possess immense talent."

Nox responded to Thorian's praise with a boisterous laugh, causing Thorian to shake his head in amusement. He then addressed the warriors once again. "I hope you won't mind, but I need to borrow Nox for a bit."

"Just take that lazy bum!" Bellafor guffawed. "All he's been doing is sitting around. It was only when that weird purple thing appeared and lots of those cat monsters came out of it that he started fighting."

"Hey!" Nox shot back. "You guys were slaying monsters too fast for me to lend a hand!"

Not wanting to entertain their squabbling, Thorian intervened. "Enough with the childish banter. We have more work ahead." He then directed his attention specifically to Nox. "Follow me. It is time for us to hunt together."

CHAPTER 44

At Thorian's command, he and Nox exited through the northern gate, setting their course towards the west. Upon reaching their intended location, Thorian initiated a dialogue with the brown kobold, detailing the same protocol that Lapis had employed with his team. Once the briefing concluded, the kobloid pack dutifully trailed their brown leader into the village, embarking on an identical tour that their eastern gate counterparts had undertaken just two hours earlier.

With the group of kobloids engrossed in accepting their quests and assessing their individual aptitudes for each class, Nox and Thorian commenced their duty as guards. Thorian adhered strictly to his previous plan, utilizing solely his Waterball spell for the entire shift. Despite Nox shouldering the bulk of the workload, Thorian's long-range assistance with his water spell was not without its merits. Nox's shadow-engulfing ability amplified the impact of Thorian's Waterball spell, turning it into a formidable weapon. Their combined powers enabled Thorian to shatter enemies' bones and blast them away with a potent shockwave.

As the hours rapidly ticked away, Nox dispatched the final rabbarian from a group that had naively attempted to penetrate the village's defensive wall. He then scaled the barrier in a single leap, swiftly joining Thorian in the watchtower.

"Thorian, why aren't you using your other skills?" Nox eventually queried, his bewilderment palpable. "It would have been so much easier if you'd fought with me down there. We could have killed even more!"

Meanwhile, Thorian was assessing the advancement of his spell.

Waterball: You summon a watery orb and launch it at your enemies, drenching them and knocking them off balance.

Proficiency: 68.3%

Not too bad, this is great progress for just two hours of work.

Thorian turned his attention back to Nox, shaking his head in response. "That's not necessary, Nox. Our current hunting pace suffices. It's more crucial to augment my skill proficiency."

Perched on the watchtower ledge, the shadowstalker cocked his head, his confusion unabated. "Why is that? It's not really a good skill. Fireball is much more powerful."

Thorian chuckled at the straightforward reasoning. "It's not as simple as that, Nox. My Waterball skill training is geared towards unlocking a more advanced class. The more basic skills I perfect, the higher the quality of classes I can access."

Nox's puzzled expression promptly morphed into surprise, quickly followed by a look of shock. "Wait, is that really how it works? Should I be focusing on Backstab more? Maybe I should get another skill and raise its proficiency too."

"That would be prudent." Thorian agreed, nodding, before falling into contemplation. "Actually, now that I think about it, you should make a point of finishing off your enemies with Backstab. Once you've slain a specific number using that skill, it will unlock a new one that can open the doors to a special class."

"Oh, you should have told me that sooner," Nox said, laughter in his voice. "But thank you. Every enemy I will kill from now on will be with Backstab."

As their conversation concluded, Thorian shifted his gaze to the vista beyond the watchtower. Foreboding howls and roars echoed from the forest's depths, yet their tranquility remained undisturbed by any immediate threat, affording them a brief respite. Thorian lifted his gaze to the sky, tracking the mid-arc transit of the twin suns across the heavenly expanse. These celestial twins, bound in a tidal system, journeyed across the sky at a synchronized pace and in approximate alignment.

Despite squeezing every drop of value from each passing second, it feels like there's an overwhelming amount of tasks yet to be done. Especially that *quest...*

The thought of the human-hunting quest had Thorian's brow wrinkling with concern. He bore no particular aversion to slaying humans—his past life was a testament to that—yet the sheer quantity required to complete the quest was staggering. If he intended for each of his men to meet the five-hundred-kill quota, they would collectively have to hunt down over thirty thousand men and women. This figure represented a significant proportion of Locksley's populace.

That can't possibly be the correct approach. Even if feasible, exterminating them would unequivocally cast me as humanity's nemesis. From a diplomatic and political perspective alone, such a course is unwise, Thorian ruminated, scratching his chin. *Furthermore, it's not in my nature. I am not a destroyer; I am a conqueror.*

Lost in contemplation, the crease marring Thorian forehead only deepened the longer he thought it over.

Eliminating a mere five hundred humans shouldn't pose a significant challenge to me, which would lead to my securing the rare evolution-

ary variant and thus ensure my dominant position. At this juncture, the majority of them likely remain oblivious to the concept of classes. And those who are aware wouldn't pose a threat to someone like me, who has already experienced his first evolution.

"Hey, Thorian."

Thorian jolted, startled back to the present by Nox's voice.

The shadowstalker continued, not noticing. "I've been meaning to ask you—when are the monsters going to stop trying to fight us? Are we just going to have to stay guarding the wall for the whole time?"

It took Thorian a few moments to dismiss his previous lines of thought before refocusing on Nox's question. "Do you recall that strange purple anomaly from which those large cat monsters emerged?" he began.

Nox's brow arched in puzzlement. "Yeah, I do. But what has that got to do with anything?"

"Those are known as portals," Thorian clarified. "As we speak, these portals are manifesting throughout the forest and across the entire country. They will persist in unleashing hordes of monsters for another day and a half."

Both Nox and Thorian cast a solemn gaze towards the forest before the shadowstalker replied, "I see. So we just need to hold out for today and tomorrow. We can do it."

Contemplating the occurrences that were set to follow the first wave, Thorian couldn't help but chuckle. "Well, it's not going to be all sunshine and rainbows after that. Some genuinely bothersome and terrifying creatures will emerge, but we will deal with them when the time comes."

Having regained his bearings, Thorian glanced back towards the village. Ventus and his orc team had cleared the area around the western gates an hour and a half ago, and now that the landscape was devoid of trees, Thorian had an unobstructed view of the village hall and the guilds.

The squad of kobloids, led by the brown kobold, were progressing from the village center towards Thorian and Nox. The former spied from a distance that the previously injured kobloids had been healed by the priests. The brown kobold leading his team bore an exuberant smile, clearly delighted at the substantial power boost his group had recently attained.

I should bestow a name upon him as well. This would ensure parity between the eastern and western gates.

Pondering this, Thorian proceeded to commend the kobloids on their newfound prowess before bestowing a name upon the brown kobold. In the end, he settled on Vivax, an old language term signifying "Energetic". It was apt for this particular kobold's disposition.

Having delegated the responsibility of guarding the western gate to Vivax and his team, Thorian's next destination was the southern gate. Saxum, Ifrit, and Inly were stationed there, and the orcs tasked with timber cutting had already made their way to it. With the brown kobloids now comfortably integrated into the tribe, Thorian felt increasingly confident about advancing his plans of assimilating the orcs.

I wonder what types of evolutions they'll gain access to once they unlock their classes. That will be intriguing to observe.

A grin spreading across his face at the prospect, Thorian strode towards the southern gate in the company of Nox. From a distance, they could witness the impact of Ventus' skill as trees toppled one after another.

As they drew nearer, they could see the orcs carefully transporting tree logs towards the village center. Even from a distance, Thorian could discern a sizable mound of timber encircling the Territory Altar.

Thorian's ears picked up a familiar voice when they stepped just past the tree line.

In the heart of woods where wild winds play,
Orcs heed the goblin's clever say,
Axe bites deep, and tall trees sway,
With the breaking dawn, we begin our day.

The melodious notes wafted from the cleared forest, and Thorian instantly identified the voice's owner. *Brix? What's he up to?* As the pair drew closer to the voice's origin, they observed the goblin in question, engaged in singing and dancing while the orcs continued their labors undisturbed. Rather than wearing stern expressions, the orcs seemed notably more relaxed and comfortable.

"A goblin that sings and dances? I have never seen something like that!" Nox exclaimed, turning towards Thorian with bright, eager eyes. "Have you seen a goblin like that? That is amazing!"

Thorian wore an intrigued expression as he watched the cavorting goblin, remarking, "That's Brix. He pleaded for mercy in the past, so I allowed him to join us."

"Oh, so he's a part of us now?" Nox's surprise was evident. "That is great to hear! I like the way he sings. His voice is really good!"

Noting that Brix was performing as instructed, Thorian navigated through the bustling orcs to reach Zogthar and Ventus. As he journeyed, the orcs cast unusual glances his way. However, instead of hostility and hatred, these gazes bore a sense of respect.

Interesting, I wonder why that is?

CHAPTER 45

As Thorian and Nox weaved through the ranks of orcs, the insistent whispering amplified. Before long, they arrived at the clearing where Ventus, the wind kobold, was employing his Gale Slash skill to fell trees. Zogthar, the burly orc, stood sentinel beside him, ready to heave the toppled timber once Ventus had completed his task. Noticing Nox and Thorian as they approved, Zogthar swiveled, his expression contorting into surprise. Caught off guard, it took him a moment to gather his wits before he inquired, "Is it true?"

Thorian's eyebrow arched at the ambiguous question. "What exactly is supposed to be true?"

"Is it true you became the king of your tribe while still just a kobloid?" He clarified hastily, flicking a surreptitious glance at Ventus. "I heard you even bested a full-grown kobold."

Thorian's gaze shifted to Ventus, a silent question in his eyes. Without requiring an explicit prompt, the kobold scratched the back of his head and chuckled. "I was just telling them about all the incredible things you have done. In just two days, no less!"

Thorian felt a twinge of surprise at Ventus' account, though he let none of it show. He merely returned Zogthar's gaze and confirmed, "Yes, what he said is indeed true. But it is not the whole story—merely the beginning."

Upon receiving Thorian's affirmation, Zogthar's eyebrows shot up in intrigue. He murmured almost to himself, "Just like the Maza-hithar."

Catching the orc's cryptic whisper, Thorian's brow furrowed. "What's that?"

"Oh, it's an old tale the elders used to regale us with," Zogthar elaborated. "An ancient orc king who supposedly claimed dominion over half the world. It's a pleasant myth to indulge in."

Carefully considering the orc's narrative, Thorian broke into a grin. "I can't say I know much about this Mazahithar, but the latter part certainly appeals." He then turned to Zogthar and proposed, "What do you think? Fancy conquering the world?"

Thorian's proposal momentarily stunned Zogthar. Grasping its implications, he brought his hand to his chest in a firm gesture and bowed slightly. "Yes! Under your rule, the whole world shall serve!"

Thorian nodded before issuing his command. "Let us formalize this, Zogthar. Gather your orcs and form a line."

"Right away," Zogthar acquiesced, springing into action immediately. He summoned the other orcs and delegated a few subordinates to retrieve those engaged in transporting the trunks to the altar.

Meanwhile, Nox, having observed the unfolding events with keen interest, finally found an opportune moment to interject. "Are the orcs going to join us too? They'll be such a formidable force once they obtain their classes!"

"That's the plan," Thorian replied with a chuckle, his gaze becoming introspective.

Ventus did an exceptional job propagating my tales amongst the orcs, and Brix managed to defuse any tension with his lively singing and dancing. Without their assistance, the integration of the orcs into our ranks would have taken considerably longer.

Thorian smiled, idly scratching his furry chin. Having capable men in his company had expedited his plans significantly. Without Nox forming an unexpected camaraderie with the brown kobloids, Thorian would have hesitated to integrate the orcs into his ranks so swiftly. He required a foundation of truly loyal followers to support him before he could contemplate expansion, and the kobloids were ideal for this role.

With the addition of the orcs, we're edging closer to our target of one hundred citizens. Once that's accomplished, all we'll need is for Lapis and Vivax to persuade their former tribesmen to join our ranks, and we can commence the village upgrade. The prospect of such a significant accomplishment on the horizon pushed a grin to unfurl on Thorian's face. *Once the brown kobloids fully evolve into their new forms, Lapis and Vivax will find it easier to convince their old companions. The allure of growth, power, and security is a potent one—few in this world could deny its call. And there's the added factor of their former leader being a tyrant...*

With confidence in his strategy, Thorian was drawn back to his surroundings. The orcs were dutifully forming a line under Zogthar's direction, while Ventus and Nox were engaged in a side conversation.

Upon noticing Thorian emerge from his contemplations, Ventus approached him. "I'm almost done cutting these stupid trees. What should I do after?"

Thorian scratched his chin before replying, "There is no need for you to continue that task. We have ample wood for now. Once we position the orcs, there's a place we need to visit."

"Oh, we're going outside the village?" Ventus' eyes sparkled with anticipation. "Are we going on a human hunt?"

"Not quite yet." Thorian dismissed with a shake of his head. "We're set to clear a dungeon first."

Before Ventus could probe further, Thorian's attention was drawn towards the orcs. Zogthar had succeeded in arranging his kin into two kneeling rows, facing Thorian.

Walking up to the forefront, Thorian directed his question at Zogthar. "Zogthar, do you pledge your loyalty to me? Do you vow to wield your sword in my name, in times of war and peace alike?"

"Yes, I swear." Zogthar confirmed, his voice soon echoed by the orcs behind him, their affirmation resonating like thunder. "We swear!"

"Good." Thorian affirmed with a nod. "From this moment forward, you are under my protection. You will serve as my spears, and I, your shield. Any who dare to wrong you will face my wrath, and any who dare harm your brethren will face yours."

Completing his declaration, Thorian let out a deep exhale. "At ease, now."

As the orcs rose, Thorian met Zogthar's gaze. The orc's face was serious, his eyebrows knit together in a steely expression.

I can't blame him. He bore witness as my flames incinerated more than half of his brethren.

Reading Zogthar's look, Thorian softened his own, giving him a gentle smile. "Welcome aboard, brother. You're one of us now."

Seeing Thorian's placid demeanor, Zogthar's taut features eased. "Thank you for welcoming us in."

"It is I who should express gratitude for your willingness to join us," Thorian countered, sweeping his gaze over the twenty gathered orcs. "Let's commemorate this moment... by bestowing upon you all new abilities."

At Thorian's pronouncement, surprise and curiosity etched themselves on the orcs' faces as a low murmur of speculation spread through their ranks.

"Are you referring to those classes Ventus mentioned?" One of the orcs queried, raising his gaze to Thorian.

"Yes, precisely those." Thorian affirmed softly, before pivoting to lead the way. "Follow me."

Their initial stop prior to visiting the guilds was the village hall. Here, the orcs could become official citizens and consequently accept their five daily quests. Concurrently, every member of the group, Ventus and Nox included, undertook the Eärendil quest, a task that had no acceptance limit. Reflecting on the brown kobloids, Thorian inquired of Melina whether they had accepted the Eärendil quest. Fortuitously, the elven lady had had the foresight to extend this opportunity to the preceding kobolds and kobloids, an offer they gratefully accepted.

Upon completing their duties at the village hall, the group proceeded towards the guilds. Their first destination was the Magus Guild, where Fizzlegrin evaluated the orcs' mana affinities with his specialized device. As expected, none of the orcs demonstrated sufficient talent in this class to merit choosing it over the warrior path. Their second stop was the Priest Guild.

Upon stepping into the recently constructed Priest Guild, a wave of tranquility washed over Thorian. The guild, freshly upgraded from its prior incarnation as a simple statue, emanated an atmosphere of serene spirituality. Constructed from a gentle, light wood, the walls were adorned with gracefully flowing patterns that inspired a sense of peace and contemplation.

In lieu of the typical training area to the left, Thorian noted the presence of a room devoted to meditation and spiritual communion. This tranquil space was decked with plush pillows and soft carpets to facilitate comfort during the rigorous spiritual exercises. The room was thoughtfully designed to assist aspirants in discovering their divine connection, a pivotal step in the journey to becoming a priest.

Merrygold, the faun guildmaster of the Priest Guild, was indeed a sight to behold. His sturdy goat-like legs, swathed in golden-brown fur, supported a robust torso garbed in robes of vivid hues. His face, wreathed in curly chestnut hair, radiated constant mirth, his eyes twinkling with wisdom and humor. A pair of magnificent horns crowned his head, adding a sense of dignity to his jovial demeanor. Seemingly inseparable from his hand was a sturdy wooden mug, habitually filled with ale.

Only two of the orcs demonstrated any inclination towards the priestly path, and even then, the deity they were most attuned to was a god of war. With this insight, Merrygold recommended that they acquire the "War Chant" skill, which bolstered their comrades' strength and constitution while mitigating their fatigue.

As they prepared to leave the guild premises, Brix nudged Thorian's leg. "Ehm, master. If it's not too bold of me, could I also attempt to become a priest?"

Thorian turned his gaze to the goblin, his eyebrows creased in thought. His initial instinct was to decline, as he had no desire to empower an individual he couldn't fully control.

Hold on, ostracizing him merely because he's not easily manipulated would be foolish. If I were to follow that course, it might be wiser to simply eliminate him.

Thorian absently scratched his chin as he considered the situation, then locked eyes with the goblin.

CHAPTER 46

"Brix... What is it that you truly desire?"

Brix, ever the anxious goblin, appeared perplexed. "Ehm, I am not sure what you mean, master. I just want to become a priest, as that class reminds me of the great elder."

Thorian shook his head, cool eyes fixed on Brix. "That's not what I mean," he clarified. "What is it that you truly desire? Be honest, Brix, as I shan't offer you infinite opportunities."

Taken aback by the intense question, the goblin faltered, struggling to articulate a response. "I... I just want to live, master. You granted me mercy and spared my life. That's more than what I could ask for."

Thorian remained silent, his penetrating gaze seeming to bore into the very essence of Brix. Sensing the impending peril, the goblin took a cautious step back, letting out a soft squeak of alarm.

"I—I just want to be like the great elder," Brix managed to stammer out. "He does everything he wants and everyone listens to him."

"So that is why you want the priest class," Thorian mused, stroking his beard before breaking into a knowing smile. "With me, Brix, you will see a world much bigger than you had ever imagined. If you prove yourself useful, you will have your authority, you will have your power, and you will have your riches." His voice grew low and icy. "But should you dare to cross me or conspire behind my back, you'll wish you had perished alongside your comrades that fateful night."

A weighty silence enveloped the duo, as Brix visibly shivered under Thorian's unwavering gaze. Only after an agonizing stretch of time did Brix muster the courage to take a deep breath and respond to Thorian's imposing proclamation.

"I will prove myself useful, and I will never betray you. I am not a fool. You possess both strength and wisdom," Brix solemnly pledged.

The goblin's reply had a smirk tugging at Thorian's lips. *So, you will remain loyal as long as I am the more powerful one? Fair enough. It's my duty to remain the strongest. I, Thorian Steelblade, will never lose to anyone else.*

His silence was eventually broken by his measured reply. "That answer is acceptable. Go, request Merrygold to initiate you into the priesthood."

At Thorian's decree, Brix exhaled a sigh of relief. As the goblin set off towards the Priest Guild's master, Thorian's eyes followed him, maintaining a watchful gaze on his back.

If I want to grow an empire, if I want to conquer the world, I cannot accept only the most loyal followers. It is my duty to ensure that everyone's interests align with mine.

Upon evaluating Brix's affinity, Merrygold discovered a strong bond between the goblin and the deity of gold and joy. Astonishingly, the guildmaster had a specialized skill scroll perfectly suited for Brix: Chanting Fortune. While not part of the base skill set, it was known that guilds occasionally held rare abilities for purchase. The availability and quantity of these unique abilities were invariably tied to the rank of the associated guild.

Chanting Fortune was a skill that demanded a lengthy casting time—at least ten seconds of vocalizing—to grant a teamwide buff that enhanced skill efficacy. Regrettably, it was incompatible with similar buffs.

Once they had concluded their business at the Priest Guild, the group redirected their course to the Assassin Guild. As expected, none of the orcs exhibited any aptitude for the art of stealth and murder.

Upon the completion of his assessment, Whisperwind detected Nox's presence and advanced towards him with a smile playing on his lips.

"How intriguing. A shadowstalker. It's been a while since I've encountered one of your kind."

"Oh, um, hello, Mr. Guildmaster," Nox nervously scratched his head and greeted. "It's just been a few hours since I evolved into one. I was a night kobloid before!"

Whisperwind's ethereal blue eyes sparkled with fascination at Nox's explanation. "Intriguing indeed. So it is possible to transition into a shadowstalker in that manner. This does shed some light on the remarkable racial diversity in this village."

Whisperwind fell into deep contemplation, his thumb absently rubbing against his smiling lips. After a brief pause, he refocused on Nox who was tilting his head in confusion.

"Well, regardless, it's commendable that you achieved such a remarkable evolution." The Assassin Guild's master chuckled. "What do you think? Would you like to engage in a friendly sparring session with me?"

Nox's eyebrow shot up before he eagerly nodded. "Sure, I'd love to! I haven't had a proper fight with someone strong since that thrikreen!"

While the pair were prepping for their duel, Thorian remained a silent observer from the sidelines. Gauging the situation's progression, he chose not to interfere and simply continued to watch.

Well now, it seems Whisperwind has taken an interest in Nox.

The orcs, sensing the imminent clash, scattered to make sufficient room for the impending duel. Having personally experienced Whisperwind's formidable strength, none held any illusions about Nox's chances of victory. Even Thorian harbored no particular optimism.

Guildmasters are towering figures—their dominance unchallenged, likely to persist for years to come. If Nox can provide even a slight challenge, it would indeed be a significant upset.

With the audience well spread out, the fight was set to begin. Yet as the orcs initiated their chants and battle cries, they were suddenly halted by Nox's peculiar behavior.

"What are you up to?" The shadowkin peered at Nox, his head cocked in puzzlement. The ebony-hued kobold had settled down on the ground and was simply regarding him with a broad, cheeky grin.

"I watched your earlier fights, and you never laid a hand on the orcs! So I thought, if you're not going to attack, then neither will I. Does that mean it's a draw?"

The crowd erupted in murmurs as the orcs exchanged glances and whispered amongst themselves, some questioning, "Is that option even possible?" Even Thorian found himself taken aback by Nox's unconventional approach.

This childish unpredictability... it's a talent in its own surprising way.

Whisperwind, the Assassin Guild's master, responded with a light chuckle before it escalated into a full-blown cackle. "Fascinating! This just keeps getting more and more intriguing. Very well, I'll indulge you. Do try to avoid getting too bruised."

No sooner had the words left his lips, the shadowkin vanished like dissipating mist. The orcs spun around, unable to discern his location, but Thorian's gaze instinctively zeroed in on Nox.

Nox swiftly rose to his feet as Whisperwind seemingly dissolved into the breeze. He spun around and, as he'd predicted, found the guildmaster materializing behind him, his towering figure casting an imposing shadow. A radiant blue light enveloped his form before concentrating in his right hand. Whisperwind shaped his fingers to resemble a dagger, the ethereal blue aura assuming a sharp, cutting edge. Only then did he launch his attack at Nox.

Despite the shadowstalker's impressive speed, his only option was to maneuver his body to avoid a lethal blow to the chest, resulting in his left shoulder absorbing the impact instead.

Nox was hurled backwards by the force of the attack, his body tumbling uncontrollably before finally coming to rest. He let out a guttural grunt of pain as he pushed off the ground with his uninjured arm, struggling to his feet. Despite his dislocated and bleeding shoulder, an unmistakable grin spread across his face.

"Your offense is as formidable as your defense. That's truly remarkable."

There was no animosity on Nox's countenance, just pure, unadulterated admiration for the shadowkin's combat prowess.

Whisperwind's eyes gleamed with surprise, followed by a light chuckle, "You're quite a character. Let's see if you maintain that bravado in the next few minutes."

In keeping with his previous tactic, the guildmaster dissolved from sight as soon as his words were spoken. However, this time Nox sprang into action without missing a beat. By the time Whisperwind materialized in his original location, Nox had already darted to safety.

Their encounter evolved into a high-speed game of cat and mouse, a spectacle only a few were capable of following. Thorian utilized his decades of experience to anticipate their next moves, while

Ventus displayed extraordinary instincts and keen visual perception. The rest of the orcs could only watch in astonished confusion.

The relentless pursuit persisted, with Whisperwind barely grazing Nox or inflicting minor wounds each time. It wasn't until over a minute had passed that Whisperwind managed to corner his elusive quarry. Hovering above Nox, he readied his attack, his hand morphed into a claw and his entire body glowing blue. Seeing the luminescent aura, Nox couldn't suppress a smile.

"Shadow's Caress."

A dark amalgamation of shadows engulfed the guildmaster's form. While Nox had previously used this skill for its enhancement effect, it also held another utility: temporarily blinding the enemy.

In a split second, Nox sprang into action, delivering a spinning back kick squarely to Whisperwind's face. The impact sent the shadowkin sprawling onto the ground.

The battlefield fell into a stunned silence as the onlookers processed the extraordinary turn of events. Even Thorian's eyes were wide in surprise as he witnessed the unexpected upset unfolding before him.

"Nox!" At that shout, the orcs erupted into ecstatic cheering, their voices echoing Nox's name with unbridled joy and exuberance. They immediately flocked to the triumphant black kobold, hoisting him onto their shoulders before tossing him up into the air. With each catch and throw, the orcs chanted Nox's name in rhythm, while the jubilant shadowstalker laughed heartily.

After several minutes of raucous celebration, Nox finally returned to the ground. Despite the pain in his shoulder and the numerous bruises scattered across his body, he made no effort to halt the orcs' festivities, choosing instead to embrace the exhilaration of the moment.

Once the crowd of orcs had dispersed, Nox was finally able to see the guildmaster. Much to his surprise, Whisperwind bore a broad smile, exhibiting no hint of humiliation over his supposed defeat at the hands of the shadowstalker.

"You're a quick one, aren't you?" he complimented. "You discerned my weaknesses rather rapidly, which is almost embarrassing on my part."

Feeling somewhat awkward, Nox chuckled and scratched his head, "No, I wouldn't say I'm smart. I just had an idea and thought it would be great if it worked. And somehow, it did!"

At Nox's modest retort, Whisperwind joined in the laughter. "And you're impressively swift too, nearly on par with a shadowstalker champion." He then fell into contemplative silence before proposing an offer, "What do you say about working for me?"

CHAPTER 47

"Working for you? How does that work?" Nox queried, his brow furrowed in confusion. Even Thorian, who had been observing from a distance, was intrigued. He had not expected a guildmaster to show this degree of interest.

"Well, you see," Whisperwind began, "These skill scrolls don't materialize from thin air. I have to personally inscribe them. Once you've fully mastered a class skill, you can inscribe them with the appropriate tools. Your task would be to do this for a few hours daily, and in exchange I will provide you with arcane coins."

"Oh, interesting," Nox responded, his voice imbued with excitement. His expression quickly shifted to one of solemnity as he looked downward, "But I haven't completely mastered any skill yet. Even Backstab is only at about 80%, and I've had that for the longest time."

"That's perfectly fine," the shadowkin reassured, shaking his head and laughing lightly. "As long as you concentrate on mastering that skill for the rest of the day, you should be able to achieve 100% proficiency. And don't trouble yourself over the other skills. Since they're racial ones, you won't be able to inscribe them."

Nox's spirits lifted at Whisperwind's encouraging words. However, before committing, he turned to Thorian, asking, "Hey, Thorian, what do you think? Should I go for it? I could purchase more skills with the arcane coins."

"It doesn't seem like a bad idea," Thorian replied thoughtfully. "If I were in your shoes, I'd seize the opportunity."

Emboldened by the king's endorsement, Nox beamed. He looked back at Whisperwind and nodded affirmatively. "Yes, I want to work for you."

The shadowkin returned a faint smile before pivoting away. "Good, follow me so we can finalize the official paperwork."

As they made their way towards the guild, Ventus, who was seated next to Thorian, clicked his tongue in mild annoyance, "Lucky Nox. He always gets the best opportunities, while I'm stuck chopping trees for four hours."

Thorian fought back a chuckle, deciding to ignore Ventus. He instead surveyed the rowdy crowd of orcs who were engaged in spirited conversation and laughter. They were reliving Nox's adventures as if they were their own.

Nox really has a knack for making everyone like him. I guess it's that childish naivety that is so endearing.

After Nox formally became the Assassin Guild's inaugural employee, the group made their way to the Warrior Guild. Rumblestone, as usual, appeared both delighted and self-satisfied about the growing number of warriors under his guild. While the financial benefits from so many members' buying skills were undeniably beneficial, his ego was soaring. After all, he was currently the master of the village's most populous guild.

The warrior orcs were divided into three factions. Of the eighteen, five selected the Taunting Shout skill, six went for Charge, and the remaining seven chose Power Strike. In general, despite their lack of long-range damage support, the group exhibited a commendable diversity and synergy as a warrior unit. In close combat, they promised to be a formidable force.

Having concluded their guilds tour, Thorian ushered the band of orcs to their next assignment: the southern gate. As they neared their post, the distant sounds of battle grew louder.

As Thorian ascended the wall, he could see a trio engaged in a fierce struggle against a horde of thumpalopes, aided by a priest in the rear. The priest, similar to the one at the northern gate, bore silver-white fur marked with moon tattoos all over his body. Bathing the two magi and the warrior in a steady stream of buffs and heals, the trio seemed invincible.

Observing the combat squad, Thorian immediately spotted something intriguing.

Ifrit was a girl?

It wasn't noticeable at first glance, so Thorian hadn't picked up on it earlier. But upon closer inspection, Ifrit's feminine attributes were undeniable.

Thorian quickly averted his gaze from the flame kobold, shaking his head. *We need to acquire some gear soon, preferably robes and armor.*

His eyes then found Saxum, who was positioned mid-range between the priest and the front liners, Ifrit, and Inly. While the pair engaged in frontline combat, Saxum provided cover fire with his Rock Bullet and also utilized his new skill. After a brief chant, the ground beneath the thumpalopes' feet would shift and latch onto their ankles, effectively immobilizing them. Deprived of their greatest strength—speed—the oversized rabbits were virtually sitting ducks.

Ifrit, employing her Combustion Touch spell, set many of the giant rabbits ablaze. Inly joined the fray, wreaking havoc with his axe. In no time, the group of rabbits was efficiently dispatched.

As the skirmish concluded, the orcs opened the gates and stepped outside. Thorian gave his orders, "From this point forward, you're responsible for guarding the southern gate. Engage wisely in your hunts, and avoid any enemy you're uncertain of defeating. In the face of such a foe, retreat immediately and dispatch people to the other gates for backup. Understood?"

"Thank you for your leniency, my lord," Zogthar responded with a slight bow.

"Raise your head," Thorian instructed. As they locked eyes, Thorian scanned the group of orcs, his gaze finally landing back on Zogthar. "These men are under your command. Do not squander this fresh opportunity you've been granted."

The orc looked earnestly at Thorian. "I won't, my lord."

"Good," Thorian acknowledged, his features softening. Looking around, he noticed the goblin engaged in conversation with a few orcs at the rear.

"Brix, come here," Thorian called out, much to the goblin's surprise. The green creature bid farewell to the orcs and hurriedly scampered towards Thorian.

"Yes, master. Do you need me for something?"

Thorian gestured towards the numerous Tthumpalope carcasses strewn across the field. "Take those inside. They'll serve as our food reserves."

"Right away, master." The goblin bobbed a nod before scampering off towards the fallen rabbits.

Realizing that the task would take ages for Brix to complete alone, Thorian turned back to Zogthar and suggested, "Could you assign some of your men to assist him? At this rate, he'll take an eternity to finish."

"Immediately, my lord," Zogthar responded, before addressing the orc warriors. "Jabath, Flamoth, go and assist the goblin."

Upon hearing their leader's command, the two orcs jumped into action. While Brix struggled with a single thumpalope, each orc managed to hoist three under their arms.

Meanwhile, the quartet of kobolds, who had been guarding the gate earlier, approached Thorian.

"Are the orcs with us now, King?" Ifrit inquired with interest.

"Yes, they are," Thorian responded with a grin. "They've all pledged their allegiance to me. They're your comrades now."

"As expected of our king," Saxum said with a chuckle. "All races seek to serve under you. They must have witnessed the same might you exhibited in the cave when you became our king."

As Saxum and Ifrit lavished Thorian with praises and laughter, Inly and the priest exchanged wary glances, observing the orcs. Finally, the priest turned back to Thorian and asked, "Can we trust them, My King?"

"They're loyal enough," he reassured. "But always remain vigilant. If you notice anything out of the ordinary, inform me immediately."

"I will be sure to do so, My King," the priest responded, punctuating his assurance with a respectful bow.

"Oh, forget about that," Ifrit interjected with a laugh. "Now that the orcs are here, what's our next move, King? Should we stay and assist them?"

Thorian regarded the scene thoughtfully before replying, "I need you to remain here for a while, Ifrit. The orcs aren't accustomed to guarding the wall, so your guidance would be invaluable."

"Oh, can I be their leader?" Her eyes sparkled at the thought.

"You can act as their advisor," Thorian responded with a sigh. "Coordinate with Zogthar and inform him that you'll be assisting them by my directive."

"Advisor, leader, it's all the same!" Ifrit exclaimed, jumping with enthusiasm before turning to approach the orcs. "Thank you, King! You're the best!"

Observing the flame kobold's nonchalant attitude, Thorian couldn't suppress his concern. He turned to the warrior, instructing, "Inly, could you please stay here and ensure everything proceeds smoothly?"

"It would be my honor, King," Inly responded, bowing slightly.

As Inly prepared to trail after Ifrit, Thorian added one final directive, "Maintain vigilance and report any developments you find noteworthy."

Inly nodded silently in response, then strode off to follow Ifrit, leaving Thorian standing with the priest and Saxum. Meanwhile, Ventus and Nox, who had been conversing nearby, joined the trio upon noticing Thorian had finished speaking.

"First, we're headed to the village hall," Thorian declared, casting a glance at Saxum and the priest. "You both need to undertake the Eärendil quest."

"Eärendil?" Saxum echoed, a puzzled expression on his face. "What is that?"

"You will know soon enough."

Upon Thorian's announcement, the group of five proceeded back to the hall, where Saxum and the priest accepted their new quest. Afterward, Thorian led the group outside the village.

As they vaulted over the wall, Nox couldn't contain his curiosity. "So, um, what's our next move?" he asked.

Thorian looked back, a smile playing on his lips. "It's time to delve into some dungeons."

INTERLUDE 3

Eleven hours ago…

"Grampa, I'm scared!" cried the small voice in Robert's ear. Locksley, typically shrouded in the quiet darkness of night, was now ablaze, an unnatural illumination reflecting off the slick, rain-drenched streets. Folktales had come alive in the most horrific of ways, as creatures of nightmares clawed their way into reality. Chasing Robert and his grandchild were goblins, snarling and snapping with an eager anticipation of their prey.

Little Roo, held tight in Robert's grip, trembled against him, each shudder a poignant reminder of their grim situation. The old man wished he could spare the breath to soothe the child's fears, but each gasp was a precious commodity, a lifeline he dared not waste. The goblins, a malicious glint in their eyes, were hot on his trail, their shrieks reverberating off the cobbled lanes, promising pain and a grisly end.

Could I have chosen differently?

The thought gripped Robert as he reflected on his decision to abandon the group of mysterious strangers at the plaza. But then, a mental image of the sinister woman emerging from the building sent shivers down his spine, reaffirming his decision. With renewed determination, he shook off the regret and pressed onward. His focus was on survival—his and little Roo's. He wouldn't let the terror of Locksley claim them tonight.

Forgoing contemplation of the past, Robert committed his full focus to the present nightmare. Suddenly spotting monsters emerging from the front as well, his eyes darted to an alley on his right. Clutching the little boy tighter and grinding his teeth in determination, he swiftly maneuvered into the lane.

As he rounded the corner, his blood ran cold. A dead end. Panic bloomed in his chest, prompting him to pound urgently on the lone door to his left, a beacon of potential safety. No matter how desperately he hammered on the cold, unyielding wood, silence greeted him from the other side.

Gods in heaven, have mercy on us.

Robert's silent plea hung in the chilly air, answered only by the shrill cries of the encroaching goblins. Without a glance backwards, he gently placed Roo in the alley's corner before finally daring to confront his grim fate.

The goblins had closed in, a horde of five ghastly green figures grinning grotesquely, crooked teeth on full display. One creature, its eyes gleaming wickedly, drew a menacing dagger, poised to strike the elderly man.

As despair threatened to consume Robert, a glint from the corner of his eye offered a glimmer of hope. A discarded piece of lumber lay nearby. Driven by desperation, the old man seized the makeshift weapon, gripping it with the fierce resolve of a swordsman.

What am I doing?

Robert's hands trembled, his hold on the makeshift weapon tenuous at best. It was apparent to him, as well as the goblin leading the pack, that he could not muster a decent swing. The creature responded with a peal of grotesque laughter, a cacophonous sound of delight at the desperate spectacle unfolding before them. Its cronies joined in, their wicked cackles echoing ominously in Robert's ears.

Gloating over, the lead goblin lunged at Robert, its dagger held high. Fear tightened its grip, freezing Robert in his tracks, his eyes instinctively squeezing shut in anticipation of the impending strike.

As he whispered a last-ditch plea to any deity that might listen, a sudden thought struck him. With no alternatives left, Robert did the only thing he could—he trusted his instincts and opened his mouth.

"Power Strike."

No sooner had he spoken the words than a surge of energy rushed from the core of his being into his hands, and then into the wooden plank. The makeshift weapon began to glow a brilliant blue, startling the charging goblin and leaving Robert himself bewildered.

With an inarticulate cry ripped from the depths of his soul, he swung. His movements were clumsy and graceless, filled with glaring flaws. But raw power needed no finesse.

Robert's now-luminous weapon viciously cleaved through the goblin with brute strength, tearing skin and sinew alike until the force of his swing had ripped through the creature from neck to midriff, laying it open like a roughly-handled doll.

Level up!

The old man's breath came in ragged, shallow gasps. Still, despite his exhaustion, he was riveted by the fading luminescent screen before him. As the glow disappeared, a rejuvenating energy seemed to replenish his depleted strength.

The sharp edge of his adrenaline-laced focus began to blur, allowing him to register new voices, previously unheard amidst the chaos.

"Charge!"

The command rang out, clear and authoritative, from a young man astride a powerful steed. A squadron of seven knights answered the call, two of them thundering forwards on their horses. Their lances, poised for attack, ensured that any goblin fortunate enough to avoid being trampled would face the deadly tip of their weapon.

As Robert's gaze fell upon the young knight sitting atop his horse outside the alley, recognition dawned on him. He knew exactly who this commanding figure was.

Is that His Grace Tristan Ravenwood? What is the prince doing here?

A solemn-faced knight rode up beside the prince, urgency lacing his voice, "Tristan, we must make haste. If we're surrounded by those creatures here, we'll find ourselves in serious trouble."

"We'll move immediately," Prince Tristan responded decisively, his eyes falling upon Robert and the young boy. "But first, we must ensure the safety of these two."

Observing the elderly man and the child huddled in the corner, the knight nodded in agreement, "Indeed. This city has plunged into chaos, and safe havens are few and far between."

With their decision made, Prince Tristan steered his horse towards Robert. Dismounting gracefully, he addressed the older man. "Sir, would you accompany me on my steed? It would be safer than remaining on foot."

Robert was momentarily taken aback by the prince's gracious offer. Stunned, he managed to stammer, "It would be my honor, Your Grace. B-But can I ask you to take little Roo too? He is just a kid."

"Rest assured, sir. I will take the child," responded the previously solemn knight, moving to scoop up Roo and secure him safely in front of him on his horse.

Despite their kindness, Robert still wore a look of surprise. Prince Tristan offered him reassurance. "Do not worry. Oswald will protect your grandson with his life, I swear it."

With a bewildered nod, Robert found himself astride the horse beside the young prince. If encountering a sentient, white-furred creature was a surreal nightmare, the current turn of events had an uncanny resemblance to a dream.

Tristan Ravenwood and Oswald Strongheart? I'd heard the rumors, but to see them in action...

The group navigated the chaotic streets, with Tristan and Oswald anchoring the formation, protected by the other knights. On occasion, a creature would break through their defenses, but the duo, despite guarding an elderly man and a small child, dispatched them with practiced ease.

"We must secure the mansion," Oswald counseled. "Once it's safe, we can coordinate rescue efforts."

With his hand stroking his chin in thought, Tristan said, "You're correct. Our efforts need structure. Haphazard actions won't do us any good."

Yet, as he spoke, he turned to Robert, his voice gentle with curiosity, "If you'll pardon my question, sir, how did you manage to defeat that monster? I distinctly remember seeing that piece of wood in your hand glowing blue."

Startled, Robert stammered before responding. "To be honest, I can't quite explain it myself. It was almost like... magic?"

"Magic?" Tristan's eyebrows furrowed, skepticism shadowing his features. "In what way?"

Robert glanced downward, gathering his thoughts before launching into his explanation, "We were at the plaza with my grandson around midnight when the earth quaked, and these enormous statues suddenly appeared. When I touched one, I... received this magic spell."

His explanation was tentative, and he was acutely aware of how fantastical it sounded. However, Prince Tristan listened attentively, his eyes never leaving Robert's face. Once the old man finished his account, Tristan turned to Oswald and stated decisively, "We need to change our plans. First, we will visit this plaza and investigate."

"I had a feeling you would say that," Oswald replied with a grin. "Perhaps we might find some answers there, determine whether the gods truly have abandoned us."

With their new course charted, the group—composed of nine knights and two civilians—spurred their horses towards the plaza. Their encounters with the monstrous goblins were frequent, as they had staggering numbers on their side, yet the skilled knights dispatched smaller groups with ease. When faced with larger hordes, they chose discretion over valor, skirting around the threat.

Upon reaching the plaza, the veracity of Robert's account was impossible to ignore. The four giant statues were a commanding presence, catching everyone's attention—some gazed in wonder, while others shrank back in fear.

"Oh, if it isn't our esteemed knights. Welcome, welcome." A new voice joined the scene.

The familiar voice caused a shiver to ripple down Robert's spine. Looking past Tristan, he saw Nalia, the woman in green, emerging from the center of the plaza with her entourage. As their eyes locked, Robert immediately averted his gaze.

"Oh, if it isn't dear Robert as well. I was so concerned when you vanished earlier. I feared the worst," she trilled, her voice dripping with false concern.

"Do you know her?" Tristan whispered, his voice barely audible to Robert alone.

"Not really," the old man responded, shaking his head. "She and her group just happened to be in the plaza at midnight. When everything went into chaos, I ran away with little Roo, leaving them behind."

Robert was about to end his explanation there, but after a pause, he added, "I didn't want to stay near them. There was something... unsettling about them."

Tristan nodded solemnly before urging his horse forward. "I've heard tell of magical happenings in this area," he began, his voice filled with feigned cheer. He gestured to the towering statues. "Are these colossi a divine gift, perhaps?"

"Indeed, they are a gift from the gods," Nalia responded, her eyes reflecting the grandeur of the statues. Her gaze swept across the plaza before settling back on Tristan. "However, once these divine gifts descend to earth, they become mankind's property."

Tristan's eyes frosted over at her words, but her smile never wavered. Before he could reply, she added an intriguing proposition, "Your Grace, might you accept a gift from me? It could grant you power beyond your wildest dreams, enough to protect all whom you hold dear."

Tristan studied Nalia intently for several silent moments before responding, "And what if I decline your gift?"

"Ah, but my prince," Nalia began, her tone as gentle as before but carrying an underlying threat. "In our world, where gods bestow gifts and monsters roam free, can we truly afford to refuse an opportunity for strength? Declining a gift isn't just a rejection of power, but perhaps... an acceptance of weakness, and all the dangers it implies."

"Insolence!" One of the knights bellowed, breaking the tense silence. "How dare you speak such words before the prince! Your tongue should be severed for this transgression!"

Just as the knight was about to lunge forward, Tristan stayed him with a hand. "Calm yourself, Sir John. Her words have caused me no offense."

Yet the prince's frosty tone contradicted his words, piquing Robert's curiosity. As he surveyed Nalia's group and the crowd beyond, he noted a throng of people filling the plaza. However, contrary to the fear and uncertainty one might expect in such a post-apocalyptic landscape, their eyes reflected an unwavering conviction.

Am I imagining things?

What truly startled Robert, making him question his own senses, was the eerie red glint that shimmered in the eyes of these men and women.

CHAPTER 48

Thorian assumed the lead, carving a path through the verdant forest, and the group fell naturally into a synchronized march. Nox, ever nimble and spry, acted as a scout, constantly a few steps ahead. Ventus and Saxum took turns securing the flanks and trailing edge, their sturdy forms cutting an imposing figure. Positioned in the heart of the formation, the priest, the group's vital lifeline, was protected by all. Thorian, with a keen eye, watched over both flanks.

The forest's inhabitants soon made their presence known. Thumpalopes and rabbarians greeted them first—relatively harmless monsters that were good for honing skills. The goblins posed a greater challenge with their sheer numbers, yet they were more than manageable. Chaskas and thri-kreens introduced an element of thrill, evidenced by their fallen forms strewn along the trail, marking the group's relentless advance.

As they ventured deeper and the forest's canopy thickened, obscuring the light, a cluster of peculiar mushrooms came into view, exuding a soft, alluring luminescence.

"A funglight lurecap," Thorian uttered, his voice barely rising above a whisper yet loud enough for his companions to hear. His eyes narrowed, captivated yet cautious as he observed the enchanting glow of the fungi.

"Fungwhat?" Ventus echoed, his brows furrowing as he gazed at the odd sight. "They look like harmless mushrooms to me, King."

"That's the point," Thorian explained. "They attract their victims with their light. Be careful not to gaze too long. Their lure is hypnotic."

"But how do they attack?" the priest asked, curiosity getting the better of him.

Thorian gestured at the ground surrounding the mushroom. "Mycelial grasp. If you get too close, they'll trap you. And they're capable of releasing a spore cloud causing several kinds of mental ailments."

As if to demonstrate, Saxum, eager to test the waters, tossed a stone near the closest lurecap. In response, the ground quivered as mycelial threads erupted around the stone, latching onto it and squeezing until it cracked. A small cloud of toxic spores burst from the mushroom's cap.

"Clever plant," Saxum mused, "or is it an animal?"

Thorian shook his head. "Doesn't matter what it is. It's dangerous. Keep your distance."

With newfound caution, the group made their way around the lurecap colony. They moved as quietly as they could, careful to avoid triggering the forest's hidden menace.

Time swiftly passed as the group adhered to Thorian's guidance. With his expertise, the creatures inhabiting the forest seemed akin to mere child's play. As long as they heeded his directions—a task they undertook dutifully—they had nothing to fear.

The forest hummed with a symphony of life and mystery. But as they ventured deeper into the dense woodland, an ethereal murmur began to intertwine with the natural orchestra. A flutter of recognition raced through Thorian's heart—he knew this spectral harmony. The whispers of the trees. They were near.

"What is this?" Nox finally inquired. "I've been hearing these weird sounds in my head."

"Me too!" Ventus joined in, voicing his concern. "It feels like my head is about to split."

"They are the Whispering Trees," Thorian enlightened them. "And refrain from talking excessively. These are the entities that will guide us."

As they progressed deeper into their exploration, the whispers took on a more tangible form. No longer a vexing whisper at the periphery of their consciousness, they became a chorus of voices just beyond comprehension. The murmurs flirted with their minds, conveying a sense of otherworldly hospitality, and yet, beneath it all, lay an unequivocal caution.

Suddenly, the whispers crescendoed to a near-deafening level. As Thorian and his group neared an overgrown archway, cradled by the intertwined boughs of ancient trees and adorned with the soft glow of age-old runes, the voices fell silent. A shiver of anticipation rippled through the group.

The leaves rustled as a wind that was not there began to blow, and the whispers returned, this time sharp and clear as a bell.

"I'm the heart of the home, yet hard as stone.

I can be warm and inviting, yet I can't be alone.

Food becomes feast when I'm put to the test.

Without me, a house would not have its zest.

What am I?"

A profound silence blanketed the forest. The riddle, hanging in the air, seemed to mute the very essence of the world. They gazed at the luminescent gateway, its cryptic power thrumming in sync with the reverberation of the words. The unuttered threat of retribution for an incorrect answer loomed over them like an impending guillotine, the blade poised ominously above their collective existence.

As Thorian fully absorbed the riddle, a smile graced his features. *This should've posed no challenge,* he thought. *The men under William should have effortlessly solved this as well.*

"You are the Hearth."

His voice echoed through the hushed forest, the woodland itself seeming to lean in to catch his response. Then, a palpable stillness befell them all. The hush deepened, the whispers dwindling to silence. The suspense was unbearable, a string pulled tight to the brink of snapping.

Suddenly, a soft sound filled the air. It was the sound of... laughter. A deep, rich laughter, full of mirth and joy, and then the Whispering Trees began to hum. It was a deep, resonant sound, filling the forest, reverberating through the very soil beneath their feet.

"Creepy..." Ventus murmured. "A tree that laughs? This is too crazy for me."

The archaic runes engraved on the archway erupted into a brilliant display, a detonation of luminescence that cast elongated, cavorting shadows around the group. The entwined branches of the archway trembled, then slowly, unyieldingly began to part, unveiling a concealed path beyond.

"Should we go inside?" Nox inquired with apprehension, his gaze directed at Thorian. The rest of the group mirrored his action, their eyes converging on their leader.

"No, not yet," Thorian decisively shook his head. "This dungeon is too hard for us currently. We will go back to it later when we are stronger."

"Heh, I have never seen you back down from a challenge before, King," Ventus remarked, a touch of curiosity in his tone as he turned his gaze back to the now-revealed sanctuary entrance. "Just what could be inside that would make you say that?"

"Ventus," Saxum admonished the wind kobloid with a stern look. "Watch your tongue."

"There are elves," Thorian expounded. "Corrupted elves. A single arrow from their quiver could pierce through the five of us."

Each member of the group looked at Thorian with a mix of disbelief and awe. His words were challenging to digest, yet given their credible source, they found it hard to refute them.

After consulting his journal, Thorian gestured for the group to follow. "We should depart now. We've completed the quest, and there's a considerably less challenging dungeon we can explore."

Guided by Thorian, the group turned back, retracing their footsteps. As they distanced themselves from the dungeon, the illumination from the archway receded, and the entrance to the sanctuary closed once more.

Eärendil's Sanctuary was nestled on the western flank of the village, neatly situated between Wolvendale and Locksley. However, the dungeon that Thorian intended to conquer was located on the opposing side.

Navigating an extensive detour, the group persisted in their perilous exploration. In addition to the creatures they had already encountered, they stumbled upon new, intriguing inhabitants of the forest. Most noteworthy among these were the shelltrotters. These fascinating hybrids of horses and armadillos stood as tall as the most formidable war horses when on all fours and could trample any adversary with their fortified hooves. Yet, it was when they curled up into a sphere that they turned decidedly more lethal. The enormous scales on their backs, sharp as steel yet remarkably pliable, facilitated a terrifying rolling speed.

Fortunately, Ventus' Gale Slash was sufficiently potent to slice through their defenses, providing Thorian a clear target for his Combustion spell. And while the shelltrotters boasted impressive speed, they were no match for Nox, who darted from one tree to another with an agility that would put any monkey to shame. Thus, despite consuming a significant amount of time, the group managed to tackle the small squadron of armored horses.

Good thing the pack did not have an evolved one amongst them. A magmastone or thunderbolt charger would have been difficult to escape from.

Thorian couldn't suppress a wry smile as he reflected on their recent encounter. However, now was not the time for nostalgia, as their destination was close at hand.

The dense forest ahead began to thin, their pace reducing as they caught sight of an immense tree towering over its neighbors. Its knotted roots sprawled outwards, and a large hollow at the tree's base served as an entrance, emanating a foreboding aura.

"That's our destination," Thorian murmured, his red fur reflecting the faint glow of the sun's rays filtering through the foliage. He stared at the dungeon entrance, his fiery eyes ablaze with unyielding determination.

"Looks creepy," Nox commented from beside him, peering towards the hollow with wide, curious eyes. The black-furred kobold was always brimming with excitement, even in the face of danger.

Ventus gave a sharp exhale, puffing out his chest. "Well, whatever's in there, we can handle it!" The wind kobold radiated a youthful aura of courage, ready to prove himself once more.

CHAPTER 49

As Thorian approached the entrance of the dungeon, a floating screen appeared in front of him.

Congratulations, you are the first to discover the small-scale dungeon: Verdant Labyrinth. You will receive double the rewards and a higher chance for extra rewards if you clear it.

Choose the difficulty layer you wish to enter.

Layer I: Recommended for a party of five at Peak Initiate Level.

Layer II: Recommended for a party of five at First Advancement.

Layer III: Recommended for a party of five at Peak First Advancement.

Layer IV: Recommended for a party of five at Second Advancement.

Layer V: Recommended for a party of five at Peak Second Advancement.

As he surveyed the screen floating before him, a smile tugged at Thorian's lips. He turned his attention back to his comrades, upon which it became apparent that they too were engrossed in a similar holographic panel.

"What do you all think?" Thorian posed the question. "Which difficulty level should we opt for?"

"I say let's go for the fifth layer!" Ventus proposed with palpable enthusiasm.

However, before he could justify his suggestion, Saxum landed a gentle punch on his head. "You really need to learn when to keep quiet."

"Ouch! Why'd you hit me? It was the king who asked for my opinion. Why do you have to butt in?"

Thorian and the priest shook their heads at the childish banter while Nox was laughing heartily on the side.

"It was my mistake to ask," Thorian grumbled. "We'll opt for the second layer. It should provide us with a good baseline to understand the layout of this dungeon."

From a technical standpoint, those recommendations assume a well-geared squad, but this shouldn't pose too much of a problem.

"But I was hoping for a challenge..."

Ignoring Ventus' grumbles, Thorian issued his command. "Since we can't yet form an official party recognized by the system, we'll need to hold hands before selecting the difficulty. Otherwise, we risk being teleported to different locations."

"Teleportation?" Nox's eyes lit up at the prospect. "Now, that's a sight I'd love to see!"

"How would that work?" Saxum asked with interest.

"You will see soon enough," Thorian said, spreading his arms, "Now take each other's hands."

Following his command, the group took each other by the hand before Thorian chose the second layer of the dungeon. With all hands linked, Thorian turned his attention back to the screen and firmly selected "Layer II." The moment he did, a radiant light enveloped the group, causing them to instinctively shut their eyes. A sensation of weightlessness swept over them, like they were being lifted off their feet. Then, just as suddenly as it began, the sensation stopped, and the brilliant light faded.

They opened their eyes to find themselves standing in a vastly different environment than the forest they'd left behind. The enormous tree that housed the dungeon was even more towering from the inside, its inner walls glowing faintly with the bioluminescence of countless fungi and moss.

"Everyone all right?" Thorian asked, scanning his companions. The others nodded, still a bit disoriented but otherwise unharmed. "Then let's proceed, with caution," he added, releasing the hands of Nox and Saxum.

Nox, being very energetic, stepped forwards with a grin. "All right! Let's see what this dungeon's got!"

"No need to rush," Thorian admonished, but there was a smile playing on his lips. He was just as eager as the rest of them to see what challenges awaited them.

As they moved from the landing area, they entered the first challenge—*The Fungal Fields*, Thorian noted. The spectacle that unfolded before them was unquestionably surreal. The fungi, in myriad colors, shapes, and sizes, each glowed with its own distinctive luminescent hue. However, the beauty of the spectacle was rapidly eclipsed by the rustling noises emanating from the towering mushrooms.

Suddenly, from the corner of his eye, Ventus spotted movement. "There!" he pointed. Emerging from the base of a large mushroom were several armored beetles, their exoskeletons shimmering with the reflected bioluminescent light.

Armored beetles? Tough creatures.

While Thorian was still occupied observing the newcomers, Nox was already in motion, his palpable excitement bubbling over. "I got this!" he declared, surging forwards with a gust of wind that stirred up loose leaves and pebbles in his wake.

"Saxum, slow him down!" Thorian called out. The earth magus quickly cast his root spell, trying to ensnare Nox, but the shadowstalker was too fast.

Nox approached the armored beetles, axe in hand, but as he brought it down, it merely clanged off the beetle's exoskeleton. The beetles retaliated in unison, their sharp mandibles snapping at the black kobold.

"Nox, run!" At Thorian's commanding shout, the shadowstalker leapt into action, sprinting away from the beetle swarm with breakneck speed. However, despite Nox's swiftness, the beetles retaliated with a volley of spikes, effectively blocking all his potential escape routes.

"Gale Slash!"

Just as the lethal barrage was about to impale the black-furred kobold, a burst of wind cleaved through the spikes, deflecting them off their intended course.

Ventus continued his relentless assault of gale slashes, the blasts of wind colliding with and deflecting the spikes away from Nox. The shadowstalker darted around the beetles, attempting to identify an opening. Concurrently, Thorian stepped forward, his fingers wreathed in flickering flames.

"Stand back!" he called out before thrusting his hands forward, a stream of fire spewing from his palm. The beetles screeched as their exoskeletons heated up, the creatures instinctively curling to protect themselves, exposing their vulnerable underbellies.

"Now, Nox!" Thorian shouted.

With a grunt of acknowledgment, the shadowstalker dashed forward, his swift movements barely visible. His blade whistled through the air as he danced among the beetles, slashing at their exposed underbellies. Each stroke of his axe was precise and deadly, leaving fatal wounds in the soft flesh of the beetles.

However, even with their impeccable teamwork, a stray spike managed to graze Thorian. A sharp yelp escaped him, his movements faltering for a moment. But before the beetles could seize this chance, Saxum stepped forward, his hands glowing a soft green.

"Earthen Grasp," he murmured, slamming his hands onto the ground. Instantaneously, the earth beneath them softened and shaped itself, ensnaring the beetles who were grounded. With the creatures immobilized, Nox could navigate with greater ease, slicing through the captive monsters effortlessly.

Still, the wound Thorian had received needed tending to. The priest, standing a safe distance away, raised his hand as a soft, silvery light began emanating from it. With a small intonation, the moonlight stretched out and enveloped Thorian. The flame kobold's grimace of pain eased as the healing magic stitched his wound together.

With their combined efforts, the party swiftly dealt with the beetle threat, leaving them panting but exhilarated. There were smiles all around, an atmosphere of camaraderie filling the air.

Level up!

Seeing the familiar pop up, Thorian let out a smile. *I forgot I was close to leveling up again. Display panel.*

Level: 12/30 (XP: 34/1350)

After checking his level, Thorian immediately closed his stat screen. His eyes then shifted towards the shadowstalker.

"Nox, you shouldn't get too excited. Understand?" Thorian said, his voice stern but not unkind.

With a sheepish grin, Nox rubbed the back of his head. "Sorry about that, guys," he admitted, glancing over at Thorian. "I got a bit carried away there. Won't happen again."

Thorian nodded, his stern expression softening. "That's all we ask, Nox. This isn't the same as just killing anything that moves when guarding the wall. We need to work as a team, to keep each other safe."

The rest of the group shared a look, the smiles on their faces betraying their relief. While the battle had been an unexpected challenge, their victory was a testament to their strength as a team. No one was seriously injured, and they'd even leveled up.

"All right, let's take a moment here," Thorian suggested, sitting down on a nearby mushroom. "We need to discuss our tactics. Nox, you need to remember to let Saxum and Ventus control the battlefield first. You're our ace, our finisher. We can't afford you going berserk from the start."

Ventus, sitting opposite of Thorian, chuckled. "Yeah, listen to the king. You nearly gave us a heart attack."

Surprisingly, even Saxum concurred. "I generally never agree with this blockhead, but you nearly ended up dead. I'm unsure where this idiot discovered such reflexes to come to your rescue so quickly."

"Hey! Who are you calling an idiot?!"

Choosing to ignore their squabble, Thorian directed his attention to the priest. "You did an excellent job with the healing. That said, remember to also utilize your other skills when appropriate. Ventus, Saxum, your battlefield control was outstanding. We should maintain that level of coordination. As for you, Nox, exercise patience. Await the opportune moment to strike."

After ensuring that everyone understood their roles, Thorian stood, the rest of the group following suit. They made their way out of the Fungal Fields, Ventus and Saxum leading the way, their senses alert to any potential danger.

As they crossed the bioluminescent sporedom, the path they were led to by the dungeon showed a clear distinction of areas. As they stepped into the second area—the Thorned Thicket—they felt a significant change in the atmosphere. The dense vegetation and the twisting ivy gave the place a claustrophobic feeling, and the quiet rustle of the leaves was a constant reminder of the lurking dangers.

They moved cautiously, Ventus' Wind Gust violently pushing aside the poisonous ivy, while Saxum kept an eye out for any movement in the dense thicket. Nox remained at the back, his gaze shifting from one side to the other, his hand never leaving the grip of his axe.

Suddenly, Saxum raised his hand, bringing the group to a halt. His eyes narrowed at a particular patch of ivy, while he conjured a Rock Bullet with his finger. The moment his magic came into contact with the vegetation, an ominous creature revealed itself. The giant vine shot out with a feral hunger, displaying fangs that gleamed threateningly under the luminescence of nearby fungi.

Ventus was quick to react, a gust of wind sending the vine flying back. Nox stepped forward, his blade slashing through the air, and with a single, swift movement, he cut the vine into two. The vine fell to the ground, writhing and hissing until it eventually stopped moving.

A voracious vine, huh?

A quiet sigh of relief went through the group. They were in the thick of it now, their every step leading them deeper into the challenges of the Verdant Labyrinth.

"Let's keep moving," Thorian said, his voice low but filled with resolve. "Stay vigilant, and we'll make it through."

CHAPTER 50

The vibrant foliage of the Thorned Thicket closed around them like a natural fortress, the glow from the bioluminescent fungi casting an eerie green light on their faces. Thorian could feel a tingle in the air, a slight increase in the magical energy that swirled around them.

"I don't like this place," the priest muttered, his eyes darting around the thicket. "Too many places for something to hide."

Thorian couldn't help but agree. His eyes scanned the undergrowth for signs of movement in increasingly wary strokes. "Stay close," he warned, his voice barely above a whisper.

The thicket was silent as they delved deeper, the only sound being their footsteps and the occasional rustle of leaves as Ventus blew a gust of wind to clear the way. The air grew thicker, the smell of damp earth mixed with the bitter tang of venomous ivy making it hard to breathe.

Suddenly, a rustling sound echoed from the undergrowth, and Saxum raised his hand, bringing the group to a halt. His eyes narrowed at a particular patch of ivy, before voicing a small chant.

Thorian felt the energy surge as Saxum cast his Rock Bullet spell. The moment the magic collided with the ivy, a voracious vine shot out, its fangs gleaming with a deadly sheen.

Reacting almost instinctively, Ventus once again sent a gust of wind that sent the vine sprawling back. Nox stepped forward, his blade swinging with deadly precision, slicing the vine in half.

The vine hissed, writhing and thrashing until it eventually stilled. As this was the second time they had to deal with this creature, the tension was still in the air but didn't hang in a suffocating veil as before. Thorian, who was already used to this level of danger and couldn't stop the quiet chuckle from escaping him. "Not as easy as killing goblins, huh, Nox?"

Nox shrugged, sheathing his weapon with a sheepish grin. "Well, those green buggers don't usually hide in the bushes."

Thorian still had a smile on his face as he said, "Let's stay vigilant," and led the group deeper into the thicket.

All seemed fine as they progressed, but a little ways in, a strange chill crept down Thorian's spine. He froze in his tracks, his eyes scanning the surrounding foliage.

Everything was still. Too still.

"Something's wrong," he murmured.

The others halted as well, their eyes wide and alert. Then, from the corner of his eye, he saw a flicker of movement. "A thorned stalker," he hissed, pointing towards the movement.

The foliage seemed to come alive as the thorned stalker emerged, its green skin making it almost invisible among the leaves. The creature's eyes were a haunting red, glaring at them with a predatory gaze.

Nox was the first to act, charging forwards with his weapon drawn. However, the thorned stalker was quick, its spiked tendrils snaking out to parry his attack.

"Nox, hold!" Thorian called out, his mind racing. The stalker was agile and cunning, and it used the dense foliage to its advantage. They needed to bring it into an open space. "Saxum, clear a field with your skill. Ventus, keep that thing at bay!"

The earth magus nodded, slamming his palms onto the ground. The earth shook violently as the hard ground turned into soft dirt, toppling the nearby trees and creating an open field. Ventus sent gusts of wind towards the stalker, forcing it into the open.

"Good!" Thorian shouted, preparing his fire magic. "Now, Nox, draw its attention!"

The black kobold nodded, dashing towards the stalker. He was a blur, his movements swift and precise, avoiding the tendrils and drawing the creature's focus.

With the thorned stalker forced into the open, Nox became a whirlwind of motion, his every move a dance of danger. The creature lunged at him, its spiked tendrils whipping through the air, but Nox dodged, his slender figure darting about with graceful agility.

"Ventus, Gale Slash, now!" Thorian ordered. Ventus nodded, pointing his finger at the enemy while articulating a small chant. A gust of wind materialized before him, spinning faster until it became a cutting blade of air. With a forwards thrust of his hand, he sent the Gale Slash spinning.

The creature reeled back, its cry echoing through the thicket as the wind magic cut across its form. In the momentary distraction, Nox closed in, his axe gleaming ominously.

"Too slow, stalker!" Nox taunted, his weapon finding its mark on the creature's exposed flank. A pained growl escaped the thorned stalker, but it quickly retaliated, its tendril swiping at Nox.

Using his superior agility, the shadowstalker sidestepped the creature's desperate attempt before shadows seeped from his hand. The dark aura completely covered the thorned stalker, blinding it momentarily.

"Good job, Nox," Thorian commended, seizing his opportunity. With the enemy incapacitated, he rushed forward, palm ablaze with swirling flames. His hand clashed against the creature's core, the infernal fire consuming the shadows, and along with it, the thorned stalker.

"Brilliant work, all of you," Thorian lauded, his gaze sweeping over his fellow combatants.

"It's nothing to write home about, this was easy," Ventus remarked, a grin tugging at his lips as he casually scratched the tip of his nose with his thumb.

"I barely got a look in," the moon priest chimed in, his tone feigning disappointment.

"Isn't that a good thing?" Saxum teased him good-naturedly. The white-furred priest simply responded with a nonchalant shrug and a matching grin.

With the stalker's demise, the party continued their cautious trek through the Thorned Thicket. The eerie green light from the fungi painted an otherworldly canvas on the forest floor, while the undergrowth's rustling hinted at the life hiding in its shadows. The air was thick with the scent of decaying leaves and wet earth.

The group reached a wide clearing, the light blue glow from the phosphorescent plants giving the area a surreal, dreamlike quality. A small spring of clear water trickled into a crystal lake pool, its surface perfectly reflecting the surrounding foliage.

"This is the Luminous Glade," Thorian began, his voice informative. "Its properties are akin to our own territory, where mana rejuvenates at a faster rate. Additionally, it aids in alleviating fatigue."

At Thorian's words, the priest felt compelled to offer his observation. "This place is very interestingly designed. It's as if they want us to clear it."

"The gods would miss their entertainment otherwise," Thorian responded cryptically.

Before the priest could offer a rebuttal, Ventus interjected enthusiastically, "Nox, let's have a swimming race across the lake. Whoever loses has to call the winner 'big brother' for a day!"

With the gauntlet thrown, the wind magus dashed towards the crystalline lake. He dove into its pristine waters, momentarily disturbing its serene beauty.

"Hold on, no fair!" Nox immediately sprang into action, trailing behind Ventus who had already seized a significant lead in their impromptu contest.

Shaking their heads at the playful rivalry, Thorian, Saxum, and the priest utilized the moment of respite to recover from the rigorous combat against the thorned stalker. Gathering around the spring, they could sense the magical energy suffusing the area, soothing their worn bodies and hastening their recuperation.

Meanwhile, at the lake's far end, Ventus and Nox were on the brink of deciding the victor. Despite Ventus initially holding the lead, Nox employed his superior agility to outswim him. Seeing his impending defeat in a competition he had instigated, Ventus gritted his teeth and aimed his palm at the shadowstalker.

"Wind Gust!"

The incanted wind spell whipped up a wave that sent the black kobold veering off course.

"That's cheating!" Nox yelled out, his voice echoing across the lake as Ventus laughed triumphantly, speeding past him. Unfazed, the shadowstalker merely grunted and resumed swimming, resolved to regain his position.

As the finish line loomed ahead, and the lake's bottom was just within reach of his feet, Ventus cast a glance over his shoulder. Seeing Nox gaining on him at an alarming pace, the wind magus clenched his teeth, fear of losing his standing urging him on. He leapt into the air, body curled in a somersault position. As he aligned himself just right, he summoned his spell and used Wind Gust as a midair propulsion. With a monumental leap, Ventus landed at the lake's edge.

Upon touching the ground, he swiveled to his left only to find Nox standing right beside him.

"I was first!" they both claimed simultaneously.

Frustrated by their inability to determine the winner, they both cast resigned glances back towards their comrades.

"King, who won?" Ventus asked, "It was me, right? I clearly jumped over the finish line before him."

"No," Nox countered, shaking his head vigorously. "While he was spinning midair, I was sprinting to the finish line! I'm the clear winner!"

"Don't burden the king with such trivialities," Saxum interrupted, a placid smile playing on his lips. "As for the victor between you two, it seemed like a draw from my perspective."

"Yes, you both arrived at the finish line simultaneously," the priest concurred.

"No, but he was cheating throughout!" Nox protested.

"There was no cheating!" Ventus shot back. "I never declared it a magic-free race."

While the two bickered, Thorian found himself chuckling and looking down, a nostalgic smile forming on his lips. Witnessing their youthful energy and camaraderie stirred fond memories of his own past.

It has been such a long time. I barely remember anything...

As the group engaged in jovial recuperation, Thorian, in contrast, was quietly steeling himself for the imminent challenge: the Quicksand Marsh, the next zone within the dungeon.

CHAPTER 51

The Luminous Glade was a sanctuary within the verdant hell, a serenity that was paradoxical to the chaos of the dungeon. The warm afterglow of their triumph lingered, fuelling their spirits for the impending challenges.

"Keep your wits about you," Thorian warned, his golden eyes reflecting the phosphorescent light. "The Quicksand Marsh is treacherous. One wrong step and you could be sinking into oblivion."

His words echoed, casting a somber veil over the camaraderie. They nodded, acknowledging the gravity of their next challenge, before venturing into the labyrinth.

The contrast between the tranquility of the Luminous Glade and the eerie desolation of the Quicksand Marsh was stark. The ground beneath their feet turned soft and treacherous, the air filled with a decaying stench, while the distant moans of the marsh's inhabitants broke the ominous silence.

The group advanced cautiously, eyes alert, and weapons ready. Thorian's hands glowed, preparing to conjure flames at a moment's notice. Suddenly, the ground beneath Saxum gave way, quicksand threatening to swallow him.

"Nox, a hand here!" Saxum called out. The shadowstalker responded with lightning reflexes, his lithe figure darting forward, arm extended. His strong grip closed around Saxum's wrist, pulling him free from the deadly trap.

"Thanks, mate." Saxum nodded, his eyes reflecting his gratitude.

The group continued on their way through the dangerous marsh, making sure to avoid the spots that looked too soft or shifty.

"Nox, what's the lead look like?" Thorian called out, breaking the ominous silence of the marsh.

The black kobold had ventured ahead, scouting for the safest path. "This way," he gestured, guiding them around a particularly large and menacing venus flytrap.

The group complied, keeping their steps light and wary. As the earth gave a little beneath their weight, Ventus voiced his concerns. "This terrain doesn't suit me well, King. Too much earth, not enough air," he quipped.

A soft chuckle rumbled from Saxum, easing the tension. "Don't worry, featherfoot. If you started sinking, Nox would quickly come and save you."

Their banter was cut short when Nox suddenly held up a hand, signaling them to halt. "Armored beetle, right at the front," he whispered, eyes narrowed at the approaching threat.

Ventus stepped forward, hands crackling with energy. "Leave this to me," he murmured, his gaze focused. With a swift movement, he extended a hand. "Wind Gust!"

A rush of wind erupted from his palms, catching the beetle off guard and flinging it sideways into a waiting flytrap. The plant snapped shut in an instant, trapping the beetle within its maw.

"You really wanted to show off with that one" Saxum rolled his eyes, while Ventus laughed sheepishly in response. The earth magus then looked to the others, a note of caution in his voice, "But we must remain vigilant. More creatures lurk in the shadows."

As if on cue, the earth beneath them began to ripple, the muddy surface bulging as creatures that looked like a giant mix of leeches and worms emerged. "On your guard!" Thorian warned, his hands already aflame.

With the ground beneath them threatening to turn into a mass of writhing worms, Nox lunged at the nearest one, his axe slicing through its segmented body with ease. Ventus, aided by Saxum, manipulated the air and earth in perfect synchronization, causing the worms to lose balance, making them easy targets.

"We have to move. Now!" Thorian commanded, leading the group through the marsh towards the safety of solid ground.

"Be ready," Thorian warned, his gaze narrowing at the uneven terrain of the shifting mounds all around them. His words echoed in the eerie silence, casting a tense air over the group.

"Something's moving," Nox whispered, his silver eyes glowing eerily in the dim light as he focused on a writhing mound. His hands tightened around his axe, prepared for the imminent attack.

Suddenly, a giant worm burst forth from the ground, lunging at Saxum with its jaws gaping wide. The earth magus, reacting quickly, thrust his palm out. "Rock Bullet." Saxum's conjured spell flew towards the incoming enemy, piercing through it instantly. The attacking worm, dead on impact, fell back into another set of mounds.

More worms burst from the disturbed ground, hissing angrily.

"Looks like we've found the nest," Saxum muttered, backing up against the group as they formed a defensive circle. Thorian's hands were aflame, casting a flickering glow across their grim faces.

"I don't like this," Nox whispered, his gaze flitting nervously over the uneven terrain of the shifting mounds. "Too many places for things to hide."

Hearing Nox's assessment, Thorian smiled. *I am not doing much, but this is perfect. Their group dynamics are shaping up well.*

"That is true," Thorian agreed with Nox, his golden eyes glowing in the eerie twilight as they scanned their surroundings. "Remember, nothing in this dungeon is as it seems. We need to stay alert and—"

Suddenly, more worms burst from the mounds around them, their bodies writhing and hissing in anger.

"Looks like we've *roused* the nest," Ventus remarked dryly, his hands crackling with energy.

Just as the wind magus was primed to cast a Gale Slash, Thorian intervened.

"Ventus, what do you say to setting this entire place ablaze?"

The wind kobold's eyebrows knit together in initial confusion before his face brightened with comprehension. "You mean to try that combo, King? It's been a while!"

"Pick a target," Thorian said cheerily, his voice ringing with anticipation. "Let's purify this forsaken realm."

"Right away, King!" Ventus responded with a grin, cracking his knuckles in preparation. He pinpointed a cluster of squirming mounds, and both Thorian and the wind magus began to summon their spells.

Ventus' Wind Gust bolted towards its target, while Thorian's Fireball trailed hot on its heels. As the elements intermingled, the fireball morphed into a cascading wave of flames.

The worms emitted high-pitched shrieks as they attempted to flee from their nests, but to no avail. The raging inferno swiftly reduced them to ashes.

"Again!" Thorian ordered, and the pair readied their spells once more. As they methodically incinerated the predatory leeches, the chorus of shrieks and squeals rose to a fever pitch. The discordant symphony was filled with inhuman cries that lacked sympathy, yet managed to elicit an instinctive, primal reaction from the heart.

Amidst this tumultuous cacophony, an unexpected notification resonated in Thorian's ear.

Level up!

Already? Thorian frowned before checking his status screen. *Display panel.*

Level: 13/30 (XP: 237/1500)

Is it because of the double rewards? Thorian's lips curved into a smile. *Hunting is first and foremost a dungeon activity. What we had been doing up until now was simply the poor man's version.*

While pondering inwardly, Thorian's gaze scanned his teammates. They all seemed absorbed with invisible screens hovering before them.

"Ah, I've leveled up twice," Saxum noted casually. "How did that happen?"

"Wait, what?" Ventus interjected, surprised. "I've leveled up twice too, but how did *you* manage that? It doesn't make sense."

"I've leveled up as well," Nox chimed in. "Not twice, but I'm close to another level up."

"The reason is because we're in a dungeon," Thorian provided an explanation. "The experience points are all shared between us. That way, even those with supportive roles get to reap the rewards."

"I wish I could offer support, but I'm just a liability," the priest sighed in self-deprecation. "Could you guys pretend to be injured so I can heal you? At least that way, I'd feel a bit more useful."

"Don't worry, mate. I got you!" Ventus reassured him, flashing a thumbs up that only added salt to the wound.

Meanwhile, Saxum shook his head, a wry smile betraying his amusement as he looked at the priest.

"I didn't realize you had that side to you," he commented. His tone might have suggested disappointment, but his expression revealed his true sentiments.

As the group continued their friendly banter, Thorian's ears perked up. He shot a glance towards his black-furred comrade, recognizing a similar hint of disquiet reflected in his eyes.

"Nox, can you scout ahead?"

With a nod, Nox darted forward, his lithe figure quickly disappearing among the shifting mounds. The others waited, their gazes scanning their surroundings, their hands tightly gripping their weapons. The stillness was only broken by the occasional rustle of leaves or a distant creature's cry.

Suddenly, Nox returned, his face grave. "We have a problem," he announced, his silver eyes darting uneasily towards a particular mound. "There's something big over there."

Before anyone could respond, the mound he had pointed at started shaking violently. With a deafening roar, a monstrous figure burst out from the ground, sending chunks of earth flying in all directions. As the dust settled, a creature, unlike any they had encountered before, stood before them.

Its body was massive, and its fur tinted a sickly green, with large fungi sprouting from its back. Its roar echoed in the air, sending a chill down their spines.

However, while everyone was surprised by the arrival of the new creature, Thorian grinned. *So you finally showed yourself, fungal bear.*

CHAPTER 52

As the dust settled, the fungal bear let out another ferocious roar, the vibrations of its cry echoing through the desolate marsh. Its eyes, a luminous green, were filled with malevolent intelligence, mirroring the predatory instincts that had been awakened within it.

The party froze, their breaths hitching in anticipation. Thorian, however, was smirking. The thrill of the challenge surged through him, his adrenaline-spiked blood singing a violent, euphoric melody. "Time for a real battle," he declared, his eyes glinting dangerously.

"Be ready," he warned, his gaze falling on the priest. "I suspect we'll be needing your help soon enough."

Before anyone could respond, Thorian lunged forward, flames dancing in his hands. He launched a fireball towards the fungal bear, striking it square in the chest. The beast growled, staggering back, but didn't fall. Instead, it shook off the singed fur, revealing a thick layer of fungi that seemed to absorb the impact.

Thorian narrowed his eyes, noting this. "It uses the fungi as a shield. Aim for its exposed parts. Nox, you're up."

The shadowstalker nodded, his figure melding with the shadows. With a burst of speed, he appeared behind the fungal bear, his axe aimed at the vulnerable points. His attack landed, his blade sinking into the flesh. As he withdrew, the shadows coiled around the beast, its figure darkening under the assassin's skill.

"Saxum, Ventus, follow up!" Thorian ordered, his voice echoing through the marsh.

The wind and earth magi needed no further encouragement. Ventus conjured a fierce gust, momentarily disorienting the fungal bear. Saxum capitalized on the distraction, sending one rock bullet after the next towards the creature. They struck true, battering the beast and furthering the damage dealt by Nox.

The fungal bear roared, reeling from the onslaught. In retaliation, it shook its body violently, launching a cloud of spores from the fungi on its back. They landed on the ground, immediately sprouting into a thicket of monstrous mushrooms.

"Fall back!" Seeing that they were about to be surrounded, Thorian signaled a retreat and led his team to a safer distance.

As they regrouped, the priest stepped forward, his hands glowing with soft, golden light. "Healing," he intoned. The comforting light washed over them, their minor wounds healing instantly.

"Thanks," Nox grunted, flexing his newly healed hand. "Now, what should we do?"

"I'm sorry, it was my fault," Ventus said, downcast. "I should have used Gale Slash when Nox gave me the chance. I would have split it in two."

"No use apologizing now," Thorian shook his head. "You will get another chance soon enough."

The flame kobold became silent for a moment, his golden eyes studying the fungal bear and its newly formed mushroom minions. "Nox, I need you to cover me," he finally said. "I will join you in close-quarters."

Thorian then looked at the earth magus and said, "Saxum, while us two are fighting, I want you to root it in place." He then shifted his gaze to Ventus. "You finish it off after that."

As he finished explaining his plan, he stood up and glanced at Ventus. "Let's set these mushrooms ablaze first."

Ventus grinned at the prospect before conjuring his wind spell. The moment his Wind Gust was fired, Thorian's Fireball followed suit, and the elements instantly intertwined. The resulting wave of flames torched the minions of the fungal bear.

With a guttural roar, the beast immediately zeroed in on the group and pounced in their direction.

Without Thorian having to give any command, the priest let out a small intonation before a brilliant moonlight showered both him and Nox.

My body feels so light. It's been so long since I felt this way.

With a grin on his face, Thorian rushed at the incoming enemy as flames swirled in his palm. At the same time, Nox merged with the shadows and dashed with mind-bending speed.

The two speeding bolts of flames and shadows darted from one side to the other, confusing the slow but powerful bear. As it looked left and right, Thorian found the most opportune moment where the bear was focusing on his friend before rushing with all his speed. With a palm full of fire, he struck at the creature's face.

The sight of the fungal bear's ferocious face recoiling from Thorian's Combustion Touch felt satisfying, the scent of burnt fur wafting in the air. Nox distracting the beast with feints and luring its attention had allowed Thorian to get close and land a solid hit.

Yet, the battle was far from over.

Thorian swiftly moved back, escaping the bear's retaliation, its paw swinging where he stood a second ago. His breath came out in harsh pants, the adrenaline pumping in his veins urging him on.

Beside him, Nox was a shadowy blur, his movements slick and fast. Every now and then, the shadowstalker would land a hit, further weakening the fungal bear and forcing it to grow more aggressive.

The gravelly voice of Saxum resounded amid their choreographed dance of flames and shadows. "Earthen Grasp." With the incantation, multiple hands made of hardened soil emerged from the ground, latching onto the fungal bear's massive paws and rooting it in place.

"Ventus, now!" Thorian called out, his golden gaze never leaving the snarling beast.

At Thorian's command, Ventus extended his hands, the air around him swirling with uncontrolled intensity. "Gale Slash!" His voice cut through the tense air like a sharpened blade.

A tornado of wind shot forward, aimed at the immobilized fungal bear. The gust tore at the fungal growths, slicing through the thick layer that served as the creature's shield. A pained roar reverberated through the marsh, announcing the success of their plan.

Suddenly, the fungal bear violently shook, throwing off the earthen hands and releasing a cloud of poisonous spores.

I was waiting for that.

With a grin on his face, Thorian launched a simple fireball at the cloud of spores. As the spell reached the glowing particles, a dust explosion engulfed the corrupted beast and sent a thunderous shockwave that threatened to lift Thorian off his feet.

"Damn, Thorian. You blasted him off," Nox remarked with a smile in his voice before his gaze shifted to an invisible screen in front of him. "I leveled up."

The group let out a collective sigh at the verbal confirmation. The fungal bear was now officially dead.

As the final flames flickered around the charred body of the fungal bear, a sense of accomplishment washed over the group. A satisfied sigh escaped Thorian's lips. Nox's announcement of his level-up was the cherry on top, confirming their victory in this part of the Verdant Labyrinth.

With a swift wave of his hand, Thorian dispersed the remaining embers. "Good work, everyone." He commended, his golden gaze sweeping over his companions. They returned his sentiment with smiles and nods, basking in their triumph.

Before they could rest for too long, Thorian's sharp eyes spotted a new pathway opening up in the distance, revealing a path scattered with golden-tinted rocks and crystals. His heart pounded in his chest as realization dawned upon him.

The boss' lair.

"Look," he pointed, catching everyone's attention. Their expressions mirrored his anticipation, a hint of fear and excitement lighting up their eyes.

Without a word, they moved, entering the path that would lead them to their final challenge of this dungeon layer. As they tred on, the glow from the golden rocks illuminated their path, casting long shadows behind them.

Suddenly, the path opened up, revealing a cavernous space that took their breath away. In the heart of this golden grotto stood a monstrous figure, a terrifying blend of beauty and menace. Its spiked tail shimmered with a golden sheen, matching the rocks and crystals of the lair.

"The gilded spiketail..." Thorian murmured, his gaze fixated on the creature. The sense of danger it radiated was intense, threatening to eclipse their triumph over the fungal bear.

"Nox," he began, his gaze trained steadfastly upon the beast, "once we engage, I want you to use your shadow skill. That should give us an opening."

The assassin nodded, his lips tugging into a confident smirk.

"Saxum, Ventus," he continued, "just like with the fungal bear, immobilize and disorient it. That will buy us some time."

The earth and wind magi nodded, their eyes mirroring Thorian's determination.

Lastly, he turned to the priest. "We'll need your healing and buffing skills more than ever. Keep us fighting fit."

With a solemn nod, the priest silently vowed to do his best.

Taking a deep breath, Thorian took a step forward, "Ventus, set a Gale Slash on it. Saxum, use your skill to slow it down when it charges. Nox, you know what to do. Let's do this."

At his command, they sprang into action. Ventus summoned a mighty gust of wind, sweeping towards the gilded spiketail. The creature roared, its attention drawn towards the threat.

Seizing the distraction, Nox slinked forward, his figure blurring with the shadows. His speed was a marvel to behold, a testament to his abilities as an assassin. At the same time, the wind kobold followed the plan and conjured his spell.

As Ventus' Gale Slash struck against the gilded spiketail, a cloud of dust billowed into the air. The creature roared, the ground shaking beneath its wrath. Thorian watched as the beast's golden spikes glinted menacingly in the light, an intimidating sight that sent a shiver down his spine.

He didn't have time to ponder over it, for his attention was drawn to Nox. The assassin moved like a ghost, merging with the darkness around them. It was as if he was one with the shadows, his movements fluid and seamless. Thorian watched as Nox crept closer to the gilded spiketail, his figure blurring with his incredible speed. His heart pounded in anticipation of the upcoming attack.

"Saxum!" Thorian called, his voice firm despite the deafening roars of the gilded spiketail. The earth magus, stalwart and calm, nodded. His hands glowed with an earthy hue as he called upon his magic. "Grasp."

With his command, the ground beneath the gilded spiketail seemed to come alive, ensnaring the creature. The spiketail struggled, its spiked tail thrashing, but the rocky bonds held firm. They had bought themselves some time, a crucial factor in their battle.

Thorian watched as the dust cloud from Ventus' attack cleared, revealing Nox's figure behind the gilded spiketail. The shadowstalker was poised, his axe glistening in the dim light. With a swift, deadly stroke, his blade sank into the spiketail's flesh.

"Backstab," Nox muttered under his breath. The effect was instantaneous. The gilded spiketail roared in pain, its body arching as it tried to shake off the pain. The beast was distracted, just as they had planned.

Meanwhile, the priest had begun his incantations. A gentle glow enveloped his hands, the soft light soothing in their chaotic surroundings. "Moon's blessing," he intoned, the light spreading to envelop them all.

Thorian could feel his body grow light and his fatigue washing away. The priest's blessing was as calming as always, a soothing balm that eased their worries.

Now it was his turn. He stepped forward, flames dancing on his fingertips. His heart pounded in his chest, a rhythm in sync with the crackling fire. He felt the power surge through him, his veins throbbing with the intoxicating sensation of magic.

"Combustion Touch," he murmured, focusing his energy in his palms. He could feel the intense heat radiating from his hands, his skin glowing with an ember-like light. With a burst of speed, he charged towards the gilded spiketail, his fiery palms extended.

Thorian landed his attack on the beast, his Combustion Touch sinking into its flesh. The spiketail roared, a chilling sound that echoed in the cavern. Its tail thrashed, managing to break the stone binds that had held it captive. Thorian quickly rolled away, narrowly avoiding a blow from the creature's lethal tail.

Even though his attack had worked, searing the giant creature's flesh and grilling its inside, the battle was still far from over.

As Thorian regained his footing, his gaze met the spiketail's glowing ember eyes. The beast roared once more, a harrowing echo that sent shivers cascading down the rogue's spine. Its golden body, even marred by Thorian's successful strike, was luminous in the grotto's eerie light, a living nightmare wreathed in gold and spikes.

As the unsettling silence stretched between man and beast, the grotto felt suddenly colder, its golden light less comforting. The gilded spiketail's predatory gaze was locked on Thorian, promising a terrifying battle yet to come.

CHAPTER 53

Thorian's eyes locked on the gilded spiketail's fiery gaze, sparking an intense stand-off in the dim light of the grotto. Despite the searing pain radiating from its ember eyes, the beast's raw strength was still palpable—perhaps even more so.

That didn't work. We need something stronger.

"Nox," Thorian hissed, his gaze never leaving the spiketail. "We need another round of Shadow's Caress."

The kobold assassin moved like a wisp in the darkness. His quiet reply floated back to Thorian's ears. "On it."

A shadow darker than the cavernous grotto itself spread over the spiketail, dulling the glow of its golden exoskeleton. Thorian could almost taste the anticipation in the air as Nox's ability took effect.

"Ventus, your move!" he called, his voice a thunderclap in the quiet.

A wild gale whipped through the grotto. The spiketail roared, spikes clattering against each other as Ventus' attack ripped through it.

Thorian saw his chance.

"Combustion Touch," he muttered, focusing his energy as he surged towards the beast. His hand glowed brighter and hotter, the fiery energy licking at his skin. He reached out, aiming for the spiketail's eyes.

But the spiketail was faster. It curled into itself, forming an armored sphere that Thorian's hand skidded off harmlessly. A curse slipped past Thorian's lips. His fiery attack flickered, then extinguished, leaving only a scorch mark on the beast's exoskeleton.

"Guys, it's regenerating!" Ventus' shout rang out in alarm, his previous attack's wound visibly healing on the spiketail's hide.

A terrifying roar echoed throughout the grotto, the sheer force of it sending Thorian stumbling back, his ears ringing. The gilded creature uncurled, its spiked tail whipping dangerously and sending debris flying.

Thorian watched in horror as the beast reared up and set its sights unerringly upon him. He stumbled backward, his heart pounding as he narrowly avoided a stalactite dislodged by the creature's tail. Mind racing, he yelled, "Saxum, now!"

Saxum's magic sprang to life, the very floor of the grotto responding to his command. "Earthen Grasp!" he bellowed. The stone beneath them waved in spreading ripples, and from the ground rose a cluster of earthen tendrils, reaching out to ensnare the spiketail.

At the same time, the soft, ethereal glow of moonlight began to gather around the priest. He extended his hands towards Thorian, the light trailing his fingertips. "Moon's Blessing!" he called out, his voice imbuing the words with divine power. The moonlight surrounded Thorian, sinking into him and fortifying his speed and agility.

The spiketail struggled against the earth kobold's magic, but the spell's tendrils only tightened their hold, limiting its movement. Thorian could see the fire in the beast's eyes dimming, replaced with confusion and frustration.

With the spiketail distracted, Thorian didn't waste any time. "Saxum, Nox, with me. We're going on the offensive!" He summoned his fire magic once more, sending a fireball hurtling towards the spike-tail.

Saxum echoed his actions, a whirl of rock and wind forming in his hands before he launched it towards the beast. The rock bullet flew in a straight line, picking up speed as it closed the distance.

In the chaos, Nox was almost invisible. With a swift movement, he slipped behind the spiketail, his axe glinting ominously in the dark. In one swift, fluid movement, he plunged his axe into the spiketail's flesh. "Backstab," Nox grunted, as the blade of his weapon dug deeper into the beast.

The spiketail wasn't down yet, however. With a deafening roar, it thrashed, dislodging Saxum's Earthen Grasp and rearing up, only to slam its body back into the ground, causing a tremor that destabilized the footing of everyone present.

"Nox!" Thorian called out in alarm as the spiketail set its sights on the smaller figure.

Just as the beast lunged, Saxum was there again. "Earthen Grasp!" he barked out once more.

Saxum's invocation echoed in the grotto, an authoritative command in the heat of battle. The cavern floor quaked and grumbled as it yielded to his will, erupting once more into an array of twisting earthen tendrils. The ground beneath the charging spiketail softened before hardening once again around it, yanking it back and arresting its assault on Nox.

Nevertheless, the spiketail's renewed fury was a terrifying sight, its fiery eyes promising certain doom to any who dared to approach. As it thrashed against the Earthen Grasp, its armored tail whipped around with vicious speed, sending shattered rock debris into the air.

With uncanny agility, Nox danced through the chaos, darting in to land a quick strike before swiftly retreating. His movements were a deadly ballet, honed from the countless battles on the wall. But even the most skillful dancer could stumble, and a sudden, careless whip of the spiketail's tail connected with the shadowstalker.

"Nox!" Thorian cried out as the kobold assassin was flung backward, slamming into a rocky outcrop with a sickening crunch. The shadowy figure slumped, his form still as the dust settled around him.

The priest's voice echoed Thorian's alarm as he called out to his comrade, but his tone held a calm determination. From his position, he extended his hands towards Nox, the gentle, ethereal light of his magic pulsing at his fingertips. "Moon's Healing," he chanted, and a beam of moonlight shot forward, bathing Nox in its glow.

As Thorian turned his attention back to the spiketail, his eyes fell on the path the beast had taken in its frenzied rush. The breath hitched in his throat as he spotted the toxic trail left in the creature's wake. It was an insidious thing, a blight on the cavern floor, eating away at the rock with a quiet, relentless hiss.

"Damn," he hissed under his breath. The situation had just become significantly more precarious. Every movement now held the potential for disaster, a misstep into the toxic trail that would leave them vulnerable to the spiketail's assault.

Gale Slash isn't enough, not even with Shadow's Caress. And the heat of my Fireball can't break through its scales.

His mind whirred at a frenetic pace, the imminent danger necessitating quick judgment. However, that disarray swiftly evaporated.

I need something more.

In a flash, he knew what should be done.

Thorian pivoted to his team, a spark of determination was ignited within his fiery gaze. "Nox, I need another Shadow's Caress. Ventus, get ready with Gale Slash. And Priest, bless me." His voice was steady, the flames in his palms flickering in tandem with his focus.

Nox, having been healed by the priest, nodded from his position. He dashed forward with his axe at the ready. "Right away," he said. He leapt into the air, melting into the shadows until even the sheen of his black fur had disappeared, becoming one with the darkness of the cave.

Moments later, a darkness more profound than the heart of the abyss spread over the spiketail. The beast roared, thrashing even harder against its earthen restraints as its glowing exoskeleton visibly dimmed under Nox's ability.

Ventus had already begun his incantation, his palms making broad sweeping gestures as the wind swirled around him, building up the power for his Gale Slash.

Simultaneously, the priest extended his hands towards Thorian, the soft light trailing his fingertips. "Moon's Blessing," he called out, his voice rich with divine power. A gentle wave of energy washed over Thorian, his senses becoming sharper, his movements quicker.

Sensing the opportunity, Thorian broke into a sprint, flames swirling around his right hand, ready for his close-quarters spell.

"Ventus, now!" he shouted.

With the elemental might of the Gale Slash building in Ventus' grasp, Thorian took a breath, steeling himself. He could feel the fiery energy of his own power thrumming along his veins, anticipation tingling in his fingers. With a determined grimace, he steeled himself, channeling all his focus into his palm.

Then, with a grunt, Thorian launched himself into the air, defying the pull of gravity in his desperate bid for victory. His flames danced, crackling with bright, fierce energy. Their light reflected off the myriad spikes and facets of the spiketail''s exoskeleton, painting a dramatic tableau of dancing shadows on the cavern walls.

As Thorian flew towards the Gale Slash, he stretched out his hand, his Combustion Touch flaring with an intensity that matched his resolve. It was a dangerous game he was playing, as Gale Slash was not something to be trifled with lightly. The sharp edges of the wind could slice through him as easily as they could the spiketail. But Thorian had made his choice.

The heat in his palm intensified, the flames licking up his arm as he neared Ventus' Gale Slash. The wind sliced past him, and he gritted his teeth against the sting. Even as the sheer force of the Gale Slash threatened to throw him off course, Thorian was resolute. He reached the back of the Gale Slash and, with a shout, drove his palm into it. The flames met the wind and, for a moment, there was resistance. Then, with a deafening roar, the two forces merged, transforming into a cataclysmic tempest of fire and wind.

The Gale Slash, now aflame, swirled with the golden hues of his Combustion Touch, flickers of bright orange and red dancing within its spinning winds. Thorian, in the eye of the storm, was a silhouette against the blinding brightness. The flames spread along the wind's razor-sharp edge, painting it with a burning aura that crackled with raw, destructive power.

With a final yell, Thorian thrust his palm forward, releasing the flaming Gale Slash towards the spiketail. It hurtled through the air, a crescent blade of howling wind and roaring fire. The grotto was filled with the ferocious hiss and crackle of the blazing wind as it cut through the stale air, carrying with it Thorian's desperate hope for victory.

The gilded spiketail roared defiantly, its fiery gaze burning into Thorian as the blazing Gale Slash rushed towards it. The raw energy of the flaming vortex was a destructive force unlike any it had ever witnessed before. The beast struggled in its earthen bonds, but Saxum's control was too strong, too unyielding.

For a moment, time seemed to stand still. The grotto fell into a hush as the kobolds held their breath, their eyes fixated on the impending collision. The spiketail's ember eyes widened, the fire within flickering with a sudden realization.

Then the moment passed, and time surged forward.

The flaming Gale Slash made contact with a deafening crash, the powerful wind driving the fire into the spiketail. The crescent blade of burning wind sliced through the air, cutting through the beast's mandible with an agonizing screech of tearing chitin. The destructive force of the combined elements was too potent, too merciless for the spiketail to withstand.

It was a terrifying spectacle, the fiery Gale Slash tearing the spiketail's head apart with terrifying precision, splitting it down the middle. The intense heat from Thorian's Combustion Touch seared into the beast's golden exoskeleton, the unbearable heat burning through the layers of chitin and into the flesh beneath.

The spiketail's roar of defiance morphed into a screech of agony as its body was engulfed in the flaming tempest until even its fiery eyes gave way to it.

Thorian landed back onto the grotto floor with a soft thud, his heart pounding as he watched the flaming Gale Slash complete its path. The golden aura around his hand extinguished, leaving behind a lingering heat that slowly ebbed away. His eyes were locked onto the spiketail, watching the destruction their combined attack had wrought.

Level up!

CHAPTER 54

"King!"

As the adrenaline rush subsided, a sharp pain immediately followed. Thorian's comrades rushed to his side, eyes wide with worry. His right hand, from palm to wrist, was a mangled mess—the unfortunate consequence of thrusting his flesh into Ventus' Gale Slash.

"Moon's Healing," the priest uttered swiftly, not daring to waste another second as the gravity of the situation became apparent. Thorian's wounds began to mend, skin and flesh knitting together to once again conceal the underlying bones. However, even as the priest's spell concluded, there remained deep scars on Thorian's hand, a stark testament to the high price of his necessary sacrifice.

"King, we were so worried," Saxum voiced, his voice heavy with concern. "Why would you risk yourself like that?"

Ventus too nodded in agreement, his expression mirroring Saxum's worry. "Yeah, King. I couldn't have lived with myself if my skill had crippled you. That was far too dangerous!"

"It was a necessary sacrifice," Thorian replied, shaking his head. "If that creature simply had a robust shell, we would have gradually weakened it and eventually brought it down with repeated uses of Gale Slash and Combustion Touch. But its rapid regeneration made any action that didn't render instant death futile."

While they understood Thorian's logic, the group couldn't shake their sense of guilt and helplessness. The image of their leader having to injure himself for their victory filled them with a mixture of remorse and frustration.

"Is your hand going to be alright?" Nox asked, his concern evident.

"Don't worry. I can move it just fine. It merely throbs a bit." A rueful smile tugged at Thorian's mouth. "Once I evolve further, these scars will vanish."

As their conversation reached its conclusion, Thorian's gaze drifted towards the twisted and shattered corpse of the gilded spike-tail. He watched as its form flickered, then dissolved into golden particles. The sparkling lights gathered in the heart of the grotto, merging into a large, luminous chest. At the same moment, an ethereal, system-like voice resounded, its echo reverberating throughout the grotto.

"Congratulations, adventurers. You have vanquished the Guardian of the Second Layer, the Gilded Spiketail. You have shown strength, courage, and exceptional teamwork. The treasure of this layer is yours to claim."

Upon hearing the nearly otherworldly voice, Thorian couldn't help but smile. Accustomed to this voice from a decade of traversing dungeons, spending even a few days without its familiar sound had felt strange to him.

"Well, brighten up," Thorian said, his voice buoyant as he began to stride towards the chest. "It is time to reap the rewards of our hard work."

Notification: Dungeon Layer Completion
You have successfully cleared the second layer of the Verdant Labyrinth. As you are the first to clear this layer of the Verdant Labyrinth, your rewards are doubled.

Total Arcane Coins Gained: 1000

Additional rewards await in the Guardian's Chest.

Reward recalibration.

"Wow, that's quite a pile of coins!" Ventus blurted out, his words breaking the heavy silence. "How many skills can I buy with a thousand, King?"

"You can afford two," Thorian responded. "However, bear in mind there will be other purchases you will need to make later. It would be wise to maintain a reserve of arcane coins. One never knows when a chance to buy something of great value might present itself."

That caught the priest's attention. "A chance? What kind of chance?"

Thorian rubbed his temples, trying to determine how much information he should provide at the moment. "They aren't available at the moment, but once our territory progresses a few levels, we'll gain access to certain vendors and merchants who offer exotic and scarce items."

"Ah, I understand..." The priest's eyes widened in realization. "You are indeed very wise, My King."

Before Thorian could respond, Nox tugged at his arm. "Hey, Thorian. Let's open the chest. I want to see what's inside."

"Oh, me too! Me too!" Ventus chimed in enthusiastically.

Their typically youthful excitement had another grin splitting Thorian's lips. Without further ado, he guided the group towards the chest and proceeded to open it. A brilliant golden light spilled out.

A golden glow? Some good rewards await us.

When the light subsided, they peered into the chest. Nestled inside, an array of items lay waiting to be claimed. Thorian's eyes gleamed with anticipation as he picked up the first item. As he touched it, a screen window popped up in front of him.

Verdant Robe

Rarity: Blue Gale

Class Requirement: Magus

Level Requirement: 10

Effect: Mana +10

Special Effect: Increases the cultivation speed of Azure Dragon Meridian by 5%

Description: A robe made from the woven fibers of a Mystic Willow Tree. It shimmers with a gentle green glow. Often favored by those cultivating the Azure Dragon Meridian.

A robe with cultivation affinity? I didn't expect to find an item like this already.

Thorian placed the rich, leaf-green robe back in the chest and picked up the next item, triggering another information window.

Gilded Spiketail Plate

Rarity: Yellow Storm

Class Requirement: Warrior

Level Requirement: 20

Effect: Strength +12, Constitution +8, Agility -5

Special Effect: Reflects 5% of physical damage back to the attacker

Description: A heavy plate armor made from the spiky tail of the rare Gilded Spiketail. It's as tough as it is majestic, offering ample protection in close combat.

A soft whistle echoed around the cave. "A formidable piece of armor," Thorian said, eyes wide as he admired the shimmering exoskeleton plate. "Our warriors would do just about anything to have it."

"Oh, what does it do?" Ventus asked, curiosity lighting up his features, while the others waited patiently for the explanation.

"See for yourself," Thorian replied, passing the plate to the wind kobold.

Ventus' expression shifted from interest to astonishment as he read through the information screen. "Forlune would kill to have this piece of equipment."

"Why? What's special about it?" Nox, unable to suppress his curiosity any longer, snatched the item from Ventus' grasp. As he too read through the details, his eyebrows shot up in surprise. "It grants fifteen stat points? That's like leveling up five times."

"That's... a significant number of levels," the priest murmured from the sidelines.

Meanwhile, Saxum turned his attention to Thorian. "King, I've been meaning to ask you. What are your plans for these rewards?"

Thorian's brow furrowed in thought before he finally settled on a balanced solution. "The items that each group retrieves from the dungeon belong to them. When distributing within the team, we first review all the items. If someone desires a specific one, they may have it. If two individuals covet the same item, the one who needs it most shall receive it. If both have an equal need, we leave it to chance. Each person can only claim one item until everyone else has received something, and then they can request a second item."

The priest nodded, impressed. "That's a remarkably fair system, My King. As always, your wisdom astounds me."

Thorian responded to his compliment with a warm smile before taking the Verdant Robe and handing it to him. "Pass it around once you've had a look."

While the group took turns examining the two pieces of equipment, Thorian progressed to the next items in the chest, each one triggering a fresh information window.

Flask of Luminescent Spores

Rarity: Green Breeze

Description: Creates a cloud of spores when thrown. The cloud of spores leads to irritation, disorientation, and even vomiting. The effects depend on the power of the target.

Earth Tremor Skill Scroll

Class Requirement: Magus

Level Requirement: 20

Use: Teaches the active skill Earth Tremor, which allows the user to strike the ground and cause area-of-effect damage to nearby enemies

Description: A weathered scroll containing the instructions to perform a certain spell. The parchment vibrates slightly when held, echoing the power within. When torn, the user learns the active skill "Earth Tremor."

A skill scroll? This one is good.

Silently, Thorian handed the parchment to Saxum. Upon reading the item's description, the earth magus' eyes widened, and he wordlessly expressed his gratitude to the king.

Meanwhile, Thorian's attention was fixated on the final two items in the chest. He swiftly retrieved them, inspecting the information screen that accompanied each.

Thorned Cloak

Rarity: Blue Gale

Class Requirement: Assassin

Level Requirement: 10

Effect: Agility +10

Special Effect: Provides a 10% chance to block a physical attack completely

Description: A dark, supple cloak adorned with small, sharp thorns. Its elusive nature resonates well with those preferring the shadows.

Bear Strength Pendant
Rarity: White Mist
No Class Requirement
Level Requirement: 5
Effect: Strength +3
Description: A simple pendant made from a bear claw. It radiates a faint, warm energy. The wearer will experience a subtle increase in strength.

While the last item was nothing to write home about, the first one made Thorian pause. *This one should go to Nox. It fits him perfectly.*

Once all the items had been examined and their information shared, the group distributed them according to individual desires and necessities. The Earth Tremor skill scroll and the Thorned Cloak found their rightful owners in Saxum and Nox, respectively, and with little deliberation. Thorian claimed the Verdant Robe, as no one else had embarked on their cultivation journey. The wind magus Ventus selected the Gilded Spiketail Plate with the express intent of exchanging it for other items once the other kobolds also had an opportunity to conquer the dungeon. Since the priest didn't express a specific preference, he ended up with both the flask and the pendant. While he planned to utilize the flask in a precarious situation, the pendant would serve as a future bartering item.

With everyone satisfied with their new acquisitions, the group began their trek out of the dungeon.

CHAPTER 55

As the group began their exit from the dungeon, Ventus cast a lingering look back at the towering tree.

"Can we go back inside, King?" His voice echoed with an undertone of anticipation. "I leveled up so much faster than when hunting goblins and giant rabbits. That big guardian made me level up twice!"

Even Saxum who loved bickering with the wind magus conceded to his sentiment with a nod. "If we could just focus on hunting here all day, we would evolve in a couple of days."

"I wish we could too," Thorian responded with a lighthearted chuckle. "However, we can only challenge a layer once per day. I want each of you to return to this first layer later with your respective groups and guide them through it."

"Can we truly manage that without your guidance, My King?" The priest's voice wavered with concern as his gaze fell on Thorian's scar-ridden hand. "The trials we faced in this dungeon were formidable, and some sacrifices were necessary."

A solemn consensus rippled through the group, acknowledging the priest's sobering words. The daunting challenge of dungeon delving was, without a doubt, a far cry from the relative predictability of monster hordes at the city walls.

But Thorian dismissed their apprehensions with a shake of his head. "The first layer is considerably simpler than the one we just traversed. It has fewer traps and fewer elite monsters, and even the guardian is significantly weaker. As long as each member of your squads has undergone their first evolution, you should encounter minimal difficulties in clearing the dungeon."

Saxum breathed a sigh of relief. "That is good to know. If we had to deal with that spiketail with a squad other than this one, we wouldn't make it back in one piece even if we had a hundred lives."

Thorian met Saxum's admission with a quiet smile, leaving his statement unanswered. He pivoted, prompting the others to fall into step behind him as they made their way back to the village. He couldn't suppress a grin as he cast a final glance at the immense tree in the distance.

Clearing the second layer on our first attempt is quite remarkable. In my previous life, it took over a month to accomplish the same feat, and even that was considered rapid progress. Even those monsters of the Thulaskar empire shouldn't be better positioned than me right now.

With this newfound conviction, Thorian guided his group towards the village. His gaze drifted skywards to the dual suns hanging in the afternoon sky, their presence signaling the passage of a few hours since their venture began. The doubled intensity from the two suns made the environment noticeably brighter than previous days, and even the temperature and humidity had increased. But none of this unsettled Thorian. To him, it was merely a return to familiarity.

As the group neared the village, they ascended a gentle hill and came to a halt at the precipice of a cliff. Their elevated vantage point unveiled the walls of Wolvendale village. The lifeless remains of the monstrous invaders formed a grisly mountain range, a grim testament to the futility of their assault. This morbid spectacle stood as a stark warning to all who dared to breach the village walls—beyond them, death was the only promise.

"We need to clear out this mess," Thorian muttered, a scowl twisting his features. "In this heat, the stench will soon become insufferable."

"I fear I can already catch a whiff of it, King," Saxum interjected with a chuckle before his expression sobered as he surveyed the pile of corpses. "If only I could control my Earthen Grasp skill a little better, I would have buried them all in no time."

"If you could do that, burying the corpses would be the least of our worries," the priest responded, his laughter rumbling in his throat. "You could just bury that giant insect guardian alive, and let it suffocate underneath the earth."

"Can't you just set them on fire, King?" Ventus inquired, his head cocked in curiosity, only to receive a puzzled look from the earth magus.

"Do you want the whole forest to burn? Our king would definitely survive the fire, but I wouldn't count on the rest of us living."

Ventus' face flushed with embarrassment at the critique. "It was just a suggestion! At least I am trying to help. Your suggestion is practically a pipe dream!"

Thorian chuckled at their playful squabble, his mirth echoed by the hearty laughter of Nox from the sidelines. The shadowstalker then turned to Thorian with a proposition. "Why don't we just do it the old-fashioned way? We can just push the bodies away with our hands."

"It's an exercise in futility for now since we will need to keep killing monsters," Thorian replied, shaking his head before shifting his gaze back to the wall. "The smell will be putrid, but it will also serve as a warning for the monsters not to keep coming towards us in droves."

As their conversation neared its conclusion, the group prepared to descend the cliff, only to be halted by Thorian.

"Priest, you are one of the few whom I have not bestowed a name upon yet," Thorian declared, his eyes locked intently on the kobold adorned with lunar shamanist tattoos. "Henceforth, you shall be known as Vigil. Your watchful nature and ability to perceive what others cannot make this a fitting title."

"Thank you, My King," Vigil replied, inclining his head slightly. "It is an honor."

Thorian reciprocated with a smile before signaling towards the village with a nod of his head. "Let's go see what the others have been up to. I am expecting some new evolutions to join our ranks."

"Oh, the brown kobloids? I want to see what they're going to evolve into too!" Nox exclaimed, his enthusiasm palpable. He descended the cliff with feline agility, Thorian and the others trailing closely behind. Upon reaching the village walls, Thorian glanced to his right to see the eastern gate, and Nox, moving with startling speed atop the wall towards it.

A smile playing on his lips, Thorian turned to the rest of the group. "We will separate for now. I would like each of you to check the other gates, evaluate the situation, and report back to me. Meet up in twenty minutes in the village hall."

"Right away, King," Ventus responded with contagious enthusiasm. "Aqua will be so jealous when he hears about how we cleared the dungeon!"

With that, he sprang up the wall and disappeared into the village. Saxum and Vigil followed suit, making their way to the western and southern gates, respectively.

His next course of action established, Thorian set out to follow Nox towards the eastern gate. Thoughts of Lapis brought an anticipatory smile to his face.

It's been a few hours now since his men received their classes. I wonder how they look now.

As he neared the gate, Thorian's gaze was involuntarily drawn to the corpses of the monsters strewn around him. While the quantity was unremarkable, some specimens among the fallen were indeed extraordinary. Thri-kreens, tailmashers, and even a few thundermashers lay in a macabre display.

It appears my high expectations were well-founded.

As Thorian ascended the wall, the raucous laughter of Nox and Lapis reached his ears. The two interacted with the ease and joviality of lifelong friends, their laughter mingling with that of the surrounding kobolds.

Lapis' contingent was a particularly impressive sight. Four individuals stood out, towering above the rest. Their fur had morphed to a deep gray, and they bore thick, rock-like plates on their bodies, acting as a form of natural armor. These protective coverings were particularly pronounced on their shoulders, forearms, and legs.

Thorian nodded his approval before his gaze slid over to another quartet. They were a bit shorter than the first group but still exceeded the average height of a brown kobold. Their muscles were more defined, their fur a deep brown, adorned with teal tribal tattoos reminiscent of those borne by Forlune's band of warriors.

Thorian then turned his attention to a group of five, easily identifiable as priests. They each possessed average kobold stature, with lean yet solid builds. Their fur had lightened to a gentle, sandy hue, suggestive of their intimate connection to the earth.

Upon closer inspection, Thorian noticed unique, greenish patterns, akin to veins of precious minerals, subtly glowing beneath their fur. These lines of energy were more densely clustered around their hands.

Finally, Thorian's gaze settled on the remaining pair. He instantly recognized them as earth kobolds, their form mirroring that of Saxum. In some ways, he felt a stronger affinity for these two magi, able to vividly imagine their abilities and the value they could bring to a battle scenario.

Among this array of impressive evolutions, Lapis' form seemed rather nondescript and unremarkable. Even Nox, with whom he chatted merrily, bore glowing silver streaks across his body, showcasing his specialness.

The gods are truly unfair. Thorian thought, heaving a sigh before shaking off his disappointment. *Well, you still have your next evolution. I hope the heavens will look favorably upon you when that time comes.*

CHAPTER 56

Lapis spotted Thorian as he nimbly descended the wall and approached the group, prompting the brown kobold to break from his conversation with Noxhim.

"Thorian, are you okay?" he kobold, concern etching his features. His gaze jumped between Thorian and the shadowstalker. "Nox just filled me in. You got roughed up quite badly in that dungeon, didn't you?"

"It's a mere flesh wound," Thorian countered, dismissively waving his scarred palm and wrist. "We were able to return safely with the spoils of war thanks to it."

"That skill combination was insane!" Nox interjected, his eyes sparkling with admiration. "I never thought something like that was possible. Setting fire to Ventus' Gale Slash made it so much more powerful—it just sliced through that Guardian like butter."

"It's a high-risk strategy," Thorian conceded, a note of pride creeping into his voice. "But the payoff is undoubtedly worth it."

As Thorian and Nox delved deeper into their exploits, Lapis, along with several other kobolds, listened attentively.

"If I may ask, what is this Guardian you two are speaking of?" Lapis interjected with an interested look.

"It's the final monster you'll have to kill to finish the dungeon and get all the rewards!" Nox exclaimed, his voice thrumming with exhilaration. "I also leveled up twice just when it died!"

"Impressive." Lapis' gaze subtly shifted to the shadowstalker's attire. "Is that where you got that green cloak? It looks very nice."

"Nailed it," Nox chuckled, proudly displaying his Thorned Cloak. Its fabric rustled softly as he said, "And it gives a solid ten-point boost to my agility," he added, before casting a glance at Thorian, who was similarly clad in a Verdant Robe. "See? We're even matching."

Thorian dismissed the superficial comparison with a shake of his head, but despite himself, a smile tugged at the corners of his lips. He then turned to Lapis and reassured him, "Don't worry, your turn to dive into the dungeon will come soon enough. Your men are developing well, just as you promised me."

"Perhaps a little too well…" Lapis murmured, his gaze lowering. A self-deprecating smile sketched itself across his face.

Thorian clapped him on the shoulder, offering a confident smile. "You'll have your own shot too. Just keep putting in the effort."

The brown kobold nodded in agreement, a gesture Thorian reciprocated. His gaze then shifted, sweeping over the rest of Lapis' men.

Clearing his throat to command their attention, Thorian asked a seemingly simple question, "Do you like it here?"

Thorian's query was met with a ripple of confusion, as the kobolds exchanged murmurs and whispers amongst themselves. It took a few moments for one of the tallest kobold warriors, his broad shoulders suggesting a formidable strength, to step forward.

"I, for one, am content here," he declared, a satisfied look softening his rugged features. "You never demand our food, and you permit us to hunt freely. I see no reason for dissatisfaction."

At the kobold's declaration, a wave of laughter and enthusiastic chortles surged through the crowd behind him.

"Flame kobold is the best!"

"You're a great leader!"

The effusion of praise was so intense that it left Thorian momentarily stunned. He had anticipated some measure of positivity, but had never dared to dream that the group would respond with such solidarity. A flicker of suspicion crossed his face, and he turned his gaze to Lapis.

Could Lapis have instructed them on what to say beforehand? No, that's unlikely. He couldn't have anticipated my spontaneous question.

As Thorian studied Lapis, his bewilderment deepened. The brown kobold seemed as taken aback as he was.

Could he be putting on an act? No, not even Brix could act so convincingly...

Left with no other plausible explanation, Thorian turned back to the crowd, his eyes wide with surprise. Despite his extensive career, he had seldom encountered a display of acceptance and jubilee like this, and the spontaneity of the moment made it all the more extraordinary.

And I didn't have to plant a single one amongst them.

Slowly, a serene smile spread across Thorian's face as priests and warriors alike expressed their gratitude for the opportunities he'd presented them. However, indulging in sentiment was not a habit of his. After gathering his thoughts, he pressed forwards with the plan he'd been concocting all along.

Turning back to Lapis, he asked a question that had been brewing in his mind for quite some time. "Lapis, can I entrust you with an important mission?"

The brown kobold tilted his head curiously. "Of course, Thorian. What would that be?"

"I would like you to bring some of the members of your tribe here."

Upon hearing Thorian's request, Lapis responded with a hearty laugh. "Is that all? They would love nothing more than to come here. How many are you hoping for?"

"As many as can be safely managed," Thorian replied.

"Are we gonna have more brown kobloids join us?" Nox chimed in, a spark of excitement lighting his eyes. "We're growing so much, it's almost hard to keep up!"

"You'll have to get accustomed to it," Thorian replied with a chuckle. "This is just the beginning."

"Should I depart immediately?" Lapis inquired. "Should my group accompany me?"

"Not immediately." Thorian shook his head. "I need to return to the village hall for a meeting with my team. Afterwards, Nox and I will return here and take your place guarding the gate."

"Alright, I understand," Lapis agreed, nodding. "Good luck, Thorian."

With that, the pair ventured back to the village hall. Upon entering, they discovered Ventus and Saxum lounging on the floor while Melina graciously offered each of them a cup of tea.

As the elven lady caught sight of Thorian and Nox entering through the door, she offered a respectful bow. "I am relieved to see your safe return, my lord."

"Thank you, Melina." Thorian reciprocated with a slight nod. "Could you assist us in submitting the quests we've completed?"

"Immediately, my lord." Melina moved towards her desk, with Thorian and Nox following in her wake. As was customary, she marked their quest parchments with her magical stamp, allowing them to claim the rewards of their arduous efforts.

Personal resources.

Arcane Coins: 1800

Just as Thorian was about to join his group, having checked his arcane coins, Melina interjected.

"Have you ventured into Eärendil's Sanctuary, my lord?" she inquired.

At her query, Thorian paused, regarding the elven lady with intrigued eyes. "Why do you ask? Are you curious about what lies inside?"

Melina averted her gaze, unable to meet Thorian's eyes. "I-I apologize if I have overstepped my boundaries, my lord."

"No, you haven't," Thorian assured her with a shake of his head. "And no, we have not entered the Sanctuary. I deemed it prudent to do so only when we've amassed greater strength."

The elf considered his response for a moment before nodding in understanding. "That is wise of you, my lord."

"Thank you," Thorian replied graciously.

With a brief nod of acknowledgment, Thorian turned and began walking alongside Nox towards the pair of magi. His smile was relaxed, his eyes holding a hint of understanding.

There is no use forcing her to speak right now. She will explain what is going on when she feels comfortable to do so.

As the pair approached Ventus and Saxum, Nox immediately noticed the absence of a certain item from the wind magus' possession. "Ventus, where's your golden armor?"

"I traded it with Forlune," Ventus responded with a chuckle. "In exchange, he promised to provide me with five items better suited to me later. Everyone heard his promise, so there's no backing out!"

"That was daylight robbery," Saxum shook his head. "Five items for one? How on earth does that add up?"

Upon hearing the earth magus' protest, Thorian tilted his head thoughtfully. *A piece of Yellow Storm equipment is worth much more than five normal items. Especially one that fits Forlune's fighting style so perfectly. They may not realize it, but it is Ventus who got the short end of the trade.*

Yet Thorian kept his thoughts to himself, recognizing that Ventus needed to learn from such experiences and grow accordingly himself.

Soon enough, the priest also rejoined the group after collecting the rewards for his quests. As each member reported back to Thorian, he gained a comprehensive understanding of the village's status. Operations at the northern gate were proceeding smoothly, with the team stationed there gradually leveling up. The western group of brown kobloids was making steady progress towards their evolution, with the three magi having already evolved—two into earth kobolds and one into a flame kobold. As for the orcs to the south, they encountered no problems under the watchful eyes of Ifrit and Inly. Their class levels had caught up with their species level, and they were now slowly approaching their impending evolution.

Once the meeting concluded, the group disbanded. Thorian and Nox headed to the eastern gate to relieve the evolved brown kobloids. As he perched himself atop the wall alongside the shadowstalker, Thorian decided to check his status.

Display panel.

Ding!

Race: Flame Kobold

Level: 14/30 (XP: 1435/1650)

Class: Magus

Level: 20/20 (XP: MAX)

Lifespan: 40 years

Cultivation Realm: Qi Gathering Second Stage (5.3%)

Stats:

Strength: 58

Agility: 62
Constitution: 35
Mana: 65
Qi: 14
Free Points: 15
Skills:
Minor Fire Affinity (passive)
Flame Resistance (passive)
Fireball (active)
Combustion Touch (active)
Waterball (active)

CHAPTER 57

Thorian was awestruck at his steady progression. *I'm already on the cusp of leveling up again. At this rate, I should evolve into a kobold champion by the end of the week.*

After taking a moment to assess his status panel, Thorian turned his concentration back to his spell.

Waterball: You summon a watery orb and launch it at your enemies, drenching them and knocking them off balance.

Proficiency: 79.5%

Not too bad considering I haven't focused on training it for the past few hours.

Satisfied with his advancement, Thorian dismissed his system screens, bringing his attention back to the present. Just as they had done before, the pair spent the next hour and a half thinning out the incoming beasts, which allowed Thorian to level up twice. During this period, his sole focus was casting his Waterball spell at every opportunity, while Nox dispatched the remaining monsters using his Backstab skill.

The intensity of the monster onslaught against the walls had undeniably dwindled. The goblins, in particular, hesitated to venture forth after witnessing the grim spectacle of their fallen comrades. Their sense of self-preservation warned them that lingering would lead to dire consequences. However, the other forest denizens lacked such cognizance. Consequently, the duo eagerly hunted any beast daring enough to approach Wolvendale's walls.

Once they had eliminated a troupe of rabbarians, Nox sprinted up to the watchtower, striding towards Thorian with a look of excitement etched on his face. "I finally finished that quest, it took so long!" he exclaimed.

"Quest?" Thorian quirked an eyebrow. "Which one are you referring to?"

"The monster hunting one, the one where we need to kill five hundred of them to finish it."

The "Revenge on the Monsters" quest? I wasn't aware someone else had it.

Brow furrowed in surprise, Thorian inquired, "When did you receive it? How did that happen?"

"Oh, um, when we saw you accept the quest, Thorian," Nox replied, scratching his head in confusion. "Were we not supposed to? I just saw you take the quest and I did the same. The other guys also took it after I did."

"No, it's good that you took it," Thorian responded, shaking his head. "I just didn't anticipate it."

I was under the impression it was a unique quest. I guess I didn't pay attention.

"So... should I go claim the rewards? They look incredible!" Nox exclaimed, his voice brimming with anticipation.

Thorian paused for a moment before replying, "If I were in your shoes, I'd wait. The 'level up' rewards tend to increase in value the longer you delay. For instance, ascending from level 26 to 27 requires more than double the experience points needed to progress from level 10 to 11."

Nox cast his gaze downward, mulling over Thorian's words. "But there is a time limit for this quest. Should I wait until around the end?"

"That could be overly ambitious," Thorian suggested, scratching his furry chin contemplatively. "My recommendation would be to delay at least until you upgrade your class. Beyond that point, it's a matter of choice. You can opt to wait longer to maximize your rewards, or claim them immediately to boost your strength as soon as possible. Each decision carries its own advantages and pitfalls."

Nox lowered his gaze, nodding in comprehension. "I see. I'll wait until closer to the deadline, then."

"It is your decision." Thorian shrugged nonchalantly. He then redirected his attention to his display panel, concentrating on his Waterball skill.

Waterball: You summon a watery orb and launch it at your enemies, drenching them and knocking them off balance.

Proficiency: 100%

Thorian grinned. *Good, I can focus on the other skills now.*

He then turned to the shadowstalker. "Nox, you'll need to carry on alone for a bit. Continue your hunt and ensure you finish off your prey with Backstab. You should be nearing the point of unlocking a new skill."

With these words, Thorian sprinted into the village, heading straight for the Magus Guild. There, he purchased the last two class skills from Fizzlegrin. The buzzlekin was delighted to see genuine customers spending arcane coins on skills, rather than merely the kobloids who were receiving their first basic skill at no cost.

Upon returning to the eastern gate, Thorian practiced using both of his newly acquired skills concurrently. He utilized Wind Gust to augment Nox's already remarkable agility, and Rock Bullet to inflict wounds on their adversaries. Of course, he targeted non-lethal areas to ensure Nox could deliver the finishing blow with his Backstab.

As the hours slipped by, the dual suns descended over the horizon, making way for a duo of moons to ascend. These twin celestial bodies sat side by side in the night sky, one a pallid blue and the other a pinkish orange. Though the sight was familiar to him, Thorian found himself still enchanted by its inherent whimsy, an element that was strikingly absent from the battleground below.

Hours elapsed as Thorian single-mindedly sought to hone his dual skills. His level was already considerably higher than his comrades' and, by extension, all the humans in the vicinity. The sole goal that eluded him was class advancement, and he was determined to close that gap as swiftly as possible.

Two hours later, Nox dispatched the final thumpalope from its herd with a deft Backstab, before he halted, his gaze fixated on an unseen screen.

"Yes! I finally unlocked it!" Nox exclaimed, glancing up at Thorian. "This is the skill, right? Whisper Step!"

Thorian smiled at the shadowstalker's infectious enthusiasm. "Congratulations, Nox. You can now proceed to upgrade your class if you wish."

Nox beamed at Thorian's confirmation. "Hang on, let me test it out first." No sooner had the words left his mouth than he vanished.

Thorian, fully aware of the skill's effect, turned to find Nox behind him on the watchtower.

Seeing Thorian's knowing gaze, Nox stammered, "H-How did you know I was here? Even I was surprised at the speed."

"I am aware of more than you could possibly fathom," Thorian responded, shaking his head. "Now, why don't you return to Whisperwind? After all, you're his employee. If you want your wages, you should at least fulfill some of his tasks."

Recalling the agreement he had made, Nox's eyebrows shot up. "Oh, I forgot about that. I will also go and advance my class, I will become stronger that way!"

With that, Nox performed a backwards somersault off the watchtower and sprinted into the village, heading for the Assassin Guild. Thorian watched him with a proud smile before redirecting his focus to the forest beyond the wall.

As per his training regimen, Thorian continued employing his two new skills to hunt the monsters that emerged from the forest depths. Only the evolved species, like the tailmasher and thri-kreens, required him to descend and dispatch them with a Combustion Touch. For the majority of the others, he simply cast a Wind Gust to disorient them before delivering the coup de grâce with a Rock Bullet.

An hour passed swiftly before the rhythmic thudding of heavy footfalls echoed from the forest. Initially assuming it was a monster horde, Thorian readied a fireball spell, but as the figures came into clearer view, he clenched his fist, extinguishing the flames. What approached wasn't a horde, but a tribe—a tribe of brown kobolds and kobloids.

Witnessing the brown-furred creatures emerge from the dense foliage, their forms bathed in the ethereal light of the twin moons, was a sight to behold. More than a hundred individuals stood before him.

From within their ranks, a brown kobold separated from the group and advanced towards him. As the kobold neared the watchtower, he sank to one knee.

"Thorian, My King," he declared, "As promised, half our tribe has heeded my words and sought you out. They are prepared to pledge their service to you, asking for your protection in return."

Lapis... You truly impress me.

Acknowledging the brown kobold with a nod, Thorian leapt from the watchtower and positioned himself before the assembly of creatures. He stood with an air of command, surveying the crowd as his gaze took in the mix of fear, uncertainty, and hope reflected in their eyes.

"Ladies, gentlemen," he commenced in a deep, authoritative tone, "You've come here, placing your hopes and trust in Lapis' words. I assure you, I am not here to let you down."

He then directed his attention to those visibly filled with fear and uncertainty: the children, the mothers, and the elderly. "If it is protection you seek, then I shall provide it. All I request in return is your loyalty—to me, and to your fellow brothers and sisters. I urge each of you to commit to hard work, so that we may all thrive together."

Thorian's assurances visibly soothed those harboring worries, as though his personal confirmation eradicated any lingering doubts.

Next, he turned his attention to the skeptics, most of whom were young and robust, potential soldiers in their prime. "For those of you who desire to become strong, to ensure no one can intimidate you or harm those you cherish, I have the solution. I can give you an opportunity to attain a level of strength beyond your wildest dreams. You merely need to strive for it, to pursue it. Those willing to work hard and risk their lives will be richly rewarded."

He cast a glance at Lapis' group of evolved kobolds and smiled in triumph. "The proof of my words stands right beside you."

The evolved kobolds reciprocated with a chuckle and proudly displayed their stature, evoking awe from the rest of the tribe. Some hooted and laughed, while others clapped in admiration.

A kobloid, bright-eyed and youthful, stepped forwards towards Thorian. "Here, become strong?"

"Yes, you will," Thorian affirmed. "With me, you will grow strong."

The kobloid's doubtful expression morphed into a broad grin. "Great! Me like!"

His voice ignited a spark in the crowd, setting off an enthusiastic cheer. Despite their rudimentary language, Thorian had no trouble recognizing their excitement.

Glancing to the side, he noticed Lapis beaming at him. With a tilt of his head, Thorian beckoned the brown kobold towards him.

"You did remarkably well, Lapis," Thorian commended, casting his gaze over the crowd. "Finally, this is beginning to resemble a true kingdom."

CHAPTER 58

Upon admitting the new contingent of brown kobolds and kobloids within the village boundaries, Thorian allocated the responsibility of the eastern gate's security to Lapis' squad. Subsequently, they shepherded the sizable group towards the hall, the locale for their citizenship ceremony. Lapis, already well-versed in the rites of integrating newcomers into the ranks of disciplined soldiers, was entrusted with this duty by Thorian. The only specific instruction he imparted to the brown kobold was for him and his kinfolk to undertake the "Revenge on the Monsters" quest.

With the necessary tasks set in motion, Thorian turned his steps towards the Territory Altar. As before, the demonic face was surrounded by heaping stacks of tree trunks. A vast, brown tide had overtaken the place, drowning the emerald green grass beneath its weight.

I should have all my men finish their tree quest before I start upgrading the village.

With a clear objective in mind, Thorian embarked on a comprehensive tour of the village. The decision to journey to the northern side came swiftly to him. Aqua, with his quick learning abilities and reliability, was the obvious choice to accompany him. He showed the water magus how to allow the altar to absorb a precise quantity of wood, then guided him from one gateway to another. At each, Thorian would assume guard duties while Aqua shepherded the group towards the Territory Altar, allowing them to accomplish their quests.

This methodical approach was replicated at each gate until all of Thorian's men had successfully completed their respective quests, earning them each a reward of one hundred arcane coins. The only remaining citizens were the newly admitted kobolds and kobloids who were still navigating their way through the guilds' aptitude tests. Thorian estimated that the latest entrants would not acquire their classes by day's end—it simply took much time, even for a compact unit like Lapis'. As a result, he redirected their efforts towards the tree quest, ensuring they capitalized on the day's quest rewards and didn't squander the opportunity entirely.

After the combined efforts of over a hundred kobloids and kobolds, resulting in the absorption of one hundred units of wood by the altar, the once dense ocean of tree trunks had dried up considerably. Now, Thorian could make out the silhouette of that demonic face even from a distance.

With all the groundwork and tedious tasks now completed, Thorian could finally concentrate on the endeavor he had been eagerly anticipating: upgrading the village.

Territory resources.

Resources:

Gathered Experience: 21.7k

Wood: 22.6k

The mounting resources had a smile unfurling across Thorian's face. This was the tangible result of a day's discipline and concerted effort. The orcs, who had been chopping trees without respite; Ventus, who had offered his assistance; the kobolds, who had vigilantly safeguarded the village, dispatching all intruders at the wall—all of them had contributed to this success.

Just how long did it take me last time to reach this state? Thorian reflected nostalgically. *Learning about the altar and knowing how to claim it was the hard part. That took three weeks, I believe. Upgrading it was much easier though, since we never had the problem of lacking citizens.*

Brushing off his nostalgic reverie, Thorian issued the command. *Upgrade village.*

Upgrade Conditions:

100 registered citizens

1000 gathered experience

Upgrade the four statues into guilds

Conditions fulfilled.

Do you wish to upgrade the Wolvendale Village to stage 2?

"Yes, I do."

Realm advancement.

A blinding sweep of blue light engulfed the village, prompting Thorian to shield his eyes. As he gradually reopened them, he surveyed his surroundings only to see that nothing had substantially altered.

Let's look at the panel. Display territory.

Wolvendale Village:

Realm: Village Stage 2

Resources:

Gathered Experience: 20.7k

Wood: 22.6k

Owned Buildings

Warrior Class Guild: The Warrior Guild exemplifies strength, resilience, and martial prowess. Acting as a bastion for combatants, it facilitates recruitment, skill sales, and martial potential assessment. Within this guild, warriors refine their combat skills and carve their destinies on the battlefield.

Magus Class Guild: The Magus Guild stands as a nexus of arcane wisdom and elemental mastery. Here, magical energies are honed, destructive spells crafted. Serving as the epicenter for magi, it offers recruitment, skill sales, and potential assessment. As the magus reshapes reality, the guild molds its members' destinies.

Assassin Class Guild: The Assassin Guild embodies the principles of stealth, precision, and cunning. As a sanctuary for those who strike from the shadows, it serves as a recruitment hub, offers lethal skill sales, and assesses potential recruits. It is in this guild that assassins perfect their craft and disappear into the shadows of their own destiny.

Priest Class Guild: The Priest Guild reflects the divine bond between mortals and gods. Serving as a haven for healers and conduits of divine power, it provides recruitment services, skill sales, and spiritual potential assessment. Within this guild, priests enhance their spiritual connection and shape their destinies through divine guidance.

Wooden Wall (Stage 1): The Wooden Wall is a sturdy barrier designed to protect the village from external threats and encroachments. Crafted from strong timber, this defensive structure forms a circular perimeter with a radius of two hundred meters from the Village Altar. The wall is equipped with watchtowers and gates to enable monitoring and control of access to the village.

Village Hall (Stage 1): The Village Hall serves as the central hub of administration, communication, and community for the village. Within its walls, the lord and villagers can gather to discuss important matters, plan for the future, and assign tasks vital to the village's growth and success. As the heart of the village, the Village Hall provides access to quests, both daily and non-daily, that help drive progress and development.

Available Upgrades

Wooden Wall (Stage 2): The Reinforced Wooden Wall, an advanced iteration of the Wooden Wall, ensures heightened security for the village. This upgraded version incorporates hardened timber and additional reinforcements, boosting the original structure's durability.

Cost: 3000 Wood Units

Village Hall (Stage 2): The Expanded Village Hall is an enhanced version of the original Village Hall, providing a larger, more advanced hub for the village's administrative and communal needs. With its expanded capacity and upgraded amenities, it facilitates more efficient planning, communication, and task distribution, while still serving as the primary access point for daily and non-daily quests.

Cost: 2000 Wood Units

Wooden House (Stage 2): The Upgraded Wooden House, an enhanced version of the Wooden Village House, offers a more spacious and comfortable living environment for the villagers. This upgraded dwelling, made from reinforced timber, boasts improved durability against the elements. It includes an expanded porch, as well as a customizable interior that caters to larger families or a more complex set of residential needs.

Cost: 1000 Wood Units

Available Buildings

Outer Wooden Wall (Stage 1): The Outer Wooden Wall is a supplementary fortification designed to provide an additional layer of security for the village. Constructed from robust timber, this secondary defense forms an extended circular perimeter with a radius of four hundred meters from the Village Altar. Similar to the inner wall, this structure is also equipped with watchtowers and gates for enhanced surveillance and access control.

Cost: 3000 Wood Units

Wooden House (Stage 1): The Wooden Village House is a simple yet cozy dwelling designed to provide shelter and comfort for the village's inhabitants. Constructed from durable timber, the house features a sloped roof to protect against the elements, a small porch, and an interior that can be customized to meet the needs of its residents. Each Wooden Village House can accommodate a small family, offering them a safe and warm place to call home.

Cost: 300 Wood Units

Cultivation Hall (Stage 1): The Cultivation Hall is a special facility designed to enhance the meditative and cultivation practices of the villagers. Its tranquil environment and purpose-built design boost cultivation speed marginally, while also enabling users to extend their meditation sessions by an additional half hour. As a place of peace and personal growth, the Cultivation Hall is instrumental in the spiritual progress of its users. Due to the effect of "Ether Lines Nexus," the cultivation speed increases significantly.

Cost: 4000 Wood Units

Blacksmith's Forge (Stage 1): The Blacksmith's Forge is a specialized facility essential for the production of tools, weaponry, and armor. Governed by a Master Blacksmith, it serves as both a production and learning hub, where villagers can undergo apprenticeships to become proficient blacksmiths.

Cost: 2000 Wood Units

Alchemist's Lab (Stage 1): The Alchemist's Lab is the cornerstone for potion brewing, herb identification, and rudimentary medicine preparation. Under the guidance of a Master Alchemist, villagers can learn to concoct a variety of useful mixtures, honing their alchemical skills.

Cost: 2000 Wood Units

Attributes

Ether Line Nexus: A powerful convergence of ether lines lies beneath Wolvendale Village, creating a nexus of magical energy. This nexus enhances the potency of magic used within the village and accelerates the recovery of mana for magi. It also promotes the growth of magical flora and fauna within the Shelderwood Forests, offering unique opportunities for research and discovery.

Upgrade Conditions:

500 registered citizens

10,000 gathered experience

Upgrade all available buildings

Thorian spent a moment studying the colossal screen before him, taking time to absorb all the information displayed. Despite his decade-long tenure as lord, many details from the lower levels had faded from his memory.

Once he had perused the entire screen, his lips curved into a triumphant grin. Without delay, Thorian issued his first command. *Upgrade wooden wall.*

Wooden Wall (Stage 1): The Wooden Wall is a sturdy barrier designed to protect the village from external threats and encroachments. Crafted from strong timber, this defensive structure forms a circular perimeter with a radius of two hundred meters from the Village Altar. The wall is equipped with watchtowers and gates to enable monitoring and control of access to the village.

Upgrade:

Gathered Experience: 2250

Wood: 3000

Do you wish to upgrade the Wooden Wall to stage 2?

"Yes, I do."

From his vantage point, Thorian watched as a massive cloud of dust billowed and shrouded the wall, the ground quaking beneath him. Emerging from the dust, the wooden wall soared to over ten meters high, its watchtowers appearing more imposing than ever.

Having reinforced the external fortifications, Thorian shifted his focus towards the village's internal infrastructure. His next move was to upgrade the village hall.

The instant transformation lent the hall an enhanced sense of grandeur and authority, which Thorian noticed immediately upon stepping inside. He observed the more spacious interior, furnished with tables and chairs scattered around for villagers to convene and converse. Melina's desk had also been upgraded, now adorned with decorations and a more expansive workspace.

"Congratulations on the upgrade, my lord." The elven lady bowed gracefully. "You've been working diligently."

Thorian returned her smile and cast a glance towards the staircase leading to the second floor. "Are the rooms upstairs operational?" he inquired.

"Currently, there is just one room on the second floor, which is well-equipped for strategic meetings," Melina stated. "If you wish, my lord, you may also access it via the rear entrance of the hall."

Thorian nodded in acknowledgment of the elven lady's explanation. His gaze then drifted towards the bulletin board, where five familiar quests instantly captured his attention.

Like I thought, the daily quests reset when you upgrade the Hall. Good thing I remembered that detail.

CHAPTER 59

Having accepted his daily quests anew, Thorian exited the hall and proceeded to review his Journal.

Show journal.

Journal:

Subjugate 20 monsters (daily)

Cast a spell 40 times (daily)

Cultivate your Qi for two hours (daily)

Gather 200 Wood Units (daily)

Clear one dungeon (daily)

Pact with the Wolven Guardians

Purification of Eärendil's Sanctuary

Revenge on the Monsters **(complete)**

Thorian gazed at his journal brimming with quests and allowed himself a satisfied grin. *Let's tackle the easier ones first, then we can concentrate on the rest.*

Given his proximity to the altar, Thorian opted to complete the wood quest first, enabling the demonic face to absorb a few fallen trees. Having accomplished this, Thorian decided to construct the one building he had been eagerly anticipating.

Build cultivation hall.

A resonant rumbling echoed from the south, just beyond the precincts of the Priest Guild, as a new structure surfaced from the earth. Thorian advanced towards the cultivation hall, a humble yet purposeful edifice now nestled within the heart of the village. Crafted from polished golden-brown wood, it exuded an aura of organic simplicity. Its gently sloping roof welcomed in an abundance of natural light and fresh air, while the intricately carved wooden door echoed the ethos of living harmoniously with nature.

At first glance, the cultivation hall might appear to be a simple hermit's abode, but upon closer inspection, its thoughtfully conceived design became evident. Elegantly carved motifs adorned the wooden panels, windows were strategically positioned to greet the morning sun, and a cleverly structured interior nurtured an ambiance of meditation and cultivation. Encircling the main hall were smaller rooms dedicated to solitary meditation, linked by a serpentine pathway bordered with saplings.

Entering one of these secluded rooms, Thorian felt the air pulsate with Ether's energy. He immediately recognized that his cultivation sessions within this domain would yield even more significant results.

The hall just affords me an additional half an hour, so I shouldn't waste it by trying to break through the Vermilion Gate. It's better if I focus on gathering more Qi.

With a clear strategy in mind, Thorian removed his Verdant Robe to keep it pristine during his meditation. He settled down cross-legged and began to breathe with deliberate intent. As he commenced his session, he could feel the world's potent energy attempting to permeate his body. Although his outer channels were more congested than those of an average human, they were significantly more receptive than when he first initiated his practice. Soon, a torrent of Ether coursed through his channels, converging in his dantian. As these Ether particles condensed into Qi drops, Thorian felt his dantian gradually becoming replenished. By the time half an hour had elapsed, Thorian knew he had made substantial progress.

Thorian issued the command immediately upon opening his eyes: *Display panel.*

Ding!

Race: Flame Kobold

Level: 16/30 (XP: 128/2200)

Class: Magus

Level: 20/20 (XP: MAX)

Lifespan: 40 years

Cultivation Realm: Qi Gathering Second Stage (21%)

Stats:

Strength: 62

Agility: 67

Constitution: 37

Mana: 67

Qi: 20

Free Points: 15

Skills:

Minor Fire Affinity (passive)

Flame Resistance (passive)

Fireball (active)

Combustion Touch (active)

Waterball (active)

Rock Bullet (active)

Wind Gust (active)

Good progress. Thorian smiled in satisfaction before scratching his furry chin in thought. *Maybe I should just focus on increasing my Qi for now. I don't need to break through my meridian nodes until I reach the first realm's bottleneck.*

With this resolution in mind, Thorian rose to his feet and utilized waterballs to cleanse his body as well as the soiled floor. After ensuring the room was clean, Thorian once again donned his Verdant Robe and exited the Cultivation Hall. Casting a backwards glance at the building, a wry smile tugged at his lips.

It's a pity we won't have access to proper cultivation skills until the next village stage. I don't want to risk Qi deviation by teaching them myself, especially since it could lead to debilitating injuries.

Shaking off the minor regret, Thorian continued his tour of the village. From a distance, he could spot the crowd of brown kobloids and kobolds trailing behind Lapis. Their sizable presence within the small village was impossible to overlook.

With a series of mental commands, Thorian manifested two new structures: the blacksmith's forge and the alchemist's lab. These buildings were critical cornerstones of any territory when it came to trade and daily life. Their current utility for Thorian, however, was rather limited since both structures necessitated an extensive assortment of blueprints and recipes to truly reach their potential.

And we need civilians with a vested interest in these professions. Having a sizable army is beneficial, but we also need those who will create and repair our military equipment.

Deciding to address these new buildings later, Thorian redirected his attention towards the exterior. As he approached the now-fortified wall, he found himself genuinely impressed. The wall had become taller, thicker, and more robust, and was armed with numerous traps. Rows of spikes were strategically positioned along the wall to deter any blind charges aimed at breaching it. The increased height made it a formidable challenge to scale, further enhancing the village's defenses.

After admiring the new fortifications for a few moments, Thorian journeyed from one gate to the next. At each entrance, he instructed one of his seasoned party members to form a squad and lead it into the

Verdant Labyrinth dungeon, where they would tackle the first layer. Thorian recognized the immense significance of this undertaking, not only for the rewards from the quest and dungeon but also for the battle experience his troops would amass. After successfully navigating it once, they would be equipped to return the following day and traverse it effortlessly with other inexperienced members, allowing the newfound knowledge and wisdom to rapidly disseminate throughout the village.

However, with five members dispatched, the remaining guard squads would struggle to perform their duties as efficiently and safely as before. Therefore, Thorian took up the mantle, assuming the guard responsibilities of the absent members. For each gate, it would take approximately forty minutes to an hour for a squad to journey to the dungeon and return.

Thus, the remainder of the day passed swiftly with Thorian transitioning from one gate to another, standing guard for the departed members. During this time, his sole focus was on honing the proficiency levels of his "Wind Gust" and "Rock Bullet" skills.

By the time the final dungeon-delving squad had returned, Thorian had achieved significant progress in mastering both spells.

Rock Bullet: You create a barrage of rocks that fly towards your enemies, pummeling them and leaving them vulnerable.

Proficiency: 39.7%

Wind Gust: You summon a powerful gust of wind that can knock your enemies off balance, extinguish fires, and enhance your speed and agility.

Proficiency: 37.4%

Good progress. At this rate, I should be done with all four skill requirements tomorrow.

Satisfied with the near-attainment of his goal, Thorian swiftly closed the screens and dashed back to the village hall. The day was on the brink of ending, and he aimed to claim the rewards for his daily quest before their expiration.

Upon entering the hall, he was surprised to see his old group, Nox, Ventus, Saxum, Vigil, and Forlune, all seated together already, sharing tales of the day's happenings.

"Oh, King?" Ventus noticed Thorian's entrance. "Have you returned to collect the rewards from the new quests?"

Forlune, appearing more confident than ever in his golden chestplate, proudly thrust out his chest and asked, "Did you get a chance to revisit the dungeon and complete that quest again? These rascals received double the rewards."

"No, I didn't." Thorian shook his head as he made his way towards the elven woman. "Though it's a pity I didn't complete that quest, it's more important that I ensure the safety of the village rather than pursue minor gains."

He offered Melina a smile upon reaching the desk and asked, "Could you assist me in claiming my quests?"

"Right away, my lord," she elegantly replied.

As usual, the elven lady stamped the quest parchments, allowing Thorian to swiftly claim his rewards. The new daily quests offered twice the rewards of the previous ones, significantly augmenting Thorian's wealth.

Personal resources.

Arcane Coins: 2200

Looking at his resources, Thorian smiled wryly. *It's a shame we don't have access to the marketplace yet. There aren't many ways to spend these coins currently.*

After closing his system screen, Thorian turned back, his gaze resting upon his group.

"Good thing you're all here," Thorian began, directing his gaze towards the staircase. "We will be having our first official meeting now."

CHAPTER 60

As the group ascended the staircase, Thorian cast a glance over his shoulder, addressing the moon kobold with a casual inquiry. "How was your day?"

Forlune gave a dismissive shrug. "Nothing special. Ever since the boys evolved, we haven't had any more trouble." With a smug grin, he puffed out his chest, the glimmer of his new equipment catching the torchlight. "But this beauty really made everything easier. Haven't taken a single scratch since the moment I put it on."

"It's really good, right?" Ventus, always eager to remind others of their shared trials, interjected. "We had to work really hard to beat that boss and get it, so you better be grateful."

"I don't have to be grateful for anything," Forlune scoffed at the suggestion, his voice dripping with dismissive scorn. "We've made a deal, pure and simple. I am going to get you five pieces of equipment that suit you, so don't go around yapping about it."

"Better follow through," Ventus shot back, his tone turning sharp. "Or I'll strip that armor you're so proud of right off your chest."

As they continued their banter, Thorian settled into a chair around the round table, motioning for everyone else to do the same. "Let's begin the meeting."

Turning to Nox, who was situated to his left, Thorian inquired, "How was your first night with Whisperwind? What have you been doing?"

Nox emitted a weary sigh before replying. "He just had me inscribing skill scrolls the whole time while he tested the new recruits." His expression then brightened considerably. "But in the end, he did let me do my class advancement ceremony. It looked so pretty, with stars and bright lights filling the room."

"Lucky you," Ventus murmured under his breath, a hint of envy coloring his words.

Vigil, however, directed a warm smile towards the shadowstalker. "Congratulations, you're the first among us to advance his class, if I'm not mistaken." His gaze then shifted to Thorian, curiosity sparkling in his eyes. "Unless you have already done so, My King."

"No, not yet," Thorian responded, shaking his head. He turned his attention to his most trusted ally. "Nox, congratulations. What kind of advancement did you get?"

Scratching his chin pensively, Nox looked up as if searching the rafters for the right words. "There were many options that I saw, but after talking with the master, we chose shadow reaper. He said that it combined my stealthy shadow skills with really strong hard-hitting spells. It felt like a good mix of the two."

Shadow reaper, huh? Whisper Step unlocks the reaper class—I guess this is a variant of it due to his racial abilities. It seems like there is a lot of synergy between races and classes.

Saxum remarked, his voice rich with admiration, "You're growing stronger by the minute, aren't you? I'm glad you're with us. You would be a terrifying enemy."

Ignoring Saxum's compliment, Forlune clicked his tongue dismissively and retorted, "I wonder if your new skills can make a dent in my armor."

Choosing to let Forlune's prideful comment slide, Thorian redirected the group's attention. "The primary purpose for this meeting is to discuss our next course of action."

"We are at your command, My King," Saxum responded readily, his loyalty evident in his tone. "Simply provide us with our directives and we will carry them out."

Vigil met Saxum's gaze, voicing his own perspective. "While I share your sentiment, I believe our king seeks more than blind agreement. Ignoring potential problems will not erase them. Instead, it only intensifies their impact when they inevitably surface."

Intrigued by the priest's comment, Thorian pursued the topic. "Do you have a specific concern in mind, Vigil?"

"Yes, I do," Vigil confirmed, nodding his head. "The forest presents real dangers. Our group can handle the tailmashers and thrikreens, particularly with a few evolved kobolds in our ranks. But it's the elusive and crafty creatures that blend into the surroundings that pose the greatest threat. Thanks to the experience you've instilled in us, I managed to navigate my men safely through a labyrinth of traps. However, less powerful groups might struggle with this. Navigating through the forest could be particularly challenging for them."

"We didn't have that issue at all," Ventus couldn't help but interject, a boastful edge to his tone. "If I don't know what I'm seeing in front of me, I just throw a Gale Slash at it. That usually solves any problem quickly."

Thorian cast a fleeting glance at the wind magus before returning his attention to the priest. "Your concern is noted. It suggests we need to reassess our approach to these excursions."

Falling into a thoughtful silence, Thorian drew on his considerable military experience to quickly formulate a plan. "Moving forward, we'll conduct dungeon expeditions with platoons of approximately fifty men each. These groups will be accompanied by between five and ten evolved kobolds. Their role will be to ensure the group's safety and navigate the forest's threats, thanks to their prior experience and familiarity with its dangers."

Once Thorian concluded outlining his plan, Forlune raised a concern. "Wouldn't this leave our village vulnerable?"

Saxum was quick to counter. "We're expecting a significant influx of new recruits soon. As they bolster their strength, we'll have plenty of manpower to secure our walls."

Thorian nodded in agreement. "Exactly. The new brown kobolds and kobloids will be distributed evenly across all four units. You'll be inundated with fresh recruits. Later in the day, once they've adequately leveled up, we'll form the two platoons. The entire operation should take around two hours—roughly one hour for each platoon to venture into the dungeon, clear it, and return."

The group took a few moments to digest Thorian's strategy before signaling their comprehension with a series of nods. Only one remained unmoved, his brow furrowed in contemplation.

"Do you have an issue with my plan, Forlune?" Thorian queried, observing the moon kobold's introspection. "Tell me. We can solve it if your concern is valid."

"It's not about the plan," Forlune replied, scratching his head in confusion. "It's about the humans—when are we planning to hunt them? Our quest deadline is fast approaching."

Remembering the challenge that all monsters had received, Nox's eyebrows shot up in realization. "That's true! If we manage to hunt five hundred, we're promised a special evolution. I wonder what form that would take?"

"We will also get a skill and lots of level-ups," Ventus chimed in.

Thorian nodded slowly in acknowledgment. "Those are valid

concerns. However, if we launch an assault on the city before ensuring the stability of our village, we risk serious complications."

He paused, gnawing thoughtfully at his thumb. Moments later, his face lit up in a grin.

"Have you stumbled upon a solution, My King?" Vigil inquired, his own smile mirroring Thorian's newfound optimism.

Thorian nodded and elaborated, "I've accepted a quest that speaks of a pack of direwolves residing within the forest. These beasts are highly formidable, swift, and most importantly, known for their unwavering loyalty. The quest instructs me to broker a pact with them. If we succeed, we can entrust the village's safety to these wolves. This way, we needn't worry about external invasions or conflicts stemming from our new recruits."

"How will we make that pact with them?" Forlune asked, his brow furrowed in confusion. "And when do you plan to do so?"

"Diplomacy is an area in which I excel, so put those concerns aside," Thorian assured, a confident smile gracing his features. "As for the timing, we will venture into the forest at the break of dawn. I will select a small, elite group to accompany me as we explore the region."

"Take me with you!" Ventus interjected eagerly, his hand shooting up. "Going outside is so much more fun than just killing the same things all day at the wall. That got really boring!"

"Certainly, Ventus," Thorian replied with an amiable chuckle. He then drew in a deep breath to introduce the final topic of discussion. "I'd like to address tonight's guarding duties. Given that each of your units will be reinforced with new members, I propose that you divide your squads. When you split the unit, ensure that each group contains a roughly equal number of veterans. The two factions will then alternate guarding duties throughout the night. One group will rest first, then halfway through the night, they'll switch with the second group.

I'll arrange for individual houses for each unit, which will help in locating the resting group."

"Houses?" Nox questioned, head tilted in confusion.

"Houses provide shelter where you can sleep without being drenched by rain all night. Additionally, they come equipped with beds, offering more comfort than the bare, hard ground."

Having covered all necessary points of discussion, Thorian concluded the meeting. The group dispersed, each kobold heading to his respective unit stationed at the village's four gates. Meanwhile, Thorian embarked on a construction spree, erecting an assortment of houses throughout the village.

Desiring to acknowledge the bravery of those consistently defending the village, Thorian prioritized the construction of several stage-two houses close to each gate. These accommodations were reserved for the selfless defenders who spent their days repelling relentless onslaughts from monstrous creatures.

For the village's remaining residents, Thorian created a substantial number of stage-one houses. Though less elaborate, these buildings exuded a welcoming atmosphere. They were clean and well-structured, and marked a significant improvement from sleeping on hard ground or within dank caves.

Once the new recruits had visited all guilds and chosen their classes, Thorian rendezvoused with Lapis. After explaining his plan to the brown kobold, they divided the fresh batch into two distinct groups. The first group consisted of civilians unfit for combat due to health issues or age restrictions. The other was composed of healthy individuals eager to demonstrate their usefulness and pursue personal growth. Impressively, the second group outnumbered the first by a ratio of four to one.

Pursuing his strategy, Thorian escorted the civilians to their new homes where they settled in for the night, while Lapis divided the fighters into four groups, each assigned to one of the village gates. Following Thorian's directive, each unit split into two, deciding on the order of their night shifts by drawing straws.

With his plans implemented successfully, Thorian raised a stage-two house for himself near the altar, a location known to his trusted inner circle of five in case of emergencies.

Finally, after what seemed an eternity of planning and execution, Thorian could retire for a much-needed rest.

INTERLUDE 4

The cacophonous din of battle reigned on the fields of Locksley, a gruesome symphony woven by clashing blades, shrieking monsters, and the anguished cries of the fallen. Tristan took a moment to survey the battlefield. Just as his sword was slick with the blood of the goblins he'd dispatched only moments ago, so too was his body drenched in their lifeblood, a morbid testament to his prowess in combat.

In the aftermath of their cryptic encounter with the enigmatic woman robed in green at the city plaza, Tristan and the warriors he'd handpicked had advanced into the heart of Locksley. Strategically positioned atop a steep incline, the inner city afforded them a commanding vantage point against the relentless flood of monstrous invaders. The formidable ring of stone walls that ensconced it provided a stalwart bastion against the monstrous onslaught.

The bastion walls of Locksley were ablaze with kinetic action. The air buzzed with the whistling of arrows as they cleaved the night sky, their lethal flight paths ending in the bodies of encroaching beasts. Knights, clad in battered armor, fought with valorous tenacity against the goblins bold enough to breach their bulwark.

But among the valiant fighters, one figure stood out in both vigor and power. The man, who was surprisingly spry even in his old age, was tearing through overgrown cats and sickly-looking goblins. The sword Tristan had previously gifted him glowed with a magical blue hue, and each swing of its blade was a death sentence for any creature unfortunate enough to be within its reach. His finesse was lacking, yet the raw might that he possessed rendered such subtlety unnecessary. As Tristan watched him, a pang of jealousy snaked its way into his heart.

Sir Robert's prowess is nothing short of awe-inspiring. I can't help but envy his miraculous capacity for growth. He is faster and stronger than me even though he is sixty years my senior.

Yet rising above this undercurrent of envy, a torrent of gratitude and respect drowned out these negative whispers. Robert had been an unwavering pillar of strength by their side, matching the relentless rhythm of battle stroke for stroke. A more steadfast ally Tristan could hardly imagine.

Looking away from the chaos of the front lines, the inner city buzzed with a different kind of intensity. Rescue squads darted in and out of the gates, bearing the wounded guards, and into the city's heart, where physicians stood ready. Arrows were in high demand, and young boys, brave despite their tender age, were kept busy distributing them. Meanwhile, the women, resilient and unyielding, brought pots of steaming stew and soup to the weary defenders.

A voice sliced through Tristan's thoughts, abruptly yanking him back to the present. "Food supplies are dwindling, Tristan. These are preliminary estimates, but it seems we have enough to last ten days at most. And that's only if everyone restricts themselves to one meal per day."

"That's too little," Tristan responded, his brows knitting together. "What about your family? They should have substantial reserves."

Oswald exhaled deeply, his head shaking in denial. "The Strong-hearts have been summoned by my father. They've barricaded them-

selves inside the manor, citing 'The Heir's Protection Act' as their jus-
tification."

Tristan's mouth hung open, disbelief clouding his face. "But…
you're the heir. Who are they attempting to protect?!"

"Father is mad at me about that," Oswald replied with a shrug.
"And it's not just my family. The Bloodworths and the Callfields have
also severed contact with the outside world. They said that they had
already accomplished their noble duties by giving us half their
guards."

"Unbelievable!" Tristan's anger flared, his thumb clamped between his teeth. "Do they not understand the situation we're in?
Monsters are ravaging the city, for the love of all gods, and they continue their power play?!"

"I don't think they've seen the situation enough to understand it."
Oswald conjectured, clicking his tongue in disapproval. "They've
spent the entire day hiding in their manors."

Gathering his composure, Tristan steered the conversation in a
new direction. "Leave them be for now. Have you been in touch with
the merchant alliance?"

"Half of them are dead, and the majority of the remaining are too
terrified to engage in discussions. They are convinced the end of the
world is nigh, and our efforts are futile." Oswald's face contorted with
distaste, but he then offered a sliver of hope amidst the despair. "However, one did express a willingness to negotiate."

"Thank the gods," Tristan exhaled, shaking his head. "Who is it?"

"The head of the alliance, Jasmine," Oswald responded, a glimmer
of a smile crossing his features. "She didn't represent the alliance when
she spoke to me, but only herself. Half of her goods are stranded on
the outskirts of the city and are irretrievable, but the remaining half is
here. She has a stockpile of spices, vegetables, and an assortment of

fresh and dried fruits. With careful rationing, it could extend our supplies for another week—perhaps even two."

"That's promising," Tristan's eyes widened momentarily in surprise before he composed himself. "And what is her asking price?"

"A seat at the table," Oswald replied, his tone sardonic. "I informed her that I would convey the proposition to you, but asked her not to hold her breath. The nobles will undoubtedly oppose her inclusion."

"I'll grant her that seat," Tristan declared, leaving Oswald visibly surprised. "If she's prepared to rise to the occasion, I'm willing to reward her handsomely. I'm confident my father would support this decision too, given the nobles' lackluster response to the crisis."

"You're in for a fierce struggle. Perhaps even more formidable than the one we're currently engaged in." Oswald sighed. "On another note, what should we do with her mercenaries? By law, we have the right to commandeer them."

Tristan only shook his head. "Let them be. They're the only leverage she has to prevent us from outright seizing her reserves. I prefer to allow her to retain this advantage, as a gesture of good faith. If she's to have a seat at the table, then it's crucial to nurture a healthy relationship from the outset. And there's no sense in shattering that trust over a mere twenty or so mercenaries."

Oswald paused, taking a moment to fully absorb Tristan's words before a reluctant chuckle escaped him. He shrugged as he said, "You have a knack for finding wisdom in the oddest of situations."

"I suppose that's just part of my charm," Tristan responded with a shared chuckle.

Their banter was abruptly cut short by an urgent call from outside. "General Henry! Open the gates!"

The gates creaked open, allowing nearly a hundred refugees to pour into the inner city. Fear and exhaustion were deeply etched onto their faces.

As the guards ushered these beleaguered souls towards temporary shelter, Oswald shook his head. "Forget about that ten-day estimate. We're looking at eight."

A laugh threatened to escape Tristan, but he swallowed it back, recognizing the inappropriateness of the moment. Trust Oswald to find macabre humor where Tristan found wisdom.

Beyond the weary refugees, Tristan caught sight of the Iron Vanguard astride their magnificent white steeds. They were seasoned warriors, their legends preceding even Tristan's birth. Each held a gaze that told tales of countless battles and hard-fought victories.

However, the man at the helm of this elite unit wore an incongruously cheerful expression. General Henry sported a warm smile that belied the grimness of their circumstances. His kindly visage coupled with his advanced age would have given the impression of a benign old man, if not for Tristan's knowledge of the truth beneath the facade.

"Your Grace! You're a sight for sore eyes," General Henry bellowed, his laughter reverberating through the air as he dismounted and advanced towards Tristan and Oswald. "What on earth happened here? This place is starting to resemble a refugee camp."

At the general's jest, Oswald laughed while Tristan simply shook his head. "It's a sign of the times, I'm afraid," the prince commented.

"A sign, indeed!" Henry guffawed, his gaze drifting beyond the inner city walls. "Who would've thought it wouldn't be the Thulaskar or those Sundawn devils that would be our undoing, but rather some monsters straight out of folklore?"

The general turned to study Oswald. "And look at you, young man. You're doing your ancestors proud! I want to see the day when you ascend to the head of your family and restore its former glory."

"I yearn for such a day myself, Sir Henry," Oswald humbly replied.

The general barked a hearty laugh, clapping Oswald on the shoulder. "You've come a long way."

Watching the older man dominate the atmosphere, Tristan queried, "You were with my father, weren't you, Sir Henry? Have you two parted ways?"

"We have indeed," the general confirmed, nodding. "He ventured west while I tackled the north. He's likely still engaged in the rescue of civilians."

"It seems to be in his nature, he can't sit idle," Tristan responded with a rueful laugh. "Though his presence would be beneficial here as well."

"The nobles are proving to be a thorn in your side, Your Grace?" the general inquired, brow wrinkled in concern.

Tristan responded with a frustrated tilt of his head. "Well, they're certainly not making things easy."

"Is that so?" General Henry laughed heartily. "Then you should count your blessings, your grace. That is more than one could hope for."

Observing General Henry's buoyant demeanor, Tristan found himself caught up in the infectious wave of optimism.

Seeing the young prince's spirits lift, Henry nodded approvingly. "Well then, why don't we go somewhere private to have a proper meeting? I'm sure you have much to tell me."

"Absolutely, Sir Henry," Tristan said, his gaze wandering over to Robert who was resting with the other guards. "But there's someone I'd like you to meet first."

Before Henry could pose a question, Tristan approached the old man, extending an invitation for him to join the upcoming meeting.

Tristan, having extended the invitation to Robert, proceeded to introduce him to General Henry. "Sir Robert has provided us with invaluable insights, many of which have proven essential and will continue to guide us," he explained. A warm smile touched his lips as he turned to Robert. "He also represents our hope against these fiendish creatures."

"That's high praise from the prince himself," Henry admitted, taken aback. "I'm intrigued as well."

The four of them made their way to Tristan's nearby manor for the meeting. As they approached the main building, Robert trailed behind the group, still reeling from the sudden turn of events. While Tristan and General Henry delved into tales of yore, Oswald gave them space, opting instead to engage Robert in conversation.

"Mister," the young knight initiated, curiosity coloring his tone, "could you elaborate on this 'level up' concept again? You mentioned it enhanced your strength, and I've witnessed that change myself. But how does it work?"

Tristan picked up on their conversation from the front and found his interest piqued. He glanced at the general, and their gazes met, followed by mutual chuckles as they realized their shared curiosity. Both were eager to hear Robert's explanation.

In response to Oswald's query, Robert delved into his understanding of the surreal events that had unfolded since the onset of the apocalypse. He explained the notion of experience points, describing how eliminating monsters augmented them, leading to these so-called "level-ups." Each level-up allowed for points to be distributed among four primary stats. He was able to grasp the roles of strength, agility, and constitution, yet the concept of "mana" still eluded him. As he allocated points to the first three stats, his physique had surpassed its former limits, achieving a state of fitness unprecedented in his six decades of life.

Their conversation continued as they climbed the manor's grand staircase and entered Tristan's strategic planning room. Dominating the space was a vast table, atop which rested a meticulous map of Locksley and its surrounding regions, speckled with a myriad of tokens and markers.

"Let's start from the beginning," Tristan suggested as he sank into his chair, his gaze fixed on Robert. "Sir, would you kindly recount the events that occurred at the plaza?"

Robert gave a nod of affirmation and embarked on his narrative, "Me and my grandson Roo, we were sitting out in the plaza, looking for a bit of fresh air and a nice view of the moon. This group of people shows up, led by this green-clad lady. We exchanged a few words with them, but I couldn't shake the sense that something was off about her. Before long, all hell broke loose."

He paused to draw a deep breath before continuing, "Amid all that chaos, me and little Roo, we were scared out of our wits. I reached out to one of the giant statues that popped up in the plaza, and that's when I got these... strange powers you've been seeing. Meanwhile, that gang was up to no good. I didn't like the look the lady shot me, so I grabbed my grandson and ran. You know the rest."

Tristan listened intently, acknowledging Robert's account with a nod before subtly gesturing for Oswald to proceed.

Rising from his chair, Oswald spoke, "The woman, named Nalia, doesn't possess a surname. She's what you'd call the queen of the underworld. Anything unsavory—slave trading, assassinations, small-time thefts, robberies—she and her lot are behind it all."

"Aha, so it's Nalia causing all the ruckus," Henry acknowledged, his brow furrowing in thought. "Then she must've known about this apocalyptic scenario in advance. I've never seen her face in public, and I looked for a long time. It's unlikely she'd be casually strolling and chatting in the plaza right as these events unfolded."

Upon hearing Henry's assessment, Oswald nodded in agreement, sinking back into his seat. "Her subsequent actions affirm this suspicion. Ever since this calamity commenced, she's been amassing followers at an alarming rate. It's as though anyone who encounters her becomes instantly enamored. Man or woman, young or old—anyone who crosses paths with her ends up joining her murderous ranks. According to the latest reports from my scouts, they number over two thousand."

"Two thousand?" The general's eyebrows shot up in surprise. "Are you sure? I know that she has a way with words, but I don't think even the king could convince so many to join so fast."

"Unfortunately, it seems that she is not only using her tongue to attract her followers, Sir Henry." Oswald shook his head. "She penetrates large districts that haven't been devastated by the monsters yet, eliminates the threats, rescues the inhabitants, and seemingly convinces all of them to join her ranks. She's been replicating this tactic throughout the day."

After a moment of quiet contemplation, General Henry voiced his skepticism. "Even if we accept she has managed to amass such a crowd using some mind-control magic, they remain ordinary civilians. Wandering around the city without the shelter of their homes is just asking to be killed."

"Nalia has monopolized the statues," Tristan clarified, shaking his head. "Those are what bestowed Sir Robert with his abilities, and they're what empowers her followers as well. Do not regard those two thousand as mere civilians. Think of them as knights with power and magic to match those creatures outside. Moreover, as per my sources, they are not only as formidable as the monsters, but they also display similar savagery. There's an unmistakable undercurrent of madness among them."

Henry sat in shock for a few seconds before he exhaled deeply. "By the gods... How on earth are we supposed to counter such a threat? If she continues to amass her forces, she'll have the city under her thumb in no time."

"That is indeed a significant problem," Tristan acknowledged gravely. Silence enveloped the room as they grappled with the enormity of their predicament.

"If only she would vacate the plaza for a few hours," Oswald mused. "We could take our men there and experience these magical abilities firsthand."

His words were cut short by a knock at the door. Rising from his seat, Oswald opened the door to find a kneeling knight. After closing the door behind him, he engaged in a brief exchange with the knight before exclaiming, "You must be joking?"

He reentered the room moments later, his face a blend of disbelief and elation. "The plaza is vacant. Nalia and her troops have moved!"

CHAPTER 61

As the sun's rays pierced through the window, heralding the dawn of a new day, Thorian roused from his modest bed. His eyes roved over the minimalist decor of the room. The sparse adornment comprised of a small desk, a humble nightstand, and a tiny chair. It paled in comparison to the opulence he had enjoyed in his past life, yet it was nonetheless a considerable upgrade from the dank cave floor he'd grown used to sleeping on.

Ready for a new day, Thorian slipped into his Verdant Robe and stepped outside. To his surprise, the village was a hive of activity, thrumming with monsters bustling about their business. Some hastened towards the village hall, eager to complete their quests, while others ventured to the guilds, ready to exchange their hard-earned arcane coins for new skills.

His attention was caught by a few evolved creatures he hadn't previously encountered. The once stocky and short orcs had transformed into towering hulks, their faces marked by battle scars and enhanced by prominent, powerful jaws. Their primal and formidable presence was a testament to their newly acquired powers.

Vivax's group should have also evolved, Thorian noted to himself with a smile. *That changes our plans a little bit.*

While Thorian's consciousness surrendered to the comforting embrace of a deep sleep, his mind tirelessly continued to churn in the background. It brewed a concoction of ideas and sifted through memories of old strategies. One such strategy pertained to the gilded spike-tail and the challenge of penetrating its armored hide without resorting to the perilous and high-risk combination skills he had to use.

How could I have forgotten such a simple trick?

Thorian chided himself for his momentary lapse but swiftly dismissed it. With the weight of countless concerns on his mind, some inefficiencies were inevitable.

Armed with a fresh strategy, Thorian traversed the village to gather his most trusted deputies. Once found, they convened in the meeting room on the second floor of the village hall. Nox, Ventus, Forlune, Saxum, Vigil, Lapis, Vivax, and Zogthar were all present.

"Thank you for joining me at this early hour," Thorian began, his voice imbued with a quiet gravitas. "I've called you here to discuss our strategy for the day. Once I have presented my plan, I invite you all to share any concerns or suggestions you might have, so that we can deliberate on them together."

Once he saw nods of assent from the gathered group, Thorian proceeded. "I observe that our new recruits are acclimating well to their environment. Can anyone report on their progress?"

"Pretty good," Forlune replied. "Mine have reached approximately level 9 in both species and class."

"Same on my end," Lapis offered.

Seeing a wave of agreement ripple through the group, Thorian reciprocated their nods. "That is commendable progress. They should be on the verge of evolution."

Pausing to draw in a deep breath, he then laid out his proposal. "Yesterday, we discussed dividing our forces into two platoons for the dungeon expedition. I believe now is the opportune moment to select the leaders for these groups."

Every gaze remained fixed on Thorian as he articulated his plan. The moon kobold, in particular, couldn't suppress a wide grin.

"Lapis, Vivax, Saxum, I entrust you with the leadership of the first platoon. This group will be divided into three units, with each of you overseeing one," Thorian commanded.

"It is an honor, My King," Saxum responded, inclining his head in a modest bow.

"We appreciate your trust, Thorian," Lapis added, gratitude resonating in his voice.

Thorian acknowledged their words with a nod, then his gaze drifted to the remaining trio. "Forlune, Nox, Zogthar, I assign you the command of the second platoon. Your roles will mirror those of the first platoon's leaders."

"That's just what I wanted to hear, Thorian!" Forlune's words echoed with unbridled enthusiasm. "How large will these platoons be? I think you said fifty yesterday?"

"I underestimated the influx of new combatants from the latest batch of recruits," Thorian admitted, shaking his head. "After tallying all four groups, we have a total of 162 fighters. Each platoon will therefore consist of 81 members, with each of you leading a team of 27."

"We appreciate this opportunity, my lord," Zogthar said, bowing slightly.

"There's no need for thanks," Thorian dismissed, shaking his head. "Now, for the second amendment to our plans. I want the first platoon to challenge the first layer without delay."

"Why is that, My King?" Vigil inquired, taken aback. "I thought our strategy was to let the fresh recruits mature before we take on the dungeon."

"I am confident they can conquer it with ease, as long as each team has an evolved kobold. Their considerable growth in strength already serves as a reliable self-defense. This strategy will also maximize efficiency, as the rookies can gain an immense amount of experience from the dungeon and edge closer to evolution. Once they evolve, tackling the second layer could become feasible."

"Isn't that too hard, King?" Ventus interjected. "The other monsters are one thing, but that guardian was really hard to deal with. Its armor is so tough we had to combine all three of our skills to kill it."

"If that's the issue, I believe we have a solution at hand," Zogthar chimed in. "Post-evolution, we've acquired a new skill called 'Lethal Strike.' It lets us bypass armor, akin to the thri-kreen."

"That is excellent news," Thorian responded, a grin spreading across his face as the rest of the kobolds looked at the high orc in admiration. "Groups with high orcs will have that advantage, but those without them aren't bereft of strategies. Reflecting on our previous encounters, I have devised a reliable method to breach the guardian's armor."

"What might that be, My King?" Vigil inquired, his interest piqued.

"You will need the Fireball and Waterball spells. Repeatedly strike the same spot with both spells, and the resulting shock from the rapid temperature change will cause the armor to fracture. Defeating it then wouldn't be as challenging."

There was a beat of silence following Thorian's explanation. Those who had accompanied him on the dungeon expedition seemed particularly stunned. Ventus arched an eyebrow in surprise and curiosity, while Saxum murmured, "We had so much trouble against it, yet the solution was so simple?"

Opting not to linger on this revelation, Thorian pressed on. "Instruct your magi to spend their arcane coins on these two spells. They will prove crucial in future engagements."

Pausing to draw a deep breath, Thorian then issued his direct orders, "Now, I want you to head to the gates and divide all the units in half to form the two platoons. Then split these platoons into three groups, each under the command of one leader."

With that final directive, the meeting was adjourned. The six leaders dispersed, heading towards the gates to initiate the formation of the two platoons, leaving Thorian, Ventus, and Vigil behind.

"It's time for us to embark on our own tasks," Thorian remarked with a smile. "Let's head out."

The trio exited the village, setting out to explore the outskirts. Guided by Thorian, they navigated confidently through the covert threats of the forest, unperturbed by the sneaky and devious dwellers lying in wait. A single Fireball or command from Thorian to unleash a Gale Slash was all they needed to neutralize most obstacles.

As they journeyed onward, Ventus couldn't help but voice his thoughts. "I should have bought the Fireball skill myself. Could you imagine the power if I could do that combo alone? I'd be invincible."

Thorian shook his head in response. "You wouldn't be able to anytime soon. Let me demonstrate."

He extended his arm towards a clearing in the forest. First, he conjured his Wind Gust and launched the spell. Without missing a beat, he began chanting his Fireball incantation, and flames ignited in front of his palm. He launched the fire spell in the same trajectory as the first, but by the time it had covered half the distance, the Wind Gust had already struck the trees and dispersed. The Fireball arrived in its wake, setting a tree ablaze.

After summoning a waterball to douse the fire, Thorian turned back to Ventus to explain, "At our current skill level, we can't cast spells rapidly enough to merge them. We would need to cast them almost simultaneously to achieve that effect."

"Your explanations are always so enlightening." Vigil chuckled.

Meanwhile, Ventus was rubbing his chin and furrowing his brow in thought. After a moment's pause, he raised his gaze to Thorian and posed a question that seemed to have been on his mind. "King, I'm sure everyone has wanted to ask you this, but how do you know so many things?"

CHAPTER 62

The moment Ventus uttered those words, even Vigil ceased his actions, turning to listen with an intensity that was rarely seen. All eyes were on Thorian searching for an answer.

Well, it's not like I didn't expect this question.

Drawing a deep breath, Thorian locked eyes with Ventus and responded, "If that information is what you desire, then so be it."

At his words, the air of anticipation around Ventus and Vigil heightened, their eagerness for an answer unmistakable. Thorian indulged in the suspense, leisurely cracking his neck, before finally offering his revelation. "It was revealed to me in a dream."

The room fell into a momentary hush before Ventus, disoriented by the unexpected reply, cocked his head to the side. "Hold on, King. I'm lost. What exactly was revealed to you in this dream?"

"It felt as though I had lived an entire lifetime," Thorian articulated, his companions hanging on every word. "That dream was both lengthy and fleeting. I can't recall all the events and the details, yet the insights I remember are tangible."

"It must be Ulvaskye's blessing." Vigil hypothesized, connecting the dots. "I recall the elders speaking of such divine revelations."

Ulvaskye? Thorian raised an eyebrow. *Oh, the wolf god.*

"Aha, that makes sense now!" Ventus exclaimed, his voice filled with enthusiasm. "That means you have gotten the god's favor. That is so amazing, King!"

"I can't say for certain if it's him, but that's how it occurred," Thorian conceded with a shrug, before setting the group back in motion.

"That also explains your change, My King," the priest observed sagely. "When we came to this world, it was as if you had become a completely different person."

Thorian took a moment to fully absorb the weight of Vigil's words. *So like I thought, this was the body of a different being before. I wonder where they are now.*

"What was I like before?" Thorian queried, intrigued by the personality of his body's previous inhabitant.

"You didn't talk much, usually." Ventus' expression reflected his puzzlement. "Now that you mention it, you really did change a lot, King."

"Who wouldn't change after getting Uldaskye's blessing?" Vigil interjected with a chuckle. "I know I certainly would."

As his companions bantered about his previous shift in character, Thorian remained quiet. He merely smiled, amused by their ability to concoct a narrative more convincing than anything he could have fabricated.

The trio of kobolds persisted on their journey, with the other two regaling stories of their old world. Thorian merely listened, offering no input. Their small party, a splinter faction of the tribe, roamed the vast lands under the leadership of Forlune. In their desolate homeland, the gods had chosen them to venture into this new world. With little instruction beyond "humans are the enemy" and the notion that "they could evolve into superior beings," they had been flung into a dimensional portal and dispatched to this unfamiliar territory.

As the hours rolled by, their journey took them further from their home village. Simultaneously chatting and hunting, Thorian limited his skill use to the two basic abilities he had yet to fully master. His

Fireball skill, combined with Ventus' Wind Gust, would only be used when they faced overwhelming odds necessitating mass destruction.

After about an hour and a half, Thorian finally noticed a sign of what they were searching for. His ears pricked up at the sound of distant howling.

"Those are direwolves," he deduced, sharing a significant glance with his comrades.

Acknowledging his conclusion, the trio sprinted towards the howling, their supernatural speed blurring the trees as they shot past. Shortly, the dense forest gave way to a large clearing.

"Wow."

Ventus' succinct remark embodied the team's shared awe as they surveyed the gigantic pack of oversized wolves before them. Each beast was twice the size of an average wolf.

Yet the denizens of these lands were far from impressed by their visitors. Five of the direwolves rose, their eyes burning with threat as they growled menacingly at Thorian's group. Any second, they could launch themselves at the intruders, primed for the kill.

"We did not come here to fight," Thorian asserted, stepping forward. "Take me to your leader."

His words, however, were not met with open arms. The moment Thorian finished speaking, the group of five lunged towards them, exuding lethal intent.

Ventus was swift to unleash his Wind Gust spell, which Thorian mirrored with his own. However, the gust of wind did nothing to halt the beasts' charge, the oversized wolves merely shaking off its effects.

Seeing that their magic was ineffective, Thorian clicked his tongue in frustration. Left with no other option, he conjured a rock bullet and hurled it towards the leading direwolf's front leg.

With a sharp yelp, the beast lost its footing and tumbled to the ground, causing the wolves behind it to fall in a domino effect. Witnessing this turn of events, the remaining direwolves, a sea of furry bodies, rose to their feet, their gaze sharp and alert.

Thorian, undeterred, made another attempt to defuse the tension. "We did not come here to fight. Please do not compel us to do so. Lead me to your leader."

The direwolves seemed set to dismiss Thorian's words again when a creature as large as a carriage made its way through the pack, parting them as if it were dividing the Red Sea.

"I am the king of the direwolves," the gargantuan beast intoned solemnly. "What do you wish to discuss with me?"

Unfazed and devoid of any hesitation, Thorian stared back at the colossal direwolf king, stating his proposition. "I am here to establish a pact with you and your pack—a pact of mutual protection."

The king let out a sound, a seemingly amused chortle that resonated more as a fearsome growl. "What value could such a pact hold when you are so weak?"

"Weak?" Ventus advanced with deliberate, heavy steps. "Let me show you who the weak one is."

"Halt," Thorian intervened, restraining the wind magus with an upheld hand. "There is no purpose in fighting now."

Having voiced his stance, Thorian steadily approached the direwolf king, all the while sweeping his gaze over the clearing. The pack of direwolves was vast—he estimated more than fifty members in their midst—yet many bore significant wounds and scars marring their bodies. Some were even handicapped, reduced to functioning with three legs.

"We are not weak, but strength is not the only thing we offer," Thorian began in a subdued tone, gradually gathering intensity and commanding the clearing with his words. "Those among you who are wounded, we have priests who can heal you. With their spells, you'll be restored to your prime condition. Those who are handicapped, we can assist you in slaying as many monsters as you need to evolve. You will emerge a superior entity, a complete being free of defects or injuries."

His gaze locked onto the wolf king's, unyielding and firm. "With me, you won't have to fear injuries. You'll have the freedom to fight to your heart's content!"

The clearing fell silent as Thorian concluded his speech, all eyes riveted on his figure. The sight was almost comical—Thorian standing tall and unafraid before the enormous wolf king. Even the king himself seemed taken aback, his eyebrows lifting in surprise.

"These are bold claims you make," the wolf king growled. "Show me this magic of which you speak, this healing power for my kin. If even a single word you've spoken proves false, your head will join the others."

The wolf king stepped aside, revealing a grisly scene. The clearing was strewn with the carcasses of various beasts and monsters. Some had already served as meals for the pack, leaving only bones behind, while others had been left to decay.

Thorian's expression remained unfazed at the sight. He simply met the gaze of the wolf king and said, "I ask for your word as a king, that if I fulfill my promise, you will form a pact with me."

"Insolent creature," the giant wolf rumbled, his tone begrudging. "Very well, if you deliver on your promise, I will enter your pact."

Thorian responded with a smile, turning his gaze back to the priest. Vigil's expression was a blend of awe and surprise.

"Show them what you can do, Vigil."

CHAPTER 63

At Thorian's command, Vigil advanced, with Ventus shadowing him closely. Although the priest demonstrated a slight hesitancy, the wind magus moved nonchalantly, displaying no fear of the pack of giant wolves who would readily liberate his flesh from the confinement of his bones.

As Vigil neared one of the injured wolves, it returned his approach with a fearsome stare and an eerie growl.

"Let him work his magic," commanded the wolf king, surprising the other wolves. "I want to see for myself whether this is true or merely the last desperate fabrication of a dying man."

The wolf reluctantly complied, permitting Vigil to draw near. With a brief incantation, he cast his Moon's Healing spell. Moonlight materialized in his palm before engulfing the injured wolf's body.

The beast yelped in surprise as the divine energy set to work, healing its gaping wound. Flesh wove itself together, concealing the exposed bone, followed by a new layer of hide and fur to camouflage any scarring.

Thorian glanced at the king of the direwolves, who was staring in disbelief at the spectacle Vigil was performing. "Is this magic...?" he murmured, awestruck. "Incredible."

"Proceed to the next one," Thorian commanded.

And so, Vigil continued healing the injured direwolves, one after the other. Over time, the skepticism and suspicion in the king's voice gradually transformed into surprise and admiration. Before long, Vigil had tended to all the visibly wounded, leaving only the crippled.

"There is one more wolf I wish you to heal," the king of the wolves spoke gravely, his tone devoid of its former arrogance. "My son."

Thorian nodded in acknowledgment, and the king led them beyond the clearing. There, next to a tree, lay a massive wolf. His size was eclipsed only by the king himself, his body worn and fatigued.

"He has been in this state the whole night," the direwolf king voiced with palpable pain. "It feels as though I'm watching my son slowly fade away right in front of me."

Without missing a beat, Vigil cast his spell once more. But as the moonlight dissipated from the wolf's body, his condition remained unchanged.

"Is he incurable?!" the king questioned, his voice a blend of fury and despair.

"Hold on a moment." Thorian furrowed his brows, meticulously examining the beast. "I think I understand what's wrong with him."

With a glimmer of hope reignited, the king urged, "Please, save my son. If you do, I swear on my name that I will form a pact with you."

Thorian nodded, then approached the languishing creature. Its eyes were half-open, but he lacked the energy to respond or react. He simply lay there, listless.

Witnessing the wolf's condition, Thorian grimaced. *It's most likely that parasite.*

Thorian then laid his hand on the beast's body, methodically examining every inch of the direwolf. He ensured he didn't overlook any part of the beast's form. As his fingers sifted through the wolf's hide, Thorian could feel the skeletal structure beneath. The creature had lost so much muscle and fat in the short time he had been suffering that Thorian could palpate the entirety of his ribcage.

All eyes were fixed on Thorian as he performed his examination. While Ventus and Vigil watched with interest, the king was utterly absorbed by Thorian's actions. A swirl of emotions was evident in the king's eyes. On one hand, he feared Thorian might inflict harm upon his son. On the other, he harbored hope, however faint, that Thorian would uncover the source of the malady plaguing his offspring.

"Found it." Finally, Thorian reached under the wolf's belly and pulled sharply.

The king was on the brink of launching into action, believing Thorian was causing his child harm, but a devilish screech froze him in his tracks. In Thorian's hand was a grotesque, small creature, its large mouth filled with a disarrayed set of teeth.

Thorian cast the creature onto the ground before incinerating it with a fireball, silencing its screeches.

"That was a vampiric leech," Thorian turned to explain. "It's a parasite that survives by draining the energy and vitality of its host. Your son was unfortunate to encounter it."

"Will he be okay now?" the king asked, his voice a combination of hope and fear.

Thorian nodded in reassurance. "He needs plenty of nourishment and time to rest, but he should return to his old self soon."

A moment of silence followed as the king reflected on his words, his eyes clouded with a myriad of emotions. After a few moments, he lifted his gaze to Thorian and stated, "Approach me. Let us solidify this pact."

Thorian complied, stepping towards the king. As he drew closer, the colossal wolf lifted its paw, puncturing it with a sharp fang. Blood began to trickle down its leg.

"We must exchange blood," the king clarified. "That's the only way we can form a genuine soul pact. A bond that cannot be broken until death."

"Let us proceed," Thorian agreed, biting his thumb. Blood trickled down his hand, which he pressed against the enormous beast's paw. A blinding light of myriad colors forced Thorian to shield his eyes.

When he reopened them, the king of the direwolves remained before him, seemingly unchanged. Yet Thorian felt a new sensation deep within his heart, both a confining shackle and a comforting connection.

"You are not as weak as I assumed." The king's words echoed in Thorian's mind.

Though momentarily taken aback, Thorian quickly regained his composure. Leveraging his familiarity with a similar skill, he responded in kind. *"You will have access to this type of power too."*

The wolf king grinned in response, asking, *"What is your name?"*

"Thorian, Lord of Wolvendale," he answered out loud this time.

The king nodded before reciprocating. "I am Harald, King of the Direwolves."

Thorian's lips curled into a subtle smile. "Well then, shall we head to your new home?"

Harald gave a nod of agreement, "I am interested to see what kind of place you have established for yourself."

"Hopefully it would be to your satisfaction," Thorian returned with a warm grin.

Harald bellowed a chilling laugh before pivoting towards his kin. "My children, from this day forward, we shall be forever bonded with Thorian and his tribe. We will defend them as they will us, echoing through the generations to come!"

The air reverberated with the unified howl of fifty direwolves, lending weight to their monarch's decree. His words bore the power of an unchallengeable celestial edict.

Chuckling at the spectacle, Thorian glanced back at his companions, Ventus and Vigil, who stood frozen in awe. "It seems we should put on a show of our own."

The small contingent intermingled with their newfound allies, with both Ventus and Vigil sealing their own soul pacts with chosen direwolves. Once finished, the group decided to linger until Harald's son regained enough strength to walk.

After half an hour, the wolf prince's pallor had entirely transformed, hinting at a resurgence of vitality. He was still far from chasing game through the forest but would at least be able to keep pace with the group.

Mounted atop Harald, Thorian guided the united band towards Wolvendale, threading their way through the dense forest. As they navigated the labyrinth of trees, Thorian decided to evaluate the development of his two abilities.

Rock Bullet: You create a barrage of rocks that fly towards your enemies, pummeling them and leaving them vulnerable.

Proficiency: 53.2%

Wind Gust: You summon a powerful gust of wind that can knock your enemies off balance, extinguish fires, and enhance your speed and agility.

Proficiency: 48.7%

Thorian's smile broadened at the tangible progress he'd made. He was inching ever closer to achieving his coveted class advancement. But as his gaze roamed across his display, another detail seized his attention.

Soul-Bound Companion: Harald (Alpha Direwolf)

A concentrated stare at this section of the interface summoned another panel, revealing Harald's statistics.

Race: Alpha Direwolf

Level: 12/35 (XP: 234/1900)

Lifespan: 50 years

Stats:

Strength: 72

Agility: 98

Constitution: 67

Mana: 23

Skills:

Feral Leadership (passive)

Howl of the Lord (active)

Wind Leap (active)

Dire Rend (active)

Bestial State (active)

He has quite a number of stat points, and they are distributed well. His skills are top-notch.

Thorian offered a nod of approval before refocusing his attention on the surrounding forest. Their party's sheer size deterred most creatures from daring to obstruct their path. The exceptions were evolved species, such as thri-kreens and thundermashers, who braved the risk. Nevertheless, Thorian provided support with his Wind Gust and Rock Bullet skills, while the direwolf pack efficiently dealt with these threats.

As they continued their journey, a distant rustle of underbrush echoed towards them. The clamor was reminiscent of a stampeding horde of monsters.

Thorian tensed, preparing for the impending onslaught. He quietly hoped the incoming creatures were of a more manageable variety.

Even their sizable group would struggle to stave off a swarm of rolling shelltrotters.

What emerged from the dense forest, however, was far beyond Thorian's wildest predictions. A tall bipedal creature, its white fur contrasted starkly against the golden armor encasing its chest, burst forth.

"Forlune...?" Thorian's voice faltered, his heart tightening with the emergence of unforeseen scenarios. "What are you doing here?"

INTERLUDE 5

Wolvendale Village, Western Gate
Some time ago…

Nox found himself perched atop the newly reinforced wall, whose broadened expanse now allowed not only for comfortable seating but also for easy conversation. His unit, composed of twenty-seven varied kobolds and kobloids, was scattered around him. Some of his comrades sat adjacent to him on the wall, others manned the watchtower, and a handful succumbed to sleep on the secure ground within the village boundaries.

One of the kobloids seated next to Nox stifled a yawn before remarking, "Man, I'm so tired. How long did we get to sleep? Two hours? Three hours?"

"Consider yourself fortunate," retorted Ifrit, a hint of resentment in her tone. "We didn't get much sleep yesterday either. The fatigue is catching up to me."

Inly, poised on the edge of the watchtower, let out a chuckle before remarking, "If anyone has the right to grumble, it's Nox. He's only got six hours of sleep in the last three days."

"It's alright," the shadowstalker replied with a dismissive shake of his head. "I got less tired when I evolved so that helped."

"You're basically calling us little bitches now, aren't you?" Ifrit retorted, rolling her eyes. "We evolved too. It didn't help that much."

"It's not just about lack of sleep," a brown kobloid interjected, clicking his tongue. "It's just that monsters don't come around as often anymore."

"And why should they?" Ifrit guffawed, her gaze sweeping over the morbid expanse of decaying corpses beyond the wall. "Not even a dumb slug would see this and dare come."

"True, but our leveling speed has taken a hit," another kobloid grumbled in response.

"Look at you complaining about monsters not wanting to kill you." Ifrit arched an eyebrow in amusement before chuckling. "But you're right. It might be a good idea to just get rid of this trash. The smell makes me want to throw up."

As Ifrit and the kobloids carried on with their playful banter and casual conversation, Nox observed them, a gentle smile gracing his features. He found their chatter enjoyable, though fatigue prevented him from participating.

Suddenly, his ears pricked at the sound of a swooshing noise. Reacting instinctively, he lunged towards one of the kobloids, his hand clutching the hilt of his axe. The recruit, a recent addition to their ranks, barely had time to register the shadowstalker's swift charge before Nox bisected the oncoming projectile with a swift swing of his weapon.

"What in the seven hells?!" Ifrit exclaimed, taken aback by Nox's abrupt movement. "Why did you do that?"

Even Inly shot him a puzzled glance, while the targeted kobloid remained speechless, too stunned to utter a word. However, as Nox lifted his axe, they all saw the noticeable dent on the kobloid's blade. Glancing down, he discovered the source of the disruption—a fist-sized rock, now split in two.

"Rock Bullet?" Nox questioned, an eyebrow arched in curiosity as the rest of the group gathered around him, intrigued by his actions. As they examined the shattered stone, Nox swiveled around to determine the origin of the unexpected attack. "Humans...?"

At Nox's utterance, the group's collective gaze followed his line of sight. Emerging from the cover of the trees were two squads of five humans each. Their attire was unassuming, similar to the clothes typically worn by village dwellers or workers. However, their recent warning shot clearly indicated they were anything but harmless.

"Finally, some action," Ifrit remarked, her knuckles cracking in anticipation. "You guys were complaining about not leveling up fast enough? Well, here's a fresh batch of experience points delivered right to our gate. We must all thank Ulvaskye for offering us such a delicious meal."

"I prefer offering my prayers after I eat," Inly remarked before launching himself off the watchtower.

"Hey, don't try to hog it all for yourself!" Ifrit retorted and leapt off the wall, her action mirrored by the remaining kobloids.

A silver-furred kobold assassin turned to Nox and asked, "Boss, you're not going to join?"

Nox chuckled, shaking his head in response. "Go ahead, enjoy yourselves. I will keep watch from here."

"As you wish, boss." The assassin promptly rejoined the group.

As anticipated, the kobolds made quick work of the human invaders. The vast disparity in abilities and skill sets was glaringly evident—five humans were no match for the ferocity of either Ifrit or Inly. Unfazed by the magi's barrage of fireballs, Ifrit would simply surge forward, incinerating her opponents with her own potent flames. Meanwhile, Inly demonstrated superior strength and vitality, a figure of unyielding resilience on the battlefield.

Even the kobloids held their own impressively. Employing their innate rock armor ability, they effectively thwarted the humans' attacks and retaliated with their own formidable skills. Their physical prowess and agility, enhanced by the substantial stat boosts from leveling up both their class and species, gave them a distinct advantage on the battlefield.

Nox observed his unit's efficient dismantling of the two human squads with a sense of pride. However, as the last human warriors made their final stand, he detected an audible rustling from the surrounding forest. From the shadows of all the trees within his line of sight, a flurry of silhouettes began to materialize.

"Fall back!" Nox's voice rang out across the field, his tone urgent. "There are a lot of them! Too many!"

The din of the battlefield made his command barely perceptible. As his fellow villagers turned towards the shadowstalker, waves of humans poured forth from the shelter of the trees, their numbers reaching into the hundreds. It resembled an army—an army comprising ordinary individuals whose eyes glowed with a wild, unhinged fervor.

Spells representing all four elements hurtled towards Nox's unit by the dozen. The kobloids bore the initial brunt of the attack, unable to evade the magical onslaught and forced to shield themselves with their comparatively weak rock armor. The kobolds, however, managed to deflect the assault and orchestrated a strategic retreat.

Observing that some of the kobloids were on the verge of being left stranded, Nox sprang into action. With a single, swift stride, he plunged into the oncoming surge of humans. Their utterances were nothing but a baying shout of "Kill!" and unintelligible battle cries.

Through a series of rapid, lethal strikes, Nox dispatched half a dozen adversaries before reaching the besieged kobloids. Scooping two of them under his arms, he made a hasty retreat towards the village, scaling the formidable wall with a single, agile leap before setting the fresh recruits safely on their feet.

Casting a backwards glance, he noted the other kobolds assisting the newer members in their desperate escape. Regrettably, some had already fallen to the human onslaught and were beyond rescue.

With a grunt of determination, Nox reentered the fray, scooping up more of the retreating kobloids. Carrying them proved faster than waiting for their clumsy attempts at running and inevitably futile efforts to scale the towering wall.

Possessing otherworldly agility, which was further enhanced by his Thorned Cloak, Nox displayed speed superior to the other two assassins, even while carrying a kobloid under each arm. His swift pace ensured that the haphazardly launched spells fell short, their sluggish trajectories failing to connect with him.

After a few quick trips, all the surviving members of Nox's unit had safely retreated within the village confines. Thankfully, most of the humans lacked the requisite strength to scale the wall. Yet Nox knew this respite was fleeting. Given time, their persistent bombardment of fireballs would inevitably breach the barrier.

"How the fuck are they so strong?" Ifrit grunted. "And why are there so many of them? It's like we kicked up an anthill."

"We need to run away, and fast," Nox commanded, his expression grave. Recalling Thorian's counsel during their meeting, he was acutely aware that this was a circumstance where retaliation would incur heavy losses, even under the best of conditions.

Turning his focus to the two assassins, he issued new instructions. "Go around the village and tell the other units we are being invaded. We need to escape into the forest and regroup with Thorian! Tell them all to go east."

"Are you out of your mind?!" Ifrit retorted, her expression a mixture of disbelief and shock. "The king left us here to protect the village, not to abandon it when the enemy comes!"

"Ifrit, mind your language," Inly reprimanded sternly, his voice resonating with authority. "Nox is our leader. Remember, it was our king who appointed him. You need to listen to his orders."

"There are too many humans," Nox explained. "I saw so many of them. It's like they covered the forest."

Just as he concluded his statement, a human hand appeared over the crest of the wall. One by one, individual humans began to scale the wall, appearing at various points. Simultaneously, the reverberating thuds and high-pitched screeching indicated that a breach was imminent.

"We need to move!"

With that directive from Nox, the group sprang into motion. The assassins diverged, one venturing north and the other south. The remaining members aimed for the furthest point from their current location—the eastern gate.

The unit of some odd seventeen kobolds and kobloids navigated through the village, but their speed was limited by the slowest kobloids. Nox and the other kobolds couldn't increase their pace by carrying them. When it came down to the ratio of kobloids to kobolds, they were simply outnumbered.

Footfalls sounded behind them, and Nox risked a glance over his shoulder. A group of fleet-footed humans were hot on their trail, brandishing an assortment of weapons from swords to axes to daggers. No doubt, they were assassins. The fastest among them exhibited a speed that could rival the slowest kobolds—a commendable achievement for a human bereft of dual leveling abilities.

As Nox's gaze turned back to sweep over the front of the village, he took in the sight of bewildered civilians going about their daily routines. There were expectant mothers, frail elders, and bemused children who hadn't even comprehended that their village was under siege.

They're going to all die at this rate.

"Ifrit, take the civilians with you and keep running," Nox gritted his teeth and issued his command. His voice was noticeably grave, a stark departure from his usual playful manner. "At this rate, they're going to catch up to us. I'm going to stop them for a bit and then re-group with you later. Don't stop or slow down more than you need to. You'll only make it harder for me."

"What the hell are you saying, Nox?" Ifrit snarled, her ire apparent. "If you're going to stay, I'm going to stay too. We either both live or we both die!"

"Ifrit!" Nox's voice thundered, taking the flame kobold aback. "I am not going to die. But if we both stay, one of us definitely will!"

"Nox," Inly's gaze bore into the shadowstalker's eyes, his tone laden with heat. "Don't you dare croak on us."

"Who do you think I am?" Nox retorted, a chuckle tingeing his words before he pivoted. The squadron of assassins storming towards his group was perilously close to the trailing kobloids. Just as one of the humans was about to plunge his blade into the back of a fellow kobloid, Nox lunged at him with a speed bordering on the spectral. The human's arm had barely stretched to deliver the fatal blow when Nox's axe claimed his neck.

With his weapon shrouded in a morbid, dark aura, the shadow-stalker made quick work of the assassin squad. With swift, lethal strokes, his adversaries were laid to rest, disemboweled and slain.

Having dispatched the group, Nox straightened up to survey the advancing horde. The humans had already breached the wall and set large portions of it aflame. They swarmed into the village like a relentless tide of ants. Wherever Nox's gaze landed, it was met with dozens, if not hundreds, of frenzied faces. Yet, rather than perceiving them as a threat, he saw them as a veritable smorgasbord.

A feral grin spread across his features as he wiped his enemy's blood off his axe, readying himself for the onslaught to come. "I'm sorry, Thorian. I might not leave you much to kill after I'm done."

CHAPTER 64

"What are you doing here?"

The moon kobold stuttered at Thorian's question, eyes wide with alarm. "King?"

At the utterance of this title, a wave of kobolds and kobloids surged from the forest. However, the sight of Thorian's band and the pack of direwolves halted them abruptly.

Thorian recognized many familiar faces among the kobolds—Bellafor, Crimen, Caedar. The presence of these figures from his tribe only added to his growing bewilderment.

"What in the world are they doing here?" Ventus chimed in from Thorian's left, perched regally atop his own direwolf.

Meanwhile, Vigil maintained his silence. The atmosphere told him something was gravely amiss.

Thorian's expression shifted from shock to an intense fury. He wrestled to keep his burgeoning rage under control.

"Who are these beings?" Harald inquired telepathically, prepared to leap into action at any sign of danger. *"Are they foes?"*

After a moment's hesitation, Thorian answered, *"No... They are my people."*

He then dismounted from Harald's back and strode towards the large group of kobolds and kobloids with a heavy determination. As his gaze swept over them, he recognized more and more familiar faces, many of them non-combatants.

"King! King!" Caedar, tears streaming down his face, ran towards Thorian and fell to his knees. "We're glad to have found you."

Now even more disoriented by the unfolding events, Thorian surveyed the scene before demanding in a low, authoritative voice, "Can someone explain to me what in the seven hells is going on here?"

A tense silence ensued. It was broken when Forlune stumbled forward, falling to one knee. "It was my fault! I was the one responsible! The humans—there was a sea of them! I ordered an escape because I didn't believe we could win."

Humans? How does that even make sense?

"Are your warriors so frail?" Harald posed telepathically. *"How could mere humans overrun them, regardless of their numbers?"*

"I intend to understand that right now," Thorian declared. He scanned the assembled crowd until his gaze settled on Aqua, the water magus, who managed to maintain a composed demeanor amidst the chaos. "Aqua, tell me exactly what happened."

The blue kobold nodded somberly. "We were guarding the wall when we heard a stampede from the forest. We thought it was just monsters at first, but they were human. Hundreds, perhaps thousands of them. They hurled all manner of spells at us, and the wall was breached by the countless fireballs thrown at it."

Thousands? Are they William's men? But how do all of them have classes? As Thorian's eyebrows drew together in deep thought, the image of an elderly man and a young child flickered into his mind, triggering another surge of fury to sweep across his features. *I should have killed them.*

Simultaneously, Aqua was expanding on his account, leaving the rest of the kobolds hanging on his every word, their breaths shallow. "No matter how many humans we killed, they continued to pour in. The village was engulfed in flames, hindering our movements. The magi continuously bombarded us with their spells, overpowering us through sheer numbers."

Thorian took a moment to inhale deeply, steadying his turbulent emotions. Casting his gaze over the crowd, he realized that while there was a considerable number of kobolds present, a significant portion of the second platoon was still notably absent.

"Where are Zogthar and the orcs?" Thorian inquired as he felt his heart clenching. "Many kobolds and kobloids are absent too. Where are Inly and Ifrit?"

"We split up," Forlune explained. "I talked with Zogthar and it became clear it was better to split up so that they couldn't catch us. Ifrit, Inly, and many of the kobolds and kobloids ran with him."

"This seems like a giant mess," Harald remarked. *"Should we go and clean up your place of those roaches?"*

"We will," Thorian affirmed with a nod. *"But there are some things we need to prepare first."*

"Forlune," Thorian addressed the moon kobold. "I want you to select a few warriors and make your way to the dungeon. Lead the first platoon and meet up with us a few hundred meters east of the gate. You should be able to track us by our scent."

"Right away, My King," Forlune agreed, eager to demonstrate his worth. He assembled a group of kobolds and set off towards the dungeon.

Thorian then turned to the water magus. "Aqua, I need you to take a few troops with you and locate Zogthar and his men. Rejoin us as soon as you find them."

"Consider it done, My King," Aqua responded, giving a curt nod before springing into action.

As Aqua was assembling his team and preparing to pursue Zogthar, one of the assassins under the shadowstalker's command stepped forward.

"King, I'm sorry for interrupting you," he stammered, a conflicted expression etched on his face.

"Speak," Thorian commanded succinctly.

"Nox!" the assassin exclaimed in a distressed tone. "Nox needs your help! He stayed behind to buy us time to escape, but he's now engaged with the entire army alone!"

Thorian's expression froze. The murmurs and groans of the surrounding kobolds receded into the background, transforming into indistinguishable white noise. As he conjured the image of his most loyal follower in his mind, an unrestrained fury ignited within the depths of his heart.

So they all want to die.

Wolvendale Village

The once vibrant village, filled with the bustling activities of the kobolds and kobloids, was now overflowing with humans. Some lay lifeless on the ground, but the majority were striding and running around, displaying no compassion or sympathy for the fallen.

Many of the dwellings Thorian had painstakingly constructed using valuable wood units had been razed by the magi's devastating flames. The wall was breached at multiple points, with large sections succumbing to the blaze. Some of the magi were casting Waterballs in an attempt to subdue the ravenous fire.

"Why are we doing this again?" The towering figure known as Ragnar posed his question to the woman dressed in vibrant green next to him.

"Do you mean extinguishing the flames?" She returned his question with one of her own, an eyebrow arched in curiosity.

Ragnar shook his head. "No, I mean why did we come here in the first place? I still don't understand this territory business. Wouldn't it have been better if we just rushed to the Ravenwood palace and claimed it?"

Nalia, the lady in green, chuckled at Ragnar's incessant questioning, "And then what? Assume control over a city of the dead?"

Her gaze drifted over the men and women around them. Their primal instincts and barbarism were barely concealed beneath a fragile shroud of civility. "These folks are a challenging lot to manage. They played their part well in breaking through the village walls and conquering it. It's only regrettable that the lord was not present for us to eliminate."

Ragnar's grin widened at Nalia's explanation, "Did you expect what we found here too? A village filled with monsters that are able to talk?"

Nalia remained silent for a beat. Her face was a mask of neutrality, but Ragnar could see through it.

"Is this something you didn't predict?" He couldn't resist the urge to taunt her. "Now, that would be a first."

"Well, nothing in my past experiences suggested such an outcome," Nalia conceded, her admission leaving Ragnar visibly taken aback. Even the lean figure walking beside them seemed startled.

"Soren," Nalia addressed the slender man. "What's the situation with the guildmasters?"

"They remain as uncooperative as ever," Soren revealed, a trace of dread in his voice. "Whenever someone enters their domain, they die a most terrifying death."

"So that speedy rat is still hiding." Ragnar clicked his tongue in disappointment. "What a pity. I would have liked to crush him myself."

Nalia disregarded Ragnar's comment and nodded at Soren's report. "That's to be expected. Without full control over this territory, they retain the right to tell us off."

"So, we need to kill the lord of this village to truly claim it?" Ragnar asked, his eyes shining with manic glee. "I wonder what he looks like? I hope he's a strong wolf, mighty enough to offer me a challenge."

"You have a one-track mind focused on combat and death," Soren rebuked, shaking his head in disapproval. "You should look to be more civilized."

"Ha! You're quite funny," Ragnar responded, laughing raucously. "Discussing civilization whilst we're surrounded by monsters. Even those among us are no different than beasts."

As Ragnar voiced these words, he cast a surveying look at the thousands of men and women crowding the village. Their eyes glowed with a sinister red light, and their breaths sounded rough, like those of wounded animals.

"Just what did you do to them?" Ragnar asked Nalia, his gaze a blend of apprehension and admiration.

"Just a slight enhancement," she responded nonchalantly. "I simply helped them tap into their true nature. In return, they gained power they could never have dreamed of. It's only unfortunate that it's temporary."

Following a moment of silence, Soren ventured to ask, "Temporary? What does that mean?"

"Power doesn't come without a price, does it?" Nalia replied, her smile enigmatic before it faded to an impassive mask. "At this moment, their demise would serve me more than their survival."

Nalia's statement caused both Soren and Ragnar to freeze, their expressions a mirror of shock. However, before they could voice their reactions, a band of men and women appeared, converging on their small gathering from all sides. These rowdy villagers, their eyes ablaze with wild fanaticism, were led by a man with fiery red hair. His stature was slender and seemingly unimposing, yet he radiated an authority rooted in an unsettling aura of dread.

"Nalia, there is something we need to talk with you about." He moved towards the woman in green with confident strides, his expression a grotesque dance of insanity. "Why don't you two have some rest and leave the rest of the matters to us?"

CHAPTER 65

As Thorian led his party towards the besieged village, a storm of anticipation swelled within him, forcing him to wrestle with an instinctive urge to immediately plunge into the fray.

Nox, just try to survive for as long as you can. I'm coming.

However, such impulsiveness was a path to ruin. It would be reckless to toss caution to the wind and leap headlong into the lion's den to rescue his ally. Such an act would merely result in a higher death toll among his own.

So, with a measured calm, Thorian began to execute his strategy. His initial command was for as many kobolds as possible to establish soul bonds with the direwolves. Fifteen of them successfully became riders, the majority of whom were warriors with the exceptions being Aqua and a swift assassin, whom Thorian had dubbed Alacritas.

"If we charge head-on, our strength might suffice to secure victory," Thorian elaborated. "But I don't desire a mere win. I want a flawless victory, with as little of us dying. Even a thousand of their lives do not equate to the value of a single one of ours."

"What should we do then, King?" Ventus inquired, perched atop his immense direwolf. "Do you have a plan in mind?"

"We will lay an ambush," Thorian declared. "Once we lure them into the forest, we can leverage our superior speed and the concealment of the trees for hit-and-run tactics. The terrain will deprive them of any defensive advantage."

"Your insight remains as profound as ever," Vigil remarked. "But where shall we stage our ambush?"

"We'll establish multiple ambush sites. Each of the six units from the two platoons will position themselves in a specific area of the forest."

"Isn't it better if we all stand together?" Ventus asked, his brow furrowing. "There is strength in numbers."

"No, that would be detrimental," Vigil countered. "If we all cluster in the same area, they could simply hurl a barrage of fireballs in our general direction. We would be ensnared in a deadly inferno. While our king might survive, many would not."

"Indeed," Thorian agreed, nodding. "Our dispersion is essential to make us less of a target. It plays into our nimbleness and adaptability."

With a strategy formulated, Thorian waited for Forlune and Aqua to rally the rest of his troops. After half an hour, the orcs, along with the kobolds and kobloids of the first platoon, regrouped with them.

According to the plan, Thorian strategically stationed each unit at various points within the forest. Some were positioned closer to the northern and southern gates, rather than the eastern gate where he resided. As for the citizens and the crippled direwolves, Thorian stationed them farther back, away from the danger of the battlefield.

With his warriors dispersed throughout the forest, waiting in ambush, Thorian rode Harald and ascended the hill, accompanied by Ventus and Aqua. From their elevated vantage point, he could see the village teeming with humans. Those camped on the pile of monster corpses outside alone numbered in the dozens. Amongst them were men and women of all ages.

Thorian spied one woman in particular whose wrinkle-free face suggested a normally gentle demeanor. She was now armed with a blood-stained axe, and a wild expression contorted her features. The level of barbarity on display, even from those who had witnessed their entire world collapse around them, was bewildering.

These are just normal citizens, Thorian thought, raising a dubious eyebrow. *I thought it would be William's men.*

Despite them being mere citizens, thoughts of mercy never grazed Thorian's mind. They had dared to show hostility and had slain his people. Such reckless individuals were destined only for death.

"Shall we extend them a small greeting?" Thorian proposed to his companions, his voice barely above a whisper.

Grasping his intention, Ventus flashed a grin. "If it's of the violent kind, I am all for it, King."

The wind and water magi readied their most potent spells, while Thorian stood on the brink of the cliff. His gaze bore into the heart of his ravaged village.

"My name is Thorian!" His voice resonated like a thunderclap, arresting the attention of all humans near or upon the wall. "And I am the lord of this village!"

No sooner had his words echoed than Ventus and Aqua unleashed their spell. The Triple Jet Stream struck first, claiming three lives instantaneously. The Gale Slash followed, leaving even greater havoc in its wake. The slicing winds tore through the crowd, cleaving limbs and rending flesh. The corpses of humans joined the pile of monsters below in a gruesome cascade.

The clamor stirred by Thorian and his troops prompted an increasing number of humans to spill from the fractured wall. Some tried to direct their spells at the kobolds, but their reach failed to ascend to the cliff's summit.

"Again!" Thorian commanded those behind him, and the pair complied. With humans surging towards the wall like a horde of ants, their spells found a mark wherever they were cast.

Yet even as their comrades fell by the dozens at their side, the humans pressed on, a peculiar frenzy fueling their momentum. Even from a distance, Thorian could discern their chants of "Kill! Kill!"

After several more volleys of spells, the human force had advanced perilously close. Thorian pivoted, and together with the three kobolds, they sped down the hill on their direwolves.

Eyeing the humans rushing from their right beneath the cliff, Thorian glanced at Ventus. "Let's incinerate them."

Understanding his intent, Ventus invoked his Wind Gust spell, unleashing it upon the approaching human throng. Thorian promptly followed with a Fireball, fusing the two spells into a colossal wave of flames.

As the fierce conflagration consumed the charging humans, a notification materialized before Thorian.

Corrupted soul extinguished.

System check.

Quest contribution accepted.

Corrupted soul?

Thorian's brow knitted together at the vaguely familiar term. He was aware that certain classes or monsters could corrupt souls under specific conditions, but neither of these possibilities seemed plausible at the moment. Such potent entities could not exist so early into the apocalypse.

Wait, I recall hearing something of the sort... As thoughts raced through Thorian's mind, he recalled a forbidden quest, one that he had heard whispers about a decade ago. *Did someone accept the "Soul Reaver" quest? But that incident happened in the capital last time.*

Thorian sensed that something was amiss, but he could not afford the luxury of deep contemplation at the moment. He had a war to win.

As the trio reached the foot of the hill, the frenzied humans charged through the fiery onslaught and lunged towards them. The moment their gazes met, the human magi invoked their spells and hurled them towards the kobolds with unwavering resolve.

Naturally, the trio didn't pause to observe. The staggering speed of the direwolves allowed them to evade the spells, using trees as cover for their retreat.

"Ease up a bit. Let them gain some ground," Thorian instructed. Harald and the other two direwolves modulated their speed, maintaining a pace fast enough to elude the humans, yet not so swift as to lose them entirely.

As the minutes ticked away, the crowd of frenzied men and women swelled in number. By Thorian's estimation, there were nearly one hundred and fifty of them.

Good, now is the time.

As if on cue, the earth magus, Saxum, unleashed his newly acquired spell: Earth Tremor. The ground beneath them shook and rumbled with the spell's casting, causing the front line of men and women to lose their footing and tumble. Those following tripped over the fallen bodies like a chain of dominos, bringing the entire group to a standstill.

Seizing the opportunity, the trio halted. Much like before, Thorian and Ventus launched their combined spell while Aqua sent his skills cascading one after another.

Simultaneously, Saxum's unit sprang forth from behind the trees, ambushing the stunned human group. The priest bestowed blessings upon the warriors, while Aqua fortified them with his Watershield.

The evolved warriors surged forward, axes at the ready. The largest of the brown kobold variants enveloped their bodies in rock armor, augmenting their defenses even further before diving into the fray. The magi, on the other hand, lent their support to the warriors with long-range firepower.

While the kobolds engaged the humans with unbridled ferocity, Thorian was careful to direct their combined spell far from Saxum's warrior unit. As the brown kobold ravaged through the human ranks from the right, Thorian and Ventus seared those on the left, leaving the humans with no escape routes.

Thorian couldn't suppress a grin as the toll of human casualties multiplied by dozens with each spell cast. The more he slew, the greater the rewards he would reap.

However, even as the group that Saxum's unit had ambushed fell, more humans charged out of the trees towards them. Soon, hundreds of ill-equipped, frenzied men and women were encircling them.

CHAPTER 66

"Fall back!" Thorian commanded, his eyes sharply trained on the encroaching wave of humans.

Saxum's unit wheeled about and made a break for their leader as Thorian and Ventus provided protective cover using their potent combination skill. Only once the last kobold had safely retreated behind them did the duo pivot on their heels and sprint towards safety.

Astride their direwolves, Thorian and Ventus swiftly closed the distance to Saxum and his warriors, then slowed to ensure that their pursuers remained within their line of sight.

"Saxum, it's time for us to part ways," Thorian ordered, his voice steady amidst the turmoil. "You head south. I'll go north. Stay true to the plan until you reach Zogthar."

"Understood, My King," Saxum responded, his tone solemn yet determined. "May fortune favor you."

With that, Saxum and his unit veered off to the south. Meanwhile, Thorian, accompanied by Ventus and Aqua, spurred their mounts northward.

Just as Thorian had anticipated, the human onslaught divided into two separate factions, each determined to intercept him and Saxum. Spearheading the group trailing Thorian and his comrades was a fleet-footed assassin, whose nimbleness rivaled Thorian's own.

The man brandished an enormous knife, a wild and frenzied gleam lighting his eyes.

Is he a first-advancement assassin? Thorian raised an eyebrow. *So like I thought, it's the Soul Reaver quest. They are getting double the experience in exchange for their humanity.*

"Ventus, turn around," Thorian commanded, twisting in his saddle atop Harald to confront the approaching foe. "Let's give them a taste of fire. Aqua, keep your sights locked on that swift vermin."

"Was waiting for you to say that, King," Ventus replied, spinning around with a wicked grin splashed across his face. Meanwhile, Aqua merely acknowledged with a curt nod.

Poised to execute their deadly combination attack, Ventus and Thorian released their abilities upon the advancing humans. The nimble assassin, however, swiftly responded to the imminent threat, launching himself skywards and allowing the searing wave to consume the assassins and warriors trailing behind him. A smug grin spread across his face as he falsely believed he had deftly evaded a fiery demise. But his self-congratulatory moment was short-lived when Aqua unleashed his spell.

Aqua's Triple Jet Stream slammed into the assassin before he had the chance to touch down, riddling his body with countless perforations. The force of the water mage's devastating spell catapulted the lifeless body back into the blaze, incinerating it along with the rest of his comrades.

The lethal display did little to quell the fervor of the frenzied humans, however. It was as if their sole focus had narrowed down to slaughtering Thorian and his kobold kin, and they seemed willing to sacrifice their lives a thousand times over to achieve that brutal objective.

Thousands of corrupted souls. Thorian cast a solemn gaze upon the surge of humans before him. The surrounding forest had succumbed to the blaze, the rising flames only serving to amplify the pandemonium they had unleashed. *Whoever accepted that quest will become a truly dangerous figure. I can't even imagine the rewards for corrupting so many.*

While their actions appeared unhinged, the humans weren't entirely bereft of strategy. They were hell-bent on taking down Thorian, but they understood that a blind pursuit would yield no results. Consequently, their mages began to hurl fireballs, igniting the surrounding forest. Their reasoning was elementary—Thorian wouldn't be able to evade them if there were no escape routes left to exploit.

This is insanity.

With a click of his tongue, Thorian turned to his two companions. "We head to Forlune's location."

At his directive, the group deftly altered their trajectory. Their direwolves, utilizing Wind Leap, leapt over the raging flames, their agile forms weaving through the inferno. Meanwhile, the humans frantically sought any possible path, some even braving the fire's wrath directly, only to swiftly realize that they lacked any form of flame resistance.

Madness...

By this stage, the ranks of the humans had noticeably diminished. Despite their initial strength in the thousands, the ones relentlessly pursuing Thorian had dwindled to mere hundreds.

Smoke and soot choked the air, making each breath a laborious gasp. However, this suffocating atmosphere served only to underscore the dire tragedy unfolding before Thorian's eyes.

Whoever is behind this is definitely ruthless. Though I'm in no position to judge them.

In a peculiar way, Thorian felt a sense of elation. The opportunity to have so many humans served to him on a silver platter was not a situation he had foreseen. His only quandary was that each corrupted soul he extinguished, inadvertently, would only serve to augment the power of the mastermind orchestrating this chaos.

And you dared to mess with what's mine. If anything unbecoming happened to Nox, I will take my sweet time stripping you of your limbs.

"King, your expression is... scary..."

Ventus' voice pulled Thorian back from his ruminations. His hand moved to touch his own face, registering the petrifying grin that had taken root there.

"We're almost at our destination," Aqua announced, steering everyone's attention ahead. In the distance, a large rocky outcrop became visible, the very location where Thorian had positioned Forlune and his unit.

After bypassing the predetermined ambush point, Thorian and his companions halted several dozen meters away, poised and patient.

They dispatched the first wave of overzealous humans with relative ease. It was only when the area began to teem with increasingly frenzied humans, that Thorian finally signaled the next phase of their plan.

"Now!"

Upon Thorian's command, the silver-furred warriors unleashed a deafening roar that resonated through the ranks of the surrounding humans, stunning them into stillness.

Without the need for verbal communication, Thorian and Ventus once again unleashed their synergistic assault, the frontlines of humans succumbing to the searing inferno. Simultaneously, Forlune and his men surged forward, eager to reap the spoils of their well-planned stratagem.

Level up!

A satisfied smile traced its way onto Thorian's lips. *Humans give a surprisingly good amount of experience points.*

"Harald, go have your fun." Thorian dismounted from his companion's back.

The towering direwolf offered a pleased growl in return. *"I was starting to lose hope of hearing those words."*

Having been given free rein, Harald bared a feral grin and revealed his true form. A blinding light engulfed him as his already imposing body swelled further in size, his dark fur gaining blazing red tips. His eyes gleamed with a golden hue as he launched towards the onslaught of humans in a powerful leap. Each swipe of his colossal paw claimed numerous human lives. His unrestrained onslaught showed no prejudice—whether child or elderly woman, flesh was torn, bones were shattered, and blood was shed indiscriminately. Indeed, in the face of death, all were deemed equal.

Aqua and Ventus' direwolves also joined their king in the fray, overwhelming their adversaries with brute force. Simultaneously, the kobolds under Forlune's command surged forward, cutting a path through enemy ranks with their superior strength and skills. All the while, Thorian, Ventus, and Aqua offered devastating long-range support with their potent spells.

Amidst the chaos of the human ranks, a heavily armored man wielding twin axes caught Thorian's attention. His wild eyes held a singular desire—to slay Thorian.

"Monster King!" He bellowed above the clamor of battle. "I will kill you! I will kill you and I will level up so much, no one will stop me!"

With surprising agility for a man of his size, he charged towards Thorian, his axes primed for a lethal blow. A powerful blue glow enveloped his weapons, amplifying the impending attack.

As the human fixed his sights on Thorian, Forlune positioned himself in the man's path, declaring, "You'll have to contend with me first."

Caught off guard, the human had no time to respond. He emitted a raw, guttural war cry and swung both axes at Forlune's chest with all his might.

Clank!

The sound of steel against steel echoed across the battlefield as the human's assault was thwarted. His axes slipped from his grasp, his arms trembling from the powerful collision with Forlune's golden armor.

Forlune's chestplate, on the other hand, remained unscathed, shimmering as brightly as the day Ventus had bestowed it upon him.

After a beat, the human warrior erupted into a horrendous scream as a bloody gash abruptly appeared across his chest, spewing forth a torrent of blood. Putting an end to the man's agony, Forlune decapitated him, his head separated from his body with a swift cleave.

The battle continued to unfold predictably. Given their clear dominance, Thorian dispatched one of the newer kobloids to notify Lapis and his unit, so they too could partake in the skirmish. This was a prime opportunity to increase their human kill count for the quest, and Thorian wasn't about to deprive them of it.

Time marched on as the kobolds and direwolves wrought havoc upon the humans. The disparity in power was simply too vast. Even on the rare occasion a kobold or direwolf sustained injury, priests were at hand to promptly administer healing.

The kobloids, however, had fewer opportunities to engage in the combat. While those who had chosen the paths of priests or magi were able to provide support from a distance, sending the assassins or warriors into the fray was tantamount to issuing them a death warrant. In their frenzied state, the humans would not show any mercy. Consequently, Thorian commanded them to hold back, instructing them to only strike when clear opportunities arose.

By the hour's end, the battlefield was strewn with hundreds of human corpses, surrounded by the raging, consuming flames of the forest. Despite Aqua's valiant attempts to halt the fire's spread with his water spells, they did little to quench the ferocity of the inferno.

CHAPTER 67

The inferno roared, wild and untamed, sending Thorian's men into fits of coughing as acrid smoke filled their lungs. Flames danced mercilessly around them, felling trees that crashed to the ground and severed their escape routes. Thorian's eyes darted about, scouring the flaming chaos for his team of assassins.

"Alacritas, come here!"

On command, the silver-furred assassin darted towards Thorian, his fur shimmering against the blaze. "Yes, King? How may I help?"

"Take the assassins with you and head south," commanded Thorian. "Search for our men caught within the fiery chaos and help them, then proceed to Saxum and Zogthar."

Alacritas nodded and sped off towards the rest of the assassin team. The kobolds, silver-furred like their leader, raced through the fiery tumult with swift agility.

Meanwhile, Aqua along with the other magi were locked in their own battle against the fire. They launched waterball after waterball into the inferno, but their attempts seemed to do little more than momentarily disturb the flames. Even Ventus, using his Gale Slash, struggled to make headway. His technique allowed him to slice through the flaming trees with relative success, but it was still insufficient to curb the spread of the relentless blaze.

The silver lining is that most of the trees within the village were felled earlier. Only the wall risks succumbing to the flames.

Yet, the potential devastation of the forest was far from an acceptable outcome for Thorian. A fire of such magnitude would ravage the land, leaving a desolate and barren landscape inhospitable for growth or survival.

Our current tactics are proving futile. It feels akin to trying to fill a sieve with water.

As he observed the magi hurling their waterballs into the inferno, the hopelessness of their strategy became painfully evident. However, the longer he watched Aqua and Ventus, the deeper the creases of his brow became. Something, a memory, itched at the back of his mind, just beyond his reach.

Ah, now I remember! I completely overlooked that particular interaction.

A new strategy forming in his mind, Thorian called out to the wind-wielding kobold. "Ventus, unleash your Wind Gust!"

Upon hearing Thorian's command, Ventus found himself puzzled. "King, that will only fuel the fire!"

"Just do it," Thorian insisted, a determined note in his voice. "I have a plan."

Putting his trust in his king's judgment, Ventus clicked his tongue and prepared his spell. As he conjured the powerful gust of wind, Thorian simultaneously manifested a waterball in the palm of his hand.

Their skills synchronized just as before—Ventus' Wind Gust raced towards the fire, closely trailed by Thorian's Waterball. The moment the waterball collided with the gust of wind, it exploded into countless tiny droplets, lending the gust an aqueous texture and a subtle bluish tint.

The unique fusion of their abilities struck the inferno, and the result was immediate. Flames wavered and diminished, their fiery wrath subdued and scattered. Yet, this victory was minor, affecting only a small fraction of the forest. The majority of the landscape remained ablaze, radiating intense heat all around.

"Yes!" Forlune's shout of triumph cut through the cacophony of the blaze. "We can defeat this fire! All hail the king!"

"All hail the king!" the other kobolds echoed, their voices creating a unified cry of hope.

Thorian was taken aback by Forlune's enthusiasm, but he had no time to dwell on it.

"All water and wind magi, replicate our strategy!" he directed, his voice booming above the roaring crackle of the flames. "We will halt the advance of this fire. *We shall extinguish it with our collective might!*"

Soon, the magi were all emulating the king's example, merging their abilities to douse the fire, one small sector at a time.

The remaining kobolds, particularly those who had evolved into the brown-furred variant with hulking frames and rock-plated shoulders, were far from idle. They used their unique abilities to expedite the process. With powerful strikes, they cratered the ground, causing the flaming trees to tumble into the hollows. This action simplified the task for the magi by negating the need to target both the canopy and forest floor. Moreover, it made the fire's path more predictable, further aiding in their strategic attack.

Observing the advancements they were making, Thorian approached Aqua and declared, "I need you to take over my position."

Aqua looked momentarily perplexed, but then comprehension dawned on his face. "Are you venturing towards the village, My King?"

Thorian's eyes harden with a furious intensity. "Yes, I am. I want to see for myself what happened to Nox."

"May fortune accompany you, My King." Aqua respectfully inclined his head in a bow.

Thorian turned, heading towards Forlune and the other warrior kobolds. Lacking any skills beneficial to the ongoing battle with the fire, their role was relegated to vigilant watchmen, standing guard against potential threats or aiding any magi in danger.

"Forlune, dispatch a scout team to spread the word," Thorian instructed. "We need the magi from the other groups to join our efforts. Halting the spread of the fire from this side alone won't suffice."

The moon kobold responded with surprising enthusiasm and authority. "Right away, King. I will take a small group with me and go immediately." He pivoted to one of the warrior kobolds at his side, adding, "Crimen, you will be taking charge here while I'm away. Don't let any harm happen to magi while they're busy using their spells, understood?"

"Understood, Forlune," Crimen responded, his voice steady. "You can depend on me."

With Forlune obediently setting about his orders, Thorian redirected his attention to the one companion he intended to bring along. "Vigil, I need your company on this journey."

The moon-tattooed priest understood the gravity behind Thorian's request and bowed, his expression solemn. "Do not yield to despair, My King. We may yet find favor with fortune."

Thorian offered only a silent nod in response, his gaze heavy with unspoken concerns. He was well aware that the shadowstalker's continued absence suggested a high probability of an adverse outcome.

"This is my first time seeing such an expression on your face," Harald strode over to Thorian with a confident gait. *"Was this person dear to you? Your emotions seem in disarray."*

As Thorian regarded Harald, flashes of Nox filled his mind's eye.

Memories of the first day when the then-night kobloid had decided to follow him, flooded his thoughts. His gaze dropped and his mouth went dry.

"I made a vow to grant him power beyond imagination," Thorian responded telepathically. *"This is only the dawn of his journey. There is much he has yet to witness."*

Harald regarded Thorian for a few heartbeats before lowering himself to the ground, an unspoken offer for Thorian to mount him. *"Let us move. There is no use losing hope yet."*

Thorian nodded and ascended onto the broad back of the direwolf king. As the wolf rose to his full stature, their combined presence was striking. The pair radiated a regal aura that befitted their status as twin monarchs.

Vigil, too, found his mount on a direwolf, and together, they commenced their journey through the blazing forest. Emboldened by the direwolves' power and swiftness, the flames held no terror for them. They effortlessly vaulted over the flaming obstacles, their path lit by the consuming fire.

Within mere minutes, the pair traversed the majority of the engulfed forest, the incinerated wall of the village becoming discernible in the distance. The bodies of humans and monsters, set aflame, were strewn across the landscape, their burning forms adding to the nauseating smog that choked the air.

At least the issue of the sea of decaying corpses surrounding the wall is resolved.

As they neared the village, a sudden foreboding clutched Thorian's heart. Looking down, he saw the ground beneath Harald's paws glowing with an intense, orange light.

Boom!

"King!" Vigil's horrified shout echoed around them as a pillar of flame surged skywards, engulfing Harald and Thorian. The surrounding roots, leaves, and grass were instantly incinerated by the furious blaze.

Suddenly, a manic cackle filled the air, emanating from an untouched thicket of bushes. From its depths emerged a man with hair as fiery as the blaze around him. His eyes glowed with a demonic light, while bone-like protrusions jutted from his forehead, resembling a fresh pair of horns.

"I killed you! Monster King—I killed you!" He raved, his voice echoing with the madness of his declaration. "Only I am king! The flame king!"

CHAPTER 68

From the heart of the inferno, a titanic form took shape. Thorian, astride his steed Harald, launched himself clear of the surprise attack. His red fur bore the scars of multiple burns, yet no trace of damage dared to breach his skin.

"Trying to surprise me with a fire attack, what a joke."

Thorian's gaze was as icy as it was unyielding, fixed on the crazed fire magus. Even under his transformation, his companion, the Direwolf King, seemed virtually unscathed. His bestial form, larger and significantly more resilient than his usual state, held steadfast against the magus' meticulously planned onslaught.

The sight of Thorian's nonchalant emergence from his explosive attack warped the human's barely contained mania into a mask of sheer insanity. With a battle cry that was half-beast and half-madman, he conjured a sphere of fire, dwarfing Thorian's Fireball. He summoned every ounce of his dwindling power, teetering on the edge of total exhaustion, before he unleashed his most devastating spell.

"How slow can an attack be?" Harald quipped, his tone veering towards tedium. As the magus released his cataclysmic onslaught, the Direwolf King employed his Wind Leap, effortlessly vaulting over the giant fireball. A luminescent green tint shimmered on his paw as he set his claws into the frail form of the fire magus.

The second Harald's claws made contact with the unhinged sorcerer, and the fire spell erupted behind them. The explosive force propelled Thorian slightly forwards from the shockwave. Twisting around, he saw a sea of flames that had claimed a vast swath of land, their fiery tendrils clawing towards the heavens.

These amateurs and their theatrics, he mused. *What self-respecting fire magus lacks control over his own flames?*

"I was concerned for you for a moment there, My King," Vigil ventured, his tone a blend of shock and exhilaration. He then directed his gaze at the lifeless form beneath Harald's gargantuan paw. "For a man with such formidable offensive power, his defenses were definitely not up to par."

"He was a fool, staying in ambush alone. A magus is never without his group," Thorian mused, shaking his head. "Still, I suppose relative to the others, his intelligence deserves some commendation."

With the immediate danger neutralized, the pair resumed their journey towards the village. As they traversed the scorched perimeter, Thorian's anxiety ebbed away upon noticing the village's interior had escaped major devastation. Homes were battered, and several facilities required repair, but the flames had not permeated the settlement. If not for the preemptive efforts of the orcs and Ventus in tree clearance the previous day, the destruction could have been catastrophic.

Thorian and Vigil, astride their direwolves, meticulously searched the village for any trace of the elusive shadowstalker. The settlement was littered with the fallen, most casualties being human, but many kobloid civilians had also tragically lost their lives in the onslaught.

Navigating the sea of debris polluting the paths of the village, they eventually arrived at the Assassin Guild. There, Whisperwind stood guard with a troubled look etched across his face. As they drew near, the guildmaster's voice reached them.

"Thorian, get over here," he commanded.

The strain in Whisperwind's tone took Thorian by surprise—the shadowkin had always been a bastion of stoicism. Quickening their pace, the pair steered their mounts towards the guild, halting at the entrance.

"Let's go inside," Whisperwind motioned towards a room to the left. "There's something you must see."

Upon entering, Thorian's face contorted in shock. The shadow-stalker was slumped next to the desk, his body a gruesome tableau of burns, deep gashes, and puncture wounds. By all logic, he should be dead, yet dark tendrils, akin to veins, coiled around his terrible injuries. In fact, Thorian could discern the faint crimson glow of blood coursing within this dark shroud.

"Nox! What has happened to him?!" Vigil cried out, horror ringing in his voice. "I will heal him right away!"

As the priest commenced his sacred chant, Thorian offered him a helpless glance. *It's futile.* Yet he held his tongue, allowing the priest to give his all. As the white-furred kobold completed his incantation, silvery moonlight enveloped Nox's battered form, but even as the illuminating glow ebbed, the grievous wounds remained undiminished. Only some of the burn scars mottling his body seemed to have been somewhat mitigated.

"Your healing spell won't be enough," Whisperwind declared, shaking his head. His luminous sky-blue eyes narrowed in a pained expression. "Only the ultimate spell of a second advancement priest has a chance. Even then, the success rate would be a mere fifty percent."

"That... No, it can't be," Vigil murmured, his gaze sinking to meet Whisperwind's grim revelation.

Thorian clenched his fists at the revelation. His heart felt like it was splintering with every step as he walked toward Nox. His movements were slow, almost hesitant, as if approaching a fragile dream he feared would shatter entirely. When he crouched to meet the shadowstalker at eye level, a bittersweet smile tugged at his lips, filled with quiet anguish. Nox's expression was so peaceful, as though he were simply enjoying a deep, undisturbed sleep far removed from the chaos of war.

Lowering his forehead to rest gently against Nox's snout, Thorian's face twisted with a storm of emotions—grief, pain, and an ever-mounting rage. *I swear, no matter where he hides or what darkness he burrows into, I will find the one who did this to you. I will see justice done.*

Drawing in a long, steadying breath, he rose to his feet. His expression hardened, determination glinting like tempered steel in his eyes. Fixing his gaze on the guildmaster, he spoke with measured resolve. "How long does he have?"

"I can maintain my skill to pump blood into his heart for ten days," Whisperwind admitted with a resigned sigh. "After that, it will naturally dissipate, and I won't be able to reuse it for an extended period."

Ten days, you say? Thorian's eyes widened, his spirits lifting as a glimmer of hope ignited within him. *Then there remains a possibility.*

With a deep breath to steady his whirling emotions, Thorian offered the guildmaster a respectful bow. "Thank you for keeping Nox safe. Thank you for sheltering him and providing protection."

Thorian was far from naïve. The lifeless human forms littering the guild's exterior painted a stark picture. The guildmaster had gone above and beyond to safeguard Nox from the frenzied human mob, even at the risk of jeopardizing his own future should Thorian's side have lost the conflict.

"He's his own savior," Whisperwind retorted. "Despite his severe injuries, he slaughtered hundreds of those brutes. It was purely fortuitous that he stumbled into my territory while unconscious. It's as if his body instinctively sought refuge."

Nodding lightly, Thorian turned back to Vigil, a strategic plan already taking shape in his mind. "Have you mastered your healing spell yet?"

Taken aback by the unexpected inquiry, Vigil hesitated momentarily before replying, "Yes. I have achieved maximum proficiency with it, My King."

Thorian acknowledged with a nod, "Good, then proceed to the Priest Guild and advance your class."

Vigil inclined his head slightly in assent before making a swift exit.

Simultaneously, Thorian's gaze returned to Nox's ghastly state. Unwilling to leave his friend on display for everyone to see, Thorian turned to Whisperwind and asked, "May I move him? I'd prefer to let him rest in his own home."

Caught off guard, Whisperwind paused before shaking his head and sighing, "Unfortunately, that's not possible. If he's too far from me, my skill won't work." He quickly offered words of consolation. "Don't worry. I'll keep him in my own quarters, away from prying eyes. It's the least I can do for him."

"Thank you for your consideration." Thorian inclined his head slightly. It was rare for Thorian to bow to anyone. However, for the man who had granted his first follower a second shot at life, he didn't mind the gesture.

As such, Thorian stepped outside the guild only to be met with a telepathic communication from Harald. *"What's your plan moving forward?"*

"First, we will halt the spread of that fire." Thorian took a second to clear his mind before responding. *"Afterward, we'll focus on the village's repair to secure our base of operations."*

"That's a sensible start," Harald agreed. *"But what comes next?"*

"I will delve into identifying the orchestrator of this attack," Thorian vocalized this time, his eyes hardening. "I believe a proper talk is in order."

No sooner had Thorian issued his veiled warning than he detected a stir from the side. Swiveling around, he spotted the goblin, Brix, scrambling towards him, gasping for breath.

"My lord, I am so glad you've returned!"

Wolvendale Village

Two hours ago...

Brix, the small goblin who had whimsically chosen the priest class, had spent several hours concealed within the foliage. He was hardly known for his speed. His late peers had often teased him for his sluggishness, but their fleet-footedness hadn't spared them from their grim fate.

When the human invasion erupted, he couldn't match the swift escape of his orc and kobloid compatriots. Left behind, he would have been an easy target and a potential feast of roasted goblin.

Recognizing his lack of speed as a considerable drawback, Brix elected to utilize his strengths. Taking advantage of his small stature and inconspicuous presence, he nestled himself amidst the bushes, careful not to make a sound. His strategy was simple—to bide his time and seize an opportunity to escape to his lord's presence when attention was diverted. He knew that that was the only place where safety was guaranteed.

As the hours ebbed away, Brix studied the invading humans. They bore little resemblance to the captives his tribe had taken and imprisoned. Those he was familiar with were typically composed, fearful, civilized, and capable of displaying a gamut of emotions. In stark contrast, the invaders displayed only crazed zeal, an insatiable bloodlust, and a desire for dominance.

They were more monstrous than any creatures Brix had previously encountered.

Only three among the crowd didn't exude that primal energy. Brix immediately singled them out as the ringleaders. A woman adorned in green seemed particularly formidable, commanding a level of fear and respect that was seldom seen by the goblin. Only his lord, Thorian, displayed such a potent influence over those in his vicinity.

It was no wonder, then, that Brix found himself dumbstruck when the trio suddenly relinquished their control, leaving the village under the guidance of one of the frenzied humans. A foolhardy red-haired man, overconfident in his newfound power.

As the trio departed, Brix's curiosity was sparked. He needed to unravel their intentions, their strategies, and the mysteries they harbored.

Thus, he made the decision to trail after them.

CHAPTER 69

As he had initially planned, Thorian returned to the forest to aid the kobold and kobloids in extinguishing the fire. This allowed Thorian to hone his Wind Gust spell, while the water magi employed their abilities to supplement the elemental interplay. Thorian also remained mindful of his final spell, "Earth Bullet," deploying it whenever a monster attempted to ambush them.

Time flowed swiftly as the flames gradually dwindled. Throughout the endeavor, Thorian reflected on his exchange with Brix. The goblin's timidity had proven to be an asset as he observed the unfolding events around the village while his kobloid counterparts had fled. His most significant revelation pertained to the orchestrator of the attack—the mysterious woman in green and her associates.

Despite racking his brain, Thorian couldn't recall ever encountering such a figure. The major factions within Locksley with whom Thorian was familiar were the Ravenwood family, the minor nobility, and the Great Temple. Rumors of a period of civil unrest stirred by the underworld had reached his ears, but William and his men had swiftly quelled the turmoil, establishing absolute control over their domain.

Out of all the people he knew from the region, there wasn't any notable figure that could be described as the "lady in green." At least not to his knowledge.

Moreover, the fact that she received the Soul Reaver quest and was able to harness its power with such proficiency is highly unusual. I've heard of no such occurrence throughout the kingdom. Only that formidable Ulfar from Thulaskar has managed anything similar.

Lost in thought, Thorian's mind was teeming with conjectures and suspicions, none of which he could verify. His situation was already anomalous—a reincarnation ten years into the past within a monster's body. Anything else paled in comparison to such extraordinary circumstances.

The forest before him was a charred wasteland, the pervasive, ashy smog was utterly nauseating. Nonetheless, they had succeeded in suppressing the rampaging flames. The protective barrier was mostly scorched, with only a few sections still partially intact.

We're going to need a lot of wood to repair all of this damage. Territory resources.

Resources:

Gathered Experience: 17.7k

Wood: 4.4k

Surveying the meager number of wood units, Thorian clicked his tongue in disappointment. Fortunately, none of the village's crucial structures had been destroyed, which alleviated some of his concerns. Only the residential areas and the protective wall required reconstruction.

Let's start with our fortifications first. Repair wall.

Just like previous occasions, the ground beneath them roared and trembled as the towering wall erupted from the earth, reminiscent of a tree sprouting forth. No matter how often Thorian witnessed this spectacle, it never lost its awe-inspiring effect.

Nevertheless, the depletion of resources that followed was a poignant sting. The construction consumed a whopping 3,000 wood units from the territory resources, leaving a meager 1,400 units to repair all other damaged structures.

That much wood was supposed to last us until the next village up-grade... It's a shame, but that is just part of running a territory. These kinds of costs are to be expected.

Having guided his past territory for over a decade, evolving it from a village to a town, then to a city and beyond, Thorian was no stranger to the bitter taste of loss in humiliating defeat. Rising above these setbacks was what distinguished genuine leaders from the pretenders.

"King, we have completed the tally!"

Thorian swiveled to see Alacritas, the silver-furred assassin, bowing beside him. His complexion was slightly ashen, his eyes dulled, and his cheeks were hollow.

"How many have we lost?" Thorian asked, taking a deep breath. "Categorize them for me by civilians, combatants, and their races."

"Immediately, My King." The assassin nodded, then swiftly tallied the numbers. "We've lost twenty lives. Ten of them were brown kobloid civilians, nine were kobloid fighters, and one was a high orc warrior."

Thorian took a moment to fully absorb the grim news before turning his gaze back to the assassin. "Summon Zogthar, Lapis, Vivax, Forlune, Ventus, and Vigil. I will convene with them at the village hall."

"Understood, My King," Alacritas acknowledged with a slight bow before darting off at an astonishing speed. Meanwhile, Thorian surveyed the scene around the village. As expected, the atmosphere was one of deep mourning, with some collapsing into tears at the loss of their friends and loved ones, while others moved around with averted gazes.

A proper funeral for those we've lost is in order.

With that thought, Thorian made his way towards the village hall.

As he pushed open the door, the stench of death greeted him. His gaze took in the numerous human corpses scattered around the room, their mouths frothing and their eyes revealing nothing but white.

"I am relieved you've returned, my lord," Melina greeted from behind her desk, delicately sipping from her teacup. "It would have posed a significant problem if I'd had to entertain these new guests any longer."

"It appears you've handled things in your own unique way," Thorian remarked, casting his eyes over the room. "We'll be using the room upstairs for an emergency meeting. Is it currently in a usable state?"

The elven woman nodded. "Certainly, my lord. No one has ventured upstairs."

"Understood." Thorian eyes lingered on the bulletin board, their focus lost in contemplation. "There's something else I've been meaning to ask. For partially completed, time-limited quests, are the rewards received automatically, or do they need to be claimed explicitly?"

"As soon as the deadline is passed, rewards corresponding to the achieved milestones are distributed automatically," Melina quickly answered. "This occurs regardless of whether you've explicitly claimed the quest or not."

"Thank you for the concise answer," Thorian expressed, a soft smile gracing his features as he thought of his loyal subordinate. *At least your efforts haven't been in vain, Nox.*

Recalling the grievous condition of the shadowstalker, Thorian clenched his teeth so hard that a fang caught on his lip and tore, causing a drop of blood to spill. His eyes blazed with an intense fury that seemed potent enough to burn holes into the ground.

After a few moments, Thorian took a deep breath and successfully transformed his furious expression into a serene one. Upon seeing this, Melina was taken aback by the sudden suppression of his previous intensity.

"I will be leading a campaign into Eärendil's Sanctuary in a week's time," declared Thorian, startling the elf.

"W-Why is that, my lord?" she stuttered in response.

"I need a specific object. 'Amelia's Crystal Tear' is the item I desperately seek."

As he noticed the elven lady's eyes widen in surprise, Thorian calmly walked towards the staircase, leaving her with a final statement. "Should a forgotten memory about the sanctuary awaken within you, I would be eager to hear it."

Without hesitating for a response, Thorian ascended the staircase, aiming for the strategic meeting room above. They had an extensive agenda to cover, and the clock was relentlessly ticking away.

"N-Nox can't be healed?"

The news struck Ventus like a blow. The meeting had just commenced, and although everyone was aware of the recent village fatalities, Nox's critical condition blindsided him.

"Healing isn't impossible," Vigil clarified, his voice marked by patience. "What we need is a second-advancement priest. That's the information Whisperwind gave us, which Merrygold later confirmed. However, even with such a strong priest, there's only a fifty percent chance of success."

Ventus gave his head a confused shake. "I get the whole special healer thing, but how on earth did Nox end up so hurt? I mean, he's fast as lightning. Nothing should've been able to touch him."

Forlune responded with a grunt. "It doesn't matter how fast you are. If they throw a thousand spells at you, you're bound to be hit by something." His gaze dropped as he bit his lip, remorse creeping into his voice. "I should have gone back for him. If the roles were reversed, I'm sure he would have."

Thorian, however, firmly shook his head. "You had a duty to fulfill, and you executed it admirably. And let's not speak of him as though he is already lost to us. We have a clear path to his salvation."

Vigil looked towards their king, skepticism clouding his eyes. "Can we really achieve the second advancement in just ten days?" he questioned. "Even if we do, our chances of saving him are just fifty percent, aren't they?"

"How is your progress in the human and monster hunting quests?" Thorian interjected.

Vigil blinked in surprise at the change in topic before answering, "Ah, well, I've hit the cap on the monster-hunting one. As for the humans, I've reached the third milestone."

"Good enough." Thorian nodded approvingly. "You'll receive all the level-up rewards, then. Don't claim them until the very last moment. We're going to rapidly elevate your class level with dungeon clears. That way, the rewards you glean from both quests will be as potent as possible."

Forlune, feeling emboldened by the strategizing, said, "Should we also aim to advance our classes? That way we're all working towards a common objective."

Thorian directed his response at Forlune. "Ensure you first unlock your Bloodlust skill. It becomes available after slaying five hundred monsters once your class reaches level 20. It's the gateway to the berserker advancement."

"Bloodlust?" Forlune's eyebrows furrowed at the unfamiliar term. He swiftly checked his stat panel, his puzzlement replaced by a triumphant grin. "Already got that skill while battling those savage humans."

"In that case, you can proceed with your advancement," Thorian responded, then swiveled his attention back to Vigil. "To revisit your earlier point—yes, using the ultimate priest skill for the second advancement only guarantees us a fifty percent chance. But there's a workaround to that predicament."

"As Thorian inhaled deeply, all eyes converged on him. "There exists an item that can amplify a skill's effectiveness twofold. However, to procure that item, we must embark on a journey into Eärendil's Sanctuary."

Smoke curled against the sky, staining it with the hues of a dying fire. Nalia stood at the cliff's edge, a predatory smile playing on her lips as she watched the flames dance below. The forest surrounding Wolvendale was a patchwork of fire and shadow, a scene of destruction that filled her with a terrible sense of peace. Beside her, Ragnar shifted impatiently, while Soren stood in quiet contemplation.

Closing her eyes, Nalia extended her arms toward the ravaged landscape. *Yaksha, please accept this offering,* she prayed silently, *May it nourish your return.* A thrill coursed through her, a sense of power that was both exhilarating and terrifying.

"We let them slip." Ragnar's gruff voice broke the silence, his tone laced with frustration. "Those monsters, they got away."

Nalia's smile widened, a hint of amusement in her eyes. "They haven't escaped me, Ragnar. They will return. They always do." A flicker of interest danced in her gaze. "The lord of that village... I'm intrigued. A kobold king claiming Raven's Nest for himself... Such a peculiarity."

"We lost more than a thousand men," Soren murmured, his voice heavy with concern.

Nalia turned to him, her expression hardening. "They were fuel for the ritual, Soren, nothing more. Their sacrifice has already been accounted for."

Turning, she began to descend the cliff, Ragnar and Soren falling into step behind her. As they entered the forest, Ragnar spoke, a calculating glint in his eyes.

"*Your* ritual, Nalia. Once you claim the rewards of that Soul Reaver quest, you'll ascend to unimaginable heights. But what will that leave the two of us, eh, Soren?"

Soren shot Ragnar a venomous glare. "Mind your tongue. Your insolence is unbecoming."

Nalia chuckled, waving a dismissive hand. "Peace, Soren. Ragnar is merely... curious. And he needn't worry. I won't be the only one to benefit from this quest. You too shall taste power beyond your current comprehension."

Their conversation was abruptly cut short by the menacing clatter of approaching monsters. A thundermasher, a pair of chaskas, and a lone Thri-kreen burst from the undergrowth, their eyes blazing with predatory intent.

Nalia's eyes flashed a brilliant blue, her voice resonating with an unnatural calm, "Still yourselves."

The monsters froze mid-stride, their hostile expressions replaced by a vacant stillness. Ragnar, seizing the opportunity, roared with laughter and charged forward, his axe a blur of motion as he hacked and cleaved, reducing the charmed creatures to lifeless heaps.

Wiping the blood from his axes, Ragnar returned to Nalia's side. "You should have used *that* on the Monster King," he sneered. "We could have taken the entire village without lifting a finger."

Soren opened his mouth to rebuke Ragnar, but Nalia's soft laughter cut him short. Her gaze drifted towards the distant city, a predatory gleam in her eyes.

"His time will come, Ragnar. But the true prize lies elsewhere." Her voice hardened with ambition. "Locksley... It's time to claim our treasure."

Books You May Like

**When a dragon-blooded emperor reaches for godhood,
Earth reaches back—with bullets.**

The plan was simple: conquer a new realm, harvest its souls, and become a god.

But nothing about Ohio is simple.

Armed with grit, ingenuity, and a lot of guns, the scrappy humans of Earth prove they're not the kneeling type. In a clash of magic and modern firepower, alliances are forged, friendships are tested, and ambitions burn brighter than the skies over the Midwest.

Can humanity stand its ground, or will the emperor's quest for divinity grind them to dust?

Grab your copy of Grimoires & Gunsmoke today! Perfect for fans of epic battles, unlikely heroes, and a healthy dose of fantasy-meets-modern warfare.

Available on Kindle Unlimited and Audible!

Thank you for reading a MoonQuill original novel. More exciting stories can be found on at www.moonquill.com.

We would greatly appreciate it if you could take a moment to leave a review. Each one helps the author and supports their ability to continue writing fantastic books for everyone to enjoy!

Scan the QR code below to subscribe to our mailing list and be notified of new releases. You'll receive 4 e-books for free!

www.ingramcontent.com/pod-product-compliance
Lightning Source LLC
Chambersburg PA
CBHW022253310726
48973CB00001B/51